B.P. DONIGAN

FATE
CLAIMED

BOUND MAGIC SERIES: BOOK 3

Fate Claimed
Red Adept Publishing, LLC
104 Bugenfield Court
Garner, NC 27529
https://RedAdeptPublishing.com/

---

1.   http://StreetlightGraphics.com

Dedicated to my dad, John M. Pontius, who taught me to love reading, writing, and all things fantasy. Miss you.

Chapter One

A blood-curdling wail pierced the air, carrying the kind of magic that twisted insides apart and sent terror riding up spines. I flinched and clapped my hands over my ears. The two agents holding the screaming woman wore earplugs, but they still jerked away from the sound, releasing the woman from their grip.

She spun in terror, but there was nowhere for her to go. The small dorm room was sealed, and there were no visible exits. She dragged in another lungful of air, and her magic-infused scream punched the air again. I leaned into my own magic and conjured a shield around the woman, cutting off the shrieking.

We all sighed in relief, and Ethan nodded at me in solidarity. I preferred to reason with newbies, but the woman was freaked out, and her magic was out of control. There wasn't much we could do until she wore herself out and calmed down enough for me to explain that developing magic was a gift and she didn't need to be afraid.

I felt bad for the woman we'd essentially snatched off the streets, but we had to help her learn to control her new abilities. After I'd freed magic, Mundanes around Boston began developing powers, and it had gone spectacularly poorly. Public panic spiraled out of control, and DODSI—the Department of Defense, Special Interests—demanded that we stop magic from spreading. Boston was quarantined until we could prove that Mundanes who developed powers could transition peacefully into a new magical world.

Dried blood streaked the woman's face and light-brown hair. She'd clearly dressed for work this morning, but her pale-pink button-down shirt hung off one shoulder, torn. A few of the DODSI agents looked a little banged up. One of them had four slashes on his face, finger-width apart. Our newbie had put up a fight, but it was good that she was a fighter. Her life was about to change in every way, and just like bringing a new life into this world, it would hurt, but the result would be worth it. I shook my head at my sentimentality—clearly, all the baby prep with Aria and Gia had gotten into my head.

Special Agent John Lennart, our assigned handler from DODSI, frowned as he watched his agents hand her off to us. Since magic had been freed, we'd seen a lot of him, and things had gotten tense. We were running out of time to prove that magic didn't need to be contained, and the government was running out of patience with our lack of progress.

"Good thing you have those disruptors," I said with a whole bunch of false innocence in my voice. "She was packing a big punch in that scream. I don't know if your team could have handled it if you'd taken any longer to get her here."

He stared down at me, all six-foot three-inch wannabe intimidation and muscle. "My job is to bring you the freaks. You should focus on yours and try to fix some of them."

Every time Lennart brought in someone manifesting new magic, he rubbed our failures in my face. All I could do was enjoy the fact that he had magic, too, but didn't yet realize it. My lips curled at the corners as I eyed the growing aura of energy around him, and Lennart's brow wrinkled as he watched me. I was really looking forward to the day his magic fully manifested. I'd happily lock him in one of our chill rooms until he stopped screaming.

Our staredown ended when Ethan took a half step in front of me, putting himself between us. With dark-brown hair and kind brown eyes, Ethan had the kind of wholesome good looks of a high school homecoming king. But he wasn't arrogant or sporty. He was constantly tinkering with magic and mundane objects—just the right kind of geeky.

In response to Ethan's slightly aggressive movement, the DODSI agents raised their magic-disrupting guns at both of us. Ethan's magic didn't rise as he faced off with Lennart, but his obviously protective movement was enough. We'd flinched first, and a cocky grin spread across Lennart's stupid face. I really wished Silas were there so Lennart would tone down the stupid alpha-male act. My hands were tied by DODSI's ultimatums, but Lennart knew Silas could put him down in a heartbeat and not care about consequences. I put my hand on Ethan's arm before he gave Lennart an excuse to shoot him.

Ethan stepped back without argument. With a small tug on my powers, I unsealed the only exit in the room, and a space the size and shape of a standard doorway opened in the wall. "Don't let the door hit you on the way out."

"Good luck." Lennart smirked. "Maybe this one will actually work out." He turned on his heel and marched out of the room, his agents falling in behind him. Ethan followed them out to make sure they actually left as I gritted my teeth in a silent snarl. We had yet to successfully transition any of the newbies back to normal life. At first, I was confident we could do it—magic was a natural part of life. I believed wholeheartedly that the world needed it, but I hadn't realized how hard it was for someone who had no idea magic existed to learn how to control it.

The government had given us three months to show the world it was possible for normal people to do just that, but we'd burned through the first month trying to quell the riots and panic in the city once they were told they'd been "infected" and Boston had been locked down. We'd spent another month working with the people who'd developed powers, but it was hard to help someone who didn't understand what was happening to them. It was awful all around, and we weren't making progress. Only a few newbies had managed to calm down enough to consciously access their magic, but they were far from being able to control it. We had only thirty days left to try and "fix" someone.

Gia, the mother of my newborn niece, walked in, holding a piece of paper. DODSI was all about paperwork. She gave me a sympathetic grimace before we turned our attention to the woman, who seemed to be winding down her freakout inside my soft bubble of protective magic.

"What's her name?" I asked.

The door sealed behind Gia as she pushed her curly black hair over her shoulder and scanned the intake paperwork. "Christine Davina of 43B Tremont Street, Boston."

Gia's previously angry and spiteful demeanor had completely disappeared after we'd made our peace over the death of my brother, Marcel, who was also the father of her baby. Over the last few months, I'd enjoyed getting to know her—and the rest of the splinter group that had moved to Alaska after my mother had died at the hands of the Brotherhood. Gia had stepped into her leadership position seamlessly as she relocated their group to our campus in the Jamaica Plain area of Boston and helped everyone settle in.

I squatted in front of the woman on the floor and softened my voice. "Christine?" Her soft brown eyes were rimmed in red as she blinked up at me. "My name is Maeve O'Neill. We're going to help you, and everything is going to be okay. I promise. What's happening to you is perfectly natural, and we're going to help you through your transition."

"I want to go home." Christine's voice was hoarse from screaming, and she hugged her knees as I unraveled the magic surrounding her.

"You can go home once your new powers are under control. I'm going to tell you everything you need to know, okay?"

DODSI had kept us from telling the world the full truth about where magic came from and how it could be controlled. Most people thought it was some kind of contagious disease and were terrified they would catch it. Christine listened silently as I laid out the facts, including that having it was a good thing. She stared at me as if attempting to process and reset her brain with every blink. I used my calm voice to give the speech I'd recited to the other newbies, but as she listened, her face drained of color.

I hit her with my big finale. "People like us are part of a new world, Christine. Our magic can be used for good, to help others and build a better world. It's a gift. You're very lucky."

With wide eyes, she took in her surroundings—a bed, a sink, a small desk, and a television mounted on the wall. No windows, no doors. We'd done our best to make it comfortable, but it was hard to disguise the lack of exits.

"Can I go home?" Her voice wobbled.

I took a deep, steadying breath. Things always went south right about there. "We have to teach you how to use your new abilities responsibly first."

"I don't want them. Please, just let me go. My son needs me. I have money—I can pay you!"

"Everything is going to be all right, Christine," Gia said in a soothing tone. "You have to stay with us until you can demonstrate control over your new abilities. You're safe with us, and we'll make sure your son is taken care of for as long as it takes."

Christine gaped at Gia, her fear palpable. She dragged in a breath as her fledgling magic rose around her.

I held up my palms. "Christine, don't—"

She screamed, and her magic punched me in the gut. I staggered backward. She inhaled again, her eyes wild. I conjured a shield around her just before her power rammed the barrier, and it remained blessedly silent on our side. She started pounding against the dome of magic with her fists, wailing and crying. I couldn't hear her words, but I could see her lips moving. *Let me go! Let me go!*

Conflicting emotions burned through me as I stood inches from the woman whose life had been flipped upside down. I felt sorry for her, but I was also angry. DODSI had tied our hands, and their ignorance kept people terrified—the whole world believed magic was scary and dangerous. The transition didn't have to be like this. Instead of telling the Mundanes the truth and allowing magic to spread naturally, they'd quarantined the entire city, forced us to contain magic within its boundaries, and refused to let us show people how magic could help. We'd had no chance to prepare them for the possibility of manifesting it. Every Mundane trapped in Boston lived in terror of catching magic.

Christine was blind with panic.

Gia shook her head. "I shouldn't have said that about her son. *Stupid.*"

"She'll be fine. She just needs time to calm herself... like the others. We'll get her there." I glanced at the clock on the wall. "Shit, I'm going to be late again. Can you handle this?"

Gia's eyes were a little wet, but she nodded. "I'll stay with her until she calms down. You should go. I know you're really busy."

I felt a little guilty, leaving Gia to handle the newbie on her own when she was clearly rattled, but I would make a point of following up with her later to let her know she was doing a good job. Our lack of progress wasn't her fault.

I unsealed the exit and found Ethan waiting on the other side. "Any progress with the others?" I asked.

"We think a few might be able to make the deadline." He grimaced, undermining his own words.

Gia and Ethan spent all day, every day, trying to work with the hodgepodge group of Mundanes who had developed magic. There were over ninety of them, and most were a mess. Several had to be almost constantly sedated. Only a small handful had shown any progress but were nowhere near being able to actively use their magic.

Not only were we not making enough progress with the newbies, but we'd also had to put our diplomatic talks with the Fae on hold. Their former leaders had leaned heavily into Fae-first separatist propaganda, and we were still working on a way to unwind all the damage and incorporate them into our community. There was a limited window to heal that damage, but we were under too much scrutiny from DODSI to incorporate the nonhuman population until things settled down.

"Gia's got this," Ethan said gently, reading the concern on my face. "She's really good with the newbies. I swear she's got some Fae blood in her. She's almost a natural Empath. She'll get Christine calmed down, and I'll come back and help later today too. It will be okay, Mae."

I couldn't help but feel a stab of guilt. People like Christine were going to have to do this the hard way because I'd freed magic and sprung it on the world without warning. I'd failed to make DODSI see reason, and I'd failed to make any progress with the Fae—or we would've had access to their Empaths and Healers, who could have helped. I was running myself ragged trying to hold everything together, but the setbacks kept piling up.

The only option left was to prove to DODSI that normal people could adjust and to show the rest of the world all the good things about magic. Once we did that, everything would be fine. Magic would be a positive in people's lives. It would all work out. It had to.

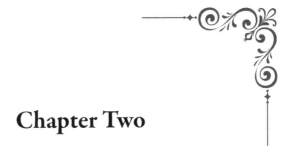

Chapter Two

Ethan and I wound through the busy former-hospital hallways and toward the converted gym for my daily training session with the Guardians. We walked in silence as my mind swirled. I'd never once said it out loud, not even to Silas, but as I thought about Christine crying on the floor, I couldn't help it. "What if the world can't handle magic?"

"Are you having second thoughts about unbinding Earth's magic?"

I instantly regretted my words as I pretended not to hear his undertone of blame. No matter how many times I'd explained it, no one quite understood why I'd freed magic. The New Alliance—a coalition of the former leaders from my sect and the members of the former Aeternal Council—had stopped just short of blaming me outright for every negative outcome since that moment, but they held me responsible in a thousand little ways. Only Silas hadn't openly questioned me, but he didn't completely agree with what I'd done, either.

I didn't regret it, exactly, but I felt bad about the way it had happened. I'd unbound all of Earth's magic all on my own, believing it the right thing to do at the time. But as I thought about Christine's son, who wouldn't see her tonight at home, guilt ate at me. My ancestors had bound all of Earth's magic and created a single source of power, and many had died to keep that power bound and out of the wrong hands... until I destroyed it.

The whole world was watching to see if our experiment would work. Outside the boundaries of the city, all the world's freaks and haters had gathered to demand entrance so they could "get magic powers" or to tell us we were about to burn in hell. At least that was one mess I didn't have to deal with—DODSI had convinced the rest of the government that they should be the ones to "handle the situation." Otherwise, we would have had every three-letter-acronym agency breathing down our necks. They brought in the rest of the government folks to patrol the borders around Boston, keep peace in the city, and manage the fallout with the Mundanes. The global politics of the whole situation were way above my pay grade—thankfully, I only had to deal with the mess inside the city.

I didn't know how to answer Ethan's question about whether I regretted what I'd done, so I forced myself to keep moving forward, literally and figuratively. "DODSI is making all of this so impossible. If the government would let us show everyone the good things magic can do, this transition would be so much easier. We're doing this the hard way, and I know everyone blames me." I swallowed hard, hating the emotion making my voice wobble. "Maybe they're right."

"Hey." Ethan stopped me in the middle of the hallway. "I know there's a lot of... um, different opinions about what you did, but you did what you thought was right. It's hard right now, but we're family, Mae. Family sticks together no matter what—through mistakes, blame, and sometimes some name calling. They'll get over it."

"Thanks." I smiled weakly, feeling a little better. Ethan always had my back even if he didn't completely agree with me. I just wished the rest of the sect felt the same way. There'd been more than "some" name calling.

"If I can offer you some advice, though? You can trust other people too. You keep all these secrets, and you don't have to. Especially when those secrets impact the rest of us." Ethan scanned my face and put his hand on my shoulder. "I'm just saying that I've got your back, and it would be nice to know that you trust me enough to let me in."

I grunted softly, neither agreeing nor disagreeing as I turned up the hall, using the motion to release myself from his grip and hide my grimace. I'd done what I needed to do, and my secrets had burned some bridges in the process. Apparently, Ethan had some hurt feelings about that, and it was hard to balance our new Anchor relationship and our past.

Ethan and I had a short relationship in high school, which he'd briefly tried to rekindle. He seemed to be moving on from any old feelings, but I still needed to keep some distance. If he tried to reignite old feelings, he would get punched in the face, and it was a fifty-fifty split whether it would be Silas or me who took that swing.

Thanks to our deal with the Fates, Silas had been gone a lot, dealing with Four's errands, and I'd been leaning on Ethan too much. I didn't want him to get the wrong idea, especially since he'd accepted a position as my Anchor, the magical equivalent of a pressure valve, which meant he was a permanent fixture in my life.

We walked for a while before reaching the converted gym inside Building Three. Silas had reorganized the Guardians after the collapse of Aeterna reduced their previously robust numbers to only a few hundred. They were split into nine groups of twenty, with a rotating schedule that included guarding the campus, manual labor to expand the gardens, renovation crews transforming the former-hospital buildings, and training. Always training.

The gym was busy. They'd doubled the amount of equipment, added a new cardio area and free weights, and organized the space into separate sections for different types of weapons. There was also an ever-changing obstacle course, where they staged mock battles that looked a lot like capture the flag with swords and magic.

Ethan and I headed to the center of the gym, which was roped off and padded for sparring. Two sets of Guardians were finishing, sweaty and out of breath as they moved out of the practice area. All four nodded solemnly at me. Early on, the Guardians had started bowing to me, showing the same deference they gave to Silas as their Lord Commander. I'd mentioned the awkwardness to Silas, and it had stopped literally the next day, replaced by the much subtler nods. Knowing that he had told them all to knock it off was only slightly less embarrassing than getting bowed at all day, but I tried not to let it bother me that everyone knew who I was only because I was sleeping with him.

Neither Silas nor Tessa was able to join me for training that day, so Ethan had stepped in. My friend, Guardian Commander Tessa D'Nali, normally trained with me several times a week, practicing hand to hand, sword work, or whatever she decided would torture me the most. Sometimes, Ethan joined us. At first, I assumed he was suffering through our grueling workouts because of a misplaced interest in me, but lately, he seemed awfully interested in a certain half-Fae First Commander. Tessa took it easier on me when Ethan was there, so it was a win-win, especially because it seemed like she might be returning his interest.

Silas joined me when he could, but between our various responsibilities and his early-morning training with the Guardians, we were lucky to spar once a week. Lately, we sometimes didn't even sleep at the same time, but that had more to do with his other responsibilities as a Fate, a subject I tried to avoid thinking about most of the time.

I toed off my shoes and started stretching on the mat. I'd learned the hard way that I needed more warm-up than when Ethan and I had trained with Casius as teenagers. As we did some light mobility work, Ethan seemed more than willing to chat, and I let him distract me from my failures with the newbies as we fell into old, familiar patterns of banter.

"There's no way." He bent his long legs into a runner's stretch. "I would never wear that."

"Oh, you definitely did. It was the red one. Remember John Marion? He was the black Ranger. You did poses and everything. I have a picture somewhere."

His handsome face twisted into an embarrassed grimace. "Please don't find it."

"You were like eleven. Power Rangers were super cool." I chuckled and began a series of cross-body rotations, stretching the primary muscle groups in my torso and shoulders.

"What did you dress up as? I don't remember."

"I—"

"If you're going to stand around and jabber, you should move off the mat." Silas stood at the edge, arms crossed over his chest, frowning at us.

I'd been so wrapped up in teasing Ethan that I hadn't noticed the silence that had fallen over the gym. Every pair of eyes was on us. Instead of snapping back at Silas's rude tone, I took a deep breath and reminded myself that he was under a lot of pressure. We both were, but on top of everything else, Silas had just gotten back from another one of Four's mysterious errands. He couldn't talk about whatever it was the Fates had him doing, but he was pissy every time.

I had handled their powers myself, and they were addictive. They made me feel disconnected from everything else, like nothing was real except the epic power coursing through me. Now, Silas was dealing with the same roller coaster because when I drained the Fate of Death's magic and used it to save his life, the Fates decided I owed them mine in exchange. Instead, Silas volunteered to keep the powers and do Four's errands for ten years. I wasn't happy about the bargain, but I was trying to be understanding about his yo-yo emotions. "We were warming up. Would you like to join us?"

He unfolded his arms. "I'd rather spar with you."

Ethan raised his eyebrows. Silas's blunt dismissal was a little rude, but Ethan shrugged good-naturedly. "That's fine. I'll go see if Gia needs help."

"Ethan, you don't have to go. We can find another partner for you."

He flashed me his signature lopsided grin as he grabbed his stuff. "I wasn't really looking forward to getting my ass kicked today, anyway. Have fun."

I watched him leave with some guilt, but with his departure, the Guardians lost interest in our drama, and the gym returned to normal activity. Plus, an all-out sparring session with Silas would be good for both of us. I'd found that working up a sweat was the best way to knock him out of a bad mood after he'd been with Four. Plus, it was a personal goal of mine to kick his ass someday, and I'd have to go all out to make him break a sweat. So far, he'd won every match, but they almost always ended with a very thorough massage afterward, which was a win in my book.

Silas stripped off his shirt and shoes. Despite the annoyance I could sense radiating from him through our Aegis bond, I immediately imagined running my hands all over his muscled torso. He had the build of someone who used his body every day, earning his hard stomach and defined, muscular arms through sweat and hard work. As a hot-blooded female, I appreciated the result, and he was ruggedly handsome on top of all that. The hint of beard on his square jaw outlined a strong masculine mouth that he knew how to use in all the right ways. His night-dark hair had been short when we first met but had grown longer, just to his ears, and begged my fingers to run through it.

My stomach did that flippity thing it did whenever I thought about alone time with Silas. I took a moment to let it soak in that he was mine and I was his. His lips twitched up at one corner, and a single eyebrow rose as he watched me drool. I wasn't trying to hide my feelings, and equal interest flared back through our Aegis bond. I bit my lip. He took a small step toward me, and the pressure between us increased like the tightening of a bow.

"Should we skip the sweaty part and move straight to the rubdown part?" I asked.

He grinned, and the expression transformed his face as the last of his coldness bled away. "Tempting." He crouched slightly, preparing to pounce, and my heart picked up speed. "But I rather like *all* the sweaty parts."

I smiled as I took off my hoodie, leaving me in leggings and my sports bra. Tighter clothing was good for sparring—I'd learned that T-shirts ended up over my head or twisted around my neck when I fought with people who had real life-and-death fighting experience.

"I thought humans didn't approve of public sex," a new voice said.

My entire body seized in panic as I looked up and saw Four standing on the practice pad with us. The Fate of Change had a very nasty habit of causing bad things to happen in my life, and his presence was like a bucket of ice water dumped over my head.

Four watched us in his strange way, absorbing our reactions as if he didn't understand the feelings behind them. "Are you embarrassed that every person in this room is watching your mating ritual? You didn't seem to care until I arrived. Is it me?"

I swallowed my panic and replaced it with righteous anger. "What the hell—why are you here, Four?"

He wore his Average Joe look, appearing just short of middle-aged, with medium-brown hair and brown eyes. Neither tall nor short, not really attractive, not ugly. Totally average. The only thing giving him away as a super-powerful and dangerous Fate was the magic radiating through his aura—or rather, the lack of it. Four was masking the insane amount of power at his disposal, and the consequence was a sort of negative space around him.

Most people had a glow reflecting their natural magical ability, and the source of that power resulted in a color. Mundanes also had a weak aura if you looked for it, but Four had nothing. It was like a black hole of energy, a space where nothing existed.

Everyone in the gym stared at us. If Four thought he was being inconspicuous by masking his powers, he was dead wrong.

"We agreed you wouldn't show up here." Silas's voice was a low growl.

"I came to tell you something, but your mating rituals are so interesting. Please continue." He circled one hand in the air, motioning for us to keep going.

I debated dragging Silas out of the room and finishing our mating rituals in private. I wished we could pretend that Four didn't exist and go on with our lives, because whatever he had to say would be terrible, a trick, or both. Four was an awful bastard, but Silas and I were stuck with him for the time being, and it was better to get it over with. Reluctantly, I asked, "What do you want to tell us?"

Silas threw me a resigned look, and I was surprised that I couldn't sense his emotions anymore. He'd shut down the bond between us when Four showed up. I didn't have a chance to worry about what that meant, but his expression reflected the same impending doom I felt.

"Mind your duties!" Silas commanded loudly.

The room suddenly returned to activity, with the Guardians attempting to act normal despite the presence of a mysterious and totally conspicuous Fate. Silas's magic rose, and a dome of energy cascaded around us, creating a bubble of impenetrable silence.

I did a little double take when I noticed his aura. Before our run-in with the Fates, his flare had been golden, reflecting his Human heritage. When I used the Fates' powers to save his life, his aura had turned white with their magic. After I unbound Earth's magic, my own had become a bright spring green, reflecting unknown Fae ancestry mixed with more prominent Human genes. His aura had re-turned to its normal color, but it hadn't faded. It was *more* intense. The brilliance of his flare was like staring into the sun, and if I squint-ed, there was a bit of a negative aura right around him, exactly like Four's. I didn't want to think about that, either.

"Your clever little magic dam has a problem." Four flashed his teeth in a way that fell just short of a smile, as if he'd practiced the ex-pression but didn't feel the emotion behind it. "The pressure of all of Earth's magic trapped in one location caused a rip between this realm and a smaller adjacent one. Creatures from that realm have entered this one. I thought you might want to know before they start eating the mortals."

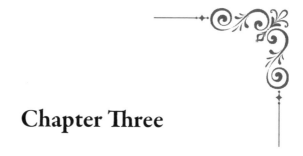

Chapter Three

A small shock ran up my ankles as I dropped from the station platform onto the tracks of the subway tunnel. I shook it off as Silas jumped down behind me. The summer air in the hundred-year-old Boston T station was stifling even in the dead of night. I flicked my long auburn braid over my shoulder and wiped sweat from my forehead.

As expected, the entire North Station terminal was empty, closed for the night, and our quick break-in went undetected. Silas took the lead as we headed into the dark tunnel without people or trains to interfere with our progress up the tracks.

"Are you sure you can build a stable portal to Aeterna? It took two circles to stabilize the last one we managed to open, and it only lasted a few hours."

He furrowed his brows. "Yes. I already told you I can do it."

"I know, but I just don't understand how this works. Four said more tears will keep happening between our realm and these pocket realms unless we release the magic barrier spell around Boston—"

"Which obviously isn't going to happen."

"Right. But how does connecting this smaller pocket realm to Aeterna fix the fact that Earth's magic is flowing into that realm?"

"It's a pressure release. Connecting the pocket realm to Aeterna will create a place for the magic to go. And Aeterna is the perfect solution, as it nullifies all magic. It isn't that complicated."

I had to ball my fists to refrain from telling him to stop being a jerk. He wasn't usually snappy with me, but he'd been borderline rude all night. The Aegis bond between us was flooded with irritation, but his annoyance wasn't about me. Silas hadn't had enough time to decompress since his last errand for the Fates. We needed time to reconnect, but instead, we'd gone off on a middle-of-the-night mission to stop beings from another realm from getting loose in ours.

"Keep your eyes peeled for creatures. Four said they were already coming through the tear, and we need to make sure they don't find their way out of the subway tunnel," I said.

"We can hunt them down if necessary. Once we establish the connection to Aeterna and release some of the pressure within the pocket realm, we should be able to return and seal the rip on this side. Nothing else will get through."

We headed north into the tunnel, past pedestrian fences and Keep Out signs, until the platform lights faded into darkness and we had to use our magic to light the way. Our footsteps echoed off the walls, sending rats scurrying just outside our circle of light. Ripper, which I used more for utility than fighting, was strapped to my thigh, and across my back in a custom holster, I carried my favorite new blade, Missy the Messer.

Missy's sheath went on like a backpack, with a belt low across my waist, enabling a singled-handed draw over my left shoulder. A sword slung across my back was a tad more conspicuous than a hip sheath, but I hated having a blade bounce against my thigh. It didn't seem to bother Silas, who'd strapped his own much longer sword to his left hip in a double-looped leather sword belt. Missy was a German-style workhorse sword with a knife-style handle and a short Nagel—a piece of metal that jutted out perpendicular to the grip and protected my hand. The single-edged blade curved at the tip into a sharp point, which was great for slashing and stabbing when the occasion called for it.

"Are you sure we shouldn't take this to the New Alliance?" I asked.

"As I said before, if we take this to the Alliance, they'll debate about it for days, probably involve DODSI, and just end up sending the two of us to do the work anyway. This is simply faster. And we're trying to keep our connection to the Fates quiet. How would you explain what we know about the rip between realms?"

"That's true," I agreed reluctantly. "Assuming your Guardians can keep their mouths shut about the visit from Four, we can at least keep our private business private."

"They'll keep closed mouths."

"Good." I always found his misuse of Earthen phrasing amusing, and some of my annoyance lifted. "What do you know about pocket realms? I didn't realize they could support sentient life."

When my sect was hiding from the Council and then the Brotherhood, we'd built our towns on pockets of strong magic to help mask our natural magic flares, but I'd assumed they were just wells of deep magic, not their own fully realized realms like Earth or Aeterna.

"Our hostile-environment training units took place in pocket realms, but most of them didn't have *evolved* beings living there. They're often rich in natural resources—water, minerals. Sometimes forests, but those are usually overrun with nasty, semisentient creatures. Hence the training units."

That was all news to me. I tried not to think about the fact that we'd drained those pockets of magic to support our own needs or what might have happened to anything living there. I really hoped that our past leaders didn't know, either, because my mother had been one of them.

"Watch out for the third rail." I pointed at the metal track running down the center of the tunnel. Accidental electrocution during a secret mission was not on my list of fun activities.

We trudged forward, and a bead of sweat trickled down the back of my neck as I peered into the darkest edges of the path, expecting an attack at any moment. The tunnel was creepy as hell, blazing hot, and smelled like a hundred years of dirt, metal and oil from the trains, and human filth.

Silas drew his sword and held it ready as we trekked deeper into the tunnel, but he didn't access his magic. Since I'd brought him back from the dead by infusing him with the powers of a Fate, he didn't do that unless he absolutely had to.

Except for Four's errands, we were doing everything we could to minimize the amount of time he used their powers. We'd both experienced the addictive nature of the power, and neither of us wanted to expose Silas to it more than absolutely necessary. We'd told the Alliance that our crazy Fate powers had faded—the situation with Four was a complication they didn't need to worry about. The only people who knew the details about our bargain with Four were Tessa, Silas's brother, Stephan, and Stephan's wife, Aria.

"Anything setting off your spidey-senses?" I whispered to Silas.

"What are spidey-senses?"

"Add Spiderman to your research list. Do you think we're not alone down here? I'm surprised we haven't run into those creatures yet."

Silas scowled at me over his shoulder. "If we *aren't* alone, then all this talking will certainly draw their attention."

I frowned at his back.

Four had sent him off twice in the past month, and we were both grumpy about it. I tried not to complain about Silas not telling me about his trips, but covering his absences with the New Alliance was getting tough. He had been released from the Acting Lord Councilor seat but was still a member of our new governing body. He oversaw the Guardians and our security on the campus, which meant he was expected to attend weekly meetings with the rest of us. Unfortunately, Four's errands had taken him away during two of those meetings that month alone, and people were asking questions.

With a silent sigh, I decided to let his bad mood go. Telling him not to snap at me or bringing up the increasingly annoyed Alliance members wouldn't help. Silas couldn't control the timing of Four's errands any more than I could. Picking a fight with him would have made things worse.

We were about halfway between North Station and Haymarket, working our way carefully around each bend of the subway tunnel and peering into every dark nook, when we rounded a slight bend in the tracks. There it was.

The rip between realms didn't look solid—I could have walked right through the little wisp of magic without physically feeling anything except the magic emanating from it. I let the power wash over me. Pure magic was like joy, wrapped in happiness and soaked in sunshine. I inhaled it, but the balance of the magic was off. The tear was like a jagged scar in the reality of our world, and instead of a hit of pure happiness, the ragged feel of it nagged at me like an itch I couldn't scratch.

I ran my thumb over Marcel's charm, which hung on a chain around my neck, and considered what Four would gain by telling us about the rip. He was a sneaky trickster with an agenda of his own, but trying to figure out the motivations of a Fate could drive a person insane. I didn't trust Four, but mending the rip between realms seemed like a good idea. I hoped we wouldn't regret it later. Second-guessing Four's motivations was pointless. We had no choice but to attempt a repair.

I glanced around to make sure something wasn't sneaking up on us in the dark tunnel. "What are the chances we're not walking into a trap?"

"Slim." His narrow-eyed stare was locked on the tear. "Four is a bastard. He's probably engineered some way for us to die in that realm."

"Scared?" I teased as I poked him in the ribs.

"No more than you are." He relaxed his harsh expression a fraction, and one side of his mouth lifted as he swept his hand toward the rip. "After you, my lady."

I snorted like the delicate lady I was and stepped up to the portal. A loud chittering sound rose from the shadows all around us. It sounded like a whole lot of rats—more rats than could possibly have been down there.

I drew Missy. "What the hell is that?"

Silas positioned himself at my back, his sword drawn. I let my magic flare brighter, illuminating the shadows around us, and gasped. The walls and ceiling of the tunnel were covered in strange, lizard-like creatures the size of large, hairless squirrels. The flare of magic drew their attention, and several of them dropped onto the tracks in front of us, hissing.

One of them rose on its hind legs, chittering and snapping. It spat a thick clump of yellow bile at us, which Silas and I both side-stepped. The glob landed on the metal rail and burned straight through.

Oh no. Their spit was some kind of super-potent acid, and if any of that landed on us, we were in serious trouble. Five more rodents dropped onto the tracks, hissing as they reared back in unison.

I was trying to figure out how to avoid a painful death by acid spit when Silas's magic flared so brightly that I had to throw my forearm over my eyes.

The flare receded, and I blinked as my vision cleared and the smell of roasted meat hit me. The charred bodies of several dozen lizard creatures lay all around us. Silas had blasted the tunnel with his power, literally cooking them all. I didn't like killing them like that, but I couldn't imagine the panic and injuries they would have caused if they'd managed to escape from the subway. I sheathed Missy.

Silas swept his hand toward the portal again. "After you."

With a last glance over my shoulder, I went into the unknown magical territory.

The pocket realm was desolate, lacking color and life. We'd landed in a forest of spiky trees with thorns as long as my hand sprouting from ominous dark-crimson trunks that looked almost black. The harsh, leafless limbs didn't provide any shade from the relentless sun, and no other vegetation seemed to have survived the arid climate. It was about twenty degrees hotter there, and the ground was sand, as if normal shrubbery couldn't withstand the sun's heat and had yielded into particles.

Just outside the knot of gnarled trees where we'd arrived, I spotted a group of boulders nestled in the sand. A large, smooth rock about the length of an SUV sat in the center. The rock surface was about waist high and would make a decent natural anchor for the gateway to Aeterna. I headed toward it and dropped my backpack onto the relatively flat surface while Silas made a loop around our immediate area, scouting for potential threats—like more of those lizards.

Either we were in the middle of a small desert, or the whole pocket realm was entirely desolate, but I didn't plan on finding out. I had no intention of staying longer than was absolutely necessary. At least there wasn't anywhere for monsters to sneak up on us—the spiky trees and smattering of boulders were the only natural features, and nothing was hiding in either of those.

"There's nothing visible for several kilometers other than sand and more trees," Silas said as he trotted back to me. "Are you ready?"

"Yep. Let's finish this and get out of here."

With a glance at the sun overhead, I reached out for him with both hands. If time moved at the same rate as it did on Earth, we had about five hours of daylight left. *Plenty of time.*

Silas took my hands and released the incredible magic coursing through him. I had to blink several times as the brilliant flood of power washed over me. His flare made my brain hurt. It also hurt my heart, and I was suddenly glad that he had shut down the emotional bond between us as he accessed his Fate powers. Those unnatural powers and the missing connection between us were a reminder that we didn't have control of our lives anymore, and I wasn't sure I could have hidden my own fear if our connection had been open.

For the rest of our sect, building a permanent portal would have taken an entire circle of people working together for hours. But Silas could build one in no time if he used his Fate powers, which was how he'd convinced me that we didn't need to involve the New Alliance.

My breath caught. The sheer amount of energy coursing between us was overwhelming. It washed over me like the rush of a river, cold and fast, exhilarating and terrifying as it almost buried me in its icy depths. A certain coldness underlay Silas's magic that hadn't been there before, and that scared me. We'd both experienced losing touch with our humanity while channeling the Fates' magic, but we kept avoiding talking about his continued exposure. We avoided talking about a lot of things lately. But I didn't know how to make it better, and bringing it up would only make it more painful.

Silas reopened our Aegis bond, and I wrapped my magic around his to anchor him from possible burnout. I nearly sighed—his magic was so strong and centered and warm, and it was a relief to find his familiar core of magic under all the vast powers of the Fates.

He built the complex first layer of the portal conjuring, weaving energy into a complex pattern of magic, then he built several other layers on top, twisting them through each other like the threads of a tapestry. Another layer came together a few minutes later, and I breathed heavily from the effort of holding that much magic.

"Do you need a break?" he asked, seemingly unaffected.

I shook my head. "Let's finish it and get out of here."

The ground rumbled, and I braced myself, examining the desolate terrain in alarm.

"Earthquake," Silas noted.

I added that to the list of reasons this realm sucked. The spiky trees seemed to be reaching for my back, and the gritty sand had worked its way into my shoes and between my toes. The relentless sun had me sweating, and a hot, dry wind had kicked up, plastering a gritty, sandy film over my entire body.

Almost an hour later, we had worked our way through all seven layers of the portal spell, including three binding midlayers. Silas had created the portal with an incredibly complex and intricate spell that he had managed from memory, but it seemed to be working. Once finished, he tied the conjuring off on the boulder in front of us then sank it deep into the stone for permanent placement before letting go.

The ground rumbled again as Silas broke our connection, and I had to brace myself against the rock. I'd exerted more energy than I realized by anchoring him, and the sudden absence of his magic felt like hitting a wall face-first. I examined the completed gateway as I recovered. Silas had formed it without a physical frame, so the result was a dome-shaped portal between realms, like an upside-down bowl on top of the rock where it was anchored. But it was solid, and I could already see magic flowing through it and into the void of Aeterna.

"Nice work," I commented, handing him a water bottle from my pack.

He took a swig then handed it back to me. "Shall we head back?"

I eyed the tear we'd come through from the subway tunnel. Once we went back, we could seal it from our side. "Yeah, let's go." I reached for my pack, but the ground rumbled and bucked violently. "What the—" I lost my footing and landed on my ass. Silas fell beside me.

The ground rose and dropped again, bouncing us around like balls on a trampoline. The boulder with the portal rose several feet off the ground. We scrambled backward as the ground shook and the boulder rose higher. The giant rock tilted forward and back, exposing more of the surface, until the entire thing emerged from the sand. I stared, frozen in my confusion, as dozens of smaller boulders hovered above the ground around us, moving together in waves as if they were somehow connected by a long string.

Holy shit! "That's not a rock!"

A giant head and then an entire creature, as large as a full-grown elephant, rose from the sand. I'd mistaken the hard, tortoise-like shell on its back for a large boulder, but that was the end of its resemblance to a turtle. The fleshy body under that hard shell was like a slug, with a blunt rounded head and three long, flat tentacles flapping off each side. Its rough, round balls of sand-colored flesh, which I had mistaken for the smaller boulders, created a patchy armor over most of its body and tentacles. The creature had no eyes, but slitted breathing flaps along the sides of its head quivered as it rose above us.

"What the fratch is it?" Silas shouted.

Screw me sideways! If he didn't know what it was, then he didn't know how to kill it.

The creature opened its full-circle mouth and roared before it rocked to one side and slammed its tentacles against the sand.

The impact lifted the ground like an ocean wave, and the entire world turned upside down. A wall of sand slammed into me, and I was tossed off my feet again. I landed hard, blinded, and I couldn't breathe through the sand shooting up my nose and into my mouth. It scraped my eyeballs as I tried to blink my vision clear. I spat and coughed as I scurried on my hands and knees away from the creature.

Boom. The ground shook, and everything tilted sideways again. I was tossed forward off my feet. I righted myself, but the air was thick with sand, and I couldn't tell where the creature was. The sky looked the same as the ground, and I could barely breathe through coughing fits. I threw my magic outward, clearing a bubble of air around me. I had no idea where Silas was but called out for him.

The creature rose right in front of me and roared. I got a close-up of four rows of needle-like teeth, each one as long as my finger.

Like a rider perched on its hard shell, the portal to Aeterna shimmered with magic as it rode on top of the bucking sand slug. The creature's tentacles whipped back as if preparing to slam down and crush me. I scrambled to my feet and ran—my magic wouldn't protect me from being crushed to death. I threw unformed magic behind me without looking, and the creature roared and flopped onto its side. The hard shell of its back slammed onto the ground, and I threw myself out of the way of flailing tentacles. The impact destroyed the gateway, and it fell apart in a colossal flare of magic.

"No!" *All that work for nothing!*

The creature twisted upward, bent nearly in half, and turned ninety degrees toward me. With surprising speed, it paddled across the sand, levering its tentacles like oars as it headed straight for me. I scrambled out of the way, but the thing was huge and hella fast. It was going to flatten me.

There was nothing between me and the enraged creature, but in the next second, Silas appeared in a brilliant flare of pure magic, glowing with the incredible powers of a Fate. He held up one palm to the creature, his magic gathered like a blazing wall of light around him, and—

Silas disappeared.

I froze, staring stupidly at the spot where he had stood a second before. He was just... gone. I hadn't felt a tug of a skimming spell or any trace of magic. *What the hell?*

The creature roared, and at the very last possible second, I recovered my wits and dove out of the way. It barreled past me, straight through the tear between our realms, and right into the Boston subway.

Chapter Four

I stared in horror at the tear leading back to our realm. The sand creature was somewhere in the Boston subway system.

"Shit! Ugh—what the hell was that!" I whirled to the spot where Silas had last stood, but he was already gone. I didn't understand how that could have happened without a trace of magic or any type of skimming spell. I reached along our bond and exhaled in relief when I sensed him. He was alive, and hot fury flamed through our shared connection. The only reasonable explanation was a four-letter word: *Four*.

Of course, Four had pulled Silas away at the absolutely worst moment and had almost gotten me killed. I let out another string of creative curse words—Silas would have been proud—before I calmed down enough to take stock of my situation. My priority had to be stopping the sand slug before someone got hurt.

If the general public discovered the nastier things about magic, especially including dangerous creatures from pocket realms, DODSI would never agree to release magic outside of Boston and would declare our "experiment" a failure. If magic in the Mundane world was going to become a reality, neither DODSI nor the Alliance could know about the colossal screwup I'd managed.

I gritted my teeth and jogged back toward the tear. I had to kill that thing before it got loose in the city, and there was nothing I could do about Silas until Four decided to send him back, which meant I was on my own. I could handle it. I tried to send a wave of reassuring feelings across the Aegis bond, letting Silas know I was fine before I went through the tear.

I took half the desert with me into the subway tunnel. We hadn't been in the other realm for very long, but night had almost passed in Boston, and even though the underground tunnels were hot, the darkness was a relief from the pocket realm's overwhelming sun.

I dumped the sand from my shoes and tried to shake the rest out of my ears and hair as I contemplated the many directions the sand creature could have taken in the interconnected maze of subway tunnels. If the creature had headed toward the city, it would hit all the major T stations and cause an unbelievable disaster—morning rush hour would start soon. It could also head toward the end of the green line and into less populated areas; multiple branches would take it to commuter hubs there too.

Luckily, the sand slug had brought the other half of the desert back with it, and once I made it past the charred lizards we'd left on the track, the trail was easy to follow. It was headed toward North Station and away from the city. *Thank all that is good in the world.* There was only one track in that direction. I glanced at my phone to check the time and realized it was later than I thought. It was almost five in the morning, and the T would be opening any minute.

I freed Missy from her sandy sheath and felt a grim smile spread over my face as I set off at a jog toward Cambridge. After a few minutes, I hit the North Station terminal where we'd started our misadventure. It was a connection point between T lines, but my luck held out, and the sand creature stayed on the north green line track. The tunnel sloped upward, and I remembered that the next two stops were above ground, right next to a major shopping center. This was very, very bad.

The night sky was beginning to lighten into early morning, and I picked up the pace. The creature was heading toward the streets of Cambridge, where the track between Science Park and Lechmere

Station became elevated and open on both sides. I bounded up the tracks at breakneck speed then had to slide to a stop as I almost collided with the slug's rear end. Ten feet in front of the creature, the narrow tracks ran out into open air. The slug had stopped there, presumably because its wide, bulky body wouldn't be able to balance on the single rail, or maybe it didn't like heights.

At my noisy approach, the slug whipped around in a ridiculous show of dexterity, folding itself nearly in half to reverse direction and face me. Its tentacles started gyrating wildly, slapping the metal walls and the ground, and the sound echoed off the tight walls of the tunnel, deafening me as it blasted down the tunnel.

The creature scrunched its fleshy body in on itself and lunged forward. I flung out my hand and sent a wave of pure energy toward it.

It was exactly the wrong thing to do. The creature reared back and smacked its hard shell into the tunnel roof. It screeched as debris rained down around us then twisted back toward the open track and plunged off the rails and onto the street below.

I ran to the end of the tunnel and gazed over the fifty-foot drop. It lay belly-up in the middle of a major highway leading into the city.

Early-morning commuters had already hit the road. The highway was full of cars, and two had been crushed when the creature fell. Horns blared, and people screamed as they abandoned their vehicles and ran. More than one idiot had gotten out of their car to point their phone camera at the creature and its flailing tentacles. The slug screeched and rocked violently, its massive fifteen-foot body rippling and twisting as it attempted to right itself.

I had to get it off the road. I raced as quickly as I could down several flights of stairs to the street. The damn station doors were locked, but I solved that with a twist of magic before I tore out of the station and onto the street.

In the two minutes it took me to reach the ground level, the sand slug had righted itself and moved off the highway. Probably scared off by the noise of the cars and panicked people, it had veered through a small business park and was heading directly for the Cambridgeside Galleria Mall.

I cleared the obstacle course of cars and raced after it, following a wide, curving pedestrian path that wound around a man-made canal complete with a decorative water fountain. The creature shimmied up the path, barreling straight for a group of moms jogging with their strollers, totally unaware of the nightmare approaching them from behind.

"Get out of the way!" I screamed, waving my arms almost as wildly as the sand slug's tentacles. "Move! Move!"

As if in slow motion, a woman at the rear of the group turned and finally noticed the otherworldly monster barreling down on them. She screamed, and the moms dove in all directions, dragging their strollers with them. Their screams of terror seemed to spur the slug along faster, as if it were trying to escape the commotion.

I twisted my magic into a protective shield and slammed it down between their group and the creature. My shield was weak and sloppy, and I wasn't sure it would hold. Right before the creature smashed headfirst into the wall of magic, it proved to be magic-sensitive as well as ridiculously agile. It levered itself on its tentacles to rise inches in front of the barrier and twist toward me.

The creature raced back in my direction, completely panicked. It was trapped between the walls of the pedestrian walkway, the canal, and the barrier of magic at its back. There was only one way out. I planted myself in its path and raised my sword. The metal glinted in the light from the morning sun, which I was sure looked striking as hell, but Missy was like a toothpick compared to the size of the thing headed my way. I wrapped my magic around the blade, prepared to get up close and personal.

Shit, shit, shit! Without access to a direct magic source, I didn't have a lot of power to draw from, and it was going to take a lot more than a blazing toothpick to stop this thing. I was capable of drawing power from every living thing around me, but taking a life with magic was a slippery slope that led to dark and tainted magic. Plus, selectively drawing magic from the environment and not the living beings around me would require finesse, and I didn't have time to be careful.

I let my magic rise, weaving threads of energy into a sphere in my left hand as I held Missy with my right. Wildly flapping tentacles propelled the sand slug toward me, and the ground shook with its frantic slaps as it closed the distance. I waited until it was less than twenty feet away before I let my magic loose. The sphere of energy hit directly over the air slits on the right side of its bulbous head. It reared back, lifting its upper body at least seven feet in the air, and screeched. Terrified onlookers gaped at the creature, pointing their cameras in our direction.

I hit it again in the same spot. It squealed again. It opened its circular mouth and gnashed its needle-point teeth. As it rose over the canal, I realized I could drive it into the water and drown it. It was a sand creature, after all, and couldn't swim. Gritting my teeth, I whipped magic at its left side again. Exhausted and running out of magic reserves, I hit it twice more before it twisted and dove into the water. Before I had time to celebrate, the sand creature's flat tentacles spread wide on either side of its body and propelled it forward in the canal.

"Oh, come on!" The universe had to have been screwing with me. The end of the canal connected with the Charles River, and from there, to the entire city of Boston. I couldn't let the swimming slug get that far. I raced after the surprisingly buoyant critter, drawing on sheer willpower to move my body faster. I panted as I ran and wove magic, but I managed to slap a barely functional wall of energy at the end of the canal, counting on the creature's instincts to turn it away from another collision with magic and back toward me. If it rammed it instead, the barrier wouldn't hold.

My plan worked. It flipped like an Olympic swimmer and headed back in my direction. I skidded to a stop halfway alongside the canal. There were only about two hundred yards to the large decorative fountain, but the slug sped up, moving faster as it pumped its tentacles like oars.

"It's going to jump!" someone yelled.

Shit! It was building up speed to make the five-foot leap out of the water and back onto land. I was exhausted and sweating, and I'd run out of magic. I couldn't keep building walls and throwing magic at the slug. I raised my sword. It was going to get messy.

The creature leapt from the water, its maw open as it arced through the air. Its massive bulk rose above the water like a freaking ballerina.

A blazing thread of golden-yellow magic wrapped around the pointed spire of the water fountain. The spire broke from the fountain, flew through the air, and slammed into the creature's unprotected neck. The heavy metal pole pierced its thick hide, ramming through and out the other side. The slug crashed onto the edge of the pedestrian walkway.

Silas walked up to me, still blazing with magic, and surveyed the slug as it gave a final shudder, went completely limp, and slid backward into the water.

All around us, people ran to the water, whipping out their cell phones and snapping photos and videos of the dead monster floating in the canal. In the distance, I could already hear sirens blaring. I rested my sword tip on the ground and stared numbly at it all.

"Did those mobile phones record everything?" Silas asked.

"Yup," I said, my voice flat. Anger rose in my chest, but I forced it down as I sheathed Missy. It wasn't Silas's fault. Four had a sick sense of humor.

"Your government insisted on secrecy as part of their agreement with the New Alliance."

"Yup." I planted my hands on my hips as I tried to drag more air into my lungs.

The creature rolled in the water, its heavy shell pulling it upside down. The broken pole from the fountain stuck grotesquely out of its fleshy neck, and its mouth gaped to fully display its four rows of spiky teeth. People gasped and continued to film.

"If we hadn't gone into that pocket realm to set up a permanent portal, that creature wouldn't have come into this realm." I turned to face Silas and realized for the first time that he was covered in yellowish gore. I didn't even ask. "Four set us up."

"Yup."

Chapter Five

"What the hell is *he* doing here?" I demanded.

Lord Elias of House Marius—former leader of the Aeternal Council, secret leader of the Brotherhood, and traitor to everyone—lounged in his chair with a satisfied gleam in his sharp brown eyes. He was an objectively handsome man with celebrity good looks and shiny dark-brown hair, but his attractiveness only ran skin deep.

"Mr. Marius is our consultant, and he's here to ensure that we're all on the same page about what exactly is actually going on," Director Pascal replied.

The tension in the former dean's office grew thick as I choked on my rage. Elias should have been in a deep hole in the darkest of prisons, not advising the head of DODSI. I was tempted to launch myself across the conference room table and take care of the mistake I'd made when I turned him over to DODSI.

"I didn't think you were an idiot," I snapped at Pascal.

Casius put his hand on my arm, warning me to stay calm, but both he and Alaric had their magic up.

Director Pascal, a dark-skinned man with cropped black hair, was dressed in his personal uniform of slacks and a polo shirt. He sat across from me, Casius, and Alaric in the small conference room in our administration building, confidently believing that he held the monster's leash. But he was fooling only himself.

Agent Lennart stood stoically behind Pascal and tried to pretend he wasn't alarmed, but he'd grown pale and quiet. He struggled to keep his eyes in one place, but they kept darting around to the various magical auras in the room. If I hadn't been so angry, I would have been delighted to see Lennart's magic progressing. *Karma is such a bitch.*

Pascal's espresso-brown eyes flashed with anger at my name-calling. "Let's focus on the real issue at hand: you exposed magic to the general public, in direct violation of our agreement."

Silence fell.

I had to fight to keep my tone civil. "It wasn't our fault. The creature escaped into our realm, and I did my best to kill it with minimal damage."

"The United States government doesn't care how it happened," Director Pascal said through clenched teeth. "Two people were crushed on the highway. That *creature* is all over the internet—as is your face—and the media are asking questions about our ability to control the situation in Boston."

"It didn't hit any major news outlets," Casius said, drawing his hand through his sandy hair. He looked tired and much closer to his actual fifty years of age than he normally did, considering that regular magic users didn't appear to age much past their thirties.

"Because we cleaned up your mess and suppressed the story under the Patriot Act!" Pascal's voice rose. "You killed it in broad daylight! There were dozens of witnesses, not to mention the actual corpse for us to deal with. What the hell am I supposed to do about the footage all over the internet?"

"Did you want me to let that creature rage all over the city? I did all of us a favor and killed it before more people got hurt." I didn't, of course, tell him that I'd been the one to disturb that poor sand slug in the first place or that Four had started the problem—again.

I didn't know why the Fate of Change wanted our alliance with DODSI to fail, but it was hard to draw any other conclusion, given that he'd told us about the tear between realms then snatched Silas away at a crucial moment, sending the sand creature crashing into our world.

"We want you to rebind Earth's magic," Pascal said.

Casius gritted his teeth and shifted in the chair next to mine. "As we've said numerous times before, we can't rebind magic. The ability to create a magic source of that magnitude died with our ancestors."

"Why can't you use the same boundary spell you used to contain magic within the city limits?" Pascal's tone was accusing despite this being an old argument.

"We kept magic from spreading outside of Boston, but that's very different from rebinding it," Casius replied with more patience than I could have mustered.

"They have the power to do it. They just don't want to." Elias raised an eyebrow at us in challenge. "Lady Maeve alone could manage it."

Everyone on my side of the room bristled as Elias leaned back in his chair and crossed his ankle over his opposite knee. Not only was he not in prison, but he was also well dressed. Even his shoes were nice. I didn't know what he had said to get out of his much-deserved imprisonment, but seeing him feed lies to DODSI about magic made me want to murder-rage. It didn't matter what Elias said—it wasn't possible to rebind magic, at least not with our current magical knowledge and powers. Not even Silas, with his Fate powers, could do it alone. We needed to set the magic free before more tears happened and more people got hurt.

I dragged my grimace away from Elias's fancy footwear and tried to keep my voice calm as I addressed Pascal. "It's not possible. I don't have the power to do it without a dedicated power source, which we don't have. And you'd better believe that if I had that kind of power, I wouldn't be sitting here, listening to this bullshit. You're focused on the wrong thing—magic is a natural part of this world. Keeping magic contained inside the city is what caused our realm to tear into that pocket realm—the magic needs a place to go. We can't keep controlling all of Earth's magic."

"You must know better than to trust the predator in your midst. He's clearly trying to create dissent between our peoples," Alaric added. The former Aeternal Councilor's tone dripped with disapproval. The angry sneer on his face and the way he'd pulled his blond hair into a tight ponytail accentuated his angular, hawkish features.

"You have yet to prove that magic can be controlled," Pascal replied stiffly.

I leaned forward in my seat. "We're training the Mundanes who manifest powers, but if people knew more about magic—that it isn't so terrible and frightening—they'd transition easier. There wouldn't be so many incidents. The world can handle it, Director Pascal, but your government has threatened and silenced us." I was raising my voice again. I took a deep breath. "Together, we can manage the return of magic. The Mundane government will have an equal voice in our shared new world if you accept a coalition with us instead of tying our hands—it solves all our problems. We just need to work together."

"If you are on U.S. soil, you'll agree to be under the jurisdiction of the U.S. government, not the other way around," Pascal said. "Magic has only caused chaos."

It was an old argument. We'd had three different meetings with all the stars and stripes of the U.S. military, but they didn't trust what they couldn't control, and magic was way outside of their control. Ultimately, they didn't want to be part of our alliance—they wanted to run it. We'd talked ourselves blue in the face trying to convince them, and in return, they'd threatened to lock us up and lose the key.

The compromise had been to turn Boston into the testing ground. It was a tense partnership with a strict secrecy clause on our part—they needed to control the message. We'd abided by that... until I accidentally brought over a creature from another realm and fought it in broad daylight. I had to admit that Pascal's anger wasn't completely unjustified, considering how we'd sworn up and down not to go public.

"You promised us that this experiment would work." Pascal tapped his index finger on his thigh with each word. He was losing his cool. "You said that people would adjust peacefully, but we are seeing no progress whatsoever. You haven't rehabilitated a single person in two months. Your plan isn't working, and now there are monsters loose in the streets. You didn't tell us about these kinds of magic creatures, and I can't help but think that you're not being fully transparent."

"Agreed," Elias added.

"Let me tell you the whole truth," I snapped. "Lennart's team drags people in here, kicking and screaming. They're terrified. It takes weeks to convince them that they're not victims of your so-called infection, let alone teaching them to control their magic! You're just as much to blame as we are for the lack of progress. What you're asking us to do is impossible."

Elias leaned over to Pascal and whispered in his ear. Pascal nodded slightly. I stiffened along with everyone on my side of the table.

"Let's focus on one issue at a time," Pascal said. "Clean up your mess in Boston, Ms. O'Neill, and then we'll talk about the progress of your rehabilitations."

The rest of his threat lingered in the air. I couldn't resist. "Or?"

Pascal's face darkened, and all sense of good humor evaporated. "Let me tell you what this looks like if our experiment in Boston fails or magic *somehow* gets loose." He rose from his chair. "Mandatory screenings and registration laws. Restricted access areas... holding facilities and terrorist watch lists. Those are just a few things that have already been discussed." There was steel in his gaze as he paused to let that sink in. He liked to project a nice-guy demeanor most of the time, but I was absolutely certain that he would not hesitate to lock us up and throw away the key.

The silence in the room was heavy. A sense of dread settled deep in my stomach because we all knew his threats were real. We had magic, but they had technology that could nullify our powers. In a war between us, there would be a lot of casualties, and I wasn't certain we would come out on top.

Casius cleared his throat. "We are citizens of the United States with rights. Are you threatening us with unlawful actions for no reason other than we're different?"

Pascal snorted. "I don't care if you're Uncle Sam. You're a threat to our national security, and you'd better remember who holds the power here. You are not legal citizens in this country. You won't get a lawyer or a phone call or anything close to due process. You'll simply disappear one day, and no one will cry about it."

Outraged and ready to argue, I shifted forward in my seat, but Casius put his hand on my arm and calmly replied, "We have over a thousand civilians and children on this campus. Just so I'm clear, you're threatening to detain all of them, regardless of their rights, although we have broken no laws and have done nothing but cooperate with you?"

Casius's calm appeared to incite Pascal further, and his voice rose as he gestured toward Elias. "Detention is the least of your worries. We have reason to believe you're holding back in your efforts."

Elias just sat there, wearing a little knowing smirk, watching us all. I didn't know exactly how he'd maneuvered himself into this meeting, whispering advice in Director Pascal's ear and wearing his fancy shoes, but it was a huge problem.

"How long do you think you can get away with lying to them?" I snarled at Elias.

"How long do you think you can escape the consequences of unleashing magic on the unsuspecting Mundanes of this realm?" Elias replied.

"You're just pissed because you wanted to use that magic to rule the world, and I said no."

Elias shrugged, but his smile looked a bit stiff around the edges.

"If I killed him right now," Silas said as he strode into the room, "no one would be sorry for it."

Lennart and his three agents all drew their disruptors and aimed them at Silas. Elias flinched, losing some of his smug demeanor as Silas stopped beside my chair.

"Try it, Highlander," Lennart snarled, his finger on the trigger of his disruptor.

Silas didn't seem particularly bothered about it as he stared down Elias. His hair and clothes were coated in a fine layer of red dust, and he looked exhausted. Wherever Four had sent him this time, he clearly hadn't cleaned up or slept since I'd seen him last—over twenty-four hours ago. I tried to school my face into neutrality, but I was burning with questions. Four's errands were becoming almost nonstop.

Casius narrowed his eyes at Silas. I'd been vague on the details of the sand-creature incident, and Casius had questions. Really good questions—like how we knew about the tear in the first place, what we were doing in the pocket realm, and where the hell Silas had gone that was more important than dealing with the fallout. I thought about coming clean, but we'd handled things with the creatures, and telling Casius about our deal with Four would only make things worse. It was better to just handle it on my own.

"Mr. Marius is an official consultant to the government, and you will not attempt to kill him," Pascal said levelly.

Silas unleashed his feral smile. "I wouldn't just *attempt* to kill him."

Years of manipulation, distrust, and anger lay between Silas and Elias, and Silas wasn't making idle threats. Elias laughed, and Silas shifted forward on his feet. He was obviously baiting Silas, and if Silas took the opportunity to squeeze the life out of Elias with his bare hands—as the feelings raging through our Aegis bond indicated he wanted to do—it would blow up our entire agreement with DODSI. Casius squeezed my elbow, urging me to get the situation back under control.

With effort, I tore my gaze away from the two men and said to Pascal, "You know Elias is going to betray you, right? It's what he does. He'll scheme and lie and *murder* until he's the only one left standing. He's lying to you, and I suggest locking him in the deepest, darkest cell you can find and not listening to anything he says."

"I have my orders." Pascal's face tightened, and it was comforting to know that he'd been ordered to work with Elias but didn't trust him.

As I hoped, Pascal's reaction was enough that Silas backed down, and the tension in the room fell a few levels.

Elias picked a piece of lint off his trousers. "You should know that everyone in this room is wielding magic right now. With a single thought, they could kill you without lifting a finger."

Pascal stiffened, and the agents around us shifted. It wasn't a lie. We all had magic, and several—but not everyone—had accessed their powers. No one on our side would try to kill Pascal. It would have destroyed our tentative alliance, and we weren't cold-blooded murderers. Unlike Elias.

"How would you even know?" I snapped back at Elias. "You're no more capable of seeing magic than Director Pascal."

The binding on his magic could never be removed, since the Source was destroyed. There wasn't a single source of magic powerful enough. To prove my point, I let my magic rise around me.

Elias had no reaction, but Lennart jerked his disruptor toward me. "She's got her magic up!"

A lot of disruptors pointed my way. I raised an eyebrow at Lennart, and he licked his lips as the agents closest to him shifted away, realizing right as he did that he shouldn't be able to see magic unless he too had been infected.

I released my magic. "Your men are getting jumpy, Director Pascal. If any of them actually had magic abilities, they'd know that I'm not doing anything with my powers." I wasn't sure why I'd decided to do Lennart the favor of giving him an explanation for his outburst, and his glare confirmed that he didn't like it, either.

Pascal grunted and motioned for his agents to lower their weapons.

Elias's lip curled, showing his teeth. But he apparently wouldn't quit until blood was spilled, and he took another shot in the dark. "I'd keep my eyes on Lord Silas, Director Pascal. He's the most volatile of the group. He earned the nickname Death's Fury—quite descriptively, I might add—while in service to the Council. The atrocities I could list..."

Pascal shifted his attention to Silas. "Exactly how many murders have you committed, Mr. Valeron?"

"I'm at least one short." Silas hadn't accessed his magic, but his fury had gone ice cold.

I shifted forward in my seat again. If Silas tried to kill Elias, I'd have to try and stop him or at least slow him down before he started a war with DODSI.

"Whatever Silas and the Guardians did was under Elias's command as the leader of the Aeternal Council, which makes *him* responsible." With a glance at Silas, I added, "Violence is not the answer."

"Are you sure?" Silas sounded perfectly calm, but the icy rage burning through our Aegis bond hadn't lessened. There was a lot of history and justified anger there, but Silas's rage was burning too hot and too long.

With Elias's smug face begging to be slapped, I was tempted to agree that violence might get us somewhere, but I had to keep the peace. The most important thing was holding together our tenuous agreement with DODSI. I tried to send calming vibes through our Aegis bond. Silas hated the amount of blood on his hands—he literally questioned the state of his soul over all the death he'd caused. Elias had aimed for maximum damage, but he must not have realized how close Silas was to actually murdering him. There was no one in the room who could stop Silas if he decided to do it.

Pascal stood. "We're done here. Unless you want the full force of the U.S. government coming down on you, you will get this situation under control. We want you to rebind the magic and fix everything you've broken."

"The keystones around Boston are keeping magic contained, per our agreement." Casius spread his hands wide, pleading with Pascal to understand. "Despite what Lord Elias says, it's too late to rebind the magic that is now free. We don't have the knowledge or power... It's not possible."

"I'll be back in three days. I expect to hear that you've figured out how to make it possible, or we'll be forced to take more drastic measures." Pascal glowered at me. "And you: if I see your face on the internet again, it's over. Stay out of sight, or there's nothing I can do to save you next time."

Chapter Six

"What's twenty-four plus"—I glanced at the campus clock tower above the administration building—"seven? Because that's how long since I've had a shower and a bed to sleep in."

Ethan frowned as he took in the sand, dried sweat, and mud on my clothes and the various bits of gods-knew-what in my hair. "You look like hell."

Silas glowered, but it was Tessa who said, "Same to you, Ethan. And you smell."

Tamara laughed quietly. Casius had asked her to join our second attempt to create a portal between the pocket realm and Aeterna because she was the one who had figured out how to finally reopen a temporary portal to Aeterna. She'd reluctantly agreed after I'd pointed out that she could watch what Silas was doing and that it might help us figure out how to make that portal permanent.

Tessa and Tamara shared an amused chuckle while Ethan sniffed himself. The two of them had spent the entire afternoon gently teasing each other, and I was beginning to think that Ethan might be out of the running with Tessa.

Our trip had been a near disaster. The sand slug had apparently been incubating a large horde of baby slug creatures. They had the same half shell, but instead of mature tentacles for moving through sand, the little creatures had six crab-like legs with cactus-like spikes on them. Hundreds of them swarmed us the second we stepped through the portal. Tessa had to hold them off for over an hour while

Silas, Tamara, Ethan, and I built the new portal between the pocket realm and Aeterna. Silas could have done it on his own, but we both agreed that using his Fate powers would draw Four's attention, and we didn't want to trigger another disappearing act.

Ethan opened his mouth, no doubt to tell me that I smelled like roses, but Silas cut him off. "We *all* smell like the—what do you call that tunnel, again? The subpar system?"

"Yeah, that works." I said, deadpan, and Ethan snorted. I loved Boston, but the T was over a hundred years old, and it really did smell bad. "I gotta shower and sleep. We have that Alliance meeting in the morning to figure out what to do about DODSI's demands."

Ethan gave me a hug. "Get some sleep. You earned it today."

Silas grabbed my hand, tugging me out of Ethan's arms. "Yes, we'll see you tomorrow. Maeve and I are going to *our bed*."

Tessa laughed outright at Silas's ridiculous display of possessiveness, and I mouthed an apology at Ethan before I let Silas drag me by the hand toward our building.

When they were out of earshot, I rounded on him. "You need to learn to be nicer to Ethan. He's my friend, and now that he's my Anchor, he's going to be around a lot. Could you please stop acting like a total caveman? You don't need to lay claim to me."

"I understand that you're fond of him because of a shared childhood, but your *friend* is in love with you. He wants to rekindle your former romance."

"We were kids. I'd hardly call it a romance, and anyway, I'm not interested in rekindling any of that. I think he likes Tessa, so be nice."

"Tessa doesn't do relationships with males," Silas replied.

"Really? I thought she liked both men and women." I glanced back over my shoulder and noticed Tessa and Tamara chatting together quietly on the quad—flirting, if I wasn't mistaken. Ethan was already gone. I was happy for my friends, but it didn't help my matchmaking plans for Ethan.

Silas shrugged. "She likes sex with both, but all of her serious relationships have been with women. She and I once both—"

"Nope. I don't want to hear that."

He chuckled. "Now who's being possessive? Earthens are so
closed-minded about sex. Would it shock you to know that all the
Guardians have coupled at some point or another? It's only physical.
It's not uncommon for all of us to—"

"No. Nope. No. I really don't want to hear how you all hooked
up in giant orgies or whatever. Just... please be nicer to Ethan. You
don't have to be best friends, but you do have to be civil."

"If you wish," he replied noncommittally.

Silas could be hard and even harsh at times, but he had a particularly sour attitude about Ethan, and I didn't love that he'd been un-
usually short-tempered lately. Our Aegis bond had been closed more
often than open, but I knew he was trying to shield me from the diffi-
culties he faced working for the Fates and tried not to take it personally. Ethan and Silas needed time to let things settle between them.
Silas was still sore about the attempted bond-mating Ethan and his
mom had tried to force on me, and Ethan was... well, Ethan had feelings that would fade in time.

I had really hoped romance was brewing between him and Tessa,
but if not, I needed to think of someone else I could hook him up
with. Whoever it was would need to be able to deal with Alannah.
Ethan's mom was a lot, and Ethan needed someone who could stand
up to her but who wouldn't run over him in the process. Someone
who would appreciate his quirky side too. I sighed and shelved my
matchmaking until tomorrow—I was too exhausted to think about
anything but the hot shower and soft bed waiting for me.

The communal showers shared by the entire floor were blessedly
empty. I took my time showering, shaving, and washing my hair
twice to get all the sand and grime off. By the time I finished and returned to our room, Silas was already sprawled on our shared double

bed, bare- chested, with only a towel wrapped around his waist. He had one arm folded behind his head and a book in his hand—*Fifty Years of American Pop Culture*. The sight was enough to stop me in the doorway.

Damn, he looked good. He was muscular but lean, wide at the shoulders from a lifetime of sword work and narrow at the waist. His abs were ridiculous. The magic sigils that I could see thanks to my Harvester background stretched from his hip across his muscular arm and over his shoulder, begging to be traced. As I stood there staring at him, he put down his book.

I literally licked my lips.

"Close the door," he said huskily.

I closed the door, dropped my shower stuff onto the small desk under the window, and arranged my features in a disapproving scowl. "You probably shouldn't walk down the hall half naked. You might be attacked."

He scrunched his brow. "You think there's another traitor on the campus? Who would attack me?"

"All the single ladies. Probably the married ones too. You're awfully tempting in just that towel. Maybe we should buy you one of these." I plucked up the hem of my fluffy blue bathrobe and bit back a laugh.

"I think I can fend off the imaginary hordes," he teased. He showcased his ridiculous abs as he leaned over the side of the mattress to scoop a small, rectangular box from under the bed. "I have something for you."

"Oh? Is this an apology gift for disappearing and leaving me to be crushed to death by a giant sand slug? Are you going to tell me what *he-who-shall-not-be-named* wanted you to do?"

He furrowed his brows as if considering what to say.

I let him squirm because I really did want an explanation of what Four had been up to. *Did he time it like that on purpose?*

Finally, he said, "You're a skilled fighter. I had confidence that you weren't in mortal danger."

Praising my fighting skills was apparently better than an apology, because I got a warm, tingly feeling in my chest. Plus, I'd felt his rage through our bond when Four had snatched him away and left me in harm's way. It wasn't Silas's fault.

I held out my hand for the present. "Gimme." He did, and I hefted the box in my palm. Not too heavy, but not light, either. "Is it jewelry?" I kept my tone neutral, but if he'd bought me something sparkly, I wasn't sure I had it in me to fake enthusiasm. I was too tired.

His eyes lit up. "You highly underestimate me."

I opened the lid and gasped at what lay inside. "How did you get this?"

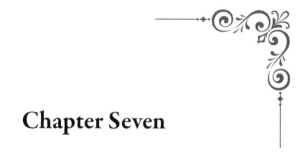

Chapter Seven

I held up the knife he'd gifted me the first time I visited Aeterna. As a distraction, I'd picked it out of a weapons shop in the lower city, and he'd had it engraved with his house sigil.

"I have my ways." He smiled, and the sight was like the sun rising on a stormy day. His smiles were rare lately and more precious than gems when they appeared. Even better, I could feel the sincerity of his happiness through our bond.

"Seriously, how did you get this? The portal to Aeterna was destroyed! Did you use the Fates' powers to do something crazy?"

"The Fates don't use portals. They only need a physical tie to that realm. I couldn't physically go to Aeterna no matter if I—" His voice choked off suddenly. He looked around the room with a furtive glance that set the hairs on my arms on edge.

"What? What's wrong?"

"I can't talk about... that." His Adam's apple bobbed as he swallowed hard. "It's no matter. You asked about the knife. I stored a few of my most valued possessions here on Earth some time ago. They were safer in this realm, protected by technology-based security measures where no one on the Council would think to look."

With a fair amount of effort, I didn't freak out about the apparent gag order I'd just witnessed stopping Silas from speaking. "The knife you gave me is one of your most valued possessions? That's sexy *and* adorable. You're like kryptonite to the cynical female heart."

He pulled me onto his lap and kissed me. I lost my thoughts for a hot minute, ready to explore where the kiss was headed.

"I love you with my entire heart, Maeve O'Neill of Earth. I will do whatever is necessary to keep you safe."

My naughty thoughts stuttered and died as I sensed his desperation through our bond. Something bad was happening. I couldn't pretend it away when Silas was nearly vibrating with troubled emotions. Whatever the Fates were making Silas do—it was bad. "Silas...What's going on?"

He leaned his forehead against mine. "You must lend me your trust. I'm doing everything I can, and I... I want to tell you more, but I can't. Please believe that I'm trying. I may not be with you for a time, but I won't leave you, no matter how desperate matters appear. I swear it."

Alarm flashed through me. "Silas, tell me what's happening. You're scaring me. What do you mean you won't be here?" My heart beat in double time as he scooted off the bed and started pacing. "Talk to me. I know you can't tell me everything, but dammit, Silas, we're partners in this. You have to let me help."

"Do you remember when you couldn't tell me about the visions the Fates gave you? Four told you that you would trigger those terrible events unless you kept everything secret, and you believed there was no other choice."

I remembered it all too well. Four had tricked me into triggering every bad event that eventually led to me killing the Fate of Death. It was exactly what he'd wanted all along, but then Four had demanded that I pay for those actions with my life. Silas traded ten years of service to Four instead. It had been a trade I didn't want him to make, and the fight we'd had afterward was epic. We'd mostly avoided the topic since then. I was still angry at Silas for making unilateral decisions that affected us both, and he was unrepentant in his desire to protect me. We loved each other more than ever, but figuring out how to navigate our current situation was tearing us apart.

With all of that festering between us, a flash of anger rose inside of me. "I never asked you to pay the price for my choices, Silas. We could have found another way."

"You're not understanding." He pinched the bridge of his nose. "I was willing to pay that price. That was my choice. My free will was the reason why I was an acceptable substitute to your bargain with Four. He backed you into that impossible situation because it had to be *your* free will. You had to choose to do what you did. He couldn't make you do it, and he couldn't do it himself."

"I don't understand. Silas, please, tell me what you're planning. Where are you going?"

He paced to the single window in our room and planted his hands on his hips as he gazed outside. "We all get to make choices. I am willing to sacrifice a period of my freedom to keep you alive. If it comes down to a matter of choice, you must know that I'll always choose you. I need you to remember that. I will always choose you."

"You're scaring me. I don't want to fight with you. We barely have any time together, and I miss you. Please don't... don't do anything crazy. I can't lose you." I couldn't stop the despair from leaking through my voice, and I couldn't stand the distance between us any longer. I moved in front of him, wrapping my arms around his chest as I turned him back toward me.

He sucked in a deep breath and let it out before he wound his arms around me. "Maeve... gods, I miss you too. I'm sorry." His whisper was filled with all the pain and longing I'd been feeling but without a shred of hope.

He buried his face in my hair, and I inhaled the spicy, clean scent of his skin and held it in my lungs until it burned. It felt like there were a limited number of breaths I'd get to take mingled with his scent. "I feel like I'm losing you."

"Ten years of my life is nothing," he said quietly. "I'm working on a way to break their ties to this realm. They're—" He swallowed hard and choked on his words again. "Fratch! I can't fratching talk about it."

"What can I do to help? It's killing me that they're doing this to you." I braced myself for the response I knew would come. He couldn't tell me.

Silas gently drew a hand through my hair. "It won't be the first time I've stained my hands to advance another's agenda. Please don't worry overly much. I'll survive."

Exhaustion suddenly overwhelmed me. It was all so damn much. "I hate this. My imagination is probably worse than reality, but I feel like I'm losing you to the Fates. We're hardly ever together anymore, and I know you can't talk about what you're doing, but I don't like it when you close down our bond." I bit my lip, waiting for the acknowledgment of the distance between us to break the fragile control we had over the situation.

"We can't let this drive us apart. We won't let Four win." His hand trailed the edge of my fluffy robe. "Promise me you'll keep fighting for us, even if it seems like there's no hope. Promise to keep me with you, and all will be right. Nothing can force us apart unless we let it. We have *free will*, Maeve. We can choose."

"I promise."

"It's you and me, forever and always."

"Forever and always. I like the sound of that." A tingle started in my stomach as his fingers traveled beneath the robe and across my bare skin. "Let's not talk about Four anymore."

He walked me backward until the backs of my knees hit the mattress, and I sat on the bed. Instead of joining me, he knelt on the floor. He grasped me by the hips and pulled me to the edge of the bed, positioning himself between my legs. My heart hammered as his deft fingers untied my robe and his lips trailed kisses up my thighs. I hummed in pleasure as his mouth and fingers stroked along my sensitive skin, teasing me. Silas draped my legs on his shoulders, and I lay back on the bed. Soon, I was gasping and panting under his enthusiastic and skilled attention.

"Shh, love. You'll bring the neighbors running."

I responded by weaving a privacy spell around our room.

Silas laughed as he rose over me, dropping his towel to the floor. "My Maeve," he said breathily.

I didn't like the hint of despair that lingered in his tone. Everything was dark and heavy, and we needed a little joy in our lives. So I dragged him on top of me and surprised him with a move I'd learned in my sparring sessions with Tessa. With a thrust of my hips, I rolled us both until I was on top, straddling him. I pinned his wrists above his head for good measure.

He could have escaped, but a wicked grin spread across his handsome face. "You've caught me. What is your plan of attack?"

I bit my lip, taking in the expanse of his delicious body beneath mine. "I'm deciding if I'll torture you first or launch a full-frontal assault."

"Whatever you do, don't hold back. Commitment is key to success."

I leaned into his neck and nibbled along the sensitive skin as I slid my body over his, enjoying the feeling of his skin against mine. He hummed deep in his throat as my lips roamed where they wanted and he pretended like he couldn't escape my hold. I sank lower, trailing kisses to the junction of his hip just below his delicious abs. "Tell me all your secrets, or I'll have to take this torture up a level."

"I'll never break," he growled. "Torture away."

I moved lower. "You asked for it."

As I focused on my torture, one of his hands broke free and slid into my hair. When I had him groaning and thrusting, I asked, "Do you surrender?"

He flipped me over so fast, I didn't see it coming. Suddenly, I was the one pinned on the bed. "Do *you* surrender?"

I wrapped my legs around his hips. "Willingly."

As our bodies connected, I felt the cool, familiar rush of his magic through our bond, and my magic intertwined with his. The rhythm of our bodies and the sharing of our magic threw me over the edge, and I cried out as my body rocked with pleasure. Silas didn't relent. He took it upon himself to torture me over and over until we were both spent, sweaty, and exhausted.

"Good thinking on that privacy spell," Silas said as he collapsed next to me on the bed. "You've got a colorful vocabulary, my love."

I flopped my hand on his chest, too tired to properly retaliate. "Please. You're equally as loud as I am."

He grunted in agreement and lifted my hand to his lips to kiss my palm. I rolled into his embrace as we both lay on the bed, completely satisfied.

"I've missed this," I said. "I miss *us*."

"It's the first time I've felt like myself in quite some time." Silas's jaw was tight, and once again, his gaze was a million miles away.

I stroked his face with the tips of my fingers as I searched his steel-gray eyes, hating the weight of all the things he couldn't tell me building between us. "What can I do?"

He brushed his lips over my knuckles then placed our intertwined hands over my heart. "Just trust me. I realize that's hard for you, but this is one thing you can't fix."

My phone chirped at the same time as his, bursting the small bubble we'd managed to carve out from reality. I picked up my phone from the little dresser and read the text aloud. "Casius wants to talk to us about DODSI's demands to rebind magic."

"I thought we were meeting tomorrow morning."

"He says he wants to talk to the two of us tonight."

Neither of us was happy as we dragged ourselves out of bed and pulled on our clothes. Instead of getting much-needed rest, we schlepped across the campus to Casius's office in the admin building.

The former college dean had left behind a giant mahogany desk in his office, and Casius had squished five chairs in front of it, which was a practical if not aesthetic adjustment to accommodate the number of people he regularly met with.

"Sorry for the late meeting. I needed to talk to the two of you privately." Casius motioned for us to sit in the circle of chairs. He sat across from us, forgoing the chair behind the desk.

"What's going on?" I asked.

"That's actually my question. It's obvious to me that something is going on with the two of you." He paused as if giving us time to admit to our nefarious secrets, but Silas and I remained silent, even as a sense of dread flooded me. "Look, I wasn't going to make a big deal about you missing meetings, Silas, but the excuses are getting thin. And then you two go off and cause this huge mess with DODSI, and I don't understand how you knew about the tears in the first place. I have a lot of questions, and you're not being forthcoming with the answers."

Silas folded his arms across his chest. "What are you implying?"

"I need to know if you're committed to being a part of this New Alliance." Casius raised his eyebrows at me.

"Of course we are," I said. "We're both working our asses off, trying to hold all of this together."

"Then I'd appreciate some direct answers, starting with how you knew about the tears between realms."

Silas leaned back in his seat. He was silent for a long time as he and Casius stared at each other. My stomach twisted in knots, but I managed to keep my mouth shut.

"Four told us," Silas finally said.

Casius nodded, unsurprised. "You still have the Fates' powers, don't you?"

Silas and I looked at each other, which was all the confirmation Casius needed.

"Why didn't you tell me?" The question was directed at me, and his betrayed tone cut through me.

I was flooded with shame, feeling like a child caught doing something I shouldn't have and being hauled into his office. "We made a deal with the Fates so they wouldn't retaliate after I killed one of them, and Silas kept their powers so he could do... whatever they needed."

"You shouldn't have kept this a secret, Mae," Casius said. "This is a big deal. We need to tell the New Alliance."

I shook my head. "The Alliance barely trust each other. We're figuring out how to govern together, and we can't afford infighting when we need to be united. We already have DODSI breathing down our necks, and if the Alliance thinks Silas has been compromised—"

"He *has* been compromised." Casius turned his attention to Silas. "What exactly does 'service' mean? Do you have to do everything they command?"

"No, of course not," I interjected quickly. Silas was being awfully quiet and wouldn't meet my gaze. I tugged on Marcel's charm as fear crawled up my throat and started to tighten its grip. "I mean, he didn't agree to do *anything* Four said. You..." I kept glancing between them, waiting for Silas to confirm my statements. "You still have your free will. You said that free will is very important to the Fates, and they can't break that. Four can't force you to do something you don't want to do... right?"

Silas's face was unreadable, and the bond between us closed again. "I'm doing this of my own free will. That's all I can tell you."

Casius's brow furrowed. "You keep acting like you're the only one who should make decisions, even when it so clearly impacts the rest of us. I can't believe you kept this a secret. What were the exact terms of the agreement?"

I flushed red at his reprimand as I searched my brain for the words Four had used. *In exchange for the life of Maeve O'Neill, Silas of House Valeron will...* "He agreed to 'willingly do Four's bidding' for a decade." I covered my mouth as the complete horror of what we'd done dawned on me. Silas had to *willingly* do whatever Four said. He'd handed over his free will, and Four could make him do anything.

"I have this under control." The expression on Silas's face was cold. "I don't want anyone else getting involved."

"We need to tell the New Alliance," Casius said.

"I would not recommend that," Silas said. "The Fates haven't forbidden me from talking about our deal, but I'm not able to talk about the specifics of their tasks. If you tell the New Alliance, they will ask questions I cannot answer. You will draw Four's attention, and that is the absolute last thing we need. Trust me."

"I don't like it," Casius replied.

"Casius, just think about it first," I pleaded. "The Alliance will freak out, and we need everyone to focus on the situation with DODSI. We have a lot to do without worrying about our situation. The deal is done, and other than not being able to control when Four needs him, Silas isn't doing anything the others need to know about. It's a pointless distraction."

Casius was quiet for a long moment. "Okay, fine. I won't make the others aware of your situation until it becomes relevant. But I won't lie to them, either. I'm not happy about this, and I'm not happy that you kept this from me. I expected more from you, Maeve."

"Thank you." I exhaled in relief, and Silas seemed to relax as well. "I'm trying to keep all of this together, but there's just so much. I don't want to distract everyone from our goals."

"I know you had good intentions, but you've made some big choices, and there are equally big consequences to what you did." Casius said. "It's not all going to be roses and ponies."

"I know. I'm doing my best."

"Let's hope your best is enough."

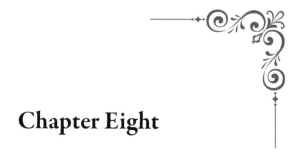

Chapter Eight

The smell of lemongrass and too many floral things tickled my nose. I sneezed, and the green-robed Fae Healer shushed me.

"Sorry," I whispered back. I tried not to breathe louder than the sound of the softly trickling water. No one else was in the spacious birthing center, which had been transformed from individual patient rooms to a centralized birthing retreat complete with a hot spring that fed into three shallow bathing pools. My nose tickled again as I looked around and found Aria floating in a basin of magic-infused water with Stephan by her side.

"Hey! Aria! Stephan!" I called out.

"Quiet!" The Healer hissed. "This space is for meditation and tranquility, not stomping around with your negative energy."

It took everything inside of me not to snap back at the awful woman. I took a deep breath and reminded myself that I was there for Aria. "Sorry," I repeated.

I was so not in the mood to deal with this. The morning after we'd spilled our secrets to Casius, I'd woken up in an empty bed. That wasn't unusual, except I'd had to deal with yet more questions about Silas's whereabouts from the Alliance members, armed only with the flimsy excuse that he was taking care of personal business. Casius had stayed silent, but I was worried about our deal with Four, and I didn't know what to do to help. With those thoughts in my head, it was no wonder the Healer believed I had negative energy. Barefoot and trailing the long green robe I'd been forced into, I padded around a stone path that wound in circles toward the pool where Aria floated. I was literally walking in circles.

"This is ridiculous." I gave up the path and stepped over a row of flowering plants onto the next ring of stones. The judgmental Healer hissed at me as I hopped over the last two circles to reach Aria, but Stephan smiled, amused at my lack of patience.

"How are you feeling? Is the baby coming?" I asked Aria.

"I am quite well. It will be several days yet until my body will be fully harmonized." Aria closed her eyes as she floated, completely re-laxed.

I stared at her in total confusion. "Uh-huh."

A light, relaxed tinkle of laughter escaped her lips. "The baby isn't coming yet. I was hoping I might ask you to attend me at the birthing. I know you're very busy with everything you oversee... but I'm hoping you can make the time."

I froze in panic. A wave of calming energy washed over me, and I half smiled at Stephan, who had to have been the source of the magic, appreciating the subtle wash of calm he exuded. Stephan was Aria's chosen life mate, the baby's father, and Silas's half-brother. His Fae lineage through his father's side had given him Empathic magic abilities.

Stephan and Silas shared a mother, and they had a strong physical resemblance. But where Silas was dark and reserved, Stephan was blond and extroverted. Stephan loved people, and people loved him back.

"I'm honored, but I don't really know about... uh, birthing stuff." Aria and I had bonded over surviving our shared kidnapping, one that I'd been dumb enough to walk into, accidentally dragging her with me. In my defense, I hadn't known much about magic at the time since my real memories had been blocked, but our experience had brought us closer together. That and the fact that she found a way out of the bond-mating agreement forced on her and Silas made her downright angelic in my book.

Aria cradled her rounded stomach, her eyes soft and doe-like. "The Healers will attend to the medical necessities. You need only be present as a comfort to me and to help me keep my mind off the labor pains."

The Healer, who had wandered closer to keep an eye on me, pursed her lips in disapproval.

"Are you sure you don't want some drugs? Or Stephan could just hit you with his calming powers. It's like a magical Xanax." I looked at Stephan hopefully, but he scrunched his brows in confusion at my reference to Mundane drugs. Aria and Stephan had been through a lot to be together, and I both liked and respected the hell out of him. Silas and I couldn't be happier that he had become the Prime of House Valeron now and that he and Aria would be carrying on the family line with the birth of this baby.

"A natural birthing process would be best for the baby," the Healer said defensively. "Primitive drugs won't be necessary."

I moved aside as the Healer helped Aria rise from the shallow pool and draped an earthy green robe around her. Stephan and the Healer gently gripped each of Aria's forearms, steadying her as she navigated out of the tub—not that she needed it. Even with an almost-full-term baby in her belly, she was agile and graceful. Aria must have had some Fae heritage in her bloodline, with her natural grace and tall, thin frame. Not that I was jealous of her innate beauty. I had... grit. And a collection of pointy things to stab people who annoyed me.

I plodded after them and watched Aria settle amongst a mountain of pillows on a raised and padded surface. She sighed happily as the Healer began rubbing her feet. I wasn't any good at foot rubbing, and I was definitely not calming. I was clearly a liability in a tranquil environment, and Aria would regret picking me over drugs during her delivery.

"You're the only female relation I have. My mother didn't make it out of Aeterna..." Aria's voice wobbled, and Stephan gave me a warning look. "Would you please do me the honor? I promise you won't be a burden."

I sighed. *Dammit*. "If you're sure you won't regret asking me when you realize you could have had drugs. They're like magic."

The Healer sniffed loudly, clearly insulted.

"I'm sure." Aria closed her eyes, completely at peace as a small smile tugged on her lips. She was ridiculously lovely, but she was also clever and stubborn. I had a sneaking suspicion she'd just manipulated me right into the place she wanted me to be—and it had probably been stupidly easy for her too. Maybe I could convince her to change her mind or, like, fall in a pit and break my neck. She'd definitely be better off with the drugs.

"Where's Silas? I sent for the both of you," Stephan asked.

I froze, unsure what to say as all of my worries about him jumped to the surface.

"Whoa, I didn't think your anxiety could go any higher, but it is astronomical. Is something the matter with Silas?" Stephan asked.

I glanced at the Healer. I didn't want to talk about Silas in front of her. Stephan and Aria already knew about our deal with the Fates, but they didn't know how bad things had gotten lately.

"Could you give us a moment, Healer?" Aria asked.

"No, no. She should stay. I don't want to interrupt the harmony stuff." I waved my hands in the air, trying to fend off this conversation, but the woman rushed off to reset her chi or something.

I swallowed thickly as I looked at Stephan and Aria. "You have enough to worry about. I don't want to put this on you—"

"Of course you'll tell us. We're family," Aria said.

"What exactly is Four making him do?" Stephan asked quietly. "He's been dodging around for weeks, acting all secretive—even more secretive than usual. Honestly, I've barely seen him."

I had no idea when or if Silas would be back, and I couldn't continue to cover for him on my own. Stephan and Aria were family, which was why we'd told them and Tessa about the deal with Four. We'd downplayed the situation and convinced them not to be concerned about it. But now... they deserved to know the full extent of the trouble we were in, and it wasn't going to be a fun story to tell. "Four's been sending Silas on errands. I don't know what he's doing, but it's not good."

Stephan and Aria wore nearly matching expressions of alarm. Now that I'd voiced my fears, I couldn't stop, and all my feelings spilled out.

"Every time he goes away, he comes back... I don't know. Distant? I don't know what's going on. The Fates have him on some kind of gag order. He can't say much, but he told me that he'd be gone for a while this time. I'm not sure if he's coming back at all, and I'm afraid of what it's doing to him long term. He's scared. I've never seen him like this. Silas tackles everything head on, and he always comes out on top—I know that—but this feels different. When I had a fraction of the Fates' powers, I started to lose touch with my humanity. I didn't care about anything, and I... well, that's when I destroyed the Earthen Source. Nothing mattered but setting the magic free, and I'm worried about what their power is doing to him."

A light brush of Stephan's worry washed over me. "I think you're right to be worried. What can we do?"

A little of the weight lifted off my shoulders, knowing that Stephan and Aria would help me figure out what was happening. I'd downplayed my concerns with Casius, but I couldn't ignore the desperation I'd sensed from Silas during our last night together, and I couldn't ignore my own fears. "Could you talk to Silas and see what you can sense from him? If the Fates' powers are really changing him, then we need to do something."

"Of course, yes. He's so stubborn, he could very well be dealing with more than he knows how to handle. He can't just shut us out."

"Thank you. We had to tell Casius, and he's agreed not to tell the Alliance, but I don't know how much longer we can keep this secret, given the amount of time Silas has been spending doing things for the Fates."

My contraband phone trilled in my bra, and the Healer's head snapped up from across the atrium. I held my breath, irrationally hoping it was a message from Silas as I glanced at the screen.

Code Red. Media Room.

Code Red wasn't a drill. It was a summons for the entire Alliance. My phone began buzzing with ETA replies, my anxiety ratcheting up with each one.

The Healer stalked toward me with her fists balled at her sides as her green robe fluttered behind her. "That's it! Out! I told you, no technology. You're destroying the balance of energy!"

I threw an apologetic grimace at Aria and Stephan and backed away before she got close enough to snatch my phone out of my hands. "I'm sorry. We'll finish talking about this later—keep this between us, okay?"

Stephan nodded warily, and Aria waved her hand, shooing me away. "Go, go. The harmonizing will be several days yet. I'll send for you once the labor begins."

The Healer's lips tightened into a thin line as I backed out of her reach. Honestly, I didn't blame her for not wanting me there. I texted my ETA and hastily retreated.

The birthing center had been set up in the west wing of the campus in Building Two, where the families from Aeterna had settled after extensive renovations, and it took me almost ten minutes to hoof it to the media room in the center of campus.

The internal hallways connecting the three main buildings had clearly been laid out by someone intent on making my life hell. They zigged when they should have zagged and were further sectioned off to accommodate the refugees from Aeterna. I swore a compass would have gotten lost without the updated signage we'd installed.

Inside the media room, the mood was tense as the members of the Inner Circle and the Aeternal Council, what we now formally called the New Alliance, gathered. Everyone was there before me except Casius, Alannah, and of course Silas.

With two-thirds of the population of our new magical community coming from Aeterna, we didn't have much choice but to incorporate the former Aeternal Counselors into our governing body, no matter how awful they'd been. At least we'd lost the worst of them with Nuada dead and Elias's magic bound.

We'd also acquired the splinter groups and their leaders—Alannah, Gia, and Levi's people, minus the real Levi, who had been tragically killed by a Fae spy. The New Alliance was a powerful group of people who were used to acting independently and had never trusted each other, and learning how to work together had made for a rough transition. The tension showed every time we were all forced together.

"Where's Casius?" I asked. "What's the Code Red about?"

I got shrugs and shaking heads all around. The political alignments were visible in the way each of the representatives had taken their positions within the media room. The former Lord Councilors congregated on one side: Lord Alaric, Aria's father and arguably the most influential of the group, stood near Lord Nero and Lady Octavia, the shifter representatives. Nero was a hulking mass of a man who transformed into a monstrously large bear, but Octavia was his opposite, delicate in frame and feature, and her animal form was a falcon the size of a large dog.

The former Inner Circle had already positioned themselves on the opposite side of the room. Tamara, our resident expert on all things magical, stood beside Jason, our diplomat. The final member of the Alliance and leader of the smallest splinter group was Gia. She smiled at me as I gently scooped my infant niece, Marcille O'Neill, from her arms and kissed the top of her tiny head. My niece was perfection. With a healthy head of curly black hair and dark-brown skin, she favored her mother's coloring, but she had my brother's hazel eyes.

"Do you know what the Code Red is about?" I asked Gia quietly. "Why are we all standing here?"

She shook her head. "No idea. I know they met with DODSI today. Maybe something happened."

"They did? No one told me."

Gia shrugged. "I think it was only Casius and Alannah. The visitors left a couple of hours ago."

I didn't know why I hadn't been told about the meeting. Even if they wanted to keep it small, I should have at least known it was happening. And why would Casius bring Alannah, of all people? I didn't have much time to dwell on my concerns as Alaric glanced in my direction and frowned.

"Where is Lord Silas?" he asked.

I stuck to the same story. "He's busy with personal matters."

My excuse was thin, and it gathered some additional looks—the two of us had become a common intermediary between the Earthen group and the Aeternal one. I bit the inside of my cheek as I rocked the baby in my arms and forced myself not to appear worried. We'd managed, so far, to keep the little issue with Four to ourselves, but now that Casius knew, maybe I could use his help to figure out a better cover story.

"Does anyone know where Casius is? I thought this was urgent." My redirect was not very subtle, but Casius and Alannah walked in, stalling any more questions about Silas. Casius scanned the room, making sure everyone was there. He paused on me and raised his eyebrows, asking silently if Silas was joining us. I shook my head slightly.

"We just got word from DODSI..." He exhaled slowly through his nose, his face pinched and pale. "More pocket realms have opened all over Boston. Magic is flooding the city."

Chapter Nine

C asius tapped a closed fist on the outside of his thigh as we watched the television screens. Boston was in utter and complete chaos. The local and national news stations were live-broadcasting a steady stream of creatures coming out of at least three new pocket realms, and people were fleeing the city despite the police blockades. They were doing their best to maintain the quarantine zone DODSI had established, but people were rioting. They wanted out.

Once again, the news channels showed cars gridlocked on the Pike and every major road out of Boston. Looters were terrorizing the downtown. The Mundane police had a lot to deal with, and that wasn't even counting the magical creatures coming from other realms, which they weren't equipped to deal with at all. Every news channel depicted a nightmare.

"There are more protesters gathering outside of the campus," Gia noted as she took baby Marcille back and settled into a chair to nurse her.

I twisted Marcel's charm between my fingers as my face was splashed across the TV screens, along with clips from the sand-slug incident. A text feed across the bottom of one channel spewed out facts about me—my name, age, and speculations about my abilities. Apparently, I was a dangerous and unstable person of interest.

"Director Pascal will not find this acceptable," Lady Octavia noted.

No shit. The news sure didn't waste time in deciding who to blame when new magical creatures showed up, and Pascal had been very clear that I needed to keep a low profile. This was insanely bad for us.

The news feeds kept switching between the three portals spewing unearthly creatures into our realm and speculations about my involvement, which quickly expanded to speculations about our compound. The first tear between realms had opened right in the Boston Common, spewing a thick swarm of lizard-looking creatures with bulbous red sacks around their necks. The second was in Kenmore Square, near the Fenway baseball stadium. There was phone video of furry creatures that scurried on four legs like rats but appeared to be able to fly short distances with sets of leathery wings. They were attacking everything within fifty feet of them, but luckily, no one had been killed yet.

The final tear was in the subway system, near where we'd finished closing the realm with the sand creature. The security footage from the station showed the morning commuter crowd fleeing the platform as a flood of snake-like creatures poured out of the tunnels.

Casius turned away from the televisions, leveling me with a look that would have inspired terror in my teenage heart. "You said you knew how to stop these tears. You said it was fixed."

"We fixed the one, but clearly, keeping all of Earth's magic trapped in one area is causing more." My tone was sharper than I intended, but at least I stopped myself from saying "I told you so."

"How fast can you fix these new tears?" he asked, completely ignoring the cause behind the rips.

"You can't just keep sending Silas out to create portals! The only way to stop this from happening over and over is to release the magic we've trapped in the city."

"Or maybe you shouldn't have unbound the source in the first place," Alannah sniped.

I started to tell her exactly what I thought of her helpful suggestion, but Jason moved between us with his palms raised. "Let's focus on the present. What can we do about the tears now?"

"We need to close them and quickly, before Director Pascal makes good on his threats." Casius said. "I managed to convince them for more time to research rebinding Earth's magic, but this is a huge setback. The public is being terrorized by magic."

"Hold a moment." Alaric leveled a suspicious gaze on me. "You implied that Lord Silas could create a portal on his own, yet you told us that his Fate powers had faded. Both of yours, in fact. How is that possible?"

Shit. I didn't have a good explanation. I glanced at Casius for help, but his mouth was set in a thin line. He'd already been clear that he wanted to tell the rest of the Alliance, and he wasn't going to help me cover this up.

I decided on a version of the truth. "We thought Silas's powers would fade like mine did... but it's taking longer than we hoped. It probably has to do with the fact that he had more of their magic than I ever did." I sounded like a Fae, carefully making truthful statements that avoided the actual truth.

Alaric's brow furrowed. "Why didn't you tell us this before?"

"Because she's incapable of *not* making things worse!" Alannah declared. "Your actions caused this, and now, there are creatures from other realms everywhere!"

I needed to redirect the train wreck before it claimed more casualties. "We didn't cause the tears! Keeping all of Earth's unbound magic trapped inside the boundary spell is creating an imbalance between our realm and others. We can't keep all of Earth's magic trapped in one area, or these rips between realms will keep happening."

"But how did you learn of the tears in the first place?" Alaric was totally locked in on the questions I hadn't been able to answer without revealing our connection to the Fates.

The entire situation was spinning out of control. "Look, I'm sorry I didn't tell the Alliance before we tried to fix that tear on our own. We thought we were helping to solve a problem before it got bigger. Yes, Silas could create more stable portals, but we'd just be putting a Band-Aid on the real problem. We have to set magic free, or this is going to keep happening."

"And where is Silas? Why didn't he respond to the Code Red?" Nero piled on.

"He's busy with a personal commitment, like I said." The lies were getting more and more complicated.

Every single member of the Alliance stared at me like I was an idiot child. Some looked confused, some outraged. Nobody was happy with my explanations or my apology, and I honestly couldn't blame them. I could drive a car through the holes in my story.

"The world isn't ready for this," Casius said finally. "We have to fix it."

I blinked at him. "What does that mean?"

He balled his left hand into a fist again. "The people DODSI brings us can't adjust. They're unable to use their powers with any control, and that's if they don't have a full mental breakdown once they realize what's happened to them. We haven't had a single person ready to return to normal life, and now this!" He flung his hand at the televisions. "This *experiment* is a failure. You made a decision for the whole world, and you were wrong."

I felt like I'd been slapped. For months, ever since I'd unbound magic in our realm, I'd sensed silent resentment from Casius and the others every time something went wrong. But I'd hammered through the kinks and twisted myself inside out to make things right. I'd done everything I could think of. I barely slept. I spent an extraordinary amount of time resolving the infighting among the Alliance members, and along with Gia and Ethan, I had dedicated nearly every waking minute to transitioning the Mundanes DODSI brought us—but it was all falling apart faster than I could hold it together.

"The problem is the government. If DODSI would just—"

"We tried it your way," Casius interrupted. "You said it yourself: containing unbound magic in Boston is causing an imbalance. We can't keep fixing the fallout. We need to find a way to bind Earth's magic into a single source again before the effects worsen. It's the only way we can appease everyone at this point. Director Pascal was right. There has to be a way."

Murmurs of agreement rose around the room. I shook my head. "The world needs to accept that magic is natural!"

Casius stayed calm as he looked me in the eye and hammered the last nail in the coffin. "You can't force the world into accepting magic, Maeve. You tried, and it didn't work. Now, we have to fix this mess before more innocents are hurt. Either help us fix what you did or stand aside."

He turned back to the others. "We have to figure out a way to rebind Earth's magic—a single source of magic kept this realm stable for a long time. It wasn't perfect, but we're better prepared this time. Our Alliance can share the power equally."

The Alliance members were listening raptly, some already nodding along.

My stomach was in knots. I couldn't believe how quickly this had gone so wrong. I couldn't believe Casius was doing this.

"We'd need enough power to rebind Earth's magic into a single source. Where could we find that kind of power?" Octavia's expression was eager as she considered the possibility of gaining access to more magic. Ever since Aeterna fell, they'd been at a disadvantage, and it didn't surprise me that the former Aeternal Counselors were hungry for more power.

Alaric pursed his lips in thought. "We have an unprecedented number of magic users in one location, and with your sect's ability to harvest magic from their surroundings... perhaps a multicircle conjuring would be able to sustain that complexity."

Tamara took a half step forward, her eyes lighting up—she loved solving a complex magical puzzle. "We've managed a three-circle connection before. I've been thinking about a way to set up a second set of three with equal power and connect them together, but we'd need someone who can hold a lot of magic to act as the focal point."

Silas and I were the only ones who could do that. "I don't agree with this plan," I said.

"What about Silas?" Nero asked. "If he has the Fates' powers, he should be able to manage it."

I couldn't believe what they were discussing. I had to turn the conversation back to the right path, but I didn't know how. They had to see that magic couldn't be hoarded by a few people. "We need to address the tears between realms, not try to rebind magic. That won't fix what's happening now."

Alaric completely ignored me. "I wish I had access to the Council's library. The founders regularly built conjurings of that magnitude. We experimented with the Aeternal Harvesters, but they were never powerful enough."

"Lord Elias was experimenting with multiple-harvesting circles in Aeterna," Octavia agreed. "He claimed that he'd managed five connected circles, but like you, he felt that the limited abilities of the Aeternal Harvesters were impeding progress. It was one of the reasons he was so driven to find the Lost Sect."

"How? When?" Alaric's face started to color, clearly irritated that Elias had gone behind his back in his area of expertise. "How did I not know about this?"

Octavia shrugged, but her expression was smug. "Lord Elias showed me a text once with the setup."

"Which obviously does not help us now." Nero waved a hand dismissively. "Ironically, we now have the Harvesters' powers, but the knowledge is lost to us with the collapse of our realm. There's no way to return to Aeterna."

All the former Lord Councilors fell silent, each wearing a different bitter expression. The reminder of the power and knowledge they'd lost with the collapse of their realm clearly burned them.

"Should we ask Lord Elias?" Alaric asked with a deep frown.

Multiple people, including me, grimaced at the suggestion, but Nero was the first to speak up. "His demands would be significant. I assume he will ask for his powers back if we succeed. I do not think putting ourselves in his debt should be our first option."

"Each of us knows a little bit," Jason said. "If we work together, we might be able to recreate the technique for binding magic, and that would restabilize the magic between our realm and all these pocket realms, like Maeve said. We might not need Elias's help at all."

Tamara's face was bright with hope. "I have all the notes from my experiments, and our ancestors' notes too. We can start there."

Heads bobbed in agreement.

I couldn't hold my tongue any longer. "Look, I know I acted on my own when I unbound magic, and I know that wasn't the best way to do it, but that doesn't mean we can't make this work. If you rebind Earth's magic, you'll make us a target for anyone who wants to control all that power, not to mention that it stunted the development of every single Mundane on Earth. They should have developed powers a long time ago, but we kept all the magic for ourselves. The world deserves a chance to accept magic—it's been less than a couple of months. I know things aren't going perfectly, but we just need more time. Don't repeat our past mistakes."

The faces around me were pinched and tight. They didn't agree with me. They only wanted the power back.

"Think of everyone who died fighting over that magic—it's too much for one group to control!"

"'Absolute power corrupts absolutely,'" Ethan quoted quietly.

"Yes, exactly! Magic belongs to the entire world. We should be figuring out a way to help magic spread peacefully. We shouldn't let DODSI force us into doing it their way."

Casius waved his hand toward the wall of television screens. "The world wasn't ready for magic, Maeve. You forced it, and look what happened."

"But—"

"No!" Alannah's perfectly manicured hand slashed through the air. "Just no, Maeve. Not this time. You don't have the right to choose for the whole world again. You wanted this New Alliance, so let's put it in their hands. I call for a vote."

All I could do was stare in shock as my desperation choked me. This couldn't be happening. Everything I'd built, everything I was trying to do, was crumbling in front of me. The future of Earth was falling apart, and I had no choice but to stand there and watch them vote.

"All in favor of attempting to rebuild the Source?" Jason asked.

Every single member of the former Aeternal Council raised their hand. From my sect, Jason, Tamara, Alannah, and Casius raised their hands. Only Ethan hadn't voted in favor. Silas wasn't there, but it was enough. Even if the three of us voted against everyone else, it was over. The vote was over. I stared at them in shocked disbelief. Binding Earth's magic had led to the Brotherhood hunting us, the Fae attacking us, and ultimately the complete collapse of Aeterna and thousands of deaths. Hundreds of my people had died defending the Earthen Source, including every single member of my family. The consequences of blocking magic from spreading outside of Boston were splashed all over the television screens in front of us, but somehow, all they saw was an opportunity to return to the way things were. They only cared about getting their powers back.

"The vote carries," Casius said. "We need to begin work right away on a joint plan for building the new source. Tamara, can you dig up everything Thomas had on the—"

"What about the rips?" I interrupted. "We have to close off those pocket realms before more people are hurt. If the Inner Circle will go with me, we can build stable portals in those pocket realms and buy ourselves more time before we do anything rash."

"We need to focus on rebinding magic," Octavia argued.

"Once we bind magic in this realm, the imbalance of power won't cause instability between the realms any longer, just as you said," Jason said more gently. "The tears may close on their own."

"But what about the creatures already on the streets—"

"Your Mundane government will deal with them," Nero said with blunt disregard for nonmagical lives.

"It's not ideal, but the damage is done," Casius said. "DODSI can sort this out, and by the time they come knocking, we'll have a plan in place to rebind magic. That's what they want from us, and once we control all of Earth's magic, we won't be at their mercy anymore. We can still salvage this situation."

"But—"

"You have a chance to redeem yourself here," Alannah said. "I know this wasn't what you wanted, but we all make mistakes. You have a chance to fix everything you broke if you help us rebind magic, and then we can move forward together."

These people were supposed to have been my family. I'd tried so damn hard to be the leader my people needed, but in the span of time it took for a single vote, they'd turned on me. They didn't care about the sacrifices I'd made or that my family had died trying to protect Earth's magic from terrible people who had tried to control the world. They didn't care that Mundanes were dying on the streets. All the New Alliance cared about was more power for themselves, and they didn't care what it cost. I refused to be part of that.

I turned on my heel and walked out.

Chapter Ten

"**S**tay alert." Tessa signaled to the group of forty Guardians we'd secretly mobilized after I walked out of the Alliance meeting, and we ran together across the Boston Common, cutting through the grass from the subway station toward the Frog Pond.

The Alliance had decided to leave the Mundanes to their own defenses, but I couldn't stomach people getting hurt when we could help them. Especially when I had a sneaking suspicion a certain four-letter fiend was behind the new tears.

The Frog Pond was a large flat patch of concrete the city filled with water for a children's splash pool in the summer and ice skating in the winter. I led us toward it quickly, eager to leave the wide-open grassy area and avoid any police patrolling the streets. It had been several hours since we'd left the campus, and most of that time had been spent making our way past the police blockades and into the city. Because of that, we'd had to make the last of our trek on foot through the closed subway tunnels before surfacing into the park. I didn't know exactly where the tear had materialized, just that creatures had started terrorizing people near the carousel in the Public Garden.

I stopped in my tracks when the carousel came into view. The iconic children's landmark had been abandoned midride, leaving riderless wooden horses and other mythical creatures bouncing and spinning on the track while tinny carnival music played over speakers. *Creepy.*

Tessa and the Guardians crouched down behind me. "What is that?" Tessa asked. "Why is it spinning?"

"It's for kids." My brain was spinning along with the blue-and-white striped top. A crawling sensation began between my shoulder blades and worked its way down my spine. "Let's shut it off and figure out where that rip is."

"Forward with caution." Tessa signaled to the Guardians, who'd split into two groups and edged around either side of the Frog Pond and toward the carousel. Their magic flared, and they drew weapons. Together, we moved toward the slowly rotating carousel to the eerie backdrop of carnival music. The carousel creatures were on their never-ending parade, and the lights were on, but...

A flicker of movement caught my attention at the edge of the Frog Pond. It was the middle of summer, and four inches of water lined the shallow splash pad. It was dark, but the water was *moving*.

One of the Guardians on the far side of the pond cried out then went down with *something* attached to his head. A dozen creatures the size of guinea pigs launched themselves from the pool. They propelled themselves with stubby wings onto the chests, faces, and legs of the Guardians closest to the water's edge, biting and scratching. Shouts and screams of pain drowned out the carousel music.

"Back! Back!" Tessa shouted.

More creatures launched out of the water, landing with squishy plops on the grass before they rose on their hind feet and scrambled toward us, gnashing pointy teeth in their elongated snouts. We scrambled back.

"Wait! Give them space," I said to Tessa. "Don't kill them!"

"Come again? I thought we were removing the threat." Tessa held up a hand, pausing the Guardians.

"They weren't aggressive until we got too close and threatened them. I think we should put them back in their own realm, not kill them."

"How do you propose we do that?" Tessa asked doubtfully.

"Through the portal." I glanced around for the rift between realms and spotted it inside the carousel. It must have been terrifying when those things came through. I could easily picture children fleeing the carousel and panicked families screaming in terror as unknown creatures poured out. It was insanely lucky that they weren't aggressive unless threatened and that no one had died.

Tessa gave me an exasperated look.

"It's the right thing to do."

She mumbled under her breath about my "ideas" but directed the Guardians to walk together, holding a shared shield in place. The barrier herded the creatures toward the carousel. They didn't like it, as they kept hissing and leaping at the shield, but it worked.

When all the creatures were back in their own realm, I planted my hands on my hips and surveyed our crew. "Here's the plan. We've got to go through that tear and build a portal to Aeterna on the other side, but we just scooted a hundred pissed-off baby-raptor things in there, so I need some of you guys to provide cover while the rest of us work on that."

I expected some complaining, but no one made a sound, which shouldn't have surprised me since that was the difference between soldiers and politicians. Tessa organized the Guardians again, and when everyone was clear on the plan, half of the group formed a shield and eased into the rip ahead of us. Tessa and I went through in the middle of the second group and emerged knee deep in a swamp on the other side. The Guardians in front of us had already erected a dome-shaped shield around the rip, keeping us safe from the hundreds of lizard creatures hissing and spitting at us as we invaded their territory.

I spotted a small island of what appeared to be dry land about fifty yards in front of us. It was full of thick, dense brush, which would make a good natural anchor for a gateway between this realm and Aeterna. I'd seen Silas create the portal to Aeterna twice, had helped the second time, and was pretty confident I could do it again. I just needed the Guardians to act as my circle. "Over there. Let's head to that island."

The Guardians in the rear of our group picked up the back edge of the shield, and on Tessa's command, we moved as a group through the swamp, slowly and carefully picking our way toward the little island through the thick mud. The lizard creatures chased us until we got farther away from the portal and apparently out of their territory. When we reached the island, the thick, spiky brush on our side forced us to skirt around, pushing up to our thighs through the muck. We waded to the other side, and I stopped dead in my tracks—a permanent portal stood there, glowing with magic.

What the hell? I absorbed the tiniest fraction of its power and inhaled in utter shock. I recognized the magic. Silas had built it.

"Where does it go?" Tessa asked, peering into its depths. It was possible to catch a glimpse of the other side of a portal, but the terrain was just pine trees. It could have led anywhere.

"I don't know, but it's not Aeterna." Nothing could live in a realm without magic, not even trees. I lowered my voice so only Tessa could hear and told her that Silas had conjured the portal, but he must have done it for the Fates. "Silas told me that connecting the pocket realms to Aeterna would help drain the pressure between our realm and the pocket realm, but I don't know what it does when the portal is going somewhere else."

"If he did this at the bequest of the Fates, you have to assume it's not good for anyone else."

"Agreed. And since all these rips opened at once, I think..." I didn't want to say that Silas had probably caused the tears on purpose. "I think we need to figure out where this portal goes. But we also need to take care of the rest of the creatures on the streets. Can you send the Guardians back into the city to take care of them while I figure out what's on the other side of this portal?"

With a plan in place, Tessa sent all but five of the Guardians back to the city, and the seven of us went through Silas's portal.

We emerged in an evergreen forest. A thick bed of pine needles blanketed the ground, ungroomed and untouched except for one set of human tracks.

"Silas?" Tessa asked quietly.

"I assume so. Let's follow them and see where he went."

The Guardians kept a watchful eye on the forest around us as we followed the trail. It lasted only a few hundred yards and led to a small pile of rocks between trees. I was very surprised to find two more portals side by side.

"That's the T," I said, peering through one into a dark manmade tunnel.

"It must be the subway station where the snake creatures were. Look at the marks here." Tessa pointed at slithery tracks leading from some rocks a few feet away and directly into the portal.

"Silas built the portals right on top of their nest. Why would he do that?" I couldn't wrap my brain around why he'd made a trek to a nest of creatures in order to build two more portals.

"Did he want the creatures to escape to Earth?" Tessa asked.

"I don't know, but it does seem intentional. None of this makes sense to me. Let's go through this other portal and see where that takes us." I pointed at the second one, which appeared to lead to some reddish rocks on a steep mountainside.

Tessa signaled the Guardians to take formation, and we traveled through the second portal, emerging on a high mountainside. The cliffside afforded a clear view of the entire pocket realm, which didn't have any human habitations or buildings. From our location, we could see one more portal not too far away from us. We climbed over to it, and it was easy enough to recognize the street near Fenway park on the other side. As before, it appeared to have been built in the middle of an empty nesting area of twigs, leaves, and clumps of gray fur matching the rat-like creatures that had emerged from the T. Despite the size of the nesting site, there weren't any scavenged animal bones, indicating that the creatures at this site weren't carnivores.

"It's a loop," I said. "Each of the pocket realms is connected to one another and to Earth."

Tessa nudged an empty nest with her foot. "If the intention was to allow magic to flow between realms, do you think he was trying to stop additional tears by making more space for the magic trapped in Boston?"

"I don't know. He caused three more tears by doing this, and we have to assume he was under Four's orders. The Fates seem to want to cause maximum conflict between us and DODSI, so I don't know why they would want to help us stop the tears from happening."

"But didn't the Fate warn you about the first rip?"

"Yeah, but I assume he only did that so we'd accidentally set that slug creature loose in Boston."

"Maybe he hoped the same thing would happen again." She shrugged. "Cause panic and damage."

"I don't know. This feels more subtle, and Four is anything but subtle. Silas went out of his way to find these little nests of relatively harmless creatures and made sure they went through the portals. What if he wanted us to find the portals, and the creatures were his way of getting our attention?"

"That does sound like Silas. So if he led us to the portals... what do they mean? What is it that we need to know?"

I ran Marcel's charm between my fingers. "I have no idea."

Chapter Eleven

W e rejoined the rest of the Guardians and built shielding around all three rips on our side to stop the creatures. Then I spent the rest of the evening alone in my room, trying to figure out why Silas would create portals between the pocket realms and Earth. I couldn't come up with an explanation. All I knew for sure was that Silas had created the portals, which had caused the tears, and magic was flowing from Boston to those other realms. Eventually, as the sun slipped over the horizon and darkness fell, I drifted into an uneasy sleep.

I was awakened by an intruder in my bedroom. My back was to them as I lay in bed, but I sensed them quietly approaching. I didn't dare move or grab for my magic and alert them that I was awake, but I had other ways to defend myself. I slipped my hand under my pillow and closed my fingers around the blade Silas had gifted me. Slowly, I drew it out, careful not to move too much. The intruder came closer and leaned over me.

I twisted around and stabbed upward with the knife, right toward the intruder's chest.

He knocked my thrust off course, and the blade went flying out of my hand and slid across the floor. I kicked out, but the blanket got in the way, and I barely managed to hit his stomach with a knee. He grunted and stumbled backward. I launched myself out of bed, untangling my body from the blanket as I slammed the man into the wall. I drew my arm back, preparing to smash my elbow into his face.

"Maeve!"

"Silas?" I wove a lighting spell and realized that it was indeed Silas that I had pinned to the wall. "What the hell are you doing?"

"I was trying not to wake you!" He looked exhausted, and he had several days' worth of scruff on his face.

"You scared the hell out of me!" I released him, but the adrenaline pounding through my veins wasn't finished. I pushed him for good measure. "You scared me! I thought you weren't coming back." The overwhelming mix of emotions—fear of an intruder, surprise and then relief at Silas's return—was too much. Tears welled. I didn't want to cry, so I punched Silas hard in the shoulder.

"Ow! What was that for?"

I balled my fists and kept hitting him in the chest. If I stopped, I was going to break down and cry.

"Shite, Maeve! What is your matter?" He grabbed my shoulders to hold me back.

"I'm so mad at you! Everything is going to hell, and you weren't here, and what the hell are you doing with those portals?"

"Shh!" He put his hand over my mouth. "You'll wake everyone in the building. I can't talk about the portals. I was sent to tell you that you have to stop Casius from rebinding Earth's magic. The—"

"You're here because Four has a message for me? I haven't seen you in days! I'm dealing with this shitshow alone because of him, and he can shove his message right up his ass. Where have you been?"

He opened his mouth to say that he couldn't tell me what he'd been doing, and I just didn't want to hear it. I *couldn't* hear it again. I didn't want to start hitting him again, so I reached up on my tiptoes and kissed him. It wasn't gentle.

My kiss was full of anger and pain, but he held me against his chest and wrapped his arms tightly around me, and my feelings flamed into hunger. I needed him. Our lips and tongues fought each other with all of our pent-up frustration. I yanked Silas's shirt over his head then pushed him back against the wall.

He grabbed the back of my neck and pulled me against him, kissing me with a hunger that matched my own. He didn't relent until I was gasping for air. His mouth moved down my neck, and the harsh scrape of his scruff along my sensitive skin lit me on fire from the inside out. I needed *more*.

I leaned back enough to take off my own shirt, and Silas surged off the wall and pushed me toward the bed. Our kisses were bruising as we tore at each other's clothing. We fell onto the bed together, our limbs tangled and our bodies wild. Neither of us relented as we rolled across the mattress, kissing and grabbing and *needing*. Naked and panting for air, I forced him onto his back and straddled his hips. With our gazes and our bodies locked together, we took and gave in equal measures until we both fell apart.

Afterward, we lay in a tangle of limbs, sweaty and satisfied, until I fell asleep.

I awoke alone the next morning. The tangle of sheets and the knocked-over lamp were the only witnesses of Silas's fleeting presence. Heartbreaking disappointment flooded me. He'd left without waking me, and I realized he hadn't opened our Aegis bond. Sex was sometimes tender and sometimes vigorous, but it was always a point of connection between us, and we'd never not shared our feelings through our bond.

I hadn't had a chance to ask him any of my burning questions—not that he would have answered them.

Rather than sit in my bed and stew, I got dressed and headed for Casius's office. I raised my fist to the door in front of me, reminded myself that I did in fact have a backbone, and knocked.

"Come in," Casius called.

The room Casius had picked for his office looked nothing like the office he'd occupied when I was a child, but the gnawing feeling in my stomach was exactly the same. Big, heavy knots of guilt and fear tried to consume me, but I forced them down because I was a gods damned adult.

Casius looked up from his laptop and sighed heavily. "I suppose we've been heading toward this conversation for a while now."

I wasn't eager to dive into the fight we both knew was coming, so I picked a gentler subject. "Any news from the city?"

"The Mundanes have barricades around the rips. So far, nothing else has come through, and the creatures seem to have disappeared—probably returning to their own realms."

I hummed noncommittally. We'd taken care of all of the creatures last night, but Casius and I weren't in a good enough place for me to disclose that.

"They've extended the shelter-in-place order, and the National Guard has doubled their numbers to keep the border around Boston secure." He closed his laptop, folded his arms across his chest, and leaned back in his leather office chair. "The situation seems stable for now."

"Any word from DODSI?"

"Not yet. I'm hopeful we'll have time to rebind Earth's magic before they shift from controlling the situation to assigning blame."

"You know this is a mistake, Casius." I'd already tried arguing every angle of why it was wrong, and I didn't bother repeating myself. He knew everything I knew. He'd lived it for longer than I had.

Casius tapped the newspaper on his desk. The front page of the *Boston Globe* had a picture of me standing over the dead sand slug. It was a stunning photo, with the creature's mouth full of pointy teeth, the broken fountain top jutting out of its neck, and my sword raised.

"'Magic Monsters Rampage Across Boston,'" Casius read aloud. "The global media connected you to our sect. The protestors outside our campus tripled overnight."

A whole bunch of viral videos had gone up after the sand-slug incident. The entire thing, almost from the moment the creature dropped onto the road until I killed it, had been captured on dozens of mobile phones, and it had all been pieced together on the internet. It wasn't a stretch for the Mundanes to realize the creatures that continued to crawl out of their subways and randomly appear in their public parks were connected to the first very large creature that had appeared. But connecting me to the sect almost overnight was a surprise. The paranoid part of me worried that someone had deliberately connected those dots for them.

"The best way to help these people is to rebind magic," Casius said.

"What gives us the right to control access to magic that belongs to the entire world?"

His face was tight as he moved from behind his desk and perched on the edge. "Mundanes can't handle magic in their lives. You tried, but you need to accept that the experiment failed. It's time to do what's best for our people."

I was so sick of the same old argument over and over. Casius and I would never see eye to eye. "You're making a mistake."

"How many people have we tried to help adjust—a hundred?"

"Ninety-two," I said flatly.

"And none of them have returned to their normal lives."

"We just need more time."

He turned back toward the window. "The government wants someone to blame. They'll whip up a riot, and the mob will come for our heads."

"We can defend ourselves from a Mundane mob. They can't get past our perimeter shield."

"You know as well as I do that DODSI's technology is a danger to us, especially when we don't have access to a powerful magic source to defend ourselves. What is happening in Boston is not progress. It's fear, and scared people lash out, Mae. It's only a matter of time until they come for us, and when they do, it won't only be DODSI. Every Mundane government in the world has their eye on us."

"What if we take down the boundary spell and set the magic free? The entire world could see for themselves the good that magic can accomplish." My voice rose in desperation.

"And then what?" He raised his eyebrows. "What do you think the government will do if we set magic loose on the entire world? How do you think people will react?"

"They can't do anything if magic is available to everyone. They'll have to let us explain what's really going on—the transition for those who inherit their magic will be much smoother if they could see the good side of our powers."

He shook his head. "It only takes one person with magic to burn down a building or rob a bank or lose control in any way, and the government will hunt down every single person with a drop of power. There will be mass panic. The religious nuts will declare it the end of days, and orderly society will crumble." He sighed and ran his hand through his sandy hair. "I'm not exaggerating when I say that your way would put the entire world in danger. Not to mention that DODSI will retaliate against *us* for breaking the terms of our deal."

"But what if it works? What if the world can adapt? We could end world hunger. No more poverty or meaningless deaths from curable diseases. The world could benefit so much from what we—"

"How can you guarantee that? Can you ensure that normal everyday humans will accept magic with open arms? Will it really make things better for them? Aeterna had magic, and they still had a lot of problems. Magic doesn't fix everything, and the crowd of people chanting outside our campus should be your first clue about the uphill battle that would be."

I wanted to say that he needed more faith in the world, that magic was natural and people would learn to live with it. But I couldn't. I couldn't promise that people wouldn't get hurt in the process. I knew too much about the way life worked, and people *would* get hurt. Chaos was entirely possible. Without the government's support, we wouldn't be successful at transitioning the world into a new reality. I still believed that it would be better for the world, but I couldn't force that outcome.

"It's a tinderbox of a world, Mae," Casius said. "I won't be the one throwing a match on it. Our only choice is to control magic until the world is ready."

"What happens if another Brotherhood or another Aeternal Council rises up and takes that magic? Not everyone will use that power for good. Hell, can you guarantee *we'll* always use it for good? We shouldn't be the ones to decide what's good for everyone."

"That's ironic, coming from you," he said.

I slumped into one of his chairs. "I did what I thought was right."

"And I'm asking you to trust that the New Alliance will do what is right until the Mundane world can handle magic, but that time is not now."

We were both quiet for a while.

"It's time for you to choose whose side you're on. If you're not going to build the future together with us, then I'm asking you to step down and let others lead the way."

I sighed. "That's it, then? After everything?"

He looked me straight in the eye. "You always have a choice, Maeve. I need you to make yours."

I didn't know what to say. Part of me burned with the righteous belief that the world needed magic, but I also felt guilty over making the unilateral decision to free magic. Casius made good points, and I couldn't guarantee that sharing magic with the world would leave it in a better place. But I also couldn't condone repeating the mistakes of our ancestors—mistakes that had cost me everything. I also had to consider that Four was trying to free Earth's magic, and whatever the Fates wanted was surely bad for the rest of us. Unless it wasn't.

My mixed feelings left me in a weird place where I was surprised to find that I had already accepted the inevitable conclusion to our situation. The New Alliance only cared about rebinding magic and restoring their control, and I couldn't be a part of that. There wasn't a happy ending where we all got to hold hands and sing campfire songs.

I gave it one last try. "You said you got more time from DODSI. Give me that time, Casius. I can fix the tears between realms and deliver a newbie in control of their magic."

He looked resigned. We both knew I was making promises I might not be able to deliver on. "I don't think DODSI is going to wait until their deadline anymore, but see what you can do."

I left his office and found Tessa in the modified gym for our morning training. She let me work out my frustration on the sparring mats while my choices, or lack thereof, circled in my head. There was nothing I could do about the Alliance voting to rebind magic, not with the tears all over Boston upping the pressure from DODSI. Casius and I had been balancing on the edge of an inevitable cliff for a long time. I didn't know what to do, and I really wished I could talk to Silas. He was my partner, and I really needed someone in my corner, but Four was driving us apart by sending Silas off on his errands and making it so we couldn't even talk to each other.

Four was behind the tears. I couldn't begin to guess why, but I needed to figure out what the Fates were up to, and I had only one option to do that.

That night, I tossed and turned alone in my bed while I compiled a mental list of all the horrible things I would rather do. That list included tearing out my own hair, poking needles under my fingernails, and listening to Alannah lecture me about the importance of leadership. Unfortunately, the appearance of the sun only a few hours after I finally fell asleep didn't bring any new solutions. All I'd concluded was that creating portals, stabilizing realms, and dealing with the motivations of the Fates were so far out of my wheelhouse that I desperately needed help.

I couldn't ask anyone in the Alliance without giving away our deal with Four, and I obviously couldn't ask Silas. Tessa, Stephan, and Aria knew about the situation with Silas, but they didn't have any more expertise in Fate motivations or secret portal networks than I did. Unfortunately, there was only one person who could help me. I got dressed in the earliest hours of the morning and forced myself to suck it up.

Gathering my magic around me, I focused on finding the no-good waste of air and space who had become my only hope of finding answers about what the Fates might be up to. Before my experience using the Fates' powers, I hadn't been able to skim to a *person*, but the experience had changed me in ways I didn't want to examine too closely. I located my target, wove my magic into a skimming spell, and held my breath as the world twisted sideways.

Elias leaned back in his seat, crossing one ankle over the opposite knee as I appeared without warning in front of him. His face crinkled handsomely. "I wondered when you'd turn up."

He didn't even have the decency to be surprised that I'd just popped into his cell. He should have been thrilled to see someone after sitting alone in a dark, dank... I looked for the first time and realized we were not in a prison cell at all.

Elias chuckled at my outraged disbelief. He should have been in a prison somewhere deep underground, surrounded by concrete and bars. But we were in a *hotel suite*. The very posh high-rise hotel was positioned so that the morning sun filtered through the windows behind him. He sat on a modern sofa, dressed in slacks and a dress shirt, shaved and groomed. He folded his newspaper then tossed it carelessly onto the glass coffee table between us. It landed with a *thwack* next to a small vase of freshly cut flowers.

What the hell? Where was the orange jumpsuit, the handcuffs, the prison bars? Elias watched with great satisfaction as I took in his surroundings. "It's amazing what cooperation and a little information will buy you in this backwater realm."

The former leader of the Brotherhood looked healthy and relaxed. He had a slight tan, as if he had spent some of his time outside recently, and I might have bared my teeth as I took in his discarded room service tray. DODSI wasn't torturing information out of him—they were pampering him.

I wanted to strangle Director Pascal, but I forced myself to rein in my anger. "I was hoping to find you in a deep, dark pit. Where are we?"

"Washington, D.C." Elias waved his hand toward a velvety wing-backed chair across from him. "Please, sit."

I had no idea what he was doing in our nation's capital. Questions swam through my head, but I held them back. From the smug little smirk growing on his face, Elias was dying for me to ask all about his sweet setup, but I decided I wouldn't give him the satisfaction.

I folded myself into the chair across from him and prepared to negotiate with the devil. "So DODSI feeds you scraps of your former power, and you just lick them right up like a good dog. How the mighty have fallen."

He frowned and picked an imaginary piece of lint off his pant leg. "As delightful as your surprise visit is, let's move to the crux of it. I have important meetings this afternoon. What favor are you here to ask of me?"

I couldn't stifle the disgust that curled my lip at the thought of him in important meetings, advising DODSI. But I could tell from the amused glint in his eye that he was intentionally pushing my buttons. I took a deep breath, counted to five in my head, then exhaled slowly, like Aria taught me. Elias was my only source of information, and I had to ask what I came there to find out.

"I need to figure out why tears are opening between our realm and others all around Boston." I'd considered my question carefully as I tossed in bed the night before. If I came straight out and asked what the Fates were up to by building a network of portals, Elias would probably lie to me. The concentration of magic in Boston had caused the first tear, but I could ask this question without any mention of the Fates. I needed to know how to repair those tears and to figure out what the Fates were having Silas do by opening the other portals.

Elias's face went blank, and he frowned. Slowly, he said, "You must be truly desperate to come to me."

Ugh, he doesn't know anything. "Never mind. This was a waste of time." I rose from my seat and started gathering my magic into a skimming spell.

"Wait!" Elias's hand shot out, but he stopped just short of grabbing me. A quick flush colored his face.

Interesting. He smoothed his features back into their usual calm mask, but it was too late. I'd seen the panic in his eyes. Channeling Silas, I raised a single eyebrow.

"I can tell you what you want to know, but I want something in return," he said.

"What do you want?"

He slowly stroked his bottom lip. "I want my powers back. Unbind my magic, and I'll tell you everything I know about building gateways between realms."

The desperate gleam in his eyes was very satisfying. I sat back down. "So your golden cage doesn't agree with you after all."

He didn't respond. He was a master manipulator who knew exactly how to get what he wanted. He'd opened with a demand I couldn't possibly agree to—restoring his magic—so I would agree to his next one, which would seem smaller and less impossible, and it would be what he really needed.

"No," I said. "I wouldn't restore your powers even if I could. You earned a lot worse than this." I waved my hand around the suite. "If I had my way, you'd be in a deep, dark hole with only a bucket to piss in."

"So crude, my lady."

"Screw you," I snapped.

One side of his mouth quirked in amusement. "It galls you to no end that I'm in the lap of luxury, doesn't it?"

"Thousands of people died because of you. The people of Aeterna trusted you, and you betrayed them."

The smirk melted off his face, and he leaned forward with his elbows on his knees. "I thought you, better than anyone else, would understand the weight of destiny on our shoulders. You also attempted to change the world—and there were casualties as a result of *your* actions. How are you less guilty than I?"

A lot of people had died because of my choices, but I swallowed the old guilt. It wasn't a path I was going to walk down any longer, especially not with him. "You wanted to subjugate everyone who wasn't Human and become the ultimate ruler of our entire world." I let my anger simmer to the surface, itching to conjure something sharp and pointy into my hand. "I was trying to save lives. I wouldn't compare the two of us if I were you."

"You and I are more similar than you realize. How do you think history will record you, Lady Maeve?"

I was sick of this little dance. "What do you want in exchange for the information about the portals?"

"Where is your Aegis?" Elias asked out of the blue.

I crossed my arms over my chest. "He had better things to do."

He leaned forward, and his sharp gaze traveled over me. He was several feet away, but the intensity in his stare filled the space between us as the silence stretched on. I wished I could leave and never see his face again, but I held his eyes.

"Lord Silas would never let you come here without him. Did you sneak away because he is jealous of our history? We had quite a promising start in my suite in Aeterna. I haven't forgotten our incredible kiss."

I snorted. "There's no history here, you snake. I kissed you as a distraction so I could steal information off your console. Silas wouldn't care one bit."

Elias's eyes sparkled. "So he *doesn't* know you're here. How very interesting."

"I'm leaving," I said. "You're messing with me, and I don't have time for this. You probably don't even know what's causing those rips."

I rose, praying that he wouldn't call my bluff. Elias was my last resort. I had no other plan and no way to find the information I needed without him.

"Come now, why don't you just ask me what you really want to know? I know how those tears came to be, and I know *who* created them. The question you want to ask me is why. What do the Fates have to gain by opening portals between realms?"

I whirled back toward him. "What do you know about the Fates?"

He shook his head. "I need you to do something for me first."

"I'm not restoring your powers."

"Tell me what deal you and Silas have with the Fates, and I'll give you the knowledge you need."

Surprise slapped me in the face, and Elias smirked. I hated that damn smirk. He was a master at reading people, and I was an open book. It had to have been so easy for him, picking the information off my face while I tried to force it back into neutral. "What are you up to, Elias?"

"Believe it or not, we're on the same side, my lady. I want magic freed as much as you do."

I glared. "Last I checked, you wanted to control all of Earth's magic and rule over the 'inferior races.' Why would you want to free magic?"

"There's no point in trying to control something that doesn't exist. You destroyed the Earthen Source, and I didn't survive this long by being inflexible. If you succeed and magic spreads across this realm, I will profit tremendously from my unique knowledge of magic. Once again, we want the same thing."

I pursed my lips. What he said made sense. Elias was uniquely positioned with information the government needed, but I didn't trust him. He always had more than one plan in motion, and just because our goals appeared to be aligned didn't mean they would stay that way. I had to be very, very careful. "If we want the same thing, then tell me what I want to know, and we'll both benefit. Helping me helps you."

"Nothing comes for free in this world." He grinned like a shark.

I glared at him, disgusted about making any deals with him, but he was obviously more in the know than I had ever guessed, and I was out of options. Information in exchange for information was the best I had. "If I tell you about the deal with Four, you'll tell me why the Fates want the portals between realms?"

"Yes." He leaned forward.

"Silas agreed to do the Fates' bidding for ten years."

Elias's eyes grew wide as he absorbed that.

"Tell me why the Fates had him open portals between our realm and the pocket realms."

"Silas opened them... interesting. So he has their powers?"

I silently kicked myself for giving away that information. "Yes. Now, tell me."

"The information you need is in a book, but I can't retrieve it myself. If you read it, you'll understand why the Fates want the portals open and why they're using Silas to do it."

I wanted to throw my hands in the air and scream, but I heroically refrained. "Why can't you just tell me?"

"I'm forbidden from telling you or anyone."

The answer was so eerily similar to Silas's response under the Fates' gag order that I actually believed him. "Where is this book?"

"It's in the Council's vault. As it so happens by a series of misfortunate events, only the Fae queen has access to the last remaining portal leading there. Unfortunately, she has rebuffed my attempts to retrieve it."

"That's impossible. I can't go back to Aeterna. No one can."

"Oh, the vault is not in Aeterna. It's here, in this realm."

Chapter Twelve

The Fells was too quiet. It was a beautiful summer evening, and the forested area located north of Boston should have been packed, but with the city on lockdown, the semigroomed trails were empty. The forest felt eerie and oppressive. Or perhaps my guilty conscience was weighing on me.

Gia, Ethan, and their team were working with the newbies, trying desperately to have someone ready to meet our original three-month deadline with DODSI. Meanwhile, I was sneaking around behind Casius's back, working with Elias so I could figure out what the Fates were up to with all the portals. Even worse, I was about to make a secret bargain with the Fae.

I'd been avoiding Casius since our last conversation. I wished I could believe that the New Alliance could control the entire world's magic without messing it up, but history proved again and again that too much power corrupted those who controlled it. If the Alliance were to rebind all of Earth's magic into a single source, it wouldn't be long before we became like the Aeternal Council.

A tug of magic shook me out of my heavy thoughts. The trees loomed over me, reaching with spindly branches that plucked at my hair and clothing. A shiver of fear raised the hairs on my arms as I looked around, my senses focusing on things I couldn't see with my eyes. Someone—or something—was watching me. My body vibrated with tension and fear.

Run! Run now!

I resisted the overwhelming urge to flee and instead let my own magic fold around me like a soft blanket of warmth and light. The pure bliss that came from using my magic flowed through me, chasing away the fear. Everything came alive. The colors in the forest were more vibrant and the air fresher. I could sense the magic aura of every living thing around me, and it filled me with joy. The anxious feelings and the desire to run flowed off me like water.

Clever. The Fae had put up a magical boundary against intruders, shooting powerful feelings of fear through anyone who came too close to their territory. I'd walked into the subtle go-away spell like a fly into the spider's web. Clear of their spell, I walked deeper into Fae territory until I found the same clearing where Silas and I had reunited Lady Treva with her daughter, Kianna. I paused, waiting for someone to show up to investigate.

I was at the edge of their territory, and the Fae should have had sentries close by, especially since I'd already tripped one of their perimeter spells. I held very still, not quite raising my palms in the air but holding them loose and unthreateningly by my sides, well away from Ripper, strapped to my right thigh, or Missy's hilt poking over my shoulder. With conscious effort and a deep breath, I let go of my magic. Completely benign, that was me. Before I could count to five, two Fae emerged from the woods. Neither had drawn their weapons, but they didn't need to—they were glowing with sky-blue magic. They stopped in front of me, completely silent.

They were both tall and thin, wearing clothing that blended into the forest, but the similarities ended there. The female had light-brown hair down to her shoulders and a magic-coated katana-style sword slung over her back. The male had a huge magic-forged broadsword scimitar sheathed on his back. It would have taken all my strength even to lift that sword. He was tall and clearly strong enough to wield the massive weapon. His longish curly hair, dark skin, and jade eyes were striking, and I recognized him right away as the Fae who had stepped forward after I killed Kianna.

He'd asked what would happen if the Fae refused to join the New Alliance. I'd told them they were free to go either way.

It wasn't a coincidence that he was there to greet me. The Fae cared about truth, honor, and debt. I'd spared this man's life, and maybe he felt he owed me something for that. Or he might have felt like I owed him my life for all the Fae who'd died in that fight. There was really no way to tell with the Fae, but tension hung between us as we stared at each other.

"Why are you here, Maeve O'Neill?" the male asked.

His greeting was downright rude for a Fae. They usually observed protocols and courtesies, and he clearly didn't think I knew that. I decided to play my part. "You know who I am, obviously, but you didn't tell me your name when I spared your life."

The female's nostrils flared.

"My name is Boone de'Fiero," he said begrudgingly.

"Nice to meet you, Boone. When I was last here, your leaders promised me safe passage as their guest. Do you intend to provide me the same courtesy? And are you going to introduce me to your companion, or must I do that myself as well?"

I'd not-so-subtly reminded them that I was a returning guest, rubbed the male's life-debt in his face, and insulted his manners at the same time. Game on.

Boone frowned, but the female's manners compelled her to speak. "I am known by Sheel de'Saritra." She inclined her head slightly. "We welcome you to Haven."

Boone glared death at his companion, who visibly paled then hung her head in shame. *That's right. I was welcomed back, and now, I'm your guest.* The chances of getting stabbed in the back had gone down exponentially. Under their strict moral code of conduct, guests were never attacked. Welcoming someone as a guest then intentionally trying to murder them would be breaking an oath, and the Fae were magic-bound to their oaths.

Boone transferred his steely gaze back onto me. "Why are you here?"

I had two ways I could play it. They might feel some obligation to humor me, since I was a guest. I could request an audience with whoever took Kianna's place as their leader and then try to convince them to help me. But I'd have to tell them about the tear between realms and how I'd bargained for Elias's help. That path would require sharing a lot of information I wanted to keep to myself. That left me with option two. "I want to strike a bargain with your leader."

Boone's eyes lit up. The Fae took negotiating deals as seriously as their personal honor and viewed bargaining as an art form. They started practicing at an early age to hone their verbal skills and avoid lying. A Fae child was encouraged to debate over everything—how much playtime they got, their educational rank, and even the amount of food they received. If they didn't haggle, they didn't receive. It was all in preparation for the oath they would take at adulthood, binding them to speak only the truth. Adult Fae were magically incapable of lying, which meant they were excellent at twisting the truth in every direction without deliberately saying anything untrue. They were masterful negotiators and manipulators.

Boone motioned for me to follow with a sideways tip of his head then marched us toward the center of the Fae Haven. Sheel fell into step behind me, eagerly escorting me toward my doom. As we walked, I started having second thoughts. I wasn't a very good negotiator, and I had very little to offer. I was on the outs with Casius and the Alliance, so I couldn't legitimately promise any of our resources or support. But I needed access to the Council's vault, so I'd have to figure out what the Fae would want in return. I just had to make sure it wasn't something I couldn't afford to lose.

As Boone led me through their Haven, I took in as many details as I could. Our path wound through the trees, but the forest was completely different from the last time I visited. It didn't feel like New England at all but more like stepping through a portal to a foreign realm. Tall, thick trees reached high above us, seeming to lean in toward each other at the tops and filtering dappled sunlight through their leafy canopies.

The trunks were thicker than I could wrap my arms around, as if they had been there for a thousand years. That might have been normal for New England, except for the vines, thick as my wrists, wrapping around and between the tree trunks, growing an entire rainbow of exotic flowers from their ropy lengths. The flowers popped up from everywhere—the ground, the trees, the vines. The array of delicate, draping blossoms and bold multicolored pedals was mind-boggling, and their heady floral musk enveloped me.

The trees and foliage fed off the Fae's elemental magic, growing wild and fast. Everything about their Haven was foreign, yet the Fae magic rolling thickly over my skin soothed me.

The Haven sat on a deep well of magic, drawing a thick cloud of it to hang all around us. Before I set magic free on Earth, the Fae had relied on the energy the Haven produced to sustain themselves in our realm. Now, the magic seemed to penetrate every pore of my skin and sink deep inside my bones, and as they led me deeper into their territory, I was invigorated and terrified at the same time.

Eventually, I started to see more Fae. They stared at me in wide-eyed surprise as we passed quietly by them. They were an interesting race—unlike Humans, they came in a wide variety of forms. The most Human-like had dark or pale skin and amethyst- or jade-colored eyes, like Boone and Sheel. Some were obviously not Human, displaying a wide variety in the colors of their skin and eyes. Some were as short as children or covered in fur. I'd heard people theorize that the Fae were not really one single race but instead a blend of magical beings who couldn't pass for any type of humanoid.

We stopped suddenly in front of a tree, its trunk as wide as a car and striped with color as if a giant had taken a paintbrush to it—wide slashes of reds, blues, greens and yellows showed in its natural bark. Boone looked at me expectantly.

"Pretty," I said dryly, "but I hope I didn't walk all that way for a painted tree."

A challenging smile spread across his face as he glanced up. I followed his gaze and realized I'd missed an entire city built into the treetops above us. Round structures, some as large as modern houses, grew out of the trees—not built but *growing* from the trees. I stared in awe at the organically shaped bark-covered structures sprouting from every trunk. Houses, shops, and walkways formed out of long limbs that stretched between the buildings, crisscrossing through open air before they joined at large flat platforms nestled in the crooks of various trunks.

Hundreds of Fae moved silently in and out of buildings, walking casually across the narrow branch bridges as if they were sidewalks and gathering on the wide platforms and generally going about their lives. Thankfully, they didn't notice me as I gaped like an idiot. I knew the entire population of Fae had left Aeterna before it collapsed, but I had no idea there were so many... or that they liked to live in trees.

Boone sprang up into the lowest branches of the painted tree in front of us. He landed on a limb at least four feet up the trunk, balancing easily on the balls of his feet. I filed away his insane leaping abilities, making a mental note not to try and escape on foot from their Haven if things went sideways. He continued, scaling a series of limbs that spiraled up the wide trunk like stairs. A quarter of the way around the wide tree, he'd already gained about twenty feet in elevation. He dashed across a branch stretching from his tree to another, navigating the foot-wide walkway with ease before he paused in the middle of the path and crooked his fingers at me.

I shook my head. "I'm not going up there."

"You are if you want to talk to Mother Nithia," Sheel replied at my back.

Surprise slapped me. They were taking me to the Queen of the Fae, a woman so mysterious I hadn't heard of anyone ever meeting her in person. She'd actually shown up briefly after Nuada captured me and forced him to hand over the supposed antidote for the poison he'd used on the Citizen Source. I'd barely glimpsed her, I was curious, and I'd come too far to turn back.

"Do you need a leg up?" Sheel's tone was perfectly polite, but her eyes danced with amusement.

She would have loved to boost me up into the tree like a child, which clearly wouldn't have put me in a great position for negotiating. I examined the closest branch four feet above my head. Boone had leapt easily onto it, but I'd have to jump up, grab it with my hands, then swing my leg over to mount it like a horse. Then I'd have to balance as I hopped from branch to branch around the tree and then somehow cross the narrow branch bridge without falling. Knowing the Fae, they'd probably lead me all around their tree-fort city until I was exhausted, sweating, and ready to trade anything for a glass of water and a ladder back to solid ground.

"Where are we headed?" I asked Sheel.

She raised her chin at a bulbous structure growing about halfway up a particularly thick trunk that rose at least one hundred feet in the air. The hollow structure was round and vertically grooved, like a wooden pumpkin growing from the massive trunk. Boone hadn't waited for me to make up my mind, and he was only about a hundred yards away from our destination. He twisted back to look at me with narrowed eyes. I focused on the platform in front of the pumpkin house, let my magic rise, and formed it into a skimming spell.

Watching from above, Boone apparently realized what I was doing and twisted back toward the pumpkin house, walking swiftly so he would beat me there.

The skim would be hard but not impossible. I could see the destination and had plenty of room to land. Casius had made me practice precision skimming hundreds of times over the years until I could land on one foot on a square piece of paper. The bridge in front of the doorway was plenty wide, but there was a height change to deal with. I just had to stick the landing... and not fall to my death.

Race you there, buddy. I locked my gaze on the pumpkin house, let the magic tug me across the space, and stuck the damn landing.

I turned my slight wobble into a mocking bow as Boone slid to a stop at the pumpkin house's entrance a second after me. I couldn't help but grin. "I'll give you a bigger head start next time."

His annoyed huff was very satisfying, and I chuckled as he unstrapped the sword from his back and stepped neatly around me to duck through the opening into the house. Boone deposited his weapon inside the doorway and bowed at the waist toward someone inside.

I followed him in without needing to duck, and as my vision adjusted to the dark interior, I stared at the Fae queen seated cross-legged on a wooden bench with her arms in her lap. As with all magic users, it was hard to pin down her age, but even without any visible magic, there was an air about her that felt heavy and powerful. Physically, she appeared to be between forty and sixty, and her delicately pointed ears peeked out from long silvery-white hair that she wore loose to her hips. Jade eyes watched me with calm confidence.

"Maeve O'Neill of the New Alliance, this is Mother Nithia, Queen of the Fae," Boone said.

"Be welcome in our Haven, child." Nithia's voice matched her kind smile.

Everything about her was grandmotherly and welcoming, and I wasn't buying it. I swallowed hard as Boone folded his large frame gracefully onto the floor, kneeling with his toes tucked under his feet, ready to spring at me. Even without his sword, I'd probably be dead the second I thought about attacking the Fae queen.

Mother Nithia was a legend. I was perhaps one of the few non-Fae to have seen her in the last hundred years. Her word was law among the Fae, and her powers were unrivaled even by the former Council members.

"I understand you have proposed a bargain. Let us discuss." Nithia raised her arm to indicate that I should sit across from her, and I stared at her hands—or more accurately, I stared at where her hands should have been. Both arms ended in round stumps at the wrists. She didn't try to hide it. In fact, she wore two black metal cuffs on each wrist, each studded with black gems. They wrapped fully around the ends of her arms, highlighting the missing hands.

It was rare to see any deformity among the Fae. Their Healers could do nearly miraculous things, including reattaching limbs, and birth defects were almost nonexistent. I wondered if someone had intentionally maimed her. She watched me watch her, and I realized that she had intended for me to notice her missing hands.

I decided not to react. The seat she'd indicated was roughly two feet in diameter and looked like a smooth root that had grown from the floor. I wasn't sure if I was supposed to sit on it like a chair or go crisscross-applesauce like the Fae queen. I decided on chair and moved to sit on the edge of the surface when the damn thing *moved*. It dropped four inches, and I yelped as I dropped hard on my ass.

Boone smirked. Nithia frowned slightly as if I'd somehow managed to mess up sitting down on my own. They were playing dirty. She had allowed me into their sanctuary because she'd assumed I'd be a bumbling Human who was terrible at negotiating, and then she'd made me literally fall on my ass. Two could play that game.

I pasted a big, dumb smile on my face. "Thanks for seeing me, Nithia."

"You will address our Queen by her title, Mother Nithia, or 'my lady,'" Boone demanded.

"Oh, sorry." I had to hold back a smile. I was slaughtering their pleasantries, and I'd just casually thanked a Fae. They took their words very seriously and very literally. While Humans threw around thanks without thought, to the Fae, formal statements of gratitude signaled a debt owed. Nithia wouldn't gain any actual advantage from my casual thanks beyond the impression that I was far, far beneath her.

She tilted her head slightly, accepting my half-hearted apology. She wore a friendly smile, but her eyes were tight. "I see the reports of your magic skill were not exaggerated." She nodded toward the door where I'd landed.

Oh, what nice compliments you give, Grandmother. "Yeah, that was cool, right? Boone thought so too."

Boone bared his teeth at me, and I smiled back sweetly. This was almost as much fun as baiting Agent Lennart, and I hoped it made me seem like an idiot who would bargain away important things without realizing it. They'd think I was an easy target and not put as much effort into negotiating every last drop of blood out of me. *Time to push some buttons.* "What happened to your hands? Were you born crippled?"

The grandma veneer slipped away, and the ancient, deadly predator across from me surfaced. I repressed a shiver as her magic rose and expanded inside the room like a thundering cloud, ready to swallow me whole. An electric current seemed to pulse through the space around us.

Two midnight-black birds glided in through a window near the domed wood ceiling, cawing as they landed on either side of Nithia. The birds moved in perfect unison as they settled into unnatural stillness beside their master, each radiating very powerful and ancient magic. I couldn't identify the species, but they were as big as large raptors, and they both had the same distinctive jade-green eyes as Nithia. I noticed the sparkle of a black-studded collar matching her metal bracelets around each bird's neck. Last time I saw her, she'd been flanked by two dog-like creatures with matching collars. Apparently, she had a thing for pets.

I swallowed hard and resisted the urge to wrap my own magic around me.

Nithia's smile became too sharp, swallowing the last remnants of friendly grandma. She looked like a feral cat who'd decided to eat me alive and spit out my bones. I took a deep breath. I needed the Fae to help me, but they would want something in return. I'd established that I was an idiot, and Nithia was pissed off, so I hoped she wouldn't be particularly careful about bargaining with me. It was time to start.

Only one thing would convince the Fae to help me. And telling them that one thing was going to be a complete betrayal of my people. The fact was, the Alliance had voted to rebind all of Earth's magic, which would be very bad for the Fae. Casius said he'd give me a chance to deliver proof that Mundanes could adjust, but as soon as DODSI put the pressure on, the Alliance would revert to that plan. Even if we managed to return all the newbies into society and DODSI backed off from their ultimatums, the temptation would always be there. At some point, the New Alliance would give in to that temptation.

I took a deep, steadying breath. There would be no going back. "The New Alliance is rebinding Earth's magic into a single magic source."

Chapter Thirteen

Nithia's face betrayed absolutely no surprise as I revealed my sect's plans to rebind Earth's magic.

I cleared my throat awkwardly. "As you know, if my people create a single source of magic in this realm, then your people won't be able to access the power that sustains you."

"We have our Haven," Boone said.

"Your Haven is impressive," I said carefully, "but it's also small. What will happen in a few generations when your children have grown and need homes of their own? When your children's children are born? The Fae don't want to be stuck in this one place when all of Earth is available... as long as magic flows freely."

Nithia hummed as if in thought, but I got the feeling she was playing along for my benefit. I was beginning to feel like the idiot they believed I was. *What am I missing?* "I can stop the Alliance from binding Earth's magic."

"I see," Nithia said. "And what are you asking in return, child?"

"I need an item from the Council's vault."

Again, she had no reaction. Boone had apparently frozen into a statue, and he didn't so much as twitch in surprise.

I needed to be very, very specific when making a bargain with the Fae, or they might help me find my way in then seal the passageway behind me. "I need to retrieve an item and return safely back out again with that item."

"Why would we help you with this?" Nithia asked.

I nodded, noting what she *didn't* say. She didn't say they couldn't do it, but she wanted to know what was in it for her. "If you help me retrieve this item, I'll help you stop the New Alliance from rebuilding the Earthen Source."

Nithia pursed her lips in the first show of emotion since I'd laid my cards on the table. The expression seemed to convey disapproval of some kind. I wasn't sure if it was directed at me or the offer I had presented, but it seemed somehow personal. With effort, I bit my tongue and waited for her reply. Any more talking and I'd be giving away my desperation.

"Whether you stop your people from rebuilding the Earthen Source is not our concern," Nithia said finally.

"But... rebinding magic would be bad for the Fae." I stretched my words as I stated the very, very obvious. I was missing something. Whatever it was, it felt big and important, and I could feel it hovering above me, ready to fall right on top of my head.

"We have already been offered equal access to the Earthen Source in exchange for joining the New Alliance and helping them to bind Earth's magic," Nithia said.

Just like that, the other shoe dropped and hit me in the face. I couldn't believe the Alliance would go behind my back and bring in the Fae. Casius was building a new power structure, and I wasn't part of it. With a pang in my chest, I realized that they had gone to the Fae *before* Casius gave me his ultimatum to help or step down.

Nithia's eyebrows rose as she watched me process all of that. "I find it interesting that you are here, offering bargains in opposition to your people. Did you break from your so-called New Alliance?"

Crap. I was giving away too much. I shoved my feelings of betrayal down deep. I was offering secret bargains in opposition to my people, which meant I could hardly be mad that they were keeping me out of the loop. I had to accept that we were on opposite sides now.

"As I see it, the Fae have two choices. You can help the New Alliance restrict access to magic on Earth and hope that your allies continue to give you access to the power you need to survive... or you can help me free magic and be truly independent." The Fae were all about their independence. I knew from dealing with Nuada how much Mother Nithia wanted the Fae to be self-reliant, and I was counting on that desire to sway her to my side.

Nithia's face was as expressive as a brick wall as she considered my words. Boone was equally stone-faced.

"Your people were stuck in Aeterna under the control of the Council for ages. If magic is freed on Earth, no one can take away your freedom ever again. All you have to do is give me access to that vault."

Nithia glanced at her lap, at her missing hands. *Interesting.* I had to remind myself to keep breathing as I watched her for any clue to her thoughts. I waited for what felt like an eternity before she inclined her head slightly. "The Fae want magic in this realm to be free. We will help you."

I exhaled as the pressure seemed to lift off my shoulders, utterly relieved to know I had at least one ally, although it was probably temporary.

"But we want something additional in return for your safe passage to the Council's vault," Nithia said.

"What do you want?" I blurted, too frayed to be subtle. I would give them whatever they asked—if it was within my power. Problem was, not a lot was.

Nithia smiled fully for the first time, and it was wicked. "We want one of your magic-killing guns."

My brow scrunched. "A disruptor? Why?"

"That is ours to know. In exchange, we will assist you in traveling safely to and from the vault. And in the future, we will provide necessary support to you, Maeve O'Neill, to ensure that magic remains freely accessible on Earth."

I tugged on my braid. Nithia's use of the word "necessary" was a loophole, but other than that, I couldn't find any double meanings. The trade was straightforward: they would help me get Elias's book, and I'd get them a disruptor. Everything else was just good-will—nothing specific was promised or offered.

Boone had knelt there the entire time like he had a rod shoved through his spine. He didn't fidget or slouch, and I wasn't getting any reaction or emotion from him. He would have been an amazing poker player.

I was lucky that all they asked for was a disruptor. I would have to retrieve Ethan's prototype from our campus, but that shouldn't be too difficult. And the damage they could do with a single disruptor wasn't alarming. No doubt they would study the technology and probably attempt to counter it. But that was DODSI's problem, not mine. And honestly, if they found a way to counter the disruptors, that could benefit us too. Ultimately, it was a reasonable request. I counted to ten in my head so I wouldn't seem overly eager. "I need your people to escort me to the vault immediately."

Nithia rose to her feet, casting a glance at Boone. "You will be given access and an escort once you have delivered the weapon. Not before."

I held back a groan. Of course they would demand the disruptor first. I could argue the point, but I was running against the clock. The Alliance was working on rebinding Earth's magic, and I didn't have time to mess around.

"You have bargained well, Mother Nithia, and I accept the terms of your offer. Let us be agreed." I lowered my head but held her eyes in the tradition of the Fae.

She blinked at me, and I smiled sweetly. *Yep, I know stuff.*

Nithia let out a loud, hearty peal of laughter that emanated from her belly and seemed to send the trees around us vibrating with sympathetic humor. Even the crows hopped from foot to foot. "You are sneaky. I like this about you. We are agreed." Magic twined around us both, binding our agreement. "Boone, when daughter Maeve returns with our disruptor, you will personally escort her through the vault to ensure her safe travels."

"No, I don't need an escort in the vault. I only require safe passage to and from the portal." I didn't want anyone coming with me, especially not the guy I'd antagonized for the past hour. I also didn't want them knowing what I was taking.

Nithia's arm rose, cutting me off, and the crows perked up again, ruffling their feathers as they prepared to take flight. "Per the terms of our agreement, we have an obligation to ensure your safe return. How can we guarantee this without someone accompanying you?"

She was smiling, but her eyes were steely. She wanted to know what I needed from the vault, and she was using my own terms against me. Unfortunately, I'd walked myself right into that corner.

"Agreed," I said, unable to keep some of the grumpiness out of my tone.

Nithia rose, assisted by Boone, and patted me on the shoulder in a return to her grandmotherly persona. "Your pretense of naivety will only work once." She tilted her head to one side then the other, and the creepy crows mimicked her movements. "You have potential. I think we shall meet again."

I stayed respectfully seated as she and the crows left. Boone followed her out then ducked back into the pumpkin house a moment later to scowl down at me.

I chuckled. "I don't like it any more than you do, buddy."

"I will escort you to the border of our Haven."

As I followed him out, Nithia was nowhere in sight, and I imagined her springing sprightly from branch to branch as soon as she was out of my eyesight. *Grandma, my ass.* Nothing was what it seemed with the Fae.

Boone led me back toward the boundary, and Sheel slipped silently behind us again. Neither spoke the entire way back, and if the tense set of his shoulders was any indication, Boone was clearly annoyed that he'd been assigned as my escort to the vault. Too bad for both of us that we were stuck with each other until we'd both fulfilled the terms of the bargain.

All things considered, I'd done all right. Giving the Fae a disruptor wouldn't cause any lasting damage. It seemed like a good bargain, but I was confident I hadn't gotten the upper hand on Nithia—not by a longshot.

The Fae queen was now aware of the rift between me and the Alliance, and my list of unreliable allies was stacking up, but I was closer to figuring out what the Fates were up to with those portals. As we walked, I brooded on the fact that the Alliance had approached the Fae without telling me. As much as I wanted to march into the circle room and demand answers, I couldn't. It was too late.

By the time Boone dispensed a gruff reminder to return with the disruptor and disappeared back into the forest, I'd decided on a plan. First, I would take the disruptor and give it to the Fae. Then, I would retrieve the book from the vault, learn why Silas was building portals for the Fates, and figure out how to stop them from doing it again. And somewhere in there, I needed to figure out how to get DOD-SI off our backs and convince the Alliance to back off of their plan to rebind magic. The last two overwhelmed me, so I focused on the things I could control, starting with taking the disruptor.

By the time I returned to campus, it was dark. I slipped through the magical barrier and held my breath, half afraid they'd altered it to keep me out. The sigil on my arm gave me access, despite my activities that day. I glanced down at the series of interconnected circles positioned over a central pair of triangles whose bases overlapped and pointed to either side. It was the access key to every protective shield over every home our people had. It had always been the symbol of home, but maybe not for much longer, at least for me.

I ran my fingers over the other tattoo on my arm, tracing the overlapping circles and thick swirling lines that formed the sigil of House Valeron, creating the Aegis bond between Silas and me. It had been days since I'd sensed him through the link... not since the sand-creature incident. I tried again to open the connection, but nothing happened because both of us had to keep it open, or it wouldn't work. I forced my disappointment aside and focused on what I could fix. Taking a disruptor shouldn't be hard.

Ethan's prototype was stashed in a weapons locker that had been keyed to all the members of the Inner Circle. I skirted my way around the campus buildings, avoiding the main quad and the busiest buildings near the center. The western building on the south side was full of classrooms, and the kids who normally attended school there would be with their families this time of night. I found the entrance on the southern side of the building and headed down the hallway toward locker 801, about halfway down the hall. I grabbed the handle, but the spell keyed to my biometrics didn't open as I twisted the lever-style handle. I let go and grabbed it again. It still didn't unlock. "What the hell?"

The hallway remained empty as I tried twice more, but the click of the lock never happened, and the handle stayed stuck. *They locked me out.* It stung, but I had to admit that they had good reason not to trust me—I was trying to steal a disruptor and ruin their plans to re-bind magic. Honestly, I felt a little less guilty because they'd *expected* me to try and defy them. It seemed somehow worse and better at the same time, but the evidence of our split solidified my resolve. It was too late to turn back—I was already on the outside.

I needed someone who could get me into the locker but wouldn't rat me out to the Alliance, and it didn't take me long to figure out who I needed to talk to.

Chapter Fourteen

E than's room was littered with half-finished projects. A random collection of stuff he'd tinkered with and infused with magic covered the small desk in the corner, and various discarded bits lay scattered across the floor. He'd squeezed a large shelf next to his desk and filled it with tools, project scraps, and finished or abandoned projects. His tinkering was mostly harmless—a shirt that folded itself, a dry-erase board that flashed through the last five things written on it before it started over, a laundry basket that magically cleaned the clothes thrown into it—which was actually genius—but most of it was useless. He just liked to tinker.

Ethan scowled at me from his desk, clearly considering my plea for help. I'd asked him to side with me against his sect and, by extension, his mother. I'd laid it all out for him—the portals Silas had been building, the book I needed, and the bargain I had struck with the Fae. I asked him to help me take the disruptor and to keep his mouth shut. Then I held my breath.

"Let me see if I've got this right. Silas is AWOL, tearing rips between our realms or whatever the Fates are making him do, and instead of going to the New Alliance with this critical information, you bargained with Elias *and* the Fae to figure out what he's up to?" Ethan shook his head. "That's... insane. You need to stop obsessing about your boyfriend and think about the big picture here."

"What the Fates are up to *is* the big picture. Whatever Silas is doing with those portals is related to the rips, and I think the Fates are behind all of it."

He snorted. "Of course you would say that. You think Silas shits sunshine."

I blinked at him. "What?"

He rose and paced to the other side of his single-sized dorm room. He only managed a few steps before he hit the end and had to turn back and face me. "Don't you think Silas should be responsible for his own actions at some point in his life? Don't look at me like that. You're completely blind to the person he really is. Jesus, Maeve. If you knew half the stuff he's done, you'd run away from him, screaming."

"I know exactly who he is, and I'm well aware of his history. More than you are, actually." Ethan's comments were way out of line. Silas and I had told each other pretty much everything about our pasts. He'd been forced to do terrible things while serving the Council and had hated it all.

He frowned. "I've tried so hard not to be the one to tell you this. I know it won't help my case, but... I just can't anymore. He's not worth it, Mae. You're willing to throw away everything we've built here for him, and he doesn't deserve it. He's not good enough for you."

On one level, I understood Ethan's concerns. Silas had a lot of blood on his hands. But beyond his past was a loyal, loving man, and I'd fallen in love with him. Silas was worth fighting for. And Ethan's not-so-secretly harbored crush on me was officially old. "You and I are not going to be a thing, Ethan, and you need to get that through your head right now."

"What? That's—I'm not—I'm not talking about my feelings!"

"You're telling me Silas isn't good enough for me because you think there's a chance you and I are going to work out."

He huffed and blushed as he looked away.

I took a deep breath and decided I didn't need to blow up our friendship over old feelings. "We were kids when we dated, and those are good memories. But that's all it is. We're not kids anymore, and life took us in totally different directions that neither of us could have imagined. I need a friend right now." I squeezed all the remaining air out of my lungs as I tried to find some semblance of internal calm. "The Alliance is trying to rebind Earth's magic. They already asked the Fae to help them."

"What?" His head whipped up. "I didn't—no. How could they... no one told me!" He plopped down in his seat, his previous anger deflating as he slumped over his knees. "Are you sure?"

"Yes, I'm sure." A totally unexpected wave of relief washed over me. Ethan hadn't known. At least he hadn't been one of the people eager to stab me in the back.

He remained silent.

"If they rebind magic, our people will pay the price. Too many have already died." I watched him process my words. The Alliance had rejected me, Silas had been missing for days, and I was all alone. Ethan was one of my oldest friends, and I hadn't realized how alone I felt until I asked him to help me. I needed him to say he would.

His voice was soft when he finally spoke. "Even if I agree with you that magic should be free, I'm not sure the world is ready for it."

"Me neither," I admitted. "But is there *ever* a good time to turn the world upside down? What I know for sure is if the Alliance rebuilds the source, someone is eventually going to try to take the power, and our sect will be the only thing standing in their way... *again*. Someday, it won't be enough, and the world will pay an even bigger price when we fail. The risk is too big."

Ethan leaned back in his desk chair, obviously turning my words over in his big, smart head. "You're right. There's not going to be a better time, and I agree there's a really high risk that the power of a single magic source would fall into the wrong hands. But are you really willing to go against the New Alliance? They're not above banishing people. Are you willing to risk that?"

"When I was inside the Source, I saw the binding our ancestors built around Earth's magic. It's hard to explain, but everything about it was *wrong*, Ethan. I know I didn't discuss it with anyone first, and people don't understand why I did it, but I made the right choice. I can't stand by and repeat the mistakes of history by rebinding magic, and I know it might mean I won't belong here anymore." I shook my head. "I'm sorry—I know this is a lot to ask. I just need access to the weapons locker. I don't need you to come with me. I can't ask you to do that."

"I still don't completely understand why you did what you did. But I know you, Mae. I know you did it for the right reasons, and I'm with you. All the way to the end."

"Friends?"

"Friends," he agreed. "And for the record, I'm not secretly harboring old feelings, at least not anymore. So you can stop flattering yourself. I said my piece about Silas, and you need to hear it, but you're an adult who can make her own decisions. I just need you to know I'm not in love with you."

A huge, relieved smile spread across my face.

He grinned. "You weren't sure your little speech was going to work, were you? Balls of Steel O'Neill was nervous."

I laughed. "Shut up."

"That's not a very nice way to talk to the guy with access to the weapons locker."

"Are you going to help me or not, smart ass?"

His laughter faded. "If we do this, I'm pretty sure we're not going to be welcomed home with open arms afterward."

The last of my own smirk melted off my face. "I just need you to open the locker then come back here and pretend you never saw me tonight."

"If you want my help, then I'm all the way in. You need all the allies you can get."

I swallowed hard. I hated asking him to join me, but a not-so-small part of me was relieved I didn't have to do it alone. I couldn't bear to pull in Stephan and Aria with their baby coming so soon, and Tessa was too conspicuous to go missing for more than a few hours. "Thank you, Ethan. This means a lot to me."

He squared his shoulders. "Okay, well... let's not waste any time. Give me ten minutes to pack my stuff then meet me at the locker."

In those ten minutes, I swung by my room. Ethan was right—there was a pretty good chance we wouldn't be allowed back home after this. I packed up my essentials then paused to scan the room I'd shared with Silas. Other than the basics, I had very few things I couldn't leave behind. I already wore Marcel's charm around my neck. I strapped Ripper's thigh holster to my right leg, picked up the memory catcher with memories of my father, then grabbed the engraved knife Silas had gifted me from the shop in Lower Aeterna and slipped them into my pack. Nothing else was irreplaceable.

It was the point of no return. I was committing to whatever it would take to set the world right, even if it meant never coming back.

I tucked a few of Silas's things in my bag too. "Okay. I'm doing this." I closed the door, hoisted my bag onto my back, and didn't look back.

I found Ethan outside the locker, looking guilty. He'd already had time to slip inside, grab the disruptor, and stuff it into the large camping backpack slung over his shoulder. Our bulky bags were conspicuous, but we couldn't do much about it. It was late enough that I hoped no one would see us.

"Try not to act so nervous," I said quietly as we walked toward the same first-floor exit I'd used earlier that night.

"I *am* nervous," he whispered. "If we get caught—"

"Someone needs to teach your friend how to look less guilty," Four said right into my ear.

I jumped and let out a very girly noise of surprise. My magic rose, but I held back as I glared at the Fate of Change standing in the hall with us. "What the hell, Four?"

He shrugged innocently, which instantly deepened my scowl.

"What do you want?"

"I'm curious what you're up to. Making deals with the Fae, sneaking around your own buildings."

Ethan gave me a confused scrunch of his brows, but I shook my head. He hadn't yet realized who Four was, and I wanted to avoid the freakout that was bound to follow if he realized he was standing in front of the super-powerful Fate I'd warned him about.

"You sure know a lot about what I've been up to. How long have you been creeping on me?"

Ethan took a small step toward Four. "Who is this guy?"

Four narrowed his eyes at Ethan and cocked his head to the side, as if considering him for the first time and questioning why he existed.

Right. Fun and games were officially over. I had to get Ethan out of there. "I have things I need to do. Nice catching up and all that." I dragged Ethan down the hallway, hoping Four would decide to go away. Whatever he was doing there wasn't going to be good for me. It never was. He was a walking catastrophe—every time he showed up, my life got worse.

Between one step and the next, Four stood in front of us, frowning. He'd done the Fate thing where he used magic, yet there wasn't a flare or an echo of it anywhere. He appeared out of nowhere, folding reality and time around his own will. We couldn't see his magic or feel an ounce of power. His entire aura, where normal people emanated a magic colored by their heritage, was basically a blank space where nothing existed.

"Whoa!" Ethan slid to a stop. "How the hell did you do that?"

I bared my teeth at Four. *Go away.*

Four bared his teeth back in that creepy way of his, mimicking human expressions without feeling the emotion behind them. "Are you going to introduce us?"

"No. Whatever terrible thing you came to tell me, just don't." Per usual, my stupid mouth moved faster than my brain. I had to get away from him. I took a ninety-degree turn and herded Ethan toward the stairs on the other side of the building.

"Mae! What the hell is going on? Is that—" Ethan froze, and his face went pale.

I was being ridiculous. There was no escaping Four if he decided to talk to me. From the moment I met him, he'd turned everything upside down in my life, and then he'd stolen a decade of Silas's, and I didn't want to deal with him. Four always ended up causing us misery. I didn't stop and think about the consequences of irritating an all-powerful being who could easily crush me out of existence. I really wished he would go away.

"Where'd he go?" Ethan asked, looking behind us.

A flash of magic pulsed right in front of us, and Ethan and I both rocked backward at the ice-cold wash of energy. We were face-to-face with Four again. His eyes glowed white with pure energy, and he bared his teeth at me again. This time, there was feeling behind it.

"Stop running from me, Maeve O'Neill." Every word was infused with magic. His power squeezed the atoms around us, suffocating the entire world.

To our eternal credit, neither Ethan nor I pissed our pants. I shivered in mortal fear, and even though every part of me ached to flee, I forced myself to let go of my magic and face the Fate because a magical showdown with Four was beyond even my level of stupid. Although Four hadn't frozen us in time, as I knew firsthand that he could. I couldn't move if my life depended on it.

Four cocked his head to the side, and his lips twisted downward, his expression turning sullen. It was a strange look on him, and I was instantly reminded of the first time I'd met him, when he sat across from me in the Elementari trap, mirroring my expressions.

"Stop mimicking me! Do you even have normal feelings?"

Four's eyes faded back to brown, and the pressure of his magic slid away, while the affable friendly-guy persona flipped back on. "You always ask me the most interesting questions, Maeve O'Neill."

"Do I?" I wised up and decided to play along, hoping a distraction would keep his nice-guy persona in place. It was a lot better than dealing with a super-scary, all-powerful Fate. Ethan was still at my side, terrified and wisely keeping silent as Four and I faced off.

"Do you remember the first question you asked me?" Four waited, seeming to expect me to remember.

It came back to me suddenly. Nuada had trapped me inside the Elementari, and Four appeared inside of it with me. He was powerful and different, but I didn't know what he was. I thought he was responsible for the kidnapping, and I asked him what he wanted. He'd treated my casual question like a personal philosophical inquiry.

"I do remember," I said. "Have you figured out what you want?"

He smiled. "Yes, I have. And to answer your other question, you *amuse* me. That is a human feeling, is it not?"

"Holy forking shirtballs," Ethan muttered beside me. His face had paled at least three shades. Four's gaze slid to him.

"Please leave my friend out of this," I said to Four.

Four shrugged. "He is irrelevant." He sounded like he was about to squash a bug and not feel bad about it. The coldness of his statement sent a familiar chill up my spine.

"I'm sorry I ran away from you. What did you want to talk to me about?" I shifted in front of Ethan, hoping he would keep his mouth shut and fade into the background. The last thing he needed was a Fate taking an interest in him.

"What are you retrieving from the vault?" Four asked.

"Don't you Fates know everything?"

"The results of your trip will not be what you want."

"How so?" I'd learned better than to take the word of a Fate at face value.

"Your bargain will bring nothing but problems."

"Am I in danger?"

He blinked. "You're mortal. You're always in danger."

The Fate mumbo-jumbo was familiar territory. We weren't getting anywhere. "It's hard to tell whose side you're on, Four."

"Fate doesn't have a side. It simply is." He winked. "What will happen is already happening."

The Fate gibberish didn't impress me. "Are you telling me I don't have a choice? Are you going to stop me from going?"

His eyes went wide for a fraction of a second. "I am not taking your free will, Maeve O'Neill." He glanced to the side as if expecting someone to jump out of the shadows and stop him from doing just that.

"Is Silas safe?"

"Choices have impacts. He makes choices, as do you."

A heady mix of anger and annoyance made me forget my earlier decision not to piss him off. Four loved dressing up and playing human, but then he would slip into all the Fate bullshit and go about merrily ruining my life. "This is why you suck, Four. What am I supposed to do with that? Are you telling me that if I go, Silas will be hurt? Are you threatening me?" I held up a hand, stopping whatever nonsense he was going to spew next. "You know what? Never mind. I don't want to know. Thank you for your warning or whatever the hell it was, but if you really cared, you'd stop keeping Silas and me apart."

He narrowed his eyes.

"Are we free to go?" I grabbed Ethan's arm, making it clear he was going with me.

"Do not disregard my words, Maeve O'Neill." Four disappeared in the biggest flare of magic I'd ever seen. The impact hit us in the chest, and Ethan and I staggered backward. Ethan hit the wall, and I almost fell on my ass.

"That was a Fate!" Ethan was wide-eyed and panicked. "You just yelled at a Fate! I can't believe we're still alive."

The intruder alarm went off. The siren blared in the hallway where we stood. The alarm would sound in every building on campus and send people to their breach posts.

"Son of a bitch! He did that on purpose. And if he winks at me one more time, I'm going to punch him in his stupid, smirking face. I don't care if he wipes me from existence. It will be worth it!"

"Come on," Ethan said. "Let's go before someone finds us with the disruptor." He leveled a very annoyed look at me. "And then we're going to have a conversation about why a *Fate* just showed up to tell you not to go to this vault."

Chapter Fifteen

"I don't like this." My toes hung just over the edge of the three-story brick apartment building in Somerville. My stomach felt like I'd already taken the plunge as I peered into the gap below, full of second thoughts about the entire plan. "Are you sure?"

Boone grunted. He stood stoically on the rooftop, his tall, bulky silhouette, including the outline of the massive two-handed broadsword strapped to his back, outlined by the city lights behind him. *So very inconspicuous, that one.*

His expression was obscured in the shadows of the setting sun, but his body language was clear. Boone was annoyed. He clearly didn't appreciate being sent on his babysitting errand any more than I wanted him to tag along.

My plan was insane if I stopped to think about it. I'd negotiated a series of shady deals, first with Elias and then with the Fae, all with the hope that I could figure out what the Fates were up to. And Four was clearly watching me. I was sure to regret all of it sooner or later—but I'd have to hope for later, because I didn't have time to second-guess myself. I had to find out what Silas was doing for the Fates and how it was related to the tears between our realms and the others, and I had to do it before the Alliance figured out how to rebind magic.

I twisted around to look at Ethan. "Seriously? Does he really expect us to jump because he said so?"

Boone sighed through his nose. "I already told you, this is an ancient portal hidden by the Fae for generations. The rooftop entrance is a security measure."

I looked down again. Somerville was a maze of houses with fences snuggling up next to each other. From the street, one wouldn't have been able to see the ten-foot gap between the buildings. The three buildings overlapped to create a perfect square of empty space with no gate or other access point, even windows, except for the rooftop.

"But, like, couldn't there be a ladder or something?" I asked. "If I jump and there's no portal there, I go splat." *I should rethink my life choices.*

Boone crossed his arms. "It's the only way to access the vault. You don't have to go."

"We should make him go first," Ethan said.

I was about to agree, but a wave of magic hit me, freezing the words in my throat as all three of us spun toward the source. My magic rose as a figure appeared on the rooftop with us.

"Silas!" I totally forgot I was a grown-ass woman and threw myself at him. I hadn't seen him for almost a week.

Boone shouted and lunged for Silas at the same time. Silas's eyes flared white, and a wall of magic slammed into my chest.

Boone froze midlunge with his sword drawn. Ethan froze also in the act of reaching for me. Everything froze.

"Silas, Boone's a friend. Don't—"

Silas raised a hand, and energy flared through his aura. Pure power. It was too bright, and I threw my hand over my eyes, unable to look at him directly, but his attention was locked on Boone.

"Silas, wait!" I shouted. "He's an ally! He was trying to protect me."

He furrowed his brows as if he didn't quite understand what I was saying. Something was wrong with him. I reached out through our Aegis bond, but it was like touching a wall of ice. Our bond was brittle and cold, impenetrable.

"Silas!" I pushed harder against our bond, and it gave way almost like an actual barrier between us. The return of our connection flooded me with his confusion, and I sighed with relief as his power lessened around us. Our magics intertwined as if an invisible reunion of our souls had occurred. I sent every warm feeling I could through our bond—love, comfort, calm. He relaxed, and the crazy amount of magic in his aura faded until the rooftop was no longer flooded with blinding power.

"Hey, welcome back." I kept my voice casual. What I really wanted was to throw myself into his arms. I wished I could tell him I was terrified of what was happening to us.

Warmth flowed through our bond as the last shreds of cold distance faded. For a moment, everything was right with the world, and I let his comforting presence wrap around me while our shared love flowed back and forth.

I waited for Silas to gather me in his arms, but he pointed at Boone. "Who is that?"

Boone stood a few feet away, frozen midlunge with his sword drawn. My brain stuttered for a second, digesting the fact that he'd tried to protect me. Because of our agreement, he was honor bound to protect me during our journey, but his instant reaction to a potential threat made me appreciate him more as an actual ally—a reluctant ally, but still.

"This is Boone de'Fiero. He's escorting me on, um, an errand."

My explanation was lame, and an awkward silence stretched between us. Whatever I said had the potential to get back to the Fates. For the same reason, I didn't dare ask him about the portals he'd created. Silas knew I wasn't telling him everything but didn't push for more information. Maybe he already knew what we were up to. The distance between us—the things we couldn't tell each other—got wider every time I saw him. It hurt my heart, but I had to lighten the mood.

I poked Silas in the chest. "You left in the middle of the night without so much as a note. Some ladies might take offense at that kind of behavior."

Silas didn't reply. I had tried to make it into a joke, but I couldn't hide the hurt in my tone. It would have taken one second to wake me up and say goodbye. Or he could have popped over at some point in the last six days and told me what he was up to or possibly given me some idea of when he would be back or that he was okay. I was so tempted to point out all the ways he could have kept me from worrying. It was useless. Four was in charge of Silas's actions, not Silas.

Silas didn't make any movement to get closer to me. "I have—what's the Earthen expression?—time off."

"Really?" I grinned. "How long do you have?"

He tried to smile, but it didn't reach his eyes. He glanced at Ethan and Boone, who were still frozen and unaware. "Until I'm needed again. I have a reprieve at least for this night and perhaps tomorrow."

He didn't seem happy about his reprieve. Four had kept us apart for so long that I wondered why he'd suddenly let Silas come back. Four's visit earlier made it weirder.

"Why are you here, Silas?" I let my suspicion color my tone. He had shown up right before I was about to do the thing Four had told me not to do. "Why did he decide to give you time off now, right at this exact moment?"

He pursed his lips, and I knew I was right. My heart fell. It was only a ploy to stop me from finding Elias's book. I was going to punch Four in the face the next time I saw him, consequences be damned. "You're here to distract me."

He clenched his jaw, and his expression said everything. He didn't want to be used like this, he knew exactly how I felt, and nothing about this situation was fair to either of us. It was all a ploy set up by Four, but I was still so tempted. I wanted nothing more than to take Silas up on being distracted for a couple of days. I would happily hole up with him forever and let the rest of this world go right to hell.

A frustrated sigh escaped me, and I took a step away from him. "I wish it had worked." I could only hope the wedge Four was driving between us wouldn't last forever as I turned back to the ledge. My heart twisted inside my chest. The fact that Silas was there meant the portal three stories below us worked and that Four *really* didn't want me going to the vault. It was all the confirmation I needed that I was doing the right thing. I risked one last glance at Silas as a deep ache burned in my chest. I almost threw myself back into his arms. "Tell Four he's a bastard."

"Maeve, wait." A wicked grin flashed across Silas's face. It wasn't the boyish grin I loved when he let his guard down but the sharp challenge of the man who had commanded legions of warriors and defied the all-powerful Aeternal Council at every turn.

It both gave me hope and terrified me. My heart rate picked up. "What?"

He licked his lips, as he did when carefully considering his words. "I was told very specifically that I had to do my best to convince you to stay without blocking your free will."

He closed the distance between us and pulled me into a rough and hungry kiss. I kissed him back with equal feeling. The Aegis bond between us was wide open, flooding me with equal parts frustration and love.

"I've always loved your strong will." His gray eyes bore into mine, urging me to understand what he couldn't say.

I nodded silently. *Free will. My strong will.* Four could do a lot to block and misdirect me, but he couldn't force me to do something against my will. I got to choose my own path, and Silas was reminding me of that.

"Come with me," I whispered. It was desperate, but I couldn't help myself.

"I'm not allowed to travel to other realms. The Fates' powers are limited to this one, and they can't—" He grimaced.

I hissed in frustration as I watched him struggle to speak, his face twisting in anger. He couldn't say or do anything Four wouldn't allow. "What about *your* free will?" I choked out.

"I gave it away when I agreed to our deal."

A flood of shame filled me. Silas had agreed to be Four's servant for a decade to save my life. Tears burned behind my eyes, but I forced them back. Silas didn't need to absorb my pain on top of his struggles. As bad as everything had been for me, I could only imagine how awful it was for him.

He took up both of my hands and lowered his voice. "I'd do it again, my Maeve. A decade of lost will for your life is an easy trade. We can't keep looking back." His eyes tightened, and he swallowed hard. "What you're doing is not going to—" His voice choked off again, and an icy rage flooded through our Aegis bond.

I reached for him, aching to pull myself into his arms forever. "I'm going to kill Four."

"Don't tell me that." He shook his head. "Don't say anything you want me to keep from them. I'm sorry I left without a word—I..." He paused. "I think it's better if we're apart until this is over. It's too confusing and just makes things worse. I won't allow them to use us against one another."

My hand drifted to his face, cupping the side of his square jaw, and his strong hands gripped my hips. "I hate this so much."

He lifted my hand from his face and kissed my palm. A flash of love and desire resonated through our Aegis bond, and my entire body ached to stay near him.

I closed my eyes and swallowed hard. "You're making it very hard to leave."

"I can't help it," he replied.

I didn't know if he was referring to Four's orders or the pain of being apart. Either way, it sucked. I intertwined my fingers with his. "I'll be back as soon as we—"

He squeezed my fingers, cutting me off. "Don't tell me."

It took a long moment for me to gather the strength to step away from him again when every part of me wanted to hang on tighter. When I finally moved back, the distance between us was more than physical. "You tried your best."

Silas nodded at me in approval, his face hard but not cold. "Be careful. I'm not able to help you there, even if your life is in danger."

"I will."

His demeanor shifted, and every inch of him went hard and commanding as his harsh power flared across the rooftop. It was like a punch in the gut as his eyes flamed pure white with the Fates' powers. Ethan and Boone came back to awareness, and Boone scrambled back as he saw firsthand the insane amount of magic coursing through Silas. Ethan managed to stand his ground.

With the return of the Fates' powers, coldness radiated from Silas again, searing me. I pushed back as much love and warmth as I could through our Aegis bond, trying to keep him grounded a little longer.

"Ethan, I'm holding you personally responsible for her safe return," Silas said.

Ethan licked his lips before he managed a response. "I don't need you to intimidate me into keeping Mae safe. *I* wouldn't abandon her when she needs me most."

A flash of irritation shot through our Aegis bond, tinged with the slightest hint of jealousy. I tensed, unsure what Silas might do.

"Good," Silas said. "I'm counting on it. And you, Boone de'Fiero. She believes you are honor bound to protect her. If you let any harm come to her, justified by some turn of phrase or loophole or for any reason whatsoever—I have your name. I will find all that you love and take it from you. You'll beg for death before I am done. Do we have an understanding?"

"Silas! I told you, he's an ally. You don't need to threaten him!"

Somewhat to my surprise, Boone bowed his head slightly. "I understand."

"I can protect myself just fine," I said. "I don't need you going all caveman on my allies."

His magic faded, and I could breathe again. His eyes returned to their normal steel gray, and his expression softened. "You are my heart, Maeve. I will do everything in my power to keep you safe."

"And then you go saying stuff like that..." I shuddered. "It's confusing and irritating and *almost* sweet."

He gathered me into his arms and kissed me fiercely. The kiss burned through me, filling me with joy and life stronger than magic. Before I could gather my wits and kiss him back properly or remember that we had an audience, he disappeared.

"Where the fratch am I?" Tessa stood on the rooftop in full battle armor, her sword drawn and pointed at Boone. She quickly glanced my way without diverting her attention from him. "Maeve?"

I forced my brain to stop spinning, and a giant sigh escaped me as I realized that Silas had sent me a babysitter.

As Tessa and Boone sized each other up, I waved my hand between them. "That's Boone," I said to Tessa. "Boone, meet Thessaly D'Nali, First Commander of the Guardians."

To Boone's credit, he hadn't tried to murder Tessa when she appeared out of nowhere and without even the flare of a skimming spell to announce her arrival, but he still had the sword in his hand and wore a freaked-out expression. He lowered his sword and nodded at her.

She sheathed her sword and narrowed her eyes. "I assume you're about to do something dangerous, and our Lord Commander didn't approve?"

I sighed through my nose. "He's feeling a little overprotective."

She jabbed a thumb at the men. "So these two didn't meet his exacting standards for your personal safety?"

Boone and Ethan let out identical grunts of male displeasure.

"Sorry to drag you into this stupidity," I said to Tessa. "You can go back to campus and—"

"No way." She grinned. "Silas knows I love dangerous stupidity!"

I shook my head in amusement, but I lost the humor just as suddenly. Everything about the situation sucked, including the fact that Silas was falling back onto his overbearing, overprotective tendencies. I was losing him, and the only choice I had was to get to the bottom of whatever was going on with the Fates before it got worse.

"You will tell me what is happening here, or I will not help you any further," Boone declared.

I sighed, deciding that Boone could at least know the part everyone else did. "A few months ago, I took the power of one of the Fates and used it to bring Silas back to life. He, uh, died. Briefly."

Boone rocked back on his heels, but his expression of shock quickly faded into narrow-eyed suspicion.

"The boost I got faded, but the effect on Silas was stronger." A lot stronger. It seemed like his powers had increased every time I saw him. I forced the thought away. Four said the Fate powers would be necessary for Silas to do his errands. They weren't stronger—my fear made my imagination run away with me. "He's feeling protective of me right now, but it's not any of your concern."

I ignored Boone's distrustful expression and very deliberately didn't look at Ethan for his reaction as I scooted back to the edge of the rooftop, grappling with my emotions. The square of empty space forty feet below loomed in front of me. I couldn't see the magic at the bottom that Boone had promised was a gateway to the vault, but a tiny trickle of hope ran through me. I had three allies at my back, two of whom I trusted with my life, and a clear plan. All I had to do was find Elias's book and figure out how to repair the rips between realms despite whatever Silas was doing for the Fates. Once I stabilized the magic, I could convince DODSI and the New Alliance to set it free. It was a plan, and it felt good to take control of things for once.

With one last glance at my unlikely trio, I gathered my free will around me and took a leap of faith right off the building.

Chapter Sixteen

The hardest part wasn't the jump—it was the landing. I instantly regretted not asking more questions about what waited for us on the other side of the portal in the realm where the Council kept their most treasured belongings... because I landed in deep shit.

I was *covered* in shit. From my armpits to my toes, the liquified excrement coated me and soaked through my clothing. I gasped and accidentally inhaled potent, moist air that burned its way down my throat. Shouts of disgust and alarm echoed off the high cavern walls as the others landed.

Holy hell. I held my breath. We were inside a huge stone cistern, and judging by the sea of brown we'd just landed in, it was a sewage dumping ground. The vile stench of an entire pool's worth of shit stung my eyes. I held my unsoiled hands over my head in a vain attempt to keep them clean.

Tessa started gagging. "Oh, gods!"

"Don't!" Ethan's hand slapped over his own mouth. "If you barf, I'm gonna barf too."

"Don't breathe!" I had to drag in another gulp of oxygen to speak, and I gagged as thick air slithered into my lungs.

Tessa tried to cover her mouth and accidentally smeared brown stuff across her face. Her eyes went wide with horror. She retched, and I had to turn away before I joined her. Boone was already silently wading away from us, holding his sword above his head in both hands, toward a ladder built into the side of the giant stone cesspit.

With burning rage in my heart, I sacrificed another breath of air to call the others, and then we climbed onto a man-made platform carved from the stone walls fifty feet above the cesspit.

I dragged in a slightly less burning gulp of air as Ethan and Tessa emerged onto the platform after me.

"Why didn't you warn us about the giant pool of shit?" I demanded.

Boone shrugged. "You didn't ask."

"You were supposed to take us to the Council's vault!" Ethan accused.

"This is the only remaining gateway to the vault. Did you not wonder why this portal had been abandoned and forgotten by all but the Fae?" Boone asked.

"You could have warned us." Now that I could breathe a little more clearly, I realized there was a strange feeling about the place, almost like my magic didn't like being there.

"This is a naturally formed portal through the stone ceiling. The walkway is supposed to extend across the cesspool. The drop was unfortunate." Boone pointed at a long metal platform bolted into the stone landing where we stood. It was connected to a rotating platform with a large metal crank, which would extend the walkway from where we stood directly under the shimmering portal—like Boone had said.

"Thanks for the heads-up," Ethan said as he spread his limbs out like a scarecrow. He held a single clean hand awkwardly above his head, trying to avoid contact with himself.

"Bullshite! I saw you land with your sword over your head!" Tessa's anger flowed in multiple languages as she flung chunks of excrement from her hair and clothes onto the ground. "You knew what was coming and didn't tell us, so don't try that bull-cocking Fae half-truth shite!"

"You didn't ask," Boone said calmly. "It's not my responsibility to inform you of every possible outcome of your actions before you take them."

I imagined several ways to murder him. At least two involved drowning him in the cesspool.

Tessa drew her sword from her hip sheath and tried wiping it on her pants, but it was a lost cause. Neither surface was clean enough not to soil the other. I grimaced as I took stock of Ripper and my thigh holster, but I didn't dare draw the Messer sword I'd strapped to my back. The hilt was high enough to avoid the pit, but everything from my collarbones down was soaked. My toes squished in my shoes, and I fought my gag reflex. Like Tessa, I tried wiping my clothes down with my hands, but it didn't help much.

I tried to let my magic rise, and a wave of nausea washed over me. "There's something wrong with my magic."

"It's the Council's security measure," Boone responded.

"What? What do you mean?"

Boone looked at Tessa. "You explain it to her. There's supposed to be a wash station nearby." He turned away, clearly above answering questions he found obvious, volunteering helpful information, or generally being a decent person.

Tessa bared her teeth at his back. "This place has a natural resistance to magic. You can still use your powers, but they'll be... hesitant. Weaker. The Council chose these types of locations for their vaults as part of their security against intruders. It's probably better if you don't try to access your powers if you can avoid it. The results may be unpredictable. Go with the flow, as you Earthens like to say."

I inhaled through my nose and about passed out from the smell as we all followed Boone toward the wash station. We took turns rinsing off, using an entire bar of the harsh chemical soap left in the wash area. The former Aeternals, Boone and Tessa, apparently felt no shame about stripping down to their birthday suits to get clean.

While they rinsed and beat their clothes against rocks without concern for their nudity, Ethan and I washed while avoiding eye contact. What I really wanted to do was burn my clothes and shave off all my hair, but we turned our pockets inside out and did what we could with our hands and the single bar of soap until we were as clean as we could be under the circumstances. When Boone pulled out a fresh set of clothing he'd brought in a waterproof satchel, I decided I truly hated him.

I took extra time with my blades until I was certain Ripper and the thigh holster were excrement free then laid them out to air dry. I ran my thumb over the sigil engraved on the base of Ripper's blade—Silas's house sigil—and swallowed hard. He was going to be fine. We were both going to be fine. I just needed to find Elias's book, and then I would have answers.

When we were mostly clean and redressed, we started our hike through the labyrinthine cave system. Boone assured us we were headed in the right direction as we climbed upward for ages, scaling a series of ladders and stairs carved into the mountain. By the time we left the stench of the cesspool behind us, we were mostly dry as we walked through man-made tunnels deep inside the mountain. We followed Boone, who seemed to have an unerring sense of direction despite the many intersecting hallways and twists that left me feeling like we were in a maze. Maybe we were. For the first time, I was grateful to have him as a guide.

As we moved quickly through the various hallways, I realized that when Elias had told me the vault was deep inside a mountain, he meant *deep down*. Twice, we took a ridiculously long stairway downward, curving around and around as we descended. We finally arrived at what Elias had quaintly described as a foyer. The large room had elaborate magical sigils carved into every wall and over the entire floor. Three stone columns stretched from floor to ceiling with two wooden doors between them. Elias had spent a long time describing the magical traps the Council had built and explained exactly how to access the real doorway in this room, avoiding the decoys that led to various and painful ways to die.

I pulled the small vial of blood Elias had given me out of my pocket and poured it into the palm of my hand.

"What is that?" Ethan asked.

"The doorway won't lead us to the correct location unless we use the blood of a former Council member. This, my friends, is the blood of a Council member."

"Ew," Tessa said. "I wouldn't touch it if I were you. Greed is contagious."

"Thanks for the warning." I put my already bloody palm against the door on the left, and it swung open with an ominous creak.

Ethan handed me a cloth to wipe my hands as we peered into the near-dark doorway.

"Let's go," I said.

"Wait... we need to be cautious." Boone stared warily at the door as he drew his sword. "The Council is notorious for its traps."

Elias had assured me that the blood would work, but he also hadn't told me about the shit pool or the magic-dampening effect surrounding the vault. "Agreed. Let's do this slowly."

"Boone can go first." Tessa drew the blade at her side and grinned in the same way Silas did before he was about to kill something.

Somewhat surprisingly, Boone didn't object. Without reliable access to my magic, I drew the Messer from its sheath. Boone took the lead, and I went next, followed by Ethan and finally Tessa. The stone-carved path circled around itself, creating a dark hole in the middle. Without a handrail, one misstep would mean a fall to the bottom, wherever that was. We slowly descended three more flights of winding stairs in tense silence until the light from the open door above us no longer illuminated our path.

"What now?" Ethan whispered.

"We need a light," I replied quietly. "These stairs are treacherous."

"This would be a lot easier with magic," Ethan replied.

It occurred to me that Ethan didn't have a weapon or a way to defend himself without magic. I handed him Ripper. Boone proved once again to be more prepared than the rest of us as he pulled a flashlight from his pack and lit the stairs as we continued downward. When we finally got to the bottom, we stood in front of a narrow bridge carved with more magic sigils. Both sides dropped into pure blackness. Elias had instructed me about which sigils were safe to walk on, and I took the lead, stepping carefully from marking to marking while the others followed.

We crossed safely but were blocked by another door. A sigil had been carved into the wood—two triangles pointing in opposite directions, one to the left and the other to the right, with a curved line above and below. I paused, unsure what to do. Elias hadn't mentioned it.

"How do we get through this one?" Ethan asked.

"Um... I actually don't know. My source didn't mention the door."

We stood there for a few more minutes, examining the possible death trap. "I can't see any spells. Maybe it's only a door, and that's why your source didn't think to mention it," Ethan suggested.

Tessa reached out and twisted the doorknob. The door swung open.

Shocked, I sucked air between my teeth. "Tessa! We have no idea what that could have done!"

She shrugged. "It's only a door."

The room behind the perfectly normal door was brightly lit with luminescent stone. A carved marble dome arched at least twenty feet above our heads. Eight alcoves were spaced evenly around the room, and an opening in the exact center of the floor held a stone staircase that descended to another level below.

We piled inside silently, not daring to speak as we examined the contents of the room. Every alcove was full of memory crystals neatly aligned on ornately carved wood shelves along the walls. Each one was nestled on a velvet cushion and labeled.

Ethan ran his finger along the neat labels. "It's just a bunch of names. What do you think this is?"

I scanned the shelf nearest me, and my attention snagged on a familiar last name. "R. Trivalent. Remus Trivalent?" I reached for it with a shaking hand. I wasn't sure I wanted to pick up a memory crystal labeled with the name of the man who had beaten me to a bloody pulp and attempted to rape Aria.

"Memories of misdeeds done by the Council's enemies," Boone said.

Ethan's mouth dropped open. "Whoa. The Council captured memories of terrible things people did and kept it for blackmail?"

I stared at the memory crystal in front of me with wide eyes. I had zero regret about killing Remus Trivalent. But the crystal, with whatever awful memory it contained, confirmed that the Council clearly knew what a monster he was and hadn't done shit about it. I stepped back and took in the entire room of crystals as a deep pit of disgust grew in my stomach. I shouldn't have been surprised that there were so many life-ruining secrets or that the Aeternal Council had collected them. It was truly disgusting. I wondered if Silas knew. "Let's keep going. We need to go to the deepest section—it should be three floors down."

We headed down the stairs to the room below, and this time Tessa led with her sword drawn as Boone brought up the rear. The second room was carved from the same glowing stone into a triangular shape. The stairs we descended put us at the base of the triangle, with the walls on either side coming together to the top point exactly opposite us. The room had hundreds of hooks on the walls, and after a quick glance, I tried very hard not to look at the items hanging from them. They were mostly body parts—ears, hands, lots of hair tied neatly at both ends, vials of blood strung up like Christmas lights. All of them were labeled. Boone stood in the center of the room, staring at a raised pedestal that contained a pale lump of flesh the size of my hand. It was protected by some kind of spell.

I looked away. "Gross, gross, gross."

Collectively horrified, we all quickly moved for the next set of stairs as I tried not to see anything or think too deeply about why the Council had collected body parts.

We took the second staircase down into another triangle-shaped room, a mirror opposite of the one above. It took my brain a second to reorient. There was a strange feeling to the space, but I couldn't quite figure out what was bothering me as the back of my neck tingled. The room felt wrong. There was something unbalanced about the entire vault.

The third level was wrapped in massive floor-to-ceiling shelves, and each one was stuffed with books of all sizes, shapes, and thicknesses and bound in leather, parchment, or cloth. There were fat tomes with golden spines and thin scrolls rolled and stacked neatly on shelves. The books were neatly arranged, spines out, with titles in various languages and some with no titles at all. We were searching for a specific text, but my fingers itched to explore them all. I made a mental note to bring Tamara back to gather whatever she thought would be helpful. It was a literal treasure trove of knowledge.

"Do you know the title?" Tessa asked.

I glanced at Boone, who was examining one of the shelves. I was hopeful I could find the book myself and somehow keep the information private, but the books weren't organized. I needed everyone to look, or I'd be down there for a month, searching for the right one. I resigned myself to the Fae knowing what I came there for.

"It's called *Origins of Fate*. But they don't seem to be in alphabetical order."

Ethan crouched to examine one of the shelves. "I think they're organized by subject. This alcove is about Hexes."

"Okay—that's a start," I said. "Let's scan each section and see if we can narrow it down."

We all turned to the shelves and scanned the titles until we could figure out the general topics, moving on if it what we found didn't seem relevant. After some time, my shoulders and neck started to ache from all the twisting and crouching. I was about to suggest that we find another approach when Tessa thrust a leather-bound tome above her head and called, "Found it!"

I took the book carefully and ran my hand over the cover, marveling at the finely filigreed gold threads worked into an elaborate symbol on the front. There must have been a preservation spell at work, keeping everything inside the vault in good shape, because it looked really old.

My sense that something was wrong flared up again. Magic pulsed across the room, and I snapped up my head. "Did you feel that?"

Ethan shook his head. "Feel what?"

"What's happening?" Tessa asked. "I didn't sense anything."

Another small wave of magic rolled over me. "It's below us!" I moved to the center of the room and turned in a slow circle as I searched for the magic washing over me like a cool wave of water. The familiar tingle set my nerves on edge, and my body strained toward the source of the magic.

"Maeve?" Tessa drew her sword. "What is happening?"

"There's a weak source of magic coming from somewhere in this room." I tucked the book into my bag then held up a hand for quiet. In the exact center of the room, the same archaic symbol etched into the first door had been carved into the stone floor—two opposite-facing triangles with a curved line above and below.

As I stood directly over the symbol, I suddenly realized what had been nagging me about the vault. "Four symbols." I pointed at the sigil carved into the ground. "The first room was a dome, then two triangle rooms. Just like this sigil. "The fourth symbol is an inverted dome, but there are only three levels. Where's the last domed room?"

"Do you think there's another room below us?" Ethan asked.

"Something is down there," I replied.

"Why can't anyone else sense it?" Boone asked.

"I don't know. It's—it's like there's a block on it. It's very faint."

"What about these other symbols?" Boone pointed to the three corners of the triangular room.

I hadn't noticed, but between all the bookshelves, symbols had been carved into the walls forming the sides of the triangle.

"It's almost like a preservation spell, but it's different.... more complex." Ethan's head cocked to the side as he examined the sigils.

"Holy gods, it's a stasis conjuring!" Tessa exclaimed.

"Stasis? Are they keeping something *alive* down there?" I asked, feeling my eyes go wide. "Does anyone know how to break a stasis spell?"

Boone and Tessa both looked mystified. Ethan's face twisted as he undoubtedly sorted through the sea of knowledge tucked inside his curious mind. "No. I don't—not really. I mean, stasis spells are used to keep things preserved. The bigger or older the item, the more magic it takes... like a plant would be minimal, but a person would take an enormous amount of magic."

"There will be a keyword to trigger the spell," Boone said. "Something relevant."

The magic vibrated again, so faintly that I probably wouldn't have noticed if I hadn't been standing right in the middle of the spell.

Tessa slammed the handle of her sword on the ground twice, right over the symbol. "Anyone down there?"

Ethan and I both jumped. "Tessa! Did you have to—"

Weak magic flared again from beneath our feet, seeming to reach for me, winding deep into my soul. "There's someone down there."

"Blasted balls of all the Fates," Tessa said as we all stared at the tiled floor.

"Keyword!" I scanned the room, fighting down my irrational panic. "We have to release the spell and get them out..."

"What is it?" Tessa demanded. "What's the keyword?"

"I don't know! There's a name placard for every other gods-damned thing they collected, but—" I gasped and smacked my own head. "That's the key!"

"What?" Ethan asked. "What's the key?"

I stood directly over the sigil carved into the tile floor and shouted the name of the person trapped down there. It came out of my mouth before I considered the impossibility. The magic washed over me, tugging at familiar connections too much a part of me to stop and question how or why or who.

"Valeron!" I shouted.

Chapter Seventeen

In complete shock, I stared at the unconscious man we'd pulled out of the stasis chamber. Lord Sergius Valeron—*Silas's father*—was alive.

He looked like an older version of Silas. He had the same olive complexion and dark hair, which ended past his shoulders, and the same strong jawline below a refined nose and proud forehead. He was wearing the same style of ceremonial armor I'd seen Silas wear at the Guardians' exposition, down to the crimson half cloak. The resemblance between father and son was so strong that I would have known who he was even without the familiar Valeron magic emanating from him.

His magic was too weak, and he'd passed out when we opened the stasis chamber. Tessa and I hadn't been able to do more than stare in shock while Ethan and Boone dragged him out of the tiny space he'd been trapped in and laid him on the floor. Tessa was completely pale and quiet, and I wasn't sure I could speak coherent words if I tried.

Everything I knew about Silas's father was wrapped up in the story about a mission gone wrong at Krittesh—*where Sergius Valeron had died*. My brain kept stuttering around the details about how he'd died. The elder Valeron had been betrayed by someone they trusted, and Silas had taken command of the Guardians and gotten them out. And of course, our friend Atticus had been attacked and framed for the failure, and he'd had to pay the price as a Traiten until we cleared his name.

The details were fuzzy, but I remembered clearly that Sergius Valeron had made Silas's life hell when Silas turned his back on the role he'd been groomed for and joined the Guardians. A lot of murky information floated around in my brain, but one thing was for certain: Silas's father was supposed to be dead.

He started to rouse, and Tessa crouched next to him. "Careful, my lord. You'll feel weak for a while longer."

"Water," he croaked.

Boone handed him a water bottle, and he drank greedily.

"Don't drink too much, or you'll be sick," I said automatically.

His steel-gray eyes were sharp, and the look he leveled on me was so *Silas*, I took a half step backward. "Who are you? Who sent you to find me?"

Tessa saluted him formally with her fist over her chest and a quick bow. "I am First Commander Thessaly D'Nali." He stared at her blankly, and she added, "I was in your son's Guardian training cohort. We've met before. Do you remember?"

"D'Nali," Sergius said slowly. "Yes, I believe so. I must apologize for not remembering one of my son's, uh, associates."

Tessa frowned slightly.

Sergius took another long drink from the bottle. "Do you have any sustenance? I've been stuck down there for days."

We all exchanged looks. I didn't know what to say. I really didn't want to be the one to tell him how long he'd been in the stasis chamber. Instead of correcting him, I dug in my pack and handed him a granola bar. He tore into it and chewed a few bites as we all stared at him.

"Where is Silas? Is my heir too busy whacking people with metal sticks to attend to my rescue?"

Tessa and I both grimaced. I was still trying to wrap my brain around all of it. *How is he alive? What was he doing in a stasis chamber?* One thing was certain: just because he was Silas's father didn't mean we could trust him. I didn't know if he would be an ally or an enemy, but Sergius Valeron was the former leader of the viper pit that was the Aeternal Council, and that made him dangerous—even if he couldn't currently stand on his own two feet.

"Do you know where you are?" Ethan asked, neatly changing the subject.

Sergius surveyed the alcoves of books. "We're in the Council's vault."

"Do you know how you got in there?" Ethan tilted his chin toward the hole in the ground.

"I was ambushed." Sergius lifted his hand as if to ward off additional questions, and his expression went hard. "And I intend to repay the responsible party. Take me to House Valeron. I need to call a special session of the Council."

Tessa frowned. "Lord Councilor, we all believed you to be dead."

"As you can see, I am quite alive, and I need to return to my House immediately. Take me to the portal."

Tessa and Ethan both glanced in my direction, but I had no idea what to say. Sergius followed their gazes and frowned. He lifted a single, disdainful brow, and I almost choked over how much he looked like Silas. That expression was a mirror image of the arrogant bastard who'd turned my life upside down before he stole my heart.

When it became clear that we weren't jumping at his orders, he wagged a finger between me and Ethan. "Who are you? You speak like Earthens."

"My name is Ethan Rourke." Ethan paused for me to speak, but I couldn't form any words. He took pity on me. "This is Maeve O'Neill. We're from Earth—uh, the Earthen Sect of Harvesters. I think you called us the Lost Sect?"

That seemed to surprise the former Lord Councilor, judging by how his eyebrows moved into his hairline. The familiar expression was too much. A sudden pang of loneliness and worry made me reach for Silas through our shared bond. It was a reflex—reaching out to connect with the man I loved.

Sergius Valeron sensed the tug on his family bond, and his eyes snapped to me. "Who *are* you, and how are you accessing my House bond?"

I swallowed hard and managed an unconvincing half shrug. "I'm Maeve O'Neill, from Earth."

He stared at me with incredulous outrage. I had no way to explain my connection to his House in a way that wouldn't blow up the whole situation. He had no idea he'd been missing for more than a decade, that I was bonded to his son, that his entire realm had been destroyed by Lord Nuada, or that the Aeternal Council was no more.

"There's a lot to explain."

His gaze was like molten steel as he judged me and clearly found me entirely lacking in every way. "Are you bedding my heir?"

His words were like a slap. "Excuse me?"

"I thought I taught Silas better. I can only assume from your brazen attitude that you've managed to get yourself pregnant with his child."

I looked at Tessa for a reality check. "Is he serious?"

Her face had gone pale. She nodded.

I ground my teeth. *Too far.* I didn't have to take this shit from anyone, not even Silas's father. *Especially* not his father. "I'm going to give you a pass this once because we just pulled you out of a hole and you don't know what's going on. You're probably in shock."

He huffed through his nose, and his expression was so irritated and impatient that I itched to smack it off his face. Valeron men knew exactly how to get under my skin.

"I'll offer double your family's annual allotment to terminate the pregnancy and never speak to my useless son again. I can't allow a bastard."

Icy rage filled me. "You've been in stasis for over ten years. Everyone in Aeterna would have died if Silas hadn't single-handedly held open the portal to Earth, so stop calling him useless. And I didn't trap your son with a pregnancy, so why don't you shut the hell up before you say more stuff you don't know jack shit about?" I was so angry that I stood and paced away from him.

Then I realized we were missing someone. "Where's Boone?"

Magic pulsed across my awareness, and this time, everyone else clearly felt it too.

"What was that?" Ethan asked.

Tessa jumped to her feet as a deep rumbling filled the chamber, and the floor started moving. The hole we'd dragged Sergius out of expanded suddenly.

"Get back!" I shouted, and we all scooted away from the opening gap in the floor. Above us, the ceiling also receded, leaving only the stone staircase traveling up through all three levels of open air. The floors kept sliding away, and the distance between us and the stairs widened.

"To the stairs!" Tessa leapt onto the stairs.

I pulled Sergius to his feet.

Ethan jumped from the other side of the room onto the stairs then reached out to me. "Jump!"

"Sergius won't make it!" After being in stasis for so long, Sergius was barely able to stand, and there was no way he could make the rapidly widening distance—it was already at least six feet. The floor kept retracting, and Sergius and I kept scooting farther away until we had our backs up against a bookshelf.

"Climb up the bookshelf!" I pushed Sergius upward. He planted one foot on the shelf ledge right as the last of the floor disappeared, and I hopped onto the same shelf.

Our combined weight tipped the bookcase forward, and we started to fall toward the gaping hole where the floor used to be.

Tessa leapt from the stairs and landed on top of our bookshelf, tipping the weight back against the wall. She reached down and helped Sergius and me to the top.

"Thanks," I said breathlessly as we all crouched on the top. "Thought I was a goner for a second there."

"No thanks required. That was great! I knew I'd get dangerous stupidity by coming along with you."

Despite our desperate situation, I laughed quietly as I surveyed the wide-open space below us. The floors had fully retracted, and the gaping pit between us and the stairs where Ethan stood was pitch black—it was impossible to know how deep. The stairs were about eight feet away, and there weren't any handrails. I turned to Sergius. "Can you make the jump?"

"I'm not entirely confident," he replied.

Given that he'd barely been able to stand as he emerged from the stasis chamber—I'd had to drag him to his feet—I doubted it. Tessa, with her half-Fae heritage, would have no problem, but it would be a big jump for me as well. I made eye contact with Tessa, who looked pointedly at the stairs. I shook my head. We weren't leaving Sergius behind.

"Any ideas, Ethan?" I called.

"Not without reliable magic. I can't even raise a first-level conjuring in here."

Boone appeared at the top of the stairs, his face darkened and looking annoyed. His power flared into an electric blue that didn't seem entirely stable. I had seen his magic before, and it was not that color—I'd never seen any magic with streaks of electricity in it. With whatever strange energy he was channeling, Boone wove a shield and tossed the threads of the conjuring at Tessa. She picked up the other side of the weave, effectively creating a walkable bridge between her and Boone.

"Maeve O'Neill, come across the void," Boone commanded.

I narrowed my eyes. "What power are you channeling? You shouldn't be able to hold a conjuring in here."

Boone crooked his fingers at me. "Come quickly."

I shook my head. "Tessa and Sergius will go first."

Boone gritted his teeth. "Make haste! I can't hold this much longer."

"Go with Sergius. I'll jump over after," Tessa said.

I grabbed the old man. "We're going together. Boone is oath-bound to keep me alive." I slid a foot out into the open air, cautiously shifting half of my weight forward onto Boone's bridge.

Ethan moved to the top of the stairs, which gave us more room. Together, Sergius and I eased off of the bookshelf and onto the bridge. I kept a firm grip on Silas's father as we hurried across to where Boone stood.

Tessa leapt onto the bottom of the stairs as soon as we stepped off Boone's bridge, and I led Sergius to the level above to make room for everyone. The retracting floors had to have been some kind of security measure, because the second level had lost its floor as well but still had everything hanging from the hooks on the walls. The central feature, the pedestal with the hand, was attached to the landing where the stairs of the second level connected to the third. The pedestal was empty.

As Boone stepped onto the platform, I twisted and kicked him in the side of the knee. His leg buckled, and he dropped onto the stone stair from the unexpected attack. I followed him down, pulled Ripper, and held it against his throat from behind. "What did you do?"

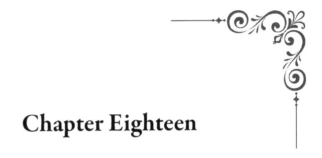

Chapter Eighteen

Boone glared at me from the base of the stairs. "There are no more traps from here to the portal. Mother Nithia's oath of safe passage is upheld." Magic flared around him, again with a strange, crackling blue energy, and he disappeared in a skimming spell.

"Shite!" Tessa drew her sword, but it was too late. Boone was gone.

"How did he do that? All magic should be dampened!" Sergius exclaimed.

"He's drawing power from whatever was on that pedestal," I said. "I noticed him looking at it when we were here before, and it's empty now."

The velvet-lined stand was clearly meant to display the center-piece of their body-part collection. I didn't want to know what used to be considered their most prized piece in the disgusting collection, but I stooped to read the plaque. "*N. de'Fiero*." My brain started buzzing... de'Fiero was Boone's last name.

Tessa gasped when she read the plaque. "Oh, hells! Did Boone steal a Hand of Glory?"

"It belonged to Lady Nithia." Sergius sat on the stairs, too exhausted or overwhelmed to stand. "This is exceptionally bad."

Holy shit. I swallowed hard. "The placard says '*N. de'Fiero*'. N for Nithia. Ugh. Of course they're related. Those green eyes were a total giveaway. I'm such an idiot!"

Tessa's face paled. "Fates curse us."

"What's a Hand of Glory?" Ethan asked.

"They're powerful dark-magic artifacts that amplify the owner's powers," Tessa explained. "Ancient Fae would make sacrifices for greater access to magic. The greater the sacrifice, the greater the magic. Human sacrifices were common, but the greatest sacrifice would have been your own flesh."

I swallowed hard. That also explained the weird magic Boone had used to escape. "I've never seen another Fae without their hands. I didn't know they did that..."

Sergius sighed. "After the Council banned the sacrificial arts, the Fae people entered into another kind of sacrifice—an oath to tell only the truth. It's a shared bond that sustains their power and ties them together."

"It's one of the reasons they hate half-blooded Fae," Tessa confirmed. "We're not tied to their weaknesses, but we can access their magic. Well, some of us." She glanced at Sergius. "There's no way the Fae Queen would have given such a powerful sacrificial item to the Council willingly."

Sergius scowled. "She didn't."

Silence hung around us as we all tried to comprehend that scenario and the consequences of what Boone had taken back to the Fae queen. There was no telling what Nithia would do with that kind of power. She already had an edge of not quite darkness but a kind of disturbing magic, and I didn't want to imagine what she'd be capable of with an artifact that amplified her powers. "Well, Boone is long gone with that hand. There's nothing we can do about it now. Let's focus on getting out of here."

"Escort me to my House. I will call an emergency Council meeting," Sergius said.

Ethan, Tessa, and I all made eye contact, but my friends were chickens, so the task of bringing Sergius into the present day apparently fell on me. "Listen, I wasn't lying. Aeterna collapsed, and the Council was disbanded. You've been missing for over a decade."

Sergius lifted his chin and literally looked down his nose at me. How he managed to do it while barely conscious and sitting on the stairs was a testament to the height of the high horse he sat upon. It was the exact expression Silas had thrown around when we first met, and it did absolutely terrible things for my temper.

"First Commander Thessaly, does this woman speak the truth?"

"Yes, my lord. We believed you had died. It's been almost eleven ani since Krittesh." Tessa paused, seeming to consider her words. "You might care to know that Lord Silas took up his seat on the Council in order to enact the Aegis bond on Lady Maeve's behalf."

Sergius's nasty expression completely disappeared as surprise flashed across his face. "How... unexpected. So my son has already acknowledged his heir, then."

"For the love! I am not pregnant with anyone's child! Are you not listening to a single word we're saying?" I threw my hands in the air and stomped up the stairs before I punched him. I could see where Silas had gotten his asshole tendencies. *Unbelievable.* I had learned to control my temper quite a bit in the last year, but Sergius Valeron was pushing all my buttons, just as Silas used to do. *Damn these Valeron men.*

Tessa helped Sergius to his feet then followed me, with Ethan bringing up the rear. "The Houses are gone, my lord. Magic can no longer survive in Aeterna, and the Council has fallen. They fled to Earth, where Lady Maeve's sect welcomed our people as refugees. She is a leader among them, and she speaks the truth."

We left the first floor with the crystals and traveled over the sigil-covered bridge before Sergius spoke again. "I'm gone for a mere decade. The entire realm falls to ruin, and my House is made destitute." He let out an undignified strangled noise. "If what you are saying is true, we must find my son before the Fates do."

Surprised slashed through me, and I stopped in my tracks. "No one said anything about the Fates. What do you know about them?"

He threw me the most Lord Asshole look I had ever seen. I thought Silas had his down pat, but this was next level. It was full of derision and annoyance, as if I were a nasty little bug that deserved to be squished... Which meant, of course, that I was onto something important.

"What do you know about the Fates and their plans for Silas?" I planted myself in front of him. "You can tell me now, or I can put you back in your hole." He'd severely miscalculated his ability to control me with his assumed superiority. I'd already pulled one Valeron lord off his high horse, and I could handle this one too. I leveled a glare right back at him and raised an eyebrow. *Bring it on, buddy.*

"My son always did like a challenge."

I couldn't figure out the game we were playing. I didn't know if he truly wanted to help Silas, but he seemed to know more about what was going on with the Fates than I did despite having been unconscious for the last eleven years. I needed to know what he knew.

Sergius stared right back at me, wearing a hard expression. "Have the Fates attempted to unbind magic in your realm yet?"

My brain stuttered. He didn't know *I* had unbound magic, but... "Why would the Fates want to unbind Earth's magic?"

He narrowed his eyes. "Why should I trust you with the information I have? I have no idea who you are or what your connection truly is to my son. You should first share all you know with me."

"For the record, I don't trust you, either. I don't know much about you, except that you made Silas's life hell. Unless you convince me otherwise, I'm considering leaving you here. I don't need to deal with your shit while I'm trying to help Silas."

Sergius's entire demeanor changed. His shoulders slumped, and the haughty air completely disappeared. "Silas is my son. If you have true feelings for him, please—tell me what is happening before it's too late to help him."

And there was the magic word. I was such a sucker for assholes who said *please*. It was a risk, but I had to do everything I could to help Silas, and if his father had the same goal, then we were allies. Temporary allies, perhaps, but I couldn't turn away from any chance to bring Silas home. "I'll tell you what I know if you tell me what you know about the Fates. Everything."

He nodded.

I organized my thoughts as we exited the foyer with the false doors and began the long trek back to the portal through the winding mountainside. "You already know I'm bonded to Silas. And for the record, I'm not trying to trick him out of his money or use him for his family name. I really couldn't care less about any of that. I love him because he's a good man with a good heart, and I'll do whatever it takes to bring him back."

Sergius's stance went stiff. "Back? Where is he?"

I took a deep breath and exhaled slowly. There was no turning back after this, but I needed to know what Sergius Valeron knew about the Fates. Trust was a two-way street, after all.

"Silas burned through all of his power—your entire familial source—stabilizing the portal between Aeterna and Earth when magic collapsed in your realm. He saved thousands of people. As you probably know, he doesn't give up when he commits to something, and he gave everything he had holding that gateway open. He actually died."

I swallowed hard, remembering the moment when they'd carried his lifeless body through the portal. "I, uh, killed a Fate and used his magic to bring him back." I glanced over at Sergius. His face had paled, but I was just getting started. "While I was hopped up on the Fate's powers, I unbound the Earthen Source and set some things into motion that came back to bite us in the ass."

I told him about our deal with Four and how Silas had created the stable portals between the pocket realms. A few of the things I shared seemed to surprise Tessa and Ethan too. I could feel their gazes on my back, burning with questions, but they graciously kept quiet while I brought Sergius up to speed.

"So now, they're using Silas to establish permanent connections between these pocket realms, and I don't know why. I need to close the rips connecting back to Earth, but I'm afraid anything I do will make it worse. In the meantime, Silas has signed over his free will to the Fates, and I don't know how to stop it because of our damned deal with Four."

"You used the Fates' powers to unbind Earth's Source, and you're not damaged?" Sergius asked. "You no longer have access to their magic?"

My thighs were burning from our ascent up the many stairs we'd descended on our way in, but Sergius seemed to be recovering his energy. "My powers faded. I used most of it up altering the past to make sure we weren't all murdered by the Fae, and then I removed the binding around Earth's magic. I was pretty tapped after that."

Sergius made a small choking sound.

I gave him a moment to come to terms. "Your turn. I want to know what you know about why immortal, all-powerful beings are making Silas do their dirty work. What do they want with him specifically, and why would they want Earth's magic unbound?"

"The Fates are not immortals. They're the remainder of a powerful race who committed so many atrocious crimes that our ancestors overcame their differences to work together and banish them to the spaces between realms. The details are thin, but our ancestors destroyed the original Fate and banned the lesser ones. Over the centuries, the remaining Fates worked together and gained some access back into a few of the magic-rich realms by sharing their powers with inhabitants of those realms. I believe it creates a sort of bridge for them, but their access is limited. Aeterna's source-based magic and Earth's fully bound magic have acted as the last remaining barriers to their freedom.

"The Fates attempted to destabilize Earth's bound magic by using those under their influence to build portals between realms. This creates an imbalance of power they hoped would destabilize the binding around Earth's magic—the binding your people put into place. But since you have freed magic on Earth and Aeterna has fallen, it would not be necessary. They will already have full access to any realms."

"Earth's magic isn't completely free," Ethan said. "We've contained it within Boston."

Sergius must have looked confused because Tessa added, "Boston is an Earthen city on the eastern coast of the American continent, a little larger than Aeterna."

"I see. Then the portals my son is creating must be an attempt to circumvent that boundary, funneling power between the city of Boston and an expanding network of other realms. Through those realms, the magic will spread across Earth, giving the Fates access to the power they need to finally break free of their imprisonment."

Nausea blossomed in my stomach. I'd believed Earth's magic needed to be freed. I'd been inside the Source and seen the wrongness of the binding around all that raw, beautiful power. But if Sergius was correct, then freeing magic was exactly what the Fates needed me to do, and I'd fallen victim to their manipulations... again.

Ethan and Tessa stayed silent as we all contemplated the new information about Earth's magic and the portals Silas was building.

Sergius paused in the long stone tunnel to catch his breath. "When I became Lord Councilor, I began to uncover the depths of this plot that has spanned centuries. There is significant evidence that the Fates cannot fully interfere in our affairs, so some element of free will is required, but in either case, they have succeeded in advancing their agenda. Silas may be the final piece of their plan. After all my work protecting my heir from the moment he was born, they still got their claws into him."

My knees were weak. "What do you mean? Why are they after Silas?"

"My son is the fourth generation of *prophesied* matches within the Valeron line. They've been using our Magisters to arrange matches that breed mortals strong enough to wield their magic. They need someone connected to each realm to join their ranks, a link of flesh and bone wielding their powers.

"It took me years to uncover evidence of their plans, but their manipulations run deep through all the Upper Houses. They've attempted dozens of assimilations of the offspring from these pairings, but none of the candidates survived. Only one person survived in recent history, but her brush with the Fates left her magic dangerously unstable. I do not believe they were grooming her genetic line, but she wanted the power desperately enough that she cut off her own hand to build up her powers."

"Mother Nithia." I gasped, suddenly realizing why her magic had been corrupted. She'd been attempting to become a Fate... and apparently failed. "She just got her hand back—well, one of them at least. Is that going to be a problem?"

His voice was hard. "She deserved a quick death for what she attempted, but I was outvoted. If she's attempting to become one of the Fates again, she must be stopped, and I won't allow leniency again. Not after what she did to me."

"Was it Mother Nithia who locked you in a stasis chamber, my lord?" Tessa asked.

"Yes, after I discovered her attempts to join the Fates and the Council voted to take her hand. Revenge is a powerful motivator."

I racked my brain for any mention Nithia might have made about the Fates, but I couldn't recall. In hindsight, the bargain to access the vault had been easy—all she'd asked from me was a disruptor. In exchange, I'd opened the vault and led them straight to her missing hand.

"Wait. Why didn't she take the hand when she put you in stasis? It was right there."

"Oh, Lady Nithia didn't physically attack me—only Council Members could access the vault," Sergius said.

I inhaled sharply. "Lord Nero." He'd been the official representative of the Fae, and he'd been doing Nithia's bidding.

Sergius nodded. "Even so, I didn't want anyone to take the Hand of Glory—especially not the other Council members, who might be tempted by the Fates. I spelled it so only I could break the stasis spell, which Lady Nithia and Lord Nero obviously didn't know at the time. That Fae who came with you must have taken hair or such from me when I came out of stasis." He sucked his teeth unhappily.

"So Nithia realized you would have to come out of stasis to get her hand back," I guessed.

"Most probably."

I am such an idiot.

We continued our journey out of the tunnels, toward the portal. "If you are capable of the things you told me about, then the Fates may have succeeded with more than one genetic line. Your powers combined with my son's would be of great value to the Fates. Are you truly not with child?"

My stomach twisted, and my knees felt weak. "No, I'm not pregnant."

"A child born to the two of you would be in great danger."

I gripped Marcel's charm so hard in my fist that it dug into my palm. Four had manipulated us every step of the way until I freed Earth's magic and brought Silas back to life with new and improved powers—Fate powers. What Sergius was saying rang true, but my brain was swimming with questions. The feeling of dread hovering over me made it hard to breathe.

"They brought Silas and me together. The prophecy about us stopping the Brotherhood, the visions Four gave me, everything. And then I freed all of Earth's magic—it was all planned by the Fates." I had to stop and draw in a couple of deep breaths. "But if they did all of that to get access to Earth's magic, why take Silas? They have everything they need."

"Their powers are strongest as a triad—they'll need a replacement for the one you killed. The Fates likely meant for you to procreate a more powerful vessel, connecting them to both Aeterna and Earth, but I'm guessing you moved up their timetable when you were able to unbind magic in your realm. With greater access to Earth's magic, they may have decided to take Silas now instead of waiting for your future offspring."

"I think I'm going to be sick."

Tessa squeezed my shoulder gently as Sergius plowed forward. "It's a hard thing to see the danger to your child and be powerless to save them. Be grateful, at least, that you were spared that pain. We need to act before it's too late to save my son."

His expression was laced with worry so bare and uncalculated that I decided right then that I could trust him to fight for his son. We would both fight for Silas because we both loved him.

He wrinkled his nose and curled his lip. "What is that smell?"

I gritted my teeth. "That, Lord Valeron, is deep shit, and it's only the beginning of what we're going to have to get through before our journey is over."

Chapter Nineteen

A laric Certus, former Lord Magister of the Aeterna Council, had threatened my life, manipulated me, and generally made my life miserable from the moment I'd met him. During his time on the Council, he'd forced a bond-mating on Silas and his daughter, Aria, that neither of them wanted. He'd redeemed himself since Atticus's death, but before that, he'd been an all-around asshat. Because of all that, I really enjoyed the expression on his face when Sergius Valeron and I walked into the circle room.

"Wha-What? How?" Color flamed up Alaric's cheeks, and he literally stopped breathing.

I bit the inside of my cheek to keep from laughing as his expression veered between terror and outrage before settling on utter shock. And if their squirming was any indication, Lord Nero and Lady Octavia suddenly found their seats around the circular stone table to be terribly uncomfortable.

Octavia recovered quicker than the other two former Councilors, rose from her seat, and bowed formally. "My lord, you're alive!"

Sergius's response was curt. "Lady Maeve rescued me from a stasis spell in the vault."

Alannah's overly styled hair bobbed stiffly as her head whipped in my direction. "I thought the vault was a rumor—is there an access point here on Earth? How did you get in?"

I decided I'd better wipe the amusement off my face and clue everyone in, especially since I needed to get back in the good graces of the Alliance if our plan was going to succeed. "The Fae have a secret portal to the vault, and they took me." I left out the details of my bargain or why I went to the Council's treasure vault in the first place, but Alannah's pinched expression said she wasn't going to be happy with fuzzy answers for long. "Everyone, may I present former Lord Councilor Sergius Valeron. He's... not dead."

Sergius raised an eyebrow at my less than elegant introduction but turned smoothly to Casius. "Lord Casius Palmer, leader of the Earthen Sect of Harvesters, I presume?"

"It's just Casius," he said slowly, clearly leery of the older Valeron.

Sergius bowed formally, flipping his little half cape behind him with a flick of his wrist. "Your sect did us a great honor, Casius. You rescued our people when Aeterna's magic collapsed. Your generosity and assistance will be remembered, and I thank you personally for what you have done for my people."

"It was the right thing to do," Casius said stiffly, clearly thrown off by the display of gratitude from a member of the Council. He glanced at me. "You should be thanking Maeve. If it weren't for her, many more lives would have been lost."

Casius gave me a hesitant curve of his lips, and I nodded in return, recognizing the peace offering. Ever since I'd freed magic, I'd been at odds with the New Alliance and with Casius. Acknowledging that I'd done the right thing by rescuing the refugees from Aeterna lifted a little of the weight between us.

"And Silas too," I said. "Your son held the portal open between realms at great risk to his own life. He brought honor to your House."

"Yes, well," Sergius said, "greatness was always his destiny, no matter how hard he tried to stop it." Pride flashed on his face briefly. He took a seat at the table—Silas's usual seat—and lost the haughty, condemning expression. "I have much to share." Sergius was in full lordly mode as all eyes stayed glued to him. He told them the history of the Fates and how they had interfered for centuries, attempting to gain their freedom. By the time he was finished, every face had gone paler, and the room was completely silent. "Tell them what you have learned about unbinding Earth's magic, Lady Maeve."

The people around the stone table used to be the closest thing I had to family. I'd turned my back on them because we disagreed over my choice to unbind magic. The decision was my own, and I was wrong. It was time to own up to my huge mistake. "I was the latest idiot to play into the Fates' plans by unbinding Earth's magic." I met the gaze of each of the Alliance members, including Alannah, as I swallowed my pride. "They manipulated me into destroying the Source. I was wrong, and I'm sorry. We need to rebind Earth's magic, or the Fates will gain their freedom again."

There were mixed reactions around the table. Some, like Ethan, seemed to sympathize with my apology, and others, like Nero, were impassive and clearly unmoved. Casius seemed thoughtful.

Sergius placed his hand on my shoulder. "We must act before the Fates build a permanent bridge into our world."

"Only one problem," Tamara said, folding her arms. "We can't figure out how to rebuild the Source. We've been trying for days, and nothing is working. I don't know what else we can do."

That brought us to what Sergius and I had planned as we traveled back to our realm. I dug Elias's book out of my bag and held it up so everyone could see the filigreed gold sigil on the front. "This book is the original guide to binding Earth's magic. If the Fates can no longer access any magic in our realm, they won't be able to escape their prison realm."

"The Fates have begun the process of establishing connections here. Once we rebind Earth's magic, we can banish them permanently," Sergius confirmed.

Tamara's eyes lit up as I handed the book to her.

Casius pursed his lips. "Is this book why you went into the Council's vault?" I must have looked guilty, because he homed in on it like a shark smelling blood. "Since the former Council Members in this room are clearly surprised, I have to assume you went behind our backs and negotiated a deal with Elias to get into their vault. That's too far, Mae. Even for you."

I didn't flinch. "You told me I would have until DODSI's deadline, but you'd already gone to the Fae and asked them to help you rebind magic."

"How do you know about that?" Alannah demanded.

I glared at them both.

Unexpectedly, Sergius stepped in. "Might I suggest that distrust on both sides led each of you to less-than-honorable actions? Let us move forward for the benefit of all."

Casius and I looked away from each other, still angry but willing to set our argument aside for the moment.

"We must discuss Lord Elias. Lady Maeve, I don't know the details of your deal, but you cannot give this book to him. He has long been interested in gaining the Fates' powers, and I'm afraid he would put it to ill use."

"I'm not planning on it, but he can't use the book anyway," I said. "His magic was permanently bound."

"Your sect did that? Impressive." His tone made it clear that he was surprised and possibly threatened that we could muster up the power to bind someone's magic.

"Mae did it on her own," Ethan piped up.

I threw him a dirty look, warning him to keep quiet.

"You"—Sergius's face paled. "*You* bound his magic on your own? How? A binding takes a direct connection to a source and at least two conjoined conjuring circles." His eyebrows rose into his hairline as he clearly reassessed my place in his power lineup.

I didn't like it at all.

I held up both hands before he hatched some manipulative scheme. "Silas and I both did it, and I don't have that kind of power anymore. None of us does."

"Not since the source was unbound," Alannah griped for the millionth time.

I ignored her as Tamara opened the book on the table and began reverently turning pages. About half the Alliance members gathered around her, eager for a peek. Alaric, Nero, and Octavia flocked to Sergius's side, eager to hear his explanation of how he'd ended up in the stasis chamber, and I was a little surprised to see Casius and Jason edging closer to him as well.

As he told his story, I wondered why Nithia had kept him alive. Killing him would have been easier and less risky. My mind circled around that question as I watched the elder Valeron. He had the same features and coloring as Silas, but he was a smooth politician, which his son was not. Silas stalked through rooms, drawing attention with his sheer presence and power. Sergius Valeron had the same magnetic draw, but he moved with deliberate intention, shaking hands and bestowing smiles.

"Something's sideways," Tessa said quietly at my shoulder.

At my confused expression, she motioned me away from the main floor and dragged me up one of the stairwells and to the viewing alcove on the first floor. The former medical theater was a completely round room with a bottom floor large enough to hold our stone table and host our usual meetings. There were four floors of viewing balconies above us with waist-high railings where medical students used to watch live surgeries. The balconies were empty now and gave us privacy.

Tessa leaned in closer, her voice low. "That whole speech—it's a classic power grab. Lord Sergius walked into the room after more than a decade without any actual authority, and within minutes, he had them all eating out of his hand—in charge yet again. He's loosed a greased pig and expects us to chase it around while he goes for the main course."

I blinked stupidly at her. "Can you translate that?"

"I'm sure he means some of it, but it's rudimentary political tactics. He's ingratiating himself into your leadership. All the 'thank you' bullshite and the bowing and his personal debt to Casius—*ph-hft*. He doesn't mean a word of it, but he needs allies. Now, he's co-opting the Councilors, and they're wrapping themselves around his little finger. Mark my words: he already has a plan hatched that puts him back in power."

Sergius worked his way around the room below us, smiling and casually touching shoulders and elbows. He introduced himself to Alannah with a charming smile and a little half bow. He was handsome and friendly, and he made a point of connecting with each person around him. *Making allies.*

"He used to drill this shite into Silas," Tessa said. "It was one of the main reasons Silas swore off politics—it's all so manipulative and insincere. Speaking of which, don't you think it's strange that he didn't remember me? I've met the man dozens of times. Only four of us graduated from our Guardian cohort."

I rubbed Marcel's charm between my fingers. "I don't know, Tessa. He just got out of a stasis spell. It's been a long time. Maybe he didn't recognize you."

She narrowed her eyes at Sergius. "Perhaps he's not who he says he is. We should test him for a Fae glamor."

"He's definitely who he says he is. I can feel his magic through the Valeron family sigil. But I don't think we should completely trust him, either."

Tessa glared down at the people below. "And Alaric chasing his approval is beyond pathetic."

"What do you mean?"

She turned her lavender eyes on me. "I forget that you are not an Aeternal and wouldn't know our history. Lord Alaric was the only survivor of his House's rebellion against the Council. He was barely out of his training years when his family was executed. The Council determined that he was innocent, but Lord Sergius wanted to make an example of the rest of them. He could have banished them, stripped their powers and their titles, but he chose the harshest punishment possible—they were all executed as traitors. Sparing Alaric's life was not a mercy but a reminder to everyone else what crossing the Council would cost them. We all expected Alaric to slink away, but he was tenacious. He insisted on maintaining his position within the Magisters, and then he clawed his way back into power."

On the main floor, Alaric's coloring seemed a little pale as he stayed on the outer edges of the crowd gathered around Sergius. Knowing that history, I had a tinge of regret for the way I'd sprung the elder Valeron's resurrection from the dead on him.

Sergius didn't seem perturbed to have Alaric there. From Silas's stories, I knew he was exactly the type of man who could decide to execute an entire family without any regrets. It probably wasn't close to the worst thing he'd done while ruling Aeterna. Maybe he hadn't been as bad as Elias, but I couldn't really know. He was obviously a man who would do whatever was necessary to get what he wanted, and I couldn't forget that. For now, we were aligned in our quest to get Silas back, but that didn't make us long-term allies.

I'd been chipping away at Silas's hard exterior since I met him, revealing the loving man beneath piece by piece, and it wasn't hard to imagine how living under the shadow of someone like Sergius Valeron had shaped him. I took a deep breath and decided I would keep some emotional distance. I didn't need to like or trust Silas's father, but I would use every resource to help Silas, no matter how I felt about Sergius on a personal level.

Tessa leaned back against the balcony railing. "Why did Nithia bother with the stasis spell at all? She hated Sergius."

"I don't know. I have a lot of questions and not very many answers. I just can't get over the fact that Silas's father is alive. Imagine if he'd never disappeared... Elias wouldn't have led the Council. The Brotherhood wouldn't have been formed. So much could have been better."

"I don't like Sergius—never have." Tessa exhaled through her nose. "But I believe he truly wants the best outcome for his people. It's his methods I don't trust." She propped her hip against the railing as we both watched him. "I can't believe he's alive. Poor Silas."

"I know things were tough between them, but won't Silas be happy to learn his father is alive?"

Tessa kept her voice low. "Stephan was lucky to have a different father and not much to do with Sergius. That man was a horrible father. He wanted to mold Silas in his own image so badly that he nearly broke his own son. The shite Silas went through in Guardian training because of his father..." Tessa shook her head.

Below us, Sergius was chatting with Tamara. Her eyes lit up as he pointed to something in Elias's book.

"He did nothing but berate and manipulate Silas. Their relationship was volatile at best... and Silas succeeded *despite* him. Things with Silas and the Fates are precarious right now. I'm not sure you should risk an additional shock."

"I can't keep this a secret. Silas deserves to know even if the news is not entirely welcome. And Sergius seems sincere in his desire to help Silas." I remembered the pride in Sergius's eyes when he'd talked about his son being destined for great things. But if Sergius was as awful as Tessa was making him out to be, I couldn't risk this being the breaking point that sent Silas over the edge.

Tessa tapped her fingers on the railing in front of us as we watched Sergius continue to make his rounds. "It's a good idea to be careful. Sergius Valeron may want to save his son, but he will use any-one and everyone to his own ends. He always has."

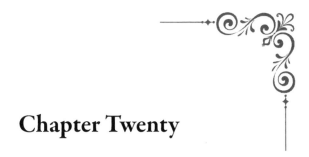

Chapter Twenty

A stream of deliciously cold water hit the back of my tongue, and I drank it down greedily. The always-cold water bottle was an ingenious invention of Ethan's, and it was particularly awesome after a hot and sweaty workout. Tessa tipped her own magic water bottle back, barely sweaty and probably ready for four more rounds with someone way more skilled than me.

I glanced quickly toward the back of the gym, where Sergius had been watching us spar for the past quarter hour, his arms folded as he leaned against the wall, his expression bland and pleasant. He wore a fitted gray suit jacket and modern-cut trousers. He was no dummy. He'd been back from the dead for less than forty-eight hours and had already figured out the modern power suit, and some lucky tailor had probably gotten a fortune for the expertly crafted wardrobe. Clearly, Sergius adapted to his circumstances and made sure he came out on top.

Every single Guardian in the training room knew who he was, and they watched him watching me. He wasn't inconspicuous in any sense of the word, and there was no way I could avoid talking to him. As the former Lord Councilor, he had been one of the most powerful men in Aeterna for longer than I'd been alive, and word had spread quickly about what they were calling his "resurrection." He was making a statement by being there, waiting patiently for me to finish my workout with Tessa.

"What do you think he wants?" I murmured to Tessa as I gathered my things.

She wiped the back of her neck with her gym towel and took another swig of water. "What all powerful people want: power, promises... more power."

I snorted and wiped loose hair off my sweaty forehead. "The usual, then."

Sergius headed our way.

"Uh oh." Tessa slipped on her shoes, quickly stuffed the rest of her items into her gym bag, and rushed toward the exit. "Gods' blessings."

"Scaredy cat," I hissed at her back.

She tossed a wave over her shoulder just as Sergius reached me.

"Gods' day, Lady Maeve." Sergius dipped his head with a quick touch of his hand over his heart. He was a lord—and the former Lord Councilor, no less—and I wasn't a lady. Technically, he didn't have to bow to me. He was being respectful and gracious, and I was sure it was all very intentional for our audience.

I hid my frown with another swig of water. I had a pretty good guess about what he wanted, and I decided to get right to the point. "You're not coming."

We had spent the last twenty-four hours coming up with a plan to rebind magic. We knew how to do it, thanks to Tamara's research in the book, but we didn't have enough raw power. Sergius had spent the better part of yesterday trying to convince us he could help, but I'd shut him down. We had a plan, and he wasn't part of it. The others agreed with me—he was an unknown, a liability. I had no doubt he was there to try and win me over, but he was going to be sorely disappointed.

He arched an eyebrow. "How can you trust Lord Elias but not me?"

"I don't trust either of you. And I can't keep my eyes on both of you while I lead the conjuring tomorrow, so you're not coming."

His steely blue eyes softened in an expression of earnest hurt. "Have I done something to earn your disfavor? Does Silas think so poorly of me that he turned you against me in my assumed death?"

I shook my head as I finished gathering my things. I refused to play his game. I didn't know him, and I certainly wasn't going to give him any information about Silas, no matter how carefully he pried. I didn't owe Sergius Valeron any explanations just because he was Silas's father. "I need to go. Other people are waiting to practice." I slipped my shoes on.

"Maeve," Sergius said, gently stretching the sound of my name.

Curse the Fates, he even sounds like Silas. I missed Silas so fiercely that my heart squeezed painfully in my chest. I focused hard on tying my shoelaces. I could only imagine what Silas was going through right now as Four and Two stripped his humanity away, moment by moment. I was losing him every second, but there was nothing I could do until I figured out how to stop them.

"Lady Maeve, I want you to trust me," Sergius said. "You are important to my son, so you are important to me. All I ask is that you give me a chance to prove my value."

His ruggedly handsome face was open and earnest as he gazed hopefully at me. The whole scene was smooth. I was supposed to be in awe of the proud, powerful leader asking me to validate him. I was supposed to feel special because he waited patiently to talk to me, and I was supposed to snatch the opportunity to have him in my debt. The very practiced and manipulative move had the opposite effect. I was furious.

Silas had been an asshole when I first met him, but he'd never been manipulative. I blinked the emotion from my eyes, willed steel to coat my heart, and gave him the truth. "It's not your value I question—it's your motives. Silas barely said anything about you, so don't think that being related to him gives you any kind of advantage with me."

Sergius's smile wavered. "I understand your caution, and I appreciate your candor. Strong relationships can be built from less than what we have in common. I'm willing to build that bridge, Lady Maeve. Are you?"

Oh, he is really good. I didn't have to stay there and be manipulated by him. I grabbed my gym bag and headed for the exit. I had a shower with my name on it. "Sorry, I don't do bullshit games. I'll let you know how it goes."

"Wait!" He reached out, almost touching my upper arm but stopping short of actual contact. Real fear shimmered behind his eyes. "Truth shared, I failed my son horribly. I steered him in the direction I believed would keep him safe from the Fates. When Silas defied me by joining the Guardians, I was scared. I interfered horribly, and... I hurt him." He knit his brows together in obvious regret, and his vulnerability didn't feel fake.

I knew that feeling. I had made decisions that had hurt others.

"I was wrong, and my mistakes cost me the last decade of my life, and now my son has been taken by the Fates regardless of all I—all *we* had to sacrifice. I need to make this right. Please, allow me to help him."

I searched for any sign that he was manipulating me, a glint in his eye that might reveal his real intentions or a flicker of pride. All I saw was deep regret. I needed time to think. I motioned for him to walk with me. As we walked silently toward my quarters, I rolled Marcel's charm between my fingers, twisting the long golden chain as I thought about my own mistakes and the burning need to fix them. I secretly wished for a do-over for myself, starting with binding my magic and my memories after my mother was murdered by the Brotherhood. That decision had cost me my entire family. But

I couldn't let my emotions cloud my judgment, and I couldn't mess this up. I couldn't afford to lose Silas.

After several minutes, Sergius spoke quietly. "Lady Nithia locked me in the stasis chamber so I could no longer interfere with the Fates' plans for Silas." He narrowed his eyes, and his expression went cold and hard. "It is no coincidence that Lord Elias rose to power after I disappeared. If he is in league with Nithia, then he was involved in the Fates' plans for Silas. I will make sure we learn all that he knows."

His honesty surprised me. In my experience, the former Aeternal Councilors didn't share information willingly. They never volunteered anything they could save for future personal benefit. "Look, tomorrow isn't about you settling your scores. You'll just be a distraction," I said with less conviction than before.

"Then let that work in our favor. You said DODSI insisted on bringing Lord Elias, but you cannot afford to be distracted by him. He will react to seeing me alive, and I will keep him occupied. While you focus on the conjuring, let me work on Elias. I know you don't have any reason to trust me, but we're both fighting for Silas. I dedicated all my considerable resources to trying to understand the Fates' motivations and unravel their plans. I have perhaps sacrificed Silas's love for me to keep him safe, and I ask you to not let that sacrifice be in vain. We must work together to stop the final steps of the Fates' plan from coming to fruition. It's not too late if we act quickly. Please. If you love him…"

Sergius was asking for a chance at redemption. He'd been an awful father, but in his mind, it had been for a good reason. And it really would be good to have Elias occupied with something other than trying to sabotage me. If Sergius could help me find information that could help Silas, then it would be worth the hassle to have him come along.

We stopped outside of my bedroom door. I was itching for a shower and a good night's rest, but I took a deep breath and let it out slowly as I made up my mind. "You can come if you promise not to attack Elias or retaliate. For now, anyway."

Sergius flashed a viciously delighted grin and bowed formally, sweeping his hand through the air behind him. "My lady, you do me a great kindness."

I shook my head but had to bite back the beginnings of an amused grin. I couldn't let my guard down, no matter how charming he was. "I'm giving you a chance to prove yourself, but I won't give you blind trust. If you betray my trust in any way, you won't get a second chance. And if I think you're a threat to Silas for any reason, I'll lock you back in that stasis chamber myself."

His face lost some of its shine, and he lowered his head slightly. "I understand. Thank you for your trust. It won't be forgotten."

I reached for the doorknob. "Do you know how to get back to your quarters?"

He nodded but seemed reluctant to leave. "Is it strange that I feel nervous to reunite with my own son? I haven't seen him in so long." He swallowed hard. "I fear that he won't forgive me for all I've done in the name of protecting him."

I sighed. I was so damn tired. I hadn't seen Silas in almost two weeks, and I couldn't remember the last time I'd had a full night's rest, but a wave of compassion overcame my better judgment. "Hang on. I have something you should see."

I pushed open the door to my room and dug into Silas's dresser. "Silas didn't have time to retrieve his stuff from Aeterna, but he had a safe here on Earth with his most valuable possessions. Ah! Here—" I grabbed the ring Silas told me was his father's and turned around.

Sergius stood in the doorway, his eyes wide as he took in our room. "Is this your quarters? *This* is the space you share with my son?"

Heat splashed across my cheeks. "Uh, yeah. This is our room." Silas and I shared a tiny patient room with a double bed. His sheathed sword leaned against the wall, and a pile of books lay on the floor on his side of the bed. The unmade bed was layered with a hodgepodge of mismatched bedding. We had a small dresser wedged into the closet, where Silas kept three sets of Guardian fatigues, neatly folded, while my stuff poked out of the other two drawers.

Embarrassment flooded me, followed by the urge to push Sergius back into the hallway and close the door. The random accessories of our lives were spread around the room—my knives, a bag with bathroom stuff, a picnic basket we used once before our lives fell apart. Compared to the luxury and opulence of House Valeron in Aeterna, we lived in a hole. His son was definitely slumming it.

I fought down those thoughts. Silas and I were happy, and it didn't matter what his father thought of our life together. I held out the ring, eager to get him out of our personal space. "Silas kept this."

Sergius took the ring and held it between his forefinger and thumb. "My father's ring."

"Listen, I know things weren't easy between you, but I know he loved you. I think if you explain things to him, he can find his way to forgiving you. He understands that people do stupid shit to protect the people they love."

Sergius's steel-gray eyes were soft. "You really aren't after our wealth, are you?"

I snorted. "No."

His mouth quirked up on one side. "Silas did nothing by half measures, including turning his back on everything I built for him." His face sagged with regret. "Was he happy?"

I blinked away the tears threatening to spill from my tired eyes. "He's not gone, Sergius. We have a plan, and it's going to work. I didn't bring him back from the dead so the Fates could take him away from me now. I'm fighting until the absolute end."

Sergius stepped away from my door and bowed formally from the hallway. "And fight we shall. Thank you... for everything."

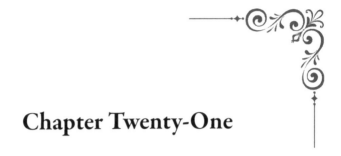

Chapter Twenty-One

T he next night, under cover of darkness, Agent Lennart and the goon squad escorted us through the military blockades around the central keystone. The electrified fencing kept trespassers away from the industrial warehouse, as did the armed guards patrolling the grounds twenty-four seven.

We had four groups, one for each keystone, and a coordinated plan to move them closer together. By tightening the spell's boundary around Boston, the magic would become more concentrated. It wouldn't be as effective as having access to a dedicated magic source, but it should give us enough power to rebind magic so the Fates wouldn't be able to break into our realm.

Our group at the central keystone was the largest and included Elias and Tessa, who brought enough Guardians to storm a castle. They were keeping a low profile to avoid alarming DODSI and had dressed in regular clothing without weapons, but they were just as deadly. Ethan and twenty others with harvesting abilities would complete our circle.

Sergius Valeron had already been useful in distracting Elias, who had almost fainted when he realized the former Lord Councilor was alive. They'd been dancing around each other, verbally sparring while Tessa watched them both like a hawk. Tamara, Casius, and Jason split between the groups headed to the other keystones positioned around the city. Alaric, surprisingly, insisted on going with Tamara's group, probably with the intent to pick her brain about the contents of Elias's book. With Sergius's help, we managed to convince Nero and Octavia to go with Jason and Casius to the final keystone.

We went through a metal detector and into the warehouse where the main keystone sat in the center of the empty, wide-open concrete floor. I was totally distracted watching Elias and Sergius banter, and I didn't notice Agent Lennart planting himself in my path until I almost ran into him. Our entire group stopped behind me as I pulled up short. Lennart towered over me with a scowl. He was too close—way inside my personal space—and I had to crane my neck to look up at him.

Tessa's magic flared, and she stepped toward him with her sword in hand. Agent Lennart's people raised their disruptors. Then the Guardians all flared with magic, which Lennart definitely saw, and his own magic flared in response. I resisted the urge to grab for my own power. The sheer amount of magic and hostility raised the hairs on my arms.

I glanced at Elias to make sure his gaggle of Mundane guards were still paying attention to him. They were well trained—I had to give Lennart credit for that. He was an asshat, but his people were reliable. They didn't take their eyes off Elias, and neither did Sergius, whose own golden magic had risen around him. *Good.*

After I confirmed that Elias wasn't going to stab someone in the back while I dealt with Lennart, I addressed him in the calm, sweet voice I reserved for idiots. "Are you trying to start a bloodbath?"

His attention lingered on the magical auras of the people around us. He had to have been aware of his own fledgling powers, but I wasn't sure the danger had sunk into his thick skull. Every single person on both sides of the standoff was a trained and capable killer, and Lennart was playing a dangerous game that could get us all killed.

"Tell me what you're really up to," he demanded.

I sighed. "I'm going to move the keystones so we can rebind magic, just like I told Pascal."

He furrowed his heavy brows into an intense frown. "*Director* Pascal bought that bullshit, but I don't believe you. You got us into this mess in the first place when you unbound the magic, so why are you suddenly helping to keep it under control?"

"Sometimes, it's not all about me. I have to do what's best for everyone." I tried to step around him, but he shifted in front of me again, and the entire entourage of trained killers twitched on both sides. "I realize you're going through your own issues right now"—I made a point of examining the magic building up in his aura—"but it's really not a good time for an existential crisis."

His expression went flat. "You're hiding something."

I held my palms out. "What, Lennart? What is your problem with me? Did I kick your dog or something?"

"Honestly? I can't decide if you're the evil villain or not."

"Do you want my opinion on that?"

"No."

"Then this conversation is stupid. You'll have to make up your own mind." I sidestepped him and continued toward the keystone.

Lennart caught up to me in two quick strides and blocked my path again. "There are a lot of people who want you dead."

"I'm hard to kill," I responded immediately.

It was Silas's line, and saying it made my heart contract in my chest. I missed him so much. It was killing me to know that Four was stripping away his humanity bit by bit, turning him into one of the Fates while I had to waste time doing stupid things like arguing with Lennart.

With that bigger purpose in mind, I waited silently for Lennart to let me pass. I didn't provoke him or do anything he could use as an excuse to keep blocking me. He was under orders to let me in, and after another tense moment, he relented and stepped to the side.

I reached the keystone without further incident. About the size of a car engine, the square hunk of creamy marble had magic sigils carved all over its surface. After I'd destroyed the Earthen Source, we'd spent a week building four matching stones and setting them up to contain magic within Boston. Power flowed between them, creating a boundary that held all of Earth's magic within their perimeter.

My job was to keep that boundary spell stable while the other groups moved the remaining three stones closer together. Besides the challenge of moving the thousand-pound stones, we had to work in such a way that it wouldn't destroy the boundary spell. Even with the enormous conjuring circle we were planning, holding that much magic while the stones moved was going to be hella hard.

Once that was done, the magic trapped inside our artificial boundary would be concentrated in a smaller area, and we would have enough power to rebind magic. As I laid both of my palms on top of the central keystone, Lennart's agents backed away with their disruptors raised. Tessa positioned herself and the Guardians at our backs, ready to fight off any threat to our safety—including the DODSI agents. Elias stood near Lennart, and I verified that multiple people were watching him before I signaled for my conjuring circle to gather around.

What I was about to do was going to be complicated, but I'd promised the Alliance I could do it. I couldn't afford to fail. If we couldn't get magic bound on Earth again, the Fates would have nothing standing between them and freedom, and I would lose Silas forever.

My group formed a circle around me, each person's aura already flaring with magic. All shades of energy glowed around me like a beautiful rainbow. It was the first time I'd been in a circle with any of the Aeternals, and their magic was unfamiliar, but we'd selected the strongest people for the task, regardless of their origins. We estimated it would take twenty minutes for the others to move their keystones. I had to hold the boundary spell together, so I shrugged off the foreign feeling of the Aeternals' magic like a slightly ill-fitting shirt and decided to get used to it.

Ethan stood behind me, prepared to keep me from expending too much of my own magic and losing myself to the addictive lure of the power. He was my safety net, and the Anchor relationship required trust. I trusted him to bring me back if I went too far, and he trusted me not to drag him over the edge and burn out his magic.

Across the circle, Sergius stared at me. It was a large circle—the biggest I had ever led—and what we were about to do was groundbreaking and complex. I frowned at the calculating expression on his face. We were on the same side when it came to helping Silas, but I didn't trust him beyond that. He was cunning and manipulative, and he was powerful.

Unfortunately, I kept working my way up to the top of his list of interesting people, and it was only a matter of time before that became a problem. There was no way for me to downplay my power at this point, and I decided that meant I needed to show him I also wasn't someone he could use for his own schemes. I'd learned a lot from dealing with the former Aeternal Councilors. Powerful people like Sergius Valeron respected strength, and I was strong.

The conjuring circle began connecting, and I let the magic flow through me, relishing the sheer joy and warmth of it. The colors around me were brighter, the smells sharper, the air fresher—everything came to life as magic filled me. My breath flowed in and out, and every living thing within a fifty-foot radius lit up in my mind like a glowing star. I could sense the energy emanating from the circle around me, the Guardians at our backs, and the DODSI agents beyond them. But the energy also came from the nature outside the warehouse, the air, the trees, and even the critters scampering in the streets. Magic was life, and all life formed the magic.

I caught Sergius's gaze and wove together a little show for him. Quickly and with confidence, I flexed the magic with both hands as

I created two fully formed spheres of magic floating above each of my palms. My time with the Fates' powers had expanded my abilities, but I'd also been practicing. Magic was a skill, and I worked on it just as much as my blade-work. Each sphere blossomed like a lotus flower, spinning and twisting itself inside out, around and around, faster and faster. *Pretty*. I added two more to orbit the first set. Sergius's face paled as he watched the display I was putting on. *Good*.

The rest of the conjuring circle, many of whom had never worked with me before, watched with a blend of awe and fear. The smug satisfaction slipped off my face as I caught their expressions. I was overdoing it. I let the orbs slow into stillness. I held my arms out, palms up, and released the magic to the conjuring circle. The spheres zipped across the circle into other hands, connecting each new person in a web of shared magic. Each person added a different colored thread of energy into the conjuring, and it grew until all twenty of us were connected through a dome of rainbow-colored magic that flexed and shimmered between us.

"Ready?" I asked Ethan.

"I've got you." He slipped his hand into mine. The physical contact wasn't strictly necessary, but it did help our magic connect faster. Things had been substantially less awkward since our chat, and I was glad to have him at my back. Besides, Sergius's eyebrows climbed into his hairline as he watched Ethan take my hand, and I liked keeping him off balance. Ethan's magic, like a warm cup of coffee on a cold morning, encircled me.

I focused on the cold, hard marble under my palm as I tapped into the boundary spell. Ethan steadied me as the full power of it hit me, and I rocked backward. Each keystone was a heavy-duty magical artifact built to contain all of Earth's magic, and holy hells, the power was heavy. It was like lifting a giant boulder over my head. I pushed back with my magic until the spell stopped resisting. It might have taken only a few seconds or a perhaps a few minutes, but I wasn't sure. Either way, I was breathing heavily before the flow of power stabilized between the keystones and me.

Carefully, I expanded my awareness across the city to the other three stones. I was prepared for the quick flex of power as I connected with each one, and I let the magic pulse through my conjuring circle until all four keystones were under my control. The magic between them and me glowed like a star, radiating life and strength.

I was an addict getting a fix—I hadn't held power like this since I tore the Earthen Source apart. I wanted to live in the pure joy forever. I was an empty well, eager to be filled, and all the magic made me feel alive. It kept coming and coming, feeding a gnawing hunger I had learned to ignore. I resisted the urge to let it consume me. When the weight of the magic thrummed in my chest until I felt lightheaded, I let some of the power ease into the others. Even that small release took an effort of will.

"I've got all four keystones," I said quietly.

Ethan took his phone off mute and told the other groups. "Go! Countdown from twenty minutes starts... now!"

I had to hold the conjuring together while they moved the giant stones closer together, but the second the stones began moving, the magic rose violently. I swayed on my feet as I realized I'd severely miscalculated—we knew the spell wasn't going to be stable while the keystones were in motion, but the amount of power flexing through the circle was more than I had expected.

Ethan wrapped his arm around my shoulder. He said something, but I didn't catch the words as I gritted my teeth and focused on holding the boundary spell together. The power coursed through my body like a second heartbeat, pounding in my skull before it released into the circle. Together, we were holding enough power to burn out our circle and level the city. I'd held back a lot from the others, but I could still feel them struggle. It was too much. If the circle fell, we would lose the boundary spell completely, and magic would be out of our control.

My body thrummed as I pulled more power into myself, taking the burden from the others, and braced myself. It hurt, but the pain didn't matter. Pain was temporary. *Just hold it together.*

Ethan squeezed my shoulders. I blinked and realized he was standing right in front of me, talking into my face. "What did you say?"

"They're moving. Six minutes. Hang in there," he said.

I nodded and forced my breath in and out in steady beats. I didn't know if I had six minutes left or only six minutes had gone by. That was an epic difference, but I couldn't form the words necessary to ask him to clarify. It hardly mattered. I couldn't focus as all that power burned through me.

My heart was beating too fast. The other members of my circle were sweating and shaking. I could feel how precariously close we were to falling apart, but I couldn't take any more of it on myself to ease the burden. I was tapped.

Ethan looked down at the live GPS on his phone, tracking the others' positions. "Almost there!"

Relief flooded me. We were going to make it.

The magic around us shifted, twisting my stomach in a familiar and nauseating way. *A skimming spell!*

I didn't have time to shout a warning before Mother Nithia appeared in a flash of electric blue magic in the center of our circle, right on top of the keystone.

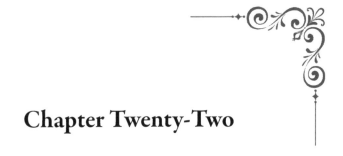

Chapter Twenty-Two

Nithia stood on top of the keystone, surrounded by a cloud of raging storm-blue magic. In a more normal flare of Fae-blue magic, Boone appeared at her side with his sword drawn. Everyone in the circle scrambled backward, and the magic of our conjuring flexed wildly. I barely managed to keep a hold on the boundary spell.

Nithia's long silver hair floated on the invisible winds of her chaotic magic like a halo around her head. "I cannot allow you to re-build the Source. Leave now, and we will be at peace."

I gaped at her perfectly formed right hand. She still wore the black, gem-studded bands around each wrist, but the bracelet on her reattached hand was attached to a matching onyx ring on her middle finger. The chain between the ring and bracelet held a smooth green stone the same color as her jade eyes.

Fifteen feet behind me, Lennart raised his disruptor toward the Fae queen. "Who the fuck are you?"

Nithia raised her arms, and magic flowed around her, sparking like electricity. Matching streaks of black energy danced like light-ning through her aura. I'd never seen anything like it. All Fae magic was elemental, but hers had turned black like the sacrificial magic the Brotherhood used.

"Kill her!" Elias yelled. "Kill her now before we all die!" He tried to grab a disruptor from the DODSI agent closest to him. "Shoot her, you imbecile!"

Boone launched himself at Elias as if propelled by invisible wings, his sword raised over his shoulder. Elias tried to take the disruptor, but the DODSI agent turned the weapon on him and fired. The wave of magic-killing energy hit Elias in the chest, and he dropped to the ground just as a vicious swipe of Boone's broadsword should have taken his head off.

The agent jumped out of the way. Boone missed Elias by less than an inch, but he recovered quickly and reversed his swing, preparing to impale Elias as he lay unconscious and defenseless.

Tessa slammed into Boone. Her shoulder knocked against Boone's larger frame, but it was enough to knock his strike off course. The tip of his sword slammed into the ground beside Elias's chest.

Boone immediately swung his sword upward, not missing a beat as he struck at Tessa.

She skipped backward, and her sword appeared in her hand with a flare of magic. She managed to parry the staggering blow, and Boone's blade smashed into hers with a deafening crash of metal. Their weapons locked hilt to hilt. Boone roared and leaned his body weight against their crossed blades, driving Tessa toward me.

With half my attention on Tessa and Boone's fight, the magic of the boundary spell flexed wildly, and someone cried out in panic. I grabbed the threads of the conjuring. I was holding the whole thing together by sheer will and focused on stabilizing it. The pressure was too much, and two of our conjuring circle had passed out. I grabbed as much magic as I could and kept pulling to take more of the weight off the others.

Boone's reach was much longer than Tessa's, and she didn't have a lot of space to move around. She swung, he parried, and on his next backswing, she stepped close to him, right against his chest. She jammed her sword hilt against his blade at a ninety-degree angle, and the flat of his sword slapped against her side, just under her armpit, trapping his sword. It was an insane and impressive move.

The magic continued to rock through the circle unsteadily, and someone else passed out. I gritted my teeth and tried to take more.

With his blade immobilized, Tessa had locked Boone's sword, and by extension his wrist, into an inescapable hold. She pushed down on her sword and twisted. Boone's eyes went wide as she pried the sword right out of his grip. She caught it before it hit the ground, and he was eye to eye with his own sword poised above Tessa's shoulder. With her right hand, she placed her blade against his neck. She was too close to him for a counterattack or a retreat. If he so much as twitched, she would cut his throat open.

An experienced swordsman shouldn't have fallen for the trick, but Boone had underestimated her. He took a half-step backward, and she followed, keeping him trapped. But Boone's big old sword was heavy, and Tessa couldn't hold it forever. They were in a stalemate until one of them slipped up or surrendered.

He sneered at her. "I'm unarmed. Are you going to kill me?"

"I'm thinking about it."

So much of my focus was needed to hold the boundary spell in place that there was nothing I could do to help my friend. Miraculously, none of the DODSI agents had tried to shoot any of us. As I hung onto the magic with sheer determination and Tessa debated what to do with Boone, Nithia rose from behind the keystone with both arms raised above her head, building a storm of magic around us.

Lennart raised his disruptor, as did several DODSI agents.

"Don't shoot! You'll hit the keystone!" I yelled.

Nithia slapped her hand onto the marble surface. The stone shattered, and an enormous wave of magic exploded out of it. Boone and Tessa were closest, and they flew off their feet. My circle fell apart, and all of us toppled in opposite directions.

Lennart and his Mundane soldiers collapsed as I grasped my head and tried not to pass out. The power of the keystones backlashed through our circle, and the magic buried me. I couldn't breathe, couldn't think. Without the central keystone, the boundary spell started unraveling in front of me. I had to stop it, or magic would flood our realm, and the Fates would have unrestricted access to our world. I called the magic to me as it poured from the central keystone, and I took everything. The magic of the keystones, Nithia's power, everything blasting over us—I took it all. My only thought was holding the boundary together.

Power coursed through every cell and atom in my body. I screamed as it burned through me. I couldn't hold it, but I hung on as it tore through my body and ripped my soul into shreds. Everything went white.

Surprise flooded me as the pain stopped. I had accidentally accessed the Fates' magic through my bond with Silas, and it felt like perfection and clarity and absolute power. Nothing else mattered—not the keystone, the shocked Fae queen standing on top of it, or the members of my conjuring circle, who lay unconscious on the ground. The Fates' magic consumed me and set me free.

It illuminated the world, and I breathed it in like air. I had lived in darkness, but I could finally see. I dismissed the insignificant people flailing around me and looked up to the stars. I felt Silas there, and through him, the Fates' powers filled me. I raised my arms to the heavens, ready to accept it all.

A familiar magic wrapped around the core of my own power, coming from a man on the ground a dozen feet from me, surrounded by sunny yellow magic. He was dripping blood from a shallow head wound. A pang of a distant emotion flicked across my awareness as he reached up for me. "Mae! Let it go! It's too much!"

"Ethan?" His magic was so warm.

Ethan's aura flared brighter, and heat filled me. I gasped. The overwhelmingly cold power released its grip on me, and I grabbed Ethan's anchor. The harsh brilliance of those foreign powers faded, burned away by warmth. I'd been so close to losing myself, but Ethan had pulled me back.

The boundary spell was still unraveling in front of my eyes. As soon as that spell collapsed, magic would spread across Earth. The Fates would be freed. I flung my arms wide and reached again for the remnants of the shattered keystone as I drove my own magic into the marble. I had to hold the boundary spell.

It had taken an entire conjuring circle to set up the spell, but thanks to the insane amount of power I'd just absorbed, I had more magic than I would need in five Mundane lifetimes. My magic snapped into place, and I became one with the central keystone, linking the boundary spell with the other keystones through me.

"Maeve! Don't!" Ethan yelled.

Crouched atop the broken keystone, Mother Nithia looked even more stunned than I was. But it was too late. I had anchored myself to the boundary spell without a circle, using my own magic to replace the shattered keystone.

Pain and power flooded through me, and I dropped to my knees with my arms outstretched. If I let go, the Fates would never give Silas back, but I also couldn't hold the conjuring together by myself. It was too much, and my mortal body couldn't channel a spell like that for long.

Nithia and I locked gazes. "Let it go, child! Set the magic free!"

"Rebuild the keystone!" I yelled. But the members of the circle were mostly unconscious. I couldn't hold the spell in place and recreate a keystone at the same time.

Mother Nithia's nostrils flared, and her face twisted in outrage. "Kill her!"

Boone snapped into action and launched himself at me. Tessa had been knocked farther away from the impact of Nithia's magic, and I couldn't defend myself—everything I had was locked into holding the keystone together. Boone charged forward, scooped his sword from the ground, and raised it above his head for a killing blow.

A familiar, heavy magic engulfed me, and a figure appeared between Boone and me with an aura of power so intense that a null space where magic didn't seem to exist surrounded him.

"Silas!" I gasped.

Boone slid to a stop. Everyone on the field paused to watch as Silas surveyed the scene without any hint of emotion on his face. His all-white eyes locked onto mine. Everything inside me was already on fire as I tried to hold the boundary spell together, but it hurt even more to look into his emotionless, foreign eyes. The feeling flooding through our bond was so cold that I almost lost my grip on the crumbling keystone. I locked down everything inside of me as I stared at him, and the weight of his magic buried me. I was drowning in an ocean of pure power, unable to look away from Silas's terrible gaze.

He grabbed my forearm, and an intense burst of pain flashed up my arm. I cried out. And then, as if I had surfaced from the water, the pressure of all the magic I had been holding popped.

I gasped and dragged in air.

"Silas, no! Don't hurt her!" Tessa slammed into Silas, knocking him back a few steps.

Silas *moved*. One second, he was standing in front of me gripping my arm, and in the next, he held his oldest friend off the ground by her throat. His eyes burned with magic as Tessa choked.

I threw myself at his legs, knocking the back of his knees as I tackled him like a linebacker. He stumbled and dropped Tessa. She jabbed her elbow into his throat as he fell. He dropped, coughing and gagging as he doubled over.

Boone chose that moment to strike. He lunged, sword first, aiming to drive his blade through my chest. Silas threw out his arm, his insane magic flared, and Boone was engulfed in Silas's power. I fell back and threw my arm over my face, shielding my eyes from the intense flash of energy. When I opened them, Boone was lying on the ground, dead.

I gasped. It had all happened so fast.

"No!" Mother Nithia screamed. Wild and furious power gathered around her. She was going to kill us.

"Silas! Go! Leave before she strikes!" Sergius ran toward us, his own golden power flowing around him. He threw a sphere of magic at Nithia, forcing her to defend herself instead of attacking us.

Surprise and then fury flashed through our Aegis bond as Silas saw his father. "No more lies!" Silas yelled at me as he yanked me to my feet and slapped me hard across the face.

The blow rocked me backward, and I hung limply in his grip as the shock of it went through me. My face and jaw flamed in pain. I should have been outraged. I should have fought back or tried to free myself from his grip, but the surprise of his blow and the rage radiating through our bond were so entirely overwhelming that I froze in shock.

A violent storm of magic flashed to my left as Sergius and Nithia fought. A wave of chaotic, electrified blue magic knocked him down then headed straight for us. The entire world spun as Silas threw me out of the way. I couldn't tell which end was up, down, or sideways, and I landed hard, slamming my entire left side into the ground. Everything went black for a long moment before I was able to pry my eyes open again.

I gazed up at the dark night sky, confused by the brilliant lights floating just above my face. Magic tingled across my skin, and I reached for the lights, realizing it was loose magic floating through the air like millions of tiny stars glowing in the night. With a groan, I pushed myself off the ground and tried to make sense of what had happened. Silas and Mother Nithia were gone, along with Boone's body. The keystone lay broken on the ground. Uncontained magic floated all around me, giving the air a glittering, ethereal quality.

Horror filled me as I realized what I had done—what Silas had forced me to do. "I let go of the keystone."

The boundary spell was no more, and magic was spreading across Earth.

My world kept spinning as Sergius came back to consciousness and Ethan helped the other members of the circle. With a throbbing head and heart, I looked down at my arm where Silas had grabbed me and gasped again. The combined sigil of our houses, our Aegis bond, was gone. Silas had broken his connection to me.

Chapter Twenty-Three

"Are you injured?" Sergius placed his hand on my shoulder. His presence was a painful reminder of everything I'd lost.

Tessa sat on my other side, rubbing her neck, which was red and bruised with Silas's handprint. I shook my head as hot tears threatened to spill. I'd let all the magic loose. I hurt in a dozen places, but my heart felt the most broken.

I wiped away my tears, unable to fully absorb everything that had happened. I didn't know how to process Silas *hitting* me. He'd tried to kill his best friend. His rage and anger toward me were so sudden and overwhelming... and he'd broken our Aegis bond. The Fates had burned away everything that made him mine. I'd lost him, and without the boundary spell holding the Fates back, I didn't know if I could get him back.

Lennart stalked over to us, his face bloody and angry. "What the hell was that? Where did he take Elias?"

Alarm blasted up my spine. "What do you mean? Who took Elias?"

Lennart's face twisted in rage. "Your Highlander! Was this the plan all along? I knew you were up to something!"

"We didn't plan any of that," Tessa replied, rubbing her throat gingerly.

Lennart calmed a bit as he seemed to remember that Silas had actually attacked us. He looked at my cheek, which I was sure was bright red. "What the hell is going on?"

"Silas isn't himself." The missing bond between us felt like a ragged hole in my heart. I didn't understand why he would sever our connection. "He's... under someone else's influence. Magically."

"This shit is so far out of my area of expertise. What the hell am I supposed to tell Director Pascal?"

"I don't know," I replied honestly.

Sergius stepped in. "Tell him the Fae attacked us, and magic is no longer contained within the boundary spell. It will spread slowly, which means we still have time to rebind magic."

Sergius was making promises we might not be able to keep, but I didn't have it in me to argue. Silas was gone. He'd turned into one of the Fates. More tears threatened to escape.

"You'll be hearing from us." Lennart signaled for his agents to leave.

Numbly, I watched them go. There was nothing I could do to fix this mess.

Tessa cleared her throat quietly. "The Fae attacked first. They have no grounds for retaliation after initiating the entire incident."

"Silas killed Nithia's heir. She's not going to let that go," Ethan said.

I touched my cheek. "The Fates are making him do things he wouldn't normally do."

"I'm not sure that's going to matter to the Fae," Tessa said.

"The Fates are working very hard to break my son," Sergius said, "but the fact that he showed up here means he has a connection to his humanity. I saw him throw Lady Maeve out of the way of Nithia's power. I believe there's a chance to save him."

My faltering hope rose again. "How?"

"With the help of your people, I can build a spell that will drain the Fates' powers. We did this with Lady Nithia, and without the Fates' influence, it's possible he could return to his normal self."

"Nithia didn't exactly turn out okay," I said.

"Unlike Lady Nithia, Silas doesn't want to be a Fate. He's fighting them."

My hope soared, but Tessa scowled at Sergius. "Why didn't you tell us about this earlier?"

Sergius regarded her silently for a long moment while I reeled. I needed to believe there was a way to bring Silas home so badly that I hadn't stopped to consider that question. But Tessa was right. If he had a way to bring Silas back, why had he delayed telling us?

"I wasn't sure whom I could trust. I had to ensure Silas hadn't acted against me in pursuit of the Fates' powers."

"What? That's insane! Silas would never do that. Why would you even think that?" I demanded.

"Because his father is a bastard who made his life a living hell," Tessa replied bluntly. "And the fact you think Silas is capable of that kind of betrayal proves just how much you don't know your son. He's not like you. He wouldn't betray his own blood for power and prestige. He didn't want any of it!" she yelled.

I couldn't blame her. Silas had told me about their relationship and about the terrible things his father had done—but Tessa had lived through those things. Her anger was firsthand and unresolved.

"I was blinded by my fears, and I didn't understand the cost of my actions. I was afraid Silas would be tempted by the Fates' offer—as so many had been—as I had been. I knew the potential Silas had, and I feared for him but also for our family line. The Fates would ruin us, using my heir for their own purposes, and I couldn't let that happen." Sergius bowed his head in shame, surprising me again with his honesty.

"I believed I was acting out of love, protecting my son, but the truth is that Silas is a better man than I. I wanted him to be too weak to tempt the Fates, and thus I undermined him and buried him in self-doubt. I didn't fully understand what I had done until I met Lady Maeve."

"Me? What did I do?"

He looked heartbroken. "You loved him. Not for his wealth or his power or his family name. Despite the efforts of the Fates, I believe your love provided the thread to which his humanity is still clinging. Even in the throes of their power, he fights to protect you." I swallowed hard against the lump in my throat as Sergius continued. "I believe we can save him, but I need the help of your people. It will be neither simple nor easy."

"Why?" Ethan snapped. "I'm sorry, but why should this be our top priority? We told DODSI we could rebind magic, and now, we've freed magic and lost Elias in the process. Not to mention that we haven't sealed the rips between realms, and people are protesting outside our campus. Magic is going to start spreading again, and there are a million other things we should be focusing on instead of rescuing Silas. The whole world is about to go to hell, and we have a responsibility to stop that."

I bristled at his angry tirade, and Tessa looked like she might stab him, but Sergius was calm. "Because, you jealous boy, if my son succumbs to the Fates' efforts at turning him into one of them and they rebuild their triad, everyone on Earth will fall subject to their powers. Now that Earth's magic is no longer contained in this city, the Fates will gain full access to this realm, and there won't be a power left that can stop them. If you let Silas fall into their hands, the entire world is doomed."

Ethan was quiet for a moment, puzzling through things. "You said the Fates can't access our realm because they'd been banished, but I saw Four at our campus. They're already in our realm."

"Those are only manifestations," Sergius explained, "projections of their own design, if you will. In their current state, they have limited ability to interact with our realm and therefore must convince others to act on their behalf, same as they convinced Lady Maeve to unbind Earth's magic—through trickery and lies."

I grimaced. I'd been such an idiot, letting Four lead me around with false visions and misleading clues until I'd been the key to them getting their hands on Silas.

Casius nodded. "Agreed. We need to get Silas out of their clutches before this spins even more out of control. How do we do that?"

Sergius clasped his hands in front of him. "I can conjure a spell that will drain Silas's powers, but we need him to walk into our trap."

Everyone looked at me.

The next morning, I stood in the middle of the room I shared with Silas, rubbing my bare forearm where the Aegis sigil used to be. My stomach was in knots. Magic was spreading, but neither the news media nor the public seemed to be aware yet. We needed to act quickly. We'd explained the situation to the rest of the Alliance, and everyone agreed that our first priority was to stop the Fates from gaining a foothold into our realm.

"Are you ready?" Sergius asked.

I let my awareness expand across the campus, confirming that everyone was in position. We'd mobilized everyone quickly and had a plan. The only question was whether it would work.

In the converted dorm rooms adjacent to my own, Ethan, Casius, and Tessa waited without accessing their magic. The rest of the New Alliance members, Tamara, Jason, Nero, Octavia, and Alaric, spread across the campus along with the Guardians, waiting for our signal.

I drew in another deep breath. *Steady. This is going to work.*

I glanced at my feet. Of course, I couldn't see the incredibly complex spell Sergius had spent all night drawing onto the floor of the room directly below us, but I took a moment to confirm that I couldn't *feel* it, either. Until I activated it with magic, Silas shouldn't be able to sense it. With his Fate-level powers, the spell alone wouldn't be enough to hold him, which was why the rest of my sect had spread across the campus, prepared to help drain his powers as soon as the trap was sprung and he couldn't escape.

I chewed on my lip. There were a lot of ways this plan could go wrong. Neither Four nor Two could act directly in our realm, but they had certainly managed to figure out ways to interfere in the past. Four was capable of a lot of interaction within our realm thanks to his ties to Silas and me. We had one shot to bring him home and prevent the Fates from building a permanent connection to our realm. If this went wrong, nothing would be able to stop the Fates from escaping their imprisonment.

"Tell me one more time that this is going to work," I said.

Sergius's eyes tightened. "It *must* work. There's simply no other option." His magic filled the small room and curled around my arm like smoke. The threads of a binding spell sank into my skin. The sting brought back memories of Silas performing the Aegis bonding spell. I'd had no idea how important that bond would become to both of us.

I gritted my teeth as Sergius's magic flooded through me. The overlapping triangles of the Valeron family sigil were the base of the bond Silas and I shared—used to share—and had allowed us to communicate our feelings with one another. The Aegis sigil Sergius shared with me was different, intended only for access to the Valeron House magic. For all intents and purposes, he'd adopted me into their House.

I was instantly flooded by magic, and I clenched my teeth to keep from automatically drawing that power into myself like a greedy sponge. I could feel everyone connected to the Valeron house—Sergius, standing in front of me, but also Stephan, Aria, and a distant awareness of Silas. Although it was nothing like the connection I shared with him through the Aegis bond, it was a relief to feel him again.

Sergius watched me with steel-gray eyes so like his son's as I struggled to find my balance inside the new Valeron bond. He took my hand and squeezed it. "It's finished. Are you ready?"

"As Silas would say, here goes *everything*." I didn't waste any time. My powers rose, drawing all the magic I'd retained from the keystones in preparation for this moment, and then I released everything back into the Valeron bond. I focused all that power in Silas's direction. He'd cut me off, but he didn't have a way to shut down the connection to his House. The Valeron magic was as much a part of him as his DNA.

As my magic flooded through the bond, the others' powers rose with mine. My breath hitched as combined energy from Aria, Stephan, and Sergius washed over me. The magic originated from each of us but flowed equally through the bond, giving me access to each of them. I could understand why Sergius had said this type of connection was rarely established even among families—it was completely intimate and exposed.

Not only could I sense each of them, but I could also manipulate their unique magical abilities if I chose, and any one of them could tap into my ability to control the individual threads of magic or use Stephan's empathic powers. It was all at our fingertips, to be used through our bond as a group.

Stephan's empathic projection flared, and just as we'd planned, I imagined opening the family bond and pouring everything I had into it. Fueled by magic, the House bond nearly vibrated with my emotions and our shared energy. I let all of it out into the open—the worry I had for Silas's humanity, the anger over what Four was doing to us, even the trembling fear that our plan to save him wouldn't work and that I'd already lost him forever. Sergius added his love for Silas, with a heady mix of sorrow and regret. Brotherly love and concern flooded us from Stephan, and from Aria came a beam of gratitude and love. We channeled all of that, focused on Silas. It was the equivalent of an emotional power hug—or perhaps a kick in the nuts.

Sergius and I waited in tense silence in my room, staring at each other as a long minute passed and then another.

"Where is he?" I whispered.

If Four and Two had already turned Silas into one of them, he wouldn't have any humanity left to care about anything we were doing. He wouldn't care about our trivial love and fears for him. He wouldn't care that he could sense his father through that bond or that I was connected to him again.

Sergius released my hand, and his expression began to crumple. "It appears we were too late."

Desperate surging fear overwhelmed me, and I felt as if my chest would crack open. We were too late. We'd lost him. Echoing feelings of loss and despair rose through our bond from Stephan and Aria.

A huge flare of cold, foreign power splashed over me as someone appeared in my room. It wasn't Silas.

Elias was still dressed in his business suit. The smug grin plastered on his face grew as he noticed Sergius standing at the far end of my bedroom. Elias's aura flared with magic so strong and bright that it created a blank space around him.

I gaped. Elias Marius, former Lord Councilor of the Aeternal Council and all-around scumbag traitor, had gotten himself turned into a Fate.

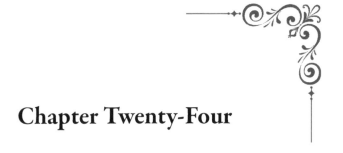

Chapter Twenty-Four

E lias executed a mocking bow in our direction. "Well met, Lady Maeve. Lord Sergius."

The amount of power radiating from him was nearly blinding, but if he'd been turned into the third Fate in their trio, then... "What happened to Silas? Where is he?" I demanded in a harsh cry.

"Did you think your little trap would actually work on a Fate?" Elias *moved*. One second, he was standing by the door, and then he had me by the arm. His magic wrapped around me, tight as ropes. It all happened so quickly that I didn't have time to cry out, and I couldn't move or fight back. His magic flared, and my stomach twisted as he started to pull me away.

Sergius grabbed for me, but Elias flicked his hand and tossed Sergius across the room to crash into the dresser in the closet. Elias sneered. "Valerons can't ever give over to the inevitable, can they? Can't give an inch for their fratching honor."

"You dishonorable shitelicker!" Sergius roared.

Elias dragged Sergius to the center of the room with his magic, dropping him in a heap at the foot of my bed. I tried to twist away from him, but I couldn't break free, and my magic was inaccessible as he held me in the grip of his power.

"I honestly wish you could see your heir, Sergius. The stubborn arse resisted and fought until the Fates broke him." Sergius tried to regain his feet, but Elias's magic forced him back down. "They scooped out Silas's brains and stuffed him full of their magic. He's nothing more than a puppet now—no feeling, no mind of his own. He's drowning in a sea of power so deep that he couldn't tell you his own name. It's the most fitting end to the Valeron line I could have imagined."

My heart squeezed painfully. "You're lying!"

"Am I? Then where is he? In exchange for these powers, all I have to do is deliver you to them, and where is your Aegis, Maeve O'Neill?" Elias laughed. "Where is your precious heir now, Sergius? I won. I got everything I wanted, and you have nothing."

Elias's magic flared, filling the room with an incredible rush of power. The spell Sergius had carefully set up to drain Silas's magic flared inside the room, exactly where Sergius lay, and he was instantly engulfed in the trap.

He screamed. I cried out, but there was nothing I could do as the spell burned golden yellow, absorbing Sergius's magic in seconds before he crumpled to the ground, unconscious. The spell was supposed to dissipate once the target lost consciousness, but it didn't. Elias laughed as he continued fueling the conjuring. The complex spell was still taking magic from Sergius, and it would kill him.

"Stop! Let him go!" I couldn't access my magic, but I grabbed a blade off the nightstand and jabbed it toward Elias's thigh.

In a physics-defying move, he moved quickly enough to grab my hand and stop the knife from stabbing him. He spun me around so we were face to face, and the blade flew from my hands with a flick of his fingers. He bared his teeth at me but then jerked in surprise, looking over my shoulder. "What are you doing here?"

I followed Elias's outraged stare, and pure joy flooded me. "Silas! You came!" I drank in the hard lines of his jaw, the strong angle of his brow, and the way his longish hair curled around his ears.

Silas didn't acknowledge my greeting. He glanced at the unconscious form of his father on the floor. He waved his hand toward the trap we'd meant for him, and the conjuring crumbled, releasing

Sergius. A crushing sense of failure overwhelmed me as Silas broke our only chance to free him from the Fates' influence, but at least Sergius's chest was moving up and down.

"What are you doing?" Silas asked Elias, his voice flat.

Elias dragged me to Silas with quick, aggressive strides, effectively trapping me between them. "Did Four send you here?"

Standing between the two of them felt like being flayed by magic, but I realized that Elias's magic wasn't as strong as Silas's. Elias radiated enough of the Fates' foreign magic to make my brain hurt, but Silas's magic blazed like a sun gone supernova. Whatever had happened to give Elias access to their magic, he wasn't a full Fate yet.

Now that Elias wasn't blocking me, my magic rose in a vain attempt to shield myself from the crushing effect of their power, but it didn't do much. Neither man paid attention to me. I didn't matter to them. I had a fraction of the power they did, and I wasn't a threat.

Through our bond, I could sense Stephan and Aria's rising concern, but I sent back a sense of patience. We still had a chance to make our plan work.

"Four wants me to be here." Silas blinked slowly as if his own words confused him.

"Go back. You can't be here, remember? You don't *want* to be here." Elias's voice was full of annoyance. "You wanted to stay away from her."

Silas furrowed his brows as he looked at me. "I won't let you manipulate me."

There was nothing kind or loving in his face. Through the Valeron family bond, there was nothing from Silas. The Fates had taken everything. The pain of that realization was so real and so sharp that I put my hand over my chest. My heart shattered into jagged pieces, stabbing me with every broken, stuttering beat as the man I loved glowed with foreign power.

They scooped out his insides and stuffed him full of their magic. He's nothing more than their puppet.

He scrunched his face as if he felt my pain, and for the first time, a hint of emotion bled into his voice. "I shouldn't be here."

"Yes, yes. Go away and it will all feel better." Elias grabbed me by the arm, and his power flared as he prepared to take me to the Fates.

"Wait! Silas!" I yelled.

"Leave her alone!" Silas grabbed my other arm, his face an angry snarl.

Elias released me and put his palms in the air. "Calm down, Silas! Four asked me to fetch her. Let's all go back and sort it out, yes? No one is going to hurt her."

Through the Valeron family bond, still amplified by Stephan's powers, I could sense Silas's confusion. I dug deep into that connection, making sure my own feelings hit him. "Silas! Snap out of it!" I grasped the collar of his shirt with both hands. "Four's been trying to make you forget who you are, but you have to fight! Fight it, Silas!"

Silas gripped both of my hands and tried to pry me loose.

"No, dammit! Remember who you are, you stubborn bastard!"

I punched him hard across the jaw. I put everything I had into it, twisting through my hips to put power behind the hit, as he had taught me. His head jerked hard to the side, and my knuckles throbbed as the impact jolted up my arm.

His eyes flamed white as a trickle of blood blossomed on his lip. He wiped at the bright-red smear. "You made me bleed."

"You told me to fight for us. This is me fighting!" I dragged in a choked breath and took a step backward at the ice-cold anger on his face and the violent rise of emotion I could sense from him.

"You really know how to win a man's heart, don't you, Lady Maeve?" Elias grabbed me by the arm again and dragged me away from Silas.

"No!" I tried to wrench free, but Elias was too powerful. His magic wrapped around me, holding me tight. If he took me to the Fates, there was nothing more I could do. "Silas! Wake up, damn you! Fight!"

Silas didn't try to stop him. The man I loved only stared at me, glowing with cold Fate magic.

Our plan was contingent on luring Silas into the trap, which had instead been used against Sergius, but I didn't have any options left. I threw all of my magic outward. Still gripping my arm, Elias flinched back, but I wasn't directing my powers toward him. Instead, I connected with my sect, waiting all around the campus. It was the signal for the next step in our plan to save Silas, and almost immediately, the combined power of all of our Harvesters fell on both Silas and Elias. We drained power from them, and they cried out as a portion of their magic was suddenly ripped from them.

With our plan in motion, Stephan burst through the door and rammed a flood of emotions through the Valeron bond, wielding his empathic powers like a weapon against Silas.

Elias didn't know where to turn. The assault was coming from every direction, and his magic flared brightly as he struggled to fight off thousands of people drawing on it. Elias sank to his knees, screaming. I grabbed the nearest heavy thing—Silas's pop culture book—and whacked Elias across the side of his head with all of my strength. He dropped to the floor, unconscious.

The onslaught of our magic, now fully focused on Silas, combined with the empathic flood of emotions through his family bond, knocked Silas to his knees.

"Stop!" Silas clutched his head with both hands. "Make it stop!"

Stephan threw everything that opposed the Fates' cold magic at his brother—love, joy, loyalty. Through our shared Valeron House bond, I added my own feelings, focused on the strongest memories of my time with him. I threw in happiness, belonging, and my love for him.

A year before, I would have tried to save him on my own. I wouldn't have thought to ask for help. I'd believed I was better off alone, but as I grabbed Stephan's hand and everyone in my sect fought to free Silas from the Fates' influence, I was part of something bigger. I was part of a family, and family stood together through the good and the bad.

Tessa burst into the room, surveyed the situation, and went to Sergius. With a burst of blue-green magic, she brought him back to consciousness. He gasped and sat up. His aura was weaker than it had been before he'd been thrown into the magic-draining trap, but his dominating presence rose within the family bond, as strong as ever.

"Make sure Elias stays unconscious!" I told Tessa, who drew her sword and held it at his neck.

Sergius scrambled over to Silas and grabbed him by the shoulders. "Son! You must resist them! You still have your free will!"

Silas's expression flared to outrage as he took in his father's face. "What is this? What are you playing at?"

As the sect continued its onslaught, I joined Sergius and Silas on the floor and fed him my most emotional memories. The passion of our first kiss on the mountain in Alaska. The joy of hearing Silas tell me how he really felt about me that first time in Aeterna. Our heartbroken goodbye when we realized there wasn't a way forward for us.

Stephan joined us, gripping Silas's shoulder. Silas bent over his knees as he tried to fight the combined weight of my sect's magic and the emotions flooding through his family bond. I put my hands on his back and drove harder, focused on the desperation of trying to save him from Four's visions then seeing his dead body emerge through the portal despite everything I'd done. Tears choked me as I remembered the precious weeks we'd spent in this very bedroom, blissfully happy and totally unaware of how little time we had together. I slammed all that emotion against the wall of ice around Silas like a sledgehammer. *Fight, Silas*!

He cried out and tried to push us away, but we wouldn't let go.

From the other side of the campus, Aria added her hope and love and positivity into the mix once more. All of us connected through the Valeron family bond as we pummeled him with our love.

Like a breaking dam, the cold, distant wall cracked. All at once, the barrier crumbled, and Silas's natural magic swelled through the bond, bright and burning with power. The cold, white power drained from his eyes until they were the same shade of gray as Sergius's.

We released him, and the pressure of the sect's magic faded.

"Father? Is it really you?" Silas's voice was choked with emotion.

"It's me, son. I'm here."

"I don't understand." Silas's eyes were wide and confused as he took us all in, kneeling around him, holding him up.

"I can explain. There's so much to tell you," Sergius said.

Silas's gaze snapped to me. I didn't dare let go of the emotional connection we all had through the Valeron bond. Moving ever so slowly, I reached out my hand.

He reached back. "Maeve?"

Tessa flew off her feet and across the room, slamming into the wall. Suddenly, Elias was on his feet, his aura burning so brightly with magic that the space around him was a blank outline. He'd somehow accessed more of the Fates' powers.

Elias bared his teeth, and his power flooded the room. Fear overwhelmed me. I should have killed him when he was unconscious.

A fraction of a second after my brain registered our imminent deaths, Silas *moved*.

I blinked to find Elias and Silas were grappling, both men bathed in the Fates' powers. All-white magic flashed from Silas, rolling through the room like thunder. My heart skipped a beat as the mag-

ic-draining conjuring flared to life in the middle of the room, powered by Silas's magic, and the trap engulfed both men.

They screamed as the spell ripped away their magic.

"Silas!" I lurched forward, but there was no way to get to him
without throwing myself into the conjuring.

Sergius grabbed me. "It's draining their Fate powers!" Sergius's
eyes were wide as we took in the sheer amount of power pouring out
of the two men and building into the conjuring. "Silas is powering
the spell directly. Incredible. Absolutely incredible."

Silas dropped to the ground inside the conjuring, his entire body
strained and his back bowed as he cried out in pain. My heart
lurched in my chest as Elias crumbled beside him, both men in
agony as power poured from their eyes, mouths, and every pore of
their bodies. The incredible weight of their magic was stored within the conjuring, but I felt like I was being crushed alongside Silas. I
couldn't breathe. Tears streamed down my face as I watched him suffer.

I couldn't imagine the soul-searing pain he was enduring, and
yet he kept going until the magic the spell absorbed had risen almost
to the top of the conjuring. As it absorbed their power, it turned
brighter and whiter. Slowly, around the edges, Silas's flare started to
change from a blazing white inferno back to his own golden-yellow
aura.

As Elias's flare drained to pale gold, he stopped convulsing and
lay still on the ground. I wasn't sure if he was alive or not, but I could
barely rip my eyes away from Silas, who had curled over his knees.
His entire body shook, but the conjuring hadn't drained all the foreign power from him yet.

"Holy hells," Stephan whispered at my side. "Can we stop it?"

"No! Silas is trying to drain all of the Fates' power from himself.
He's breaking himself free," Sergius said.

I examined all the power the conjuring had already taken from Elias and Silas as it filled the conjuring like a pitcher. "Is the spell going to be able to hold it all?"

"I don't know. Silas is powering the conjuring now. He's keeping it going."

"What if it doesn't hold? That's one hell of a backlash. I'm not sure we could survive that. Should we evacuate the campus?" Stephan asked.

"To where? There's nowhere we'd be safe from this much power," I said.

Silas clenched his fists tightly against the sides of his head and rocked back and forth on his knees while his entire body shook. With a choked cry, he curled into the fetal position, and I crouched in front of him on the outside of the conjuring, desperately wishing I could somehow help him. A sob escaped me as I felt his anguish through the House bond. I had no idea how he was conscious. Tessa's hand found mine and squeezed as we waited for his suffering to end.

Stephan put his hand on my shoulder. "Almost there."

"It's going to hold," Sergius said quietly, his eyes on the fullness of the conjuring spell.

"Get him out!" I demanded.

"Silas is the one holding it! There must be no trace of the Fates' magic left to break their hold. He's close," Sergius said.

I couldn't breathe as the torture continued until finally—*finally!*—we couldn't see any trace of the Fates' magic in his aura. Silas released the conjuring. It shivered out of existence, taking with it the incredible power it had stored.

I practically threw myself on top of him, rolling him over to face me. "Silas! Are you okay? Silas?"

He blinked up at me and dragged in a ragged breath. "Maeve?"

I was unable to speak as my sobs choked me.

He pulled me into his chest as tears rolled down both our cheeks. "My Maeve."

Tessa checked Elias's pulse. "He's alive."

"Give me your sword," Silas croaked.

Tessa gave it to Silas without question. He pushed to his knees, raised the sword above Elias's chest, then thrust it down, spearing him through the heart. Elias jerked, and blood blossomed across the floor under him, soaking into the carpet. He didn't open his eyes or make any noise, and he never would again. Elias Marius, former Lord Councilor of the Aeternal Council, orchestrator of the Brotherhood, traitor to his own people and ultimately the entire world, was dead.

No one objected to his sentence. He died alone without any last words or anyone who would mourn him. He deserved it, but I didn't relish it. An unexpected wave of anger washed over me. All the suffering and death he'd inflicted because of his own greed... it was all so pointless. So tragically without meaning.

Silas sat back on his butt, bracing himself on one arm. "I think I need a nap." His eyes rolled back in his head, and he passed out.

I caught his head before it hit the floor and gently laid him down.

"Don't worry, Valerons are hard to kill. All will be right with him." Sergius flashed a small hopeful smile. "We all will."

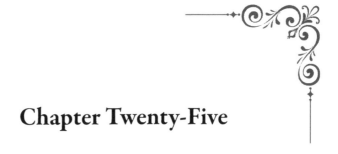

Chapter Twenty-Five

Silas's face was haggard and lined with exhaustion when he opened his eyes eighteen hours later. He furrowed his brows when he saw me sitting on the edge of our bed. I reached out to touch him, needing to reassure myself that he was okay, but he flinched back. I lowered my hand. It all seemed so impossibly fragile. Without our Aegis bond, I couldn't sense any emotions from him. I ached to see the smile that softened the hard lines of his face, to hold him, and to hear him say it would all be fine.

"You're free of the Fates, and everything is going to be okay," I whispered like a promise to both of us.

My heart broke as I took in the distrust on his face. There were things between us that Four had broken. I didn't yet know everything Silas had gone through, but it clearly had been brutal.

I placed my hand on his. He didn't pull away, but his exhaled breath was shaky. He held my gaze, searching for something. "I can feel you through my family bond. I can sense all of you, including my father. Is that real?"

"Yes. I know it's going to take some adjusting, but—" My voice broke, and I had to swallow hard around the lump in my throat. "Four can't get to you anymore. We broke their ties to our realm. You're safe."

"You're not going to try and convince me to turn you into a Fate?"

I couldn't keep the surprise and disgust off my face. "Why the hell would I want to be a Fate?"

The tightness in his face softened, and a hint of the smile I'd been aching to see appeared on his face. "I have no fratching idea why anyone would want that, either." He lifted my hand to his lips and kissed the back of my knuckles. "It really is you, then. My Maeve."

He opened his arms, and I crawled into them. I buried my face in his chest as tears slipped down my cheeks. There was so much to discuss and so much pain to address, but I needed this—*we* needed this moment to reconnect.

"I'm so, so sorry, Maeve," he whispered into my hair. "I couldn't stop them. I wasn't strong enough and I... I almost killed you. I didn't know what I was doing."

"Shut up, Silas."

He huffed against my scalp. "Not quite the response I was expecting."

I leaned back enough to look into his eyes. His reflexive clutch on my arms told me he needed me close as much as I needed to be in his arms. "I can give you the it-wasn't-your-fault speech if you want. Or I could tell you how scared I was as you got colder and colder and I couldn't make it stop." Some heat colored my tone. "Or how about yelling at you for apparently deciding to stay away from me 'for my own good' or whatever stupid thinking led you to decide you couldn't be around me?" That last one did sting, and a real flare of anger and hurt rose inside me.

A flicker of amusement brightened his gaze. "I missed you scolding me. Feels normal." He looked away, losing the flash of humor as quickly as it had appeared. "Maybe Four should have tried *that*."

"What did Four do to you?" My voice was barely a whisper.

He didn't respond for a long time. When he did, his gaze was locked on the ceiling, not meeting my eyes. "Two and Four needed me to complete their triad, but they couldn't force me to accept becoming one of them permanently—I had to choose it. My free will was the last barrier to their plans, but I wasn't tempted by their promises of power and immortality. I wouldn't accept their offer. Unfortunately, it didn't take Four very long to pinpoint my weakness."

The raw pain I saw in his face burned a hole in my heart. He stopped talking, seemingly unsure how to continue, but I had a sinking feeling I knew what Four had used against him. I needed to know what had happened to Silas, and he needed to tell me, or it would fester between us.

I gathered his hands between mine, forcing him to release his clenched fists. "I was your weakness, and that's why you needed to stay away from me."

"My love for you was the one remaining connection to reality, and Four tried to use that against me. I was so close to giving over. He said that all I had to do was accept the role he wanted for me, and you and I could be together. Forever. I wanted to be with you, but it was also wrong. It *felt* wrong.

"They pummeled me with visions of you. You tried to convince me to join them. You cajoled, begged, and demanded I join them—so I could make you one of us. You demanded eternal life at my side. But Four's version of you was all wrong. You would never care about the prestige, or the power the Fates could offer. Four fundamentally can't understand someone who doesn't want power for themselves. You would never ask me to sacrifice the world's freedom for our own immortality."

He paused and searched my face. I squeezed his hands and waited for him to continue. "When that didn't work, they made me live through your death. You died a thousand different ways, each time because I wouldn't save you from your own mortality. I couldn't tell what was real, so I decided I had to stay away from you. That's why Elias came after you. Four said I could choose to be one of them, or they would turn you into a Fate instead. He said they hadn't groomed your line, but you were a candidate."

"That's another thing I don't understand. Why did the Fates want one of us instead of Three? Four orchestrated everything that led to your death and then bringing you back with their powers."

"Three was the weakest of the triad. Four believed that they'd be stronger with a mortal groomed to handle more power."

"And the Fate of Death never saw it coming?"

Silas shrugged one shoulder. "Maybe he did but simply accepted his fate. Maybe Four tricked him too. All I know is that the Fates are full of lies and manipulations, and we can't believe any words that fall from their lips."

"I couldn't agree more."

"I don't know what I would have done had Elias taken you to them. Probably anything they wanted. I couldn't bear to watch you suffer any more." He swallowed hard.

I placed my hand over his heart, hurting from the pain I could hear in his voice. "Oh, Silas. I am so, so sorry. None of that was real."

He turned my arm over and ran his palm over the bare flesh where his sigil used to be. "Part of it was. I was so deep in my own personal hellscape, I wasn't sure what was real, and when I saw you with my dead father, I thought Four was tricking me again. I didn't understand how Four had managed to replicate our bond, and I was so *angry* that he'd found a way to defile our most intimate connection. I was afraid I'd lost any ability to discern what was real from his deceptions. I wanted to kill him, but instead, I hurt you." He cupped the side of my face, where he had hit me.

A tear leaked from the corner of my eye.

He wiped it away with his thumb. "I couldn't tell what was real anymore, and so I simply refused to interact with you—the fake versions of you. I wouldn't give the Fates my free will. Eventually, they gave up and went for brute force. I... I couldn't fight them. Their magic was so overwhelming. I couldn't think, I couldn't escape. It was like drowning in a cold, bottomless pit of magic until there was nothing left of me. I couldn't *feel* anymore, which was a blessing, I suppose. But I lost myself."

"I'm so sorry, Silas. I didn't realize what was happening to you, and I should have. I could feel you slipping away, but I didn't realize what it meant."

"When I finally *felt* you through my House bond, it was like a fire burning in my chest, painful but more real than anything I had experienced in what seemed like so many lifetimes trapped inside those horrid visions. I remembered you before I remembered myself."

I kissed both of his hands as tears continued to stream down my face. "I blame Four for every awful thing that happened, not you. Never you. We can fix all the damage Four did."

"Can we start by restoring our Aegis bond?" His face softened. "I missed having you with me. I miss feeling your presence. With your permission, of course. I wouldn't want to brand you like an animal."

I shook my head at the reminder of the first time he'd initiated the bond between us. I'd agreed to accept his protection, but I didn't fully understand what that entailed, and I'd accused him of branding me like a cow. "You have my enthusiastic consent to reinstate our Aegis bond."

He kissed me, and I let the happiness of that moment wash away any lingering hurt. Our kiss drained away all the fear I'd stored as I worried about Silas, the Fates, the Fae, DODSI, and everything horrible that had happened. Silas was back, and he was in my arms. For a few brief moments, as our lips moved together and our souls reconnected, it didn't matter what else was happening in the world.

When we pulled apart, his magic rose, golden and strong, as his palm slid up my left forearm. His magic sank into my arm, which stung briefly, but our new bond flared wide open, flooding me with love. Silas's magic wrapped around me like a cool rush of water, and

I nearly gasped with joy. The magic was all him, no longer tainted by the Fates' powers, and it was strong and steady and good and perfect. It felt so damn right in every way. I inhaled all that power and sent my own back to him, sharing my magic through our renewed connection.

Silas groaned hungrily, and my own eager anticipation rose along with the butterflies fluttering in my belly. Our mouths moved as our magic flowed, and his hands roamed as eagerly as mine. We shed our clothes as our mutual hunger became a frenzy. He kissed down my neck, and I crawled on top of him. As his clever fingers caressed my breasts, he pushed more magic into our shared bond. I arched into his hands as the magic around us flared golden and blue-green, mingling our magic and engulfing us in our shared power.

I was breathless and aching. "Are you sure you're feeling up for this? You should probably rest for like a month after what you went through." I was honestly concerned, but I glanced at the door, wishing I'd thought to lock it. If someone came to check on Silas, they'd get an eyeful of me straddling him, buck naked.

"Oh yes, I'm definitely up for it." A wicked grin spread across his face as he ground his hips against mine, illustrating his point.

He pulled me down to his mouth as I lowered myself onto him, and we both groaned at the amazing feeling of our bodies joining and the shared magic flooding through our bond. I rocked on top of him, building a delicious friction. He gripped my hips as our bodies moved together, building pleasure deep inside of me. Our hands and bodies loved each other until the feeling—the love—between us was too big to hold back any longer. Just as I was about to fall over the edge, Silas's magic flared and my own rose to meet him, grabbing us both and sending us flying.

Afterward, we lay in the bed for a long time, tangled together in a sweaty, satisfied heap. The gentle thumping of his heart and the soft strokes of his fingers on my bare back were like heaven.

He sat up suddenly, his expression intense. "Marry me."

I blinked stupidly at him. Aeternals didn't do marriage. They did bond-matings brokered by their Houses to ensure political alignment or to produce the most powerful offspring. "Is that a Mundane proposal? Because you forgot the ring and the getting-on-your-knee thing." I was hoping to lighten the mood, but he frowned as if I had rejected a serious proposal. "You don't have to marry me. We're already bonded for life, remember? You're stuck with me. I'm not going anywhere, and neither are you."

"I want to tie myself to you in every possible way, Maeve. You're an Earthen—why not honor the tradition? An Earthen marriage is another bond we can share."

"Weddings are a nightmare. I'd have to find a big white dress, and there's flowers and food... it'll cost a fortune."

Silas cocked an amused eyebrow at me. "I have money to pay for these things. I can get you the ring, and I promise to get on my knees anytime you're in the mood."

I rolled my eyes and smacked him lightly on the chest. "You'd have to dress up, too, and I know how fond you are of big fancy parties..."

"I want you to marry me the Earthen way." He was serious.

I shook my head, trying to understand his urgency. I didn't know everything that was happening, but I could feel his desperate desire through our bond. I didn't have a problem marrying Silas—I was happy to tie myself to him in every way, and if it would make what he had gone through a fraction less painful, then it was worth the ridiculous hassle. "Okay. Let's do it. I'll marry you the Earthen way."

He leaned in and kissed me with a passion that stole my breath. I kissed him back with all the feeling in my heart. When he pulled back, we were both breathing heavily.

"When?" he asked.

I laughed. "Whenever you want, but traditionally, you need to put a diamond on my finger first. Maybe we start there? I need to get you a ring also, and there's the dress... Ugh, we should elope."

Silas grinned with boyish delight, and he jumped out of bed and started digging in our dresser. He dug into the very back of his lone drawer, lifted out a crystal the size of a golf ball, then clambered onto the bed and held it out to me.

"What is that?" I stared at the almost perfectly round crystal in his palm. It looked heavy.

"The diamond is a family heirloom. It's called the Heart of Valeron. I want you to have it for your marriage ring."

"Diamond? That's a freaking diamond?" I backed away from him. "Nope. No way. You can't give me that!"

"I'll have it set into a ring." He held it out again, bouncing it lightly in his palm as if it wasn't worth more than I would ever earn in my entire life.

"That's not a ring. It's a giant paperweight. Holy shit—was that just sitting in your drawer this whole time? You need to put that in a vault or Fort Knox or something. That's gotta be worth a bazillion dollars. I can't wear it as a ring!"

Silas frowned at the diamond. "It is a bit large. It can be a necklace if you prefer." He placed the ridiculously oversized gem in my palm, and I cupped it with shaking hands.

It was heavy and cool in my grip, and as I gazed into the faceted stone, I realized it was pulsing with magic. Beautiful golden energy swirled within the diamond. "It's tugging on my magic. Is this..."

"It's an amplification stone. My family has used it for generations, and now that Aeterna is gone, it's the only remnant of magic from the original Valeron Source." He wrapped his hands around mine, closing the diamond within our shared grip. "My heart is yours, Maeve O'Neill of Earth. It's fitting that you have the physical representation of that."

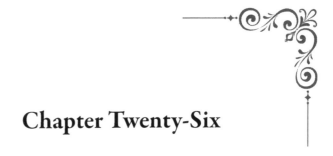

Chapter Twenty-Six

Aknock on the door broke us out of our tender moment. Before either of us could answer, it swung open. Sergius stood in the doorway with his hands clasped behind his back. Behind him, Stephan had his arm around Aria, who cradled her large pregnant belly, and just beyond them, Tessa stood in the hallway. None of them seemed embarrassed about interrupting our obvious naked cuddle. In fact, Tessa wore a face-splitting grin.

The tender happiness radiating from Silas flared into confusion and alarm. He swung his long legs off the side of the bed, surging to his feet totally naked. "You! I'm going to kill you, you bastard!"

"Silas!" I grabbed the closest portable thing and threw it at him. He caught my bra out of reflex then stared at it in complete confusion. My face flamed red when I realized what I'd chucked at him, but it was enough distraction to keep him from murdering his father. "Silas, that's really your dad! It's not Four."

"It's me," Sergius confirmed.

"This isn't another illusion?"

The Aegis bond between us started to close. Sheer panic grabbed me around the throat, and I slammed our connection wide open. It was overkill, but every instinct in my body demanded that I not lose my link to him again.

"Sorry, love... I was surprised. I didn't mean to shut you out." The bond between us reopened. "Is it really him?"

I swallowed hard and tried to let go of the overwhelming fear that had flooded me when I felt him slipping away again. The reality of what Four had done to us was just starting to sink in, and it was going to take a long time for both of us to recover. "It's really him. Can you sense him through your House bond?"

Silas went wide-eyed.

"There's a lot to catch you up on, but I swear it isn't a trick. And also, you're completely naked. Maybe you should, you know, *not* be naked?"

More than one of the Aeternals chuckled as Silas grabbed his pants off the ground and pulled them on. My clothes were scattered everywhere, but I found his shirt within reach and covered myself while everyone crowded into our little room. Everyone seemed to relax, but I could sense Silas's ongoing confusion through our bond and a rising anger I didn't quite understand.

Silas planted his hands on his hips and faced his father. "Tell me what happened. How are you not dead?"

"I was trapped in a stasis spell... but Maeve found and freed me." Sergius didn't move or try to get closer as the tension stretched between them.

Silas's anger was rising. Stephan's empathic powers flared to life, flooding us all with a sense of calm. "We're all here with you, brother. This is real, and it's actually him."

"I see," Silas said neutrally.

In addition to the shock of discovering his father alive, there was a lot of history between the two men, reflected in Stephan's tone. Neither brother seemed overly eager to have Sergius back in their lives, and even Tessa frowned at the older man's back. The damage inflicted by the elder Valeron had clearly been wide and deep.

Sergius cleared his throat. "Since Maeve and her companions freed me, I've—*we've*—been working to release you from the Fates.

Son, I know this is confusing, but I am alive, and I have a lot to explain. Please give me a chance to set things to rights."

Silas's shoulders were rigid as he stared at his father. Silently, I relayed my support through our Aegis bond. If my own past had taught me anything, it was that family could be messy and hard, but those connections were worth fighting for.

"I'm aware of the Fates' interference in our family line, and I'm also aware that you knew all of this and chose not to warn me." His voice had started cold but began to rise. "You intentionally sabotaged me and kept me in the dark. My lack of knowledge made me vulnerable to their manipulations. Was I so lacking as your heir that you thought it was best simply to sacrifice me?"

Sergius jerked backward as if he'd been struck. "How could you accuse me of such a heartless act?"

"I think you know quite well how I could think that. Shall I cite examples for you?"

This was going downhill fast. Someone needed to intervene before they said something that couldn't be repaired, but I had no idea what to do.

"I know my actions have wounded you, but everything I did was for you, son. I—"

"*Stop calling me that!* You didn't want me as your son. You wanted an heir to mold in your own image. You did everything in your power to break me and keep me under your control to protect the Valeron legacy. What kind of father sabotages their own child at every turn until they have no choices left? I know how you used your connections to try and make me fail out of Guardian training. I didn't need your name or your influence then, and I don't need you now!"

My phone trilled with the tone that meant Casius had sent an urgent alert. Silas's phone, charging on our desk, chimed along with Sergius's. I glanced at mine, and the blood drained from my face.

"What is it?" Silas asked.

I read the text out loud. "The Fae attacked Boston."

Every member of the New Alliance crowded into the media room, where live news coverage showed Mother Nithia standing outside of Trinity Church. The Fae had taken over the iconic stone church, holding the priest and parishioners hostage. The entire place was surrounded by police and media.

Nithia looked into the news cameras, scanning each one slowly. The hood of her robe was up around her head but carefully pulled back to show a circlet of twisted gold on her brow and the tips of her pointed ears. She looked like something straight out of a fairy tale.

"The Fae now rule this city, and all Humans who do not leave by midnight will forfeit their lives." She raised her arms dramatically, paused, then dropped them.

An explosion from somewhere off-screen shook the camera, and Nithia smirked before turning and going back into the church. The news channel broke to various reporters stationed around the city as live reports came in about dozens of simultaneous explosions. Every church, synagogue, and temple in the city seemed to have blown up at the end of her speech.

The sheer horror of it was more than I could absorb. "We have to stop her."

"Agreed." Casius read my look of surprise and added, "We can't stand on the sidelines and hide anymore. The stakes are too high for all of us."

"Take a legion of Guardians into the city," Sergius said. "Remove Lady Nithia, and the rest of the Fae should be easy to deal with."

Silas shook his head. "Your history with Lady Nithia is coloring your response. We should attempt to talk her down."

They stared at each other, angry and tense from their unresolved argument, as news reports continued to flash on every channel.

Octavia broke the standoff. "Take the legion and talk to her. Strike if the negotiations fail."

"I'll go with you," I said. "I've bargained with her before."

"As have I," Sergius said.

"I'm pretty sure you haven't trained for hand-to-hand combat," I replied. "No offense, but you're not going to be helpful in a fight, and we'll just have to assign someone to watch your back."

"Queen Nithia is dangerous and desperate to become one of the Fates. Do you know how to stop her? Because I do." Sergius had the same stubborn set to his jaw I'd seen a hundred times on Silas. He wasn't going to budge.

We had an unstable Fae Queen who held unspeakable dark powers on our hands and no one who really knew the full extent of what she was capable of except possibly Sergius Valeron. I sighed in acceptance, and Silas watched his father with narrowed eyes, but no one else objected.

"We'll send out multiple scout parties. Maeve, Silas, and Sergius can head to Back Bay and try to negotiate with her," Casius said.

"And if negotiations fail?" Sergius asked.

Silas and Casius exchanged a hard look.

"We'll be prepared. Be ready within the half hour," Silas said.

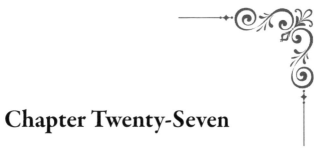

Chapter Twenty-Seven

Two hours after Nithia's news debut, seventy-five Guardians, Sergius, Silas, Tessa, and I piled into our converted school bus and headed into the city. The police roadblocks and gridlocked traffic forced us west and away from Back Bay, where Trinity Church was located, until we had to cross over to the Cambridge side of the Charles River.

After an hour of anxiously monitoring the news from my mobile phone and unable to cross bridges blocked with people trying to get out, we abandoned the bus and walked along the river on the Cambridge side until we were across from Back Bay. The sun had already set as we stood on the bank, gazing across the river to the city, which was burning in half a dozen places, with plumes of dark smoke rising into the gradually darkening sky. Along the water's edge, fifty-foot-tall oak trees had sprung out of the ground, spaced about a hundred feet apart. They had appeared suddenly and accomplished decades of growth within hours.

"The trees have some kind of conjuring running between the trunks. It's definitely elemental," I informed the others.

Silas's magic rose. "I haven't seen anything like that before."

Sergius hummed in agreement.

"I think it's some kind of boundary spell," I said.

Tessa grunted. "I've never heard of an elemental spell this large. It must be powered by the trees—"

"Like the Fae Haven," I guessed.

I sent a quick update text to Casius, and he confirmed that the other scouting parties had found the same barrier all around the city. The entire city from the North End, across Back Bay, and down to South Boston was ringed by the Fae trees. I relayed to the others that the perimeter skirted around Jamaica Plain, where we had our campus, carving out a little pocket of the city and effectively leaving us outside of the area the Fae had claimed.

"Do you think we can make it past the tree line?" I asked.

"Let's send a scout in first. It could be a trap," Silas replied.

He sent two volunteers to swim across the calm but frigid waters of the Charles. The Guardians emerged from the river, dripping wet as they raised their swords and their magic to approach the trunks. I held my breath as one of the Guardians, a woman, eased toward the tree line while the other held his position closer to the bank.

The magic between the trees flickered and grew brighter.

"Get back!" I yelled.

A blast of energy shot out of the treetops like lightning and hit the woman in the chest. She jerked like a fish on a hook, her arms and legs flailing wildly in the air until the blast of magic ended and she fell to the ground. The other Guardian's magic flared as he rushed forward to help his fallen companion. Another blast of energy shot from a different tree, and he dropped to the ground near her. Stunned silence fell over our group, even as magic built up again between the trees.

"It's going to strike again!" I called.

My entire body was strung tight, and several of the Guardians on our side had already started to wade into the river, ready to swim across and help.

Silas held up his hand, and the Guardians paused. "They're unconscious. A passive boundary conjuring shouldn't detect them as a threat any longer."

As if spurred on by his words, two more bolts of magic hit the unconscious Guardians, jerking their bodies violently. I swore, and every one of the Guardians tensed. They were ready to dive into the river and rescue their comrades, and I desperately wanted to do the same.

"That's Lieutenants de'Kidder and Fenian," Tessa said through clenched teeth. "Fenian is a first-year trainee. I can't tell if they're still breathing—they're too far away. I'll go over." She looked at Silas for permission.

He shook his head slightly. "We need a better plan, or you'll end up on the ground with them."

Damn it. No one had a chance against those defenses. None of the Guardians would be able to help. My throat tightened. "I can get them." I pulled magic and wove it into a skimming spell. Without direct access to a source, skimming wasn't possible for anyone else, but I'd gotten quite a hit of power when Nithia destroyed the keystone and I tried to hold the boundary spell together. I had enough to skim there and back with the three of us.

Silas grabbed my arm. "You'll get hit! We don't know what that spell is capable of doing!"

"I'll skim in and out before it has a chance to hit me." He started to shake his head, but I pointed at my chest. "High-powered magic mojo, remember? It's what I do. And there aren't any better options. We have to move fast."

Silas reluctantly nodded and released me.

"Your life is more valuable than some Guardian's," Sergius said. "You mustn't risk—"

I snarled at him, disgusted beyond words, and pushed power into the conjuring spell. The magic wrapped around me, and I landed on the beach next to the woman who had fallen at the tree line.

Above my head, a whining noise sounded exactly like a disruptor charging up. About twenty feet up, each tree had a black box attached to its trunk. I didn't have time to examine it closer as the small hairs on my arms rose and the air seemed to electrify.

I grabbed the woman's ankle, establishing physical contact, and threw magic into a conjuring spell. The man was too far away. I wouldn't be able to grab them both, and I was out of time. The power flashed, and I slammed magic into the spell and skimmed us both to the other bank, where I tumbled over the unconscious woman and landed on my ass in the mud.

On the Boston side of the river, the ground was smoking where we'd just been. If I'd moved a heartbeat slower, we'd have been fried.

The Guardians surrounded their comrade, checking her vitals as Silas helped me to my feet. "Are you injured?"

"No, but it was close." I flinched as another blast of energy hit the Guardian who had collapsed closer to the shoreline. "I didn't have enough time to get him."

"Where are those blasts coming from?" Silas demanded. "Why is it attacking unconscious people?"

"The trees have some kind of boxes in them... I couldn't see them until I was really close, but I could hear it recharging like the disruptors." Actually, the magic was *exactly* like disruptors. A terrible sinking feeling landed in my gut. "I gave Nithia one of DODSI's disruptors in exchange for access to the Council's vault. They must have used it as a model for their barrier."

The magically enhanced technology was still attacking the unconscious Guardian on the shoreline. Every couple of seconds, another blast hit him.

"We have to get Lieutenant Fenian off the shore before the blasts kill him," Tessa said. "They seem to have a recharge cycle similar to the disruptors. We can swim across and run for him during the period when it's charging."

"We can't wait that long. I can skim again." My magic rose, and I formed another skimming spell. I was tired, but I had enough power to do it.

Silas frowned. "No. I'm sending someone else. That was too close."

"I'm the only one who can skim! Swimming across the river is too slow."

Silas swore, but he couldn't argue with my logic. "If they're using the same tech as the disruptors, we need as many shields around you as possible. Each one will deflect a blast. Land at the river's edge and wait until our shields are in place. It appears to be on a five-second cycle, which should be enough time to close the distance."

Silas barked orders at the Guardians then turned back to me. "Wait until the shields are in place before you run."

I wove energy into the skimming spell and crossed the river, but the second my feet touched the ground, a disruptor blast slammed into the ground in front of me, throwing me off my feet. I slid several feet in the mud, right down into the water.

I might have blacked out, because when I opened my eyes, everything hurt. I couldn't feel my arms or legs, and my ears were ringing as cold water lapped at me. The hit had been like a two-by-four to the face, and blood gushed from my nose. I tried to access my magic but couldn't get a handle on it. Another blast of magic hit barely beyond my feet on the shoreline, and I scrambled backward into the river as a third bolt landed in almost the same spot as the last. We'd badly miscalculated how far the disruptors could reach, but I was just beyond their range in the water.

I crawled to my hands and knees in the river. Lieutenant Fenian lay only ten feet away. I could run for the unconscious trainee, but without my magic, I couldn't skim us back to safety.

Unfamiliar magic wrapped around me and built into a second shield. A third and fourth shield glowed around me from the

Guardians on the other side. Human, Fae, Shifter—every combination of magic surrounded me with multiple layers of protection.

The high-pitched whine of the disruptors recharging pierced through the ringing in my ears as I rose to my feet and ran for Lieutenant Fenian. I tried to dodge the next blast, but the lightning-fast pulse of energy hit me straight on. Before I could even breathe, a second slammed into my chest, throwing me off my feet. I slid several feet in the mud and stumbled to my knees as the hit tore through the first two shields. It hurt, but I stayed conscious.

More magic wrapped around me, as tangible as if the remaining Guardians had thrown their own bodies between me and the disruptors.

I flung myself forward, closing the last few feet between me and the lieutenant.

Multiple disruptors wailed as I flung myself on top of him. The bolt of energy hit us, and I screamed as the last of my shields disintegrated. I didn't have any of my own magic to protect me. I grabbed Lieutenant Fenian's ankles and dragged him down the bank and toward the water as the whining recharging of disruptors chased us. He was heavy, but my adrenaline fueled me as I dragged us both into the frigid water.

More blasts of energy hit along the shoreline, but they couldn't reach us. Safely in the water, I planted my hands on my knees and tried to catch my breath as I considered what to do next. Fenian's breaths were shallow and weak. He needed help, which meant we had to swim. I hooked my arms under his armpits and pulled us deeper into the river. I gasped as freezing water rose up to my hips and then my chest until I could float the trainee on his back. The Guardians swam out to meet us and helped carry him to the Cambridge side of the river.

I was exhausted and shivering as we dragged Lieutenant Fenian out of the muddy water and laid him on the ground. Several other

Guardians—the ones who had protected me with their magic—were unconscious but breathing.

As we turned him over, I realized that Fenian's eyes were open and staring blankly up at the sky. I sank to my knees in exhausted defeat. It was all for nothing. He was dead.

One by one, the Guardians gathered around Lieutenant Fenian. Silas drew his sword then drove it into the ground and dropped to one knee. The rest followed suit until the lieutenant's body was ringed in swords.

Tessa placed a fist over her heart as she knelt in front of her sword. "For honor in battle."

"For glory in death," a chorus of Guardians replied, their heads lowered. Their magic rose together, and the body sank into the ground.

I wanted to scream. He shouldn't have died... but there was nothing I could do to make it right. Behind me, the city continued to burn. We were in a waking nightmare, and there was nothing I could do to make any of it right.

A flash of pure-white magic brought me to my feet as Four appeared at the bank of the river.

"You!" In my anger, I almost launched myself at Four, but Silas grabbed me and held me back.

Four cocked his head to the side and examined me in all my muddy, dripping-wet glory. "You are angry, Maeve O'Neill, but it is I who should be angry with you. You broke our deal."

"You're not welcome here," Silas said. "Leave."

"I've come to collect on the debt owed—a life for a life." Four looked at me. "If you will not pay her debt, then Maeve O'Neill will come with me and accept her fate."

Silas pushed me behind him, and his magic rose. Tessa pulled her sword from the ground, and all the Guardians followed.

"No," Silas said. "I don't accept that. You manipulated Maeve into taking the Fate of Death's power. You put our lives in danger over and again and did everything in your power to take away our free will. I don't accept your false consequences. Maeve is not going with you. Not willingly."

Talking to a Fate like that made Silas either the bravest or the stupidest person alive, but he'd gained an intimate understanding of what the Fates could and couldn't do in our realm, and the power of free will was important. More important than I'd realized.

Four bared his teeth, reminding me of Elias's angry snarl. An incredible, cold power rose around us and pressed down on me like a weight. "Come with me, Maeve O'Neill, and settle your debts, or you will face the consequences."

"No!" I reached for Silas's hand, drawing strength from our ability to stand together. "I'm not going with you willingly."

"Your power in this realm is limited after I broke the connections you have here," Silas said. "You cannot take her against her will."

Four stared at us. "You will come to regret this moment." He disappeared, and his magic followed.

"Holy fratching balls! You told off a Fate!" Tessa laughed. "That was legend!"

I was shaking, wet, and too exhausted to celebrate. Silas put his arm around me, and I folded into his chest. After everything we'd been through with the Fates and their manipulations of our lives, Silas understood both the risk and the victory we'd claimed. We were truly free of Four.

After a minute, I regained my composure and checked the time on my phone. "What do we do now? It's almost midnight."

"We're not making it into the city tonight," Tessa said. "Perhaps we head back to the—"

The ground shook violently beneath our feet, and a deep, rumbling bass filled the air. The Guardians all raised their weapons and magic as we looked for the source.

A tidal wave of muddy-brown water rushed up the river, coming from the bay. We backed up onto Memorial Drive as the water rose.

"What the hell is that?" I yelled over the continuous rumbling bass.

We couldn't see the bay from our spot on the empty highway, but the source of the noise became visible as massive icebergs rose out of Boston Harbor, surrounding the city.

"Holy shit!" We all scrambled back again as the unnatural wall of ice continued to rise.

"It's the Fae!" Tessa exclaimed.

The white wall kept growing until it was higher than the downtown skyline. We watched in shock until it stopped hundreds of feet above us, and everything fell silent. In the aftermath of so much noise, the silence weighed on me like a deep snowfall—thick and deafening.

I craned my neck upward, gaping at the sheer walls of ice as my brain tried to comprehend the insanity of what I was seeing. The Fae had raised an entire glacier around Boston, and like the trees, it glowed with elemental magic. Between the tree boundary with their disruptors and the glaciers, no one was getting into their city.

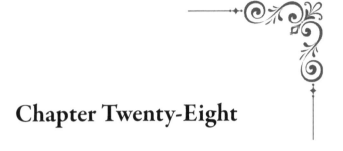

Chapter Twenty-Eight

When the sun rose the next morning, hundreds of heads on pikes lined the Charles River. Anyone who had not evacuated had been murdered by the Fae. Exhausted news anchors, many of whom had stayed live all night, were openly crying on air. The country's shock turned to horror and outrage. Every branch of the military and all the three-letter agencies tried to get into the city, but they were stopped by the elemental protections the Fae had erected. Their jets fell from the sky, and the glacier proved impervious even to missile strikes. Troops on the ground died in foolhardy attempts to break past the tree line on foot.

The president of the United States declared martial law in Boston, and they sent in tanks. Mother Nithia made international news when she crushed one of those tanks with her magic then used it to smash the other two. Speculation and rumors flew across every news channel and social media site, and nearly every country in the world dealt with mass hysteria.

At a quarter past four that afternoon, Director Pascal drove onto our campus. He brought Special Agent Lennart and several dozen DODSI goons with him, all armed with disruptors. We met him and Lennart in the circle room with every member of the New Alliance: Casius, Alannah, Jason, Tamara, Alaric, Nero, and Octavia. Sergius had also gotten himself invited, which didn't bother me since including him in the leadership was all but inevitable, but Silas bristled when his father took the seat next to me at the circular stone table.

Pascal and Lennart sat as Lennart's goon squad lined the walls on either side of the exit on the main floor. The upper balconies of the circle room were eerily empty, an unusual event when we gathered, but Casius had called a closed session because shit was about to hit the fan with DODSI.

Casius sat at my other side, facing off with Director Pascal from across the table. Silas positioned himself along the wall behind me by the door, presumably to prevent us from being blocked in. Despite not having his sword, he was clearly prepared to fight his way out of the room if necessary. The air was so thick with tension that a less mature person would have started whistling Wild West showdown music. I didn't have it in me after spending the night watching my city fall to the Fae.

The head of DODSI looked like he hadn't slept, either. His shirt was rumpled, his tie was loose around his neck, and his normally rich, dark complexion was ashen. He didn't waste time on pleasantries. "You broke our agreement."

"We didn't free magic intentionally," Casius responded carefully. "The Fae—"

"The Fae are killing innocent people and terrorizing our nation. We had to evacuate the city, and some of our people didn't make it out." Pascal's voice was gravelly, intense, and full of terrible consequences. He pointed at me. "*Her* face is all over the news again. Tell me, were you working with the Fae all along to release magic, Miss O'Neill?"

The situation was escalating quickly, but I'd promised Casius that I would let him take the lead, so I sat on my hands and stayed quiet.

"Our work on the keystones didn't free magic," Casius said. "We tried to stop the Fae—Agent Lennart can attest to our efforts."

"Oh, I have a full report and bodycam footage. I know exactly who did what, including *that man* taking Mr. Marius out of our custody." Pascal pointed at Silas, and I had to force myself not to flinch. The video footage was news to me. "We want him back."

Casius and I exchanged a cautious look. "We don't have him."

Pascal's eyes narrowed. "That's a lie."

"No," Silas said immediately. "Lord Elias is dead."

"You admitting to murder, Highlander?" Lennart leaned forward, eager to catch Silas in a punishable crime.

Silas didn't take the bait. I couldn't see his expression as he stood behind me, but Lennart's narrow-eyed stare was locked angrily on him.

Pascal's nostrils flared. "You killed our consultant?"

"Nobody said we killed him. Just that he's dead," I replied.

Lennart sneered. "Let me guess, Highlander's sword 'slipped.'"

"Where's the body?" Pascal demanded.

"What do you want with his body?" Silas snapped.

"We have nothing else to say," I said. "If you want to question us about a missing person who never officially existed in this realm, then you'll need an arrest warrant."

Casius gaped in surprise. I shrugged. Watching all those crime dramas had to pay off sometime. DODSI wouldn't really have a legal way to charge us for a murder of someone who never officially existed in our realm.

Pascal rubbed the furrow between his brows. "We will be revisiting this subject, but we have more pressing problems right now. Magic is infecting major cities across the Eastern Seaboard. New York City has declared martial law. Riots broke out in Chicago and most of the neighboring cities. North Korea and China are threatening a nuclear response to stop the spread. Our allies globally are closing their borders and detaining American citizens in case they're infected." Pascal's gaze narrowed on me. "Is this what you wanted all along?"

"I didn't want *this*." The picture Pascal was painting was dire. His accusation hurt, because I *had* believed magic should be freed. The whole world should have had access to the joy and beauty of magic. But instead, people were terrified, and the Fae were destroying the city I loved.

"We're prepared to help," Casius said. "Magic will spread slowly. There's time to rebind it."

"Help? It's a bit late for that, don't you think? We lost seven agents last night just trying to get past the damn trees!" Pascal's voice rose to a yell, and he had to visibly settle himself before he continued. He leaned forward, placing a fist on the table. "Do you know what I was discussing with the president all night? Whether or not wiping you all off the face of the Earth would fix the 'magic problem.'"

An alarmed murmur rose from our side of the table. My stomach clenched. They had the means, and given the current state of Boston, they would probably throw a parade afterward.

"I assume, since we are all sitting here, that you decided against that course of action," Sergius said calmly.

"Do you want to know why you're waking up this morning? I told the president and Joint Chiefs you could fix this. I convinced them you're more useful alive." Pascal looked around the room, pausing to meet my eyes again. "I'm here to deliver an ultimatum from the president of the United States: you have seventy-two hours to get the Fae out of Boston."

Pascal didn't have to spell out the threat behind the ultimatum. He'd already made it clear that the government was willing to wipe us off the face of the Earth.

Under the table, Casius tapped his fingers on his thigh, but he somehow kept the stress off his face, and his voice was calm. "How are we supposed to do that?"

Pascal sat back in his chair. "Honestly, we don't care how you do it. You said you could rebind magic—start there. I trust you'll come up with something.

"We tried to make it into the city and lost one of our own too. We can't get in there any more than you can. What you're asking is impossible," Casius said quietly.

"This isn't a request." Pascal's tone was hard. "This is the last opportunity for you to fix your mistakes and prove you're not in league with the Fae terrorists."

I waited for Casius to deny Pascal's outrageous claim about being in league with Nithia. He needed to explain the impossible timeline and the limitations of our abilities. He needed to make them understand that their demands weren't possible.

"We understand," Casius said. "We didn't cause this mess, but we'll do everything we can to help you reclaim the city."

A surge of desperate alarm flooded through me, but Casius put his hand on my knee under the table, urging me to stay quiet. I had to bite my tongue hard to keep from speaking up. There was no way for us to force the Fae out of Boston, but there was also no way for us to tell DODSI no.

Pascal rose to his feet. "Agent Lennart's team will be stationed outside. Coordinate with him if you need to leave this compound. I don't think I have to impress upon you the consequences of failure."

"You've made yourself clear," Casius said.

"You have seventy-two hours." Pascal scowled at me before he walked out the door.

Lennart waited stoically as the DODSI agents filed out. When they were all gone, he met my gaze, and his mouth thinned into a tight line. I got the distinct impression that he wanted to say something. He glanced around then extended four fingers on his right hand and tapped them against his thigh. I had no idea what he was trying to tell me. I glanced at Silas, the only other person who was paying close enough attention to Lennart to see the strange gesture, but he furrowed his brows in confusion.

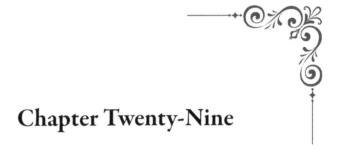

Chapter Twenty-Nine

I traced the tip of my finger along the giant crack running through the stone table in front of me. The carved magical sigils used to represent the access points to Earth's magic, before I broke the binding around that power and set it free. Now, it was only a broken table.

Silas, seated next to me at the table, squeezed his hand into a fist. "How are we supposed to force the Fae out of the city when we can't make it past their borders?"

"It's not possible," Tamara said. "We've been working for months, trying to come up with a way to counter the disruptor technology, but we have nothing viable."

Casius drummed his fingers on the stone table. "We have to figure it out. They just threatened to eradicate us."

With that fresh reminder, people started talking all at once. More than one person suggested that we run and hide and let the Fae and the Mundanes sort it out. I slumped in my chair. I was so tired of living the same cycle over and over. All the other times, I'd held on to the conviction that it was better to face our enemies. I'd always believed there was something we could rally around, a way out, or a clever solution. At the least, we would go down fighting. But this time, it was different. The Fae had taken over Boston, and hundreds were dead. The big secret about magic was out, and not in the peaceful, transitional way I'd envisioned. The government was threatening to kill us, it would be impossible to do what they wanted, and the world was never going to accept magic peacefully. I couldn't see a way out of our mess, and I'd never felt more hopeless. Not to mention the ongoing problem of the Fates. We'd stopped them from getting their hands on Silas—or me, for that matter—but with magic spreading, they would gain access to our realm soon enough.

"The Mundanes gave us an impossible ultimatum," Octavia said. "We must strike first, before they take punitive actions against us." Until then, all the other former Aeternal Council members, seated on one side of the round table, had been suspiciously silent. Even Silas, who had taken the seat next to me when Sergius got up to pace, hadn't spoken. Octavia leaned forward in her chair. With her petite features and narrow shoulders, she seemed almost fragile next to Nero, but her gaze was steel. "The seat of their government is defenseless against us. They will not expect an attack."

No one responded. Not a whisper of a noise.

"We don't kill innocent people to get what we want." I gave her a long look to be sure she got the message.

Octavia took in the horrified expressions on the faces of those who hadn't ruthlessly ruled an entire magical society and shrugged one shoulder. "If you are unwilling to crush your enemies, then you'll be forced to negotiate from a weaker position."

"Is it an impossible ultimatum?" Silas asked. "If we cannot take the city by force, then can we not negotiate with Lady Nithia? Surely, we can find something the Fae want more than the Mundanes' city."

"All Lady Nithia wants is to become one of the Fates," I said, "which we obviously can't allow."

Silas's mouth twisted in thought. "Then let us use that to our advantage. If she believes we are capable of offering her the opportunity to become a Fate, it may be enough to get us inside their boundary. Once inside…" He shrugged. "Negotiations are sealed with either the pen or the sword."

"That just might work," I agreed. "She knows both of us have access to the Fates' powers. If she's eager to inherit their power, she'll at least want to talk to us. And if we can't figure out a peaceful way into the city, you and I can absorb enough power to skim our forces in."

Silas frowned. "The Fae are more than capable fighters, and they'll outnumber us."

"Why should we concede to the Mundanes' demands at all?" Nero cut in, folding his arms over his broad chest. "The Fae are not our enemy. We should ally with them against the Mundanes."

"They killed hundreds of innocent people!" Alannah snapped.

"They didn't attack *our* people," Nero replied.

"They attacked innocents who couldn't even defend themselves," I said.

Nero's eyes took on a slightly yellow sheen, as if he might shift into his animal form. "It was a strategic strike. But we might have to make reparations first for Lord Silas's killing of the Fae Queen's heir.

"Boone tried to kill me." I glared at him.

"As her Aegis, I was within my rights to act in Maeve's defense," Silas said calmly. "Boone then attacked *me*, and I defended myself. Lady Nithia doesn't have a claim to retribution."

Nero lifted an eyebrow in challenge. "Lady Nithia may not see it that way, given that Boone was frozen in place when you killed him."

Silas remained stone-faced, but his irritation flooded through our Aegis bond.

"She has a few grudges to choose from, don't you think?" I replied. "What makes you think she'd want an alliance with any of you after you cut off her hands?"

"She removed her own hand as a sacrifice to the Fates," Octavia said with a small, indignant sniff. "The Council simply removed the second one to keep her from doing it again."

"Don't you think she might be upset that you cut off her *other* hand?" I raised my eyebrows at the former Council members.

"We were merciful." Sergius's voice was cold. "The Council spared her life when we should not have. While I would very much personally like to see her pay for all her sins, we need her alliance more."

Heads bobbed around the table, and I found myself at a loss for words. I was sure Nithia wouldn't feel quite so casual about them taking both of her hands instead of her life. I was also surprised that Sergius was willing to set aside his personal vengeance after she had him stashed in a stasis spell for ten years.

"The Fae killed innocent people in cold blood." Alannah jabbed a finger into the stone tabletop as she stared down the Aeternals. "They put heads on pikes! We will not agree to an alliance with them."

I found myself nodding.

"They gave an appropriate deadline to evacuate," Octavia replied. "Lady Nithia could have razed the entire city without warning in retaliation for"—she glanced at Silas—"the retribution they believe they are owed. That was an intentional show of restraint, while your Mundane government leaders have already threatened to erase us from existence if we cannot do the impossible. They respect only power and destruction, and they fear us. The bigger threat is clear."

I glanced at Casius. He listened with furrowed brows and a tense jaw but didn't seem intent on weighing in. Neither did Jason or Tamara, who had stayed silent the whole time. Silas's expression was unreadable as he leaned back in his chair, silently surveying the others seated at the table.

Sergius sat and raised his palms. "I understand emotions are high right now, but there is logic to an alliance with the Fae. I am willing to set aside the penance owed me for Lady Nithia's actions for the greater good. Lord Nero is right—we need strength against those who would seek to eradicate us. If we fight against each other, we are vulnerable to attack, but no Mundane government could stand against a united magical front."

"The Mundanes always seek to destroy what they fear. History repeats itself," Nero added in his rumbling bass.

Alaric, Nero, and Octavia were all on the same page, which never happened. Ever. They'd clearly come to an agreement beforehand, and I was certain Sergius was to blame. It was possible that he'd convinced them that an alliance was the best way to protect themselves—or it could be something more.

"Why are all of you agreeing to an alliance with the Fae?" I asked.

"It is the obvious solution," Nero replied. "Your government's impossible demands will not end. They fear our powers, and they will not stop until they believe they control us. Unless you join forces with the Fae, you are powerless against them and their *technology*."

I shook my head. "What you're proposing would bring every Mundane government in the whole world down on us. We'd be the most hunted people on Earth."

"Do you truly trust your Mundane allies not to turn on you?" Silas quietly asked me, and silence descended as the others waited to see what I would say.

I took a moment to consider my answer. I didn't trust DODSI, but allying with the Fae would start the next world war, with my sect at the center of the fallout. "I don't trust them... but I also don't trust the Fae. I do know DODSI will retaliate if we make an alliance with Nithia. And there's no reason to think the Fae are going to want an alliance with us, anyway. Not after everything."

"The Fae have already agreed to ally with us against the Mundanes," Sergius said. His quiet words were like an explosion in the room, and everyone around the table started talking at once.

"You met with the Fae? When?" Casius demanded.

Alannah jumped to her feet. "That is completely unacceptable! You don't have the authority to make deals on behalf of this alliance."

I couldn't muster up enough surprise to be outraged like the rest of them. Of course the former Lord Councilors had this planned. Silas also looked surprised, and I could feel his concern through our bond. He'd been out of commission while in Four's clutches, but I wondered if he was alarmed about his father's power grab or about being left out of their plans.

Sergius wore a sympathetic expression as he listened to the commotion. With the former Councilors united for the first time in a long time, I couldn't underestimate what they were capable of. They were each dangerous on their own, but together and with Sergius pulling the strings, they were going to be a huge issue.

After several minutes of chatter, Sergius placed both of his palms on the table and rose to his feet. He looked earnestly into each person's face until it was quiet. "I only intended to forge the path forward in case we decided on this course of action. If the leaders of this alliance believe we can reclaim the city by force, we need not agree to any bargain with the Fae."

Sergius was a tricky bastard, all right. He'd just laid out a way out of our impossible situation with DODSI, but there was a hook in that bait. "What did you promise them?" I asked.

Sergius inclined his head in my direction. "Our alliance would include a guarantee to come to their aid against the Mundanes, if necessary, and Nithia wants access to the Fates."

I had an immediate and visceral reaction and rose to my feet. "Absolutely not!"

"That's what we've been trying to avoid," Casius said more levelly.

Sergius raised a palm. "Not for the reasons you think. She no longer wants to become a Fate. She wants revenge."

"What?" I sat back down, deflated and confused.

"Lady Nithia sacrificed much to gain the Fates' favor and their powers, but she has since realized they lied to her. She is not physically capable of joining their ranks, yet they let her believe it was possible. She did many works at their behest—including attacking me and leading her people to abandon Aeterna. But she has now learned that her lineage is not compatible."

An alliance with the Fae would mean Nithia getting away with all the terror and death she'd caused. I frowned as I scanned the room to see what everyone was thinking. Casius was laser focused on Sergius, likely tempted by a way out from under DODSI's thumb. Jason's face was lit up with hope, while Alannah pursed her lips in thought. She didn't seem completely sold on the idea, but the sharp edges of anger had drained from her face. Everyone in the Inner Circle was at least considering allying with the Fae.

"If we have the upper hand, we could bargain with DODSI for a truce," Casius said slowly. "It would be a long road, but it puts us on more equal footing."

"The Fae can't just walk away," I said. "Not after yesterday."

"I agree," Alannah said. We glanced at each other, uncomfortable being on the same side of an argument for probably the first time ever. "And we're not making a deal until we understand exactly what you're getting out of it, because the Aeternal Council only does the things that benefit you the most and screw everybody else."

Sergius raised his eyebrows. His face was the picture of earnest honesty. "I cannot speak for the time after I was Lord Councilor, but I assure you that our only intention is mutual benefit."

My phone chirped. I glanced down to read a text message from Stephan. *It's time!*

"Aria's having her baby!" I popped up from my seat, startling Sergius, who had leaned over like a nosy bastard to read my private message.

"We'll convene and take a vote tomorrow morning," Casius said quickly, taking advantage of my outburst to try and maintain control over the situation. It was a good idea to stall for time and really think through the proposal.

When everyone agreed to a break, Silas and Alaric both followed me out of the circle room. I paused, unsure what to say to Alaric. He was Aria's father, but he hadn't been invited to the birth, and I didn't want to put myself in the middle of their complicated family situation. If Aria didn't want him there, that was her business.

"Now is not the best time," I said gently to him. I didn't have anything nice to say about Alaric abusing his position as Lord Magister to misinterpret a prophecy in order to force Silas and Aria into a bond-mating. He'd tried to make up for it, but his relationship with Aria was... not my business.

His face started to color as he looked down his long nose at me. "I didn't intentionally hurt her, you know. I tried to... The prophecy *could have* been about Aria. I truly believed it was, and I only wanted the best for her."

Silas snorted, and his face went hard. "You wanted what was best for your House, not your daughter."

"I apologized to Aria." The flush over Alaric's skin burned a shade deeper. "I was wrong, but I swear upon my forefathers that I thought the prophecy was about my House as well as yours."

"Is that an acknowledgment of a penance owed to my House?"

His face flamed fully red. "If you need it to be, I will acknowledge such a debt formally."

Silas didn't respond, neither accepting nor refusing the apology, but I could feel his anger settle a tiny fraction.

Alaric's face was pleading. "Aria hasn't spoken to me since she almost died. I've tried everything I can, but she doesn't understand that all I did was for her. I only want to see my grandchild."

I remembered what Sergius had done to Alaric's entire family when he was the Lord Councilor and had a flare of sympathy for him. Offering a penance to the Valeron House had to really hurt. He was a selfish asshat most of the time, but he really did love Aria. And he'd been better since leaving Aeterna, working with us to rebuild a shared life for all of our people. "Maybe you should give the explanations a break and do some listening," I suggested gently.

The phone dinged again with a message from Stephan. *Where are you?*

"I'm sorry. Now is not the right time to try and make amends with your daughter. You have to respect her wishes, but I'll tell her you want to see her and the baby."

By the time Silas and I reached the birthing center, I found the ornery Healer waiting for me with her hands on her hips. She held a green robe in her hand, but she didn't offer it to me as she looked Silas over from head to toe and deepened her scowl. "You have not been invited."

Silas stopped short. "I'm—"

"I know who you are, and you're not invited." She planted a fist on her hip.

"But Stephan—"

"Did not invite you. I don't care what your family name is. You're not going in that birthing room without permission from the parents."

I put my hand on Silas's arm as I addressed her. "It's a misunderstanding. Silas wasn't back home until yesterday, so I'm sure they just didn't have a chance to tell you he's invited."

My phone trilled again. The Healer glared as news alerts hit my phone back-to-back, vibrating and chirping. I scanned through several major media outlets with growing horror. Someone had released footage of Nithia's attack at the keystone, but the video had been edited all to hell—it looked like Silas had been working *with* Nithia and attacking the government agents.

Silas watched the footage over my shoulder. "My memory is a little blurry, but I don't remember killing those people."

"You didn't." I ground my teeth. The clip had gone viral in less than an hour. I swore under my breath as I scrolled through it all with rising outrage. They hadn't yet identified Silas—without an identity on Earth, that would be quite difficult—but the video showed *my* face very clearly, and the news outlets had already connected me yet again to the "magical terrorists." A lead weight settled in my stomach. We were being set up. DODSI was laying the foundation to blame us for everything if we couldn't take the city back. Given Pascal's threats, I didn't have to guess too hard what would happen next.

The Healer snapped her fingers and held out her hand. "That's enough. Give me all your technology! I won't have you destroying the harmony of this birth."

I clutched the phone. I had to *do* something. We needed to figure out what DODSI was up to and how to avert the looming crisis. I needed to talk to Casius and figure out our strategy.

"If you want to go into the birthing room, you'll give it over. The trouble will still be here when you return."

I took a deep breath and let it out slowly through my teeth. I couldn't be everywhere all at once, and I couldn't fix everything by myself. "I need to be with Aria right now. This video is just pressure tactics from DODSI," I told Silas. "Can you make sure Casius knows about this? Pascal is the only one who could have produced this footage, and he's gone to a lot of effort to make it look like we're working with the Fae."

"They're turning on us," Silas said gravely.

"Yeah, looks like it." Reluctantly, I held out my phone.

The Healer snatched it out of my hand and tossed it into a basket on the side table. It clanked against other devices, and I cringed at the possibility of all the broken screens.

"You'll get it back when you leave. Focus on the present," she advised.

"It's fine, Maeve," Silas said. "I'll let you know of any critical developments."

I sighed as I watched Silas go then pulled off my shoes and slipped the robe over my shoulders. With a glance at the Healer blocking the doorway to the birthing center, I took a deep breath and tried to clear my negative aura or whatever. She pursed her lips in general disapproval, but after a moment, she opened the door and let me in. "Your time here can do you good. Try to find your inner balance."

The calming sound of gurgling water and the serene scent of herbs flowed over me. I inhaled deeply and reminded myself to focus on what mattered right then. *Family.*

Aria's low, keening cry carried across the open space, and I found her on all fours in a shallow stream, slowly rocking back and forth. Two Healers and Stephan knelt at her side, rubbing her back in slow circles and coaching her.

I took another deep breath. I had no idea what I was doing in a birth situation, but Aria needed me, so I would be there for her. It was the most important thing I could do.

Chapter Thirty

The baby's little button nose scrunched, and she opened her rosebud mouth slightly as she slept trustingly in my arms. A tiny, perfect hand curled into a fist next to her face. I inhaled the scent of newborn baby and felt ready to burst with love.

Alaric, sitting in a chair to the side of Aria's recovery bed, placed a soft kiss on his daughter's brow. "She's absolutely perfect."

Maybe it was left over from the Fates' magic or the pure joy on Alaric's face after having been forgiven by his daughter, but there was tangible power in the unlimited potential of new life. The girl would be capable of great and wonderful things.

The exhaustion of her overnight labor showed under Aria's eyes as she smiled at me. "Thank you for staying with me. I know you have other matters to deal with."

"I wouldn't miss it for the world." The love glowing in the room was what life was about. The mess with DODSI and the Fae and the Fates was raging outside those walls, but in that moment, all that mattered was being with family.

A pang of longing hit me. I wanted that. I wished for a family of my own—a child I could pour my heart into. I wanted it so badly my chest ached.

Silas wrapped an arm around my shoulder and squeezed gently. "What will you call her?"

"Her name is Sariah," Stephan said from his perch next to Aria's bed.

Sergius, dragged to the recovery room by Silas, had been lingering at the back, and his head snapped up. "After your mother?"

Stephan nodded. "Sariah Westerlan Certus Valeron. My mother's house, Aria's house, and... yours."

Silas turned to his father. "An appropriate name for the future Prime of House Valeron."

Everyone's attention shifted to Sergius. Given the tension between them, I'd wondered why Silas had dragged his father along, but as the tense silence stretched on, I realized that Stephan and Silas had planned the moment.

We all waited for Sergius's reaction to the fact that Stephan and Aria's child would be the future Prime of his House. *Stephan's child, not Silas's.* Alaric tensed at Aria's side, his eyes wide as he perhaps waited for violence to erupt.

The older Valeron's jaw was so tight that I could see his muscles clench as he digested that the future heir had none of his blood. It was the moment that could break the family apart. Stephan had adopted the Valeron last name when Silas made him the Prime of House Valeron, but they were half brothers through their mother. Sergius was finding out just how thoroughly Silas had rejected his birthright and his father's legacy.

With his eyes on Silas, Sergius exhaled through his nose and unclenched his jaw. "So witnessed."

Stephan and Silas visibly relaxed, and Alaric remembered how to breathe as the collective tension in the room plummeted. Aria's eyes got watery as Stephan wrapped his arm around her.

Silas took the precious bundle from me and planted a gentle kiss on the baby's forehead as he settled her in Sergius's arms. "Thank you, Father."

Sergius shook his head as he gazed at his future heir. "My bullheaded efforts to ensure the success of our family line have only led me to losing the very legacy I sought to protect. I'm sorry, Silas. I shouldn't have pushed you down the path I assumed would protect you. I should have been honest with you about the threat the Fates posed to our House, to our family." He smiled at the baby and took a deep breath. "When you chose to join the Guardians, I was harsh. My efforts were meant to ensure you were safe, but I only ensured that you despised me and turned away from everything I had built."

Silas placed a hand on his father's arm. "We've both changed. There is much history to unlearn between us, but I'm willing to try."

"As am I, son."

The manly emotion hanging between them was too much for my smart mouth. I took the baby out of Sergius's arms. "Oh, just hug it out already, will you?"

I cradled the precious bundle as father and son—so alike and yet so very different—embraced each other. Many people who would love and protect baby Sariah. Unfortunately, she was going to need every ounce of it.

After the birth, I'd managed to get a few hours of sleep and up-dates from Silas and Casius. Things in Boston were worse. "Uniden-tified government sources" had confirmed that we were responsible for the "disease" spreading across the eastern seaboard and that we had aided and abetted the Fae terrorists in Boston. Fear was fueling the media, and the mob of protestors outside campus had tripled in size. Several major religions had officially renounced us as Satan worshippers. DODSI was setting us up as the ultimate bad guys. If they decided to eliminate us from the face of the Earth, as Pascal had threatened, the rest of the world would cheer them on.

Aria and Stephan's child was only hours into our world, and she already needed to be shielded simply because of who she was and what she was capable of. She wouldn't stand a chance without people to protect her from the prejudice and fear of Mundanes who didn't understand our magic. The very powerful people surrounding Sariah would do anything to protect her, but I wasn't sure it would be enough. We couldn't withstand attacks from all sides forever.

The solution to both our problems was obvious. I didn't love it, but looking down at the precious new life in my arms, I knew it was the right choice.

"We have to think about the future," I said. "DODSI will never trust us because we're too different and our powers are too dangerous. If magic spreads across Earth, the Fates will figure out a way to gain access. We don't really have a choice."

"What are you proposing?" Alaric asked.

We couldn't handle DODSI and the Fates on our own. But with the Fae—with the murdering, backstabbing Fae—we had a chance. As much as I wanted to punish Nithia for what she had done to my beloved city and for the lives she'd taken, we couldn't afford to stand alone.

I looked around the room full of my chosen family and accepted what needed to be done to secure a future for all of us. "We need an alliance with the Fae."

B y the next morning, the mob outside our campus had grown to an unbelievable size. People led chants on bullhorns, and protestors carried signs renouncing us as Satanists, demons, and magical terrorists. News cameras lined the streets, keeping a twenty-four-hour watch on the mess. My face was on at least half the signs, usually with red devil horns. Only our shield kept them from storming the campus.

If it hadn't all been so terrifying, I might have been amused by the small group of fans dressed in ridiculous black robes who'd decided we were their new prophets. Unfortunately, they weren't really helping our cause by painting bright-red pentagrams on the sidewalks and celebrating as they ushered in the apocalypse.

Casius called an emergency meeting. I'd spent the better part of the day in the circle room, trying to convince the New Alliance to ally with the Fae.

"It's the only way," I said to the few remaining skeptics.

"DODSI isn't going to be happy with us if we help the Fae escape justice," Gia pointed out. "I don't see how we can play both sides here. Either we side with DODSI or with the Fae."

Her tone was thoughtful, and heads bobbed around the table, which was a huge improvement from that morning, when I'd suggested going forward with an alliance and Alannah had immediately started yelling. It was strange to find myself on the side of the former Aeternal Councilors, but being at odds with Alannah was nothing new.

"With the Fae's help, I believe we can rebind magic. That will give us enough power to hold them off, and it will take care of the problem with the Fates," I said.

"We'll be in a better position to bargain after we have our power back and DODSI can't just threaten to murder us all if we don't do what they want," Jason said, nodding.

I placed my hand on the top of the broken stone table—the evidence of all I'd torn apart—as hope began to build in my chest. We had a shot. "Let's put it to a vote. I propose an alliance with the Fae."

"I second the proposal for an alliance," Sergius said quickly.

I swallowed. This was it, the moment that would define our future for generations to come. If we could pull it off, we had a shot at stopping the Fates. But if not... I stopped that thought and let go of my doubts. Our plan had to work.

"All those in favor of a treaty with the Fae?" Jason asked formally.

All the former Lord Councilors, including Silas and Sergius, voted to ally with the Fae, as did Casius, Tamara, Jason, and Gia. I raised my hand, and we had the majority.

"The motion carries," Casius declared. "We'll accept an alliance with the Fae."

Alannah had not voted in favor, but she stayed quiet as we moved forward with our plans.

"We have arranged to finalize the terms tomorrow within the city boundaries," Sergius said.

My annoyance surged, and the frowns on several faces said I wasn't the only one rubbed the wrong way by Sergius making plans with the Fae before our actual vote. "Who said *you're* going to negotiate the terms of our deal?" I demanded.

"I've built a relationship with the Fae over decades. They won't accept a stranger into their midst for negotiations."

"I'm not a stranger. I've bargained with Mother Nithia before, and she knows who I am."

Alannah clicked her tongue. "No offense, but I don't think either of you is a good choice. We need to send in a strong negotiator who will represent all our interests equally. I nominate Jason."

"Rude," I said under my breath.

"I said no offense," she replied dismissively.

"I have to disagree," Casius told her. "Sergius and Mae represent both sides of our New Alliance. Mother Nithia knows them individually, and Sergius has clearly already established the lines of communication. Changing that up now will signal internal disagreement, and the Fae will try to exploit that."

Alannah scowled, and my heart went all warm and glowy as my mentor expressed his trust in me.

"I concur," Silas said. "And I will accompany them both for the negotiation."

Sergius flinched. "No. Mother Nithia will try to kill you on sight as retribution for her heir's death."

"Exactly. The issue needs to be addressed. I was acting under my rights as Maeve's Aegis when I killed Boone. But if Nithia believes I have wronged her, then it needs to be settled either way."

"And if she doesn't agree with your assessment of the situation?" Sergius pushed.

Silas's feral smile spread across his face. "We'll have to agree to disagree."

I tugged on Marcel's charm hanging around my neck. "Silas, your father's right. We're trying to forge an alliance, not piss her off. I don't think you should come."

"Addressing the issue is the only path forward."

"You're right, but I think that might go better without you actually being there," I said gently.

Sergius was quick to agree. "Yes, I can address the question of retribution on behalf of our House."

Silas scowled as he looked between me and his father, and I realized this was about more than Boone's death. Although they'd agreed to move forward, there were many decades of distrust and anger between Silas and his father. I was headed into enemy territory, where Nithia might choose to retaliate against us, and Silas wouldn't be there. I sent calm vibes through our bond. "I've got this. It will be fine."

Silas puffed air from his lungs, clearly unhappy, but he let it go.

Alannah cleared her throat. "Not that I'm doubting our dear Maeve's abilities or questioning the loyalties of a former Lord Councilor we all thought was dead..." She paused long enough to make it clear that was exactly what she was doing. "But we should keep working on a way to rebind magic in case we can't come to terms with the Fae."

I ached to slap the smugness right off her face, but she wasn't wrong. A backup plan was smart.

"That would be wise," Sergius agreed easily. "But since the single most powerful magic user in this community will be occupied negotiating with the Fae, you'll need to figure out a way to recreate the Earthen Source without Lady Maeve." He smiled at her, and it wasn't friendly. "Unfortunately, she can't do everything for you."

The flustered scowl on Alannah's face was perfect, and I decided Sergius could stick around for a while longer.

"We can share the Ascension with them," Silas suggested.

Sergius rocked back in his seat and crossed his arms. The rest of the Aeternals were suddenly very, very alert as they watched Silas and his father.

"What's the Ascension?" I asked.

Sergius and Silas seemed to be having a staring match, and neither answered me. I cleared my throat.

"It's a power amplification spell that is unique to each House," Alaric said. "They're very closely guarded and passed down from Prime to Heir."

"The Valeron Source is gone," Silas said to his father. "There's no power left to hoard. We need every advantage we have if we're to rebind magic and stop the Fates."

I held my breath. It was clearly some kind of test between Silas and his father, and sharing this information was apparently the proof Silas wanted that his father was willing to change.

"Very well," Sergius said, his voice tight. "If you think that is the best course of action."

"When we're ready, I can make one large enough for two people," Silas told Casius.

Silas looked expectantly at his father, who sighed loudly. "I can conjure another one of equal size, and with enough time spent in the Ascension circle, they should be able to amplify the power of an entire circle almost twofold."

"Does every House have one?" I raised my eyebrows at the rest of the Aeternals.

There was some shifting around in seats until Sergius nodded. "Yes, and they will each be happy to perform these amplification spells, should they be needed. Am I correct?"

Mumbled and hesitant agreement followed, which made both Silas and me smirk. Even Sergius had a glint in his eye, though he was trying hard to hide it.

"We'll take every advantage we can," Casius said. "Tamara, can you get the conjuring circles planned and figure out who should spend time inside the amplification circles?"

With everyone agreed on our next steps, Casius ended the meeting, and people started leaving. I told Silas I'd catch up with him that evening then mustered up my courage as I caught Casius's eye. "Can I talk to you for a second?"

"Sure, Mae. What's going on?"

I waited for the last couple of stragglers to leave. "I just wanted to say that, um, well, I know things have been tense between us, and I'm sorry for my part in that."

"You already apologized for your mistakes. You don't need to beat yourself up about it. We'll fix things together."

"I hope things will be okay between us. You're my mentor, and... I really value your opinion of me, and I know that, well, we both went behind each other's backs."

Casius sighed. "I'm sorry about that. I was wrong to force you to choose between what you thought was right and being part of this sect. We're family, no matter what. I'm proud of you, kiddo. Your mom would be proud of you too."

Tears welled up in my eyes. "That means a lot to me."

"Ah, don't cry. Come here." Casius pulled me into a hug and planted a kiss on the top of my head. "We've been through a lot, you and I. We're probably going to go through a lot more before this is over, but we're going to have each other's backs from now on. Deal?"

"Deal."

Chapter Thirty-One

The Cambridge Public Library outside of Harvard Yard was eerily empty and quiet. Sergius liked my suggestion to change the location to a neutral site outside of the Fae-controlled city, and he also suggested changing the time to right after dark. He said making several demands would "establish dominance" in the negotiations. I wasn't sure how his twisted logic worked, but meeting in the abandoned library in the middle of the night was creepy.

The entire front side of the library was a giant glass wall overlooking a large grassy park. The interior was lit only by the emergency lights near the stairs, and the floor-to-ceiling wall of night-dark glass windows reflected my own image staring at me. Behind me, rows and rows of bookshelves lined the open floor. In my teenage years, I'd spent a fair amount of time there, pilfering free internet or otherwise staying warm until the library closed and I had to find a spot to sleep for the night—

I stopped that thought in its tracks. Those memories were only partially true. I'd never actually been homeless. After I'd chosen to bind my magic and my memories to hide among the Mundanes, the magic had filled in the gaps of my forgotten past. I was still working to untangle the memories. I *had* spent a lot of time in the library, but only after my father brought us to Boston. We hid here, but I'd never lived on the streets. I'd been loved by my family and educated by my sect in both secular and magical knowledge—not to mention a robust training in self-defense.

A pang of regret hit me. I'd chosen to run and hide from the pain of my mother's murder. It had led to a lot of problems, but I'd come to terms with my responsibility in that, and with Silas's help, I'd managed to let go of a lot of misplaced guilt. But I missed my family. My parents and my brother had died fighting the Brotherhood. My Aunt Deanna, who had helped me unlock my memories, had died trying to protect our control over Earth's magic.

I let the past go with the breath I'd been holding and turned away from the glass. I didn't need to revisit those mistakes. I wasn't responsible for everything that had happened since my fateful decision to run and hide so many years ago. As I'd told Silas after regaining my memories, I was a different person than I used to be.

Sergius appeared silently at my side. I jumped at his reflection in the glass, and he threw me a concerned look. "Is all right?"

"Yeah. It's just creepy to be here at night." And I was lost in the past when I should have been focused on the future. Specifically, I should have been preparing for the meeting with Nithia, or there would be no future. "Are they here?"

As if on cue, Mother Nithia emerged from the book stacks like the living incarnation of a Fae queen from a fairytale, shrouded in a hooded cape that brushed across the floor. The deep cowl hid everything but her chin as her magic, prickling and dancing on the edge of violence, made my skin tingle. *Unstable.* My own magic rose in response, and Sergius's familiar power, strong and reassuring, also glowed around us.

When I'd first met Nithia in the Fae Haven, she'd played up her age, gray-haired and maternal. As I suspected, she was far from grandmotherly or feeble. She'd sabotaged our plans to rebind magic and had ordered Boone to kill me, and a righteous anger rose in my chest as I thought about the heads on pikes along the edge of the river.

Two others followed Nithia out of the darkness. They both had straight, black hair cropped above their shoulders and unusual almost-all-black eyes. They were identical, and a chill snaked up my spine as they moved into place on either side of Nithia in perfect sync. They were utterly wrong and inhuman.

Nithia pushed the hood off her head, draping the velvety fabric around her shoulders. Silver hair crowned her head like the halo of some dark angel. "Sergius Valeron. I was surprised to receive your message of peace, and I find myself further surprised to see you standing here without a legion of Guardians. Are you sure that's quite wise?"

"Lady Nithia"—Sergius inclined his head—"didn't we sufficiently warn you against breeding your *aberrations?* Animals should not be given human forms."

A chill skittered down my spine as I realized the pair flanking Nithia were shifters... but not humans who could turn into animals. They were animals that had somehow been given the ability to stay human. I'd last seen them as giant ravens, but I'd also seen them with her in the forest outside their Haven as large black cats. Even now, they moved stiffly and unnaturally, as if Nithia had twisted the shape-shifting magic to somehow control them. I looked at the black collars around their necks and the matching bracelets on Nithia's wrists. Whatever she had done to the poor creatures, they were tied to her, and they weren't entirely animal or human.

"Are you offering me a Child of Fate in their place? Or perhaps as penance for your heir killing mine?" She smiled at me, and the expression was purely violent.

"Your heir attacked my son, and this after he attacked Lady Maeve, an Aegis of House Valeron, whom we have the right to defend unto death," Sergius said. "Are *you* offering penance for this unprovoked attack, or perhaps for your attack against me a decade past?"

The wicked smile disappeared from Nithia's face. Although nothing changed in their blank expressions, the twins shifted onto the balls of their feet, and their bodies tensed as if ready to attack. If they had been in animal form, they would have had their ears back and their hackles up. Nithia's power crackled with strange energy that raised the hairs on the back of my neck.

The twins' magic rose, and I was more than a little alarmed to see the same dark power flaring through their auras. I stared in fascinated horror. Mother Nithia was somehow feeding her powers to them, controlling them with her magic. I'd never seen anything like it. I hadn't brought any weapons and wished I had as her magic crackled like an electric storm waiting to crash down on our heads. The unstable cloud of power raised goose bumps on my arms as the twins shifted a few steps to subtly flank us.

Sergius and I both tensed.

"My great-grandson is dead, and you came here to claim retribution?" Nithia said.

"We are not claiming retribution," Sergius said. "We came in a show of good faith to discuss a treaty between our people. Let us do that in peace."

"Very well." Nithia's magic receded as quickly as it had filled the room. The grandmotherly smile emerged on her face, and the twin creatures relaxed. "I am so intrigued by your offer, Lord Councilor. I had not realized you were capable of looking past your own self-interest to negotiate with me. A decade is a long time, even for us. So much changed in your absence."

I sucked in a breath. She was throwing what she had done in Sergius's face, completely unrepentant.

He narrowed his eyes. Showing an amazing amount of restraint, he nodded at her missing hand. "Was it retaliation, then?"

Her smile was tight. "You punished me for my desire to become a Fate, but what of your sins? Who would punish you?"

Every word she said was true, but she wasn't telling the whole truth. I wasn't sure how I knew there was more to it than simple revenge, but something had been bothering me. "Why didn't you kill Sergius, then? Why go through the effort to put him in stasis?" I glanced at Sergius. "No offense. I'm glad you're still alive, but it seems like a lot of extra work, and I want to know why."

"The Fates wanted Sergius Valeron alive. Like a fool, I did not ask for their reasoning. I now know it's because they were grooming his line—if the next generation didn't work out, they intended to start again with Sergius. Like a rutting horse."

He frowned but didn't reply to the insult. She sounded angry, and as Sergius had said, she was clearly bitter that she had done the Fates' bidding but they hadn't delivered on their promises to make her one of them.

"You couldn't handle their magic," I said.

Nithia hissed through her teeth, and her eyes went tight with anger. The dangerous instability of her powers felt like rubbing a cat the wrong way. The twins bristled at her sides.

"You aren't descended from one of the lines they groomed to be able to handle their powers," Sergius said. "The Fates have been manipulating the Valeron line for generations to ensure offspring who could. You couldn't become one of them, and they used you anyway."

She inclined her head, and some of the heat behind her eyes dissipated. "I know now, yes. They lied to me and used me. They had me doing their bidding, running their *errands*, until I grew wise to their lies."

Sergius looked thoughtful. "What do you intend now, Lady Nithia? You hold a Mundane city, taken by force. They will retaliate, and defending this land of concrete and steel will take many resources from your people. Without a dedicated source of power, you do not have enough magic to withstand them indefinitely."

Nithia's eyes narrowed, and she cocked her head. The creepy twin animals moved with her. Sergius had pretty much hit the nail on the head—the Fae were in a dilemma. "As Lady Maeve so aptly pointed out to me, we need room to expand. We need defensible land where our children and their children will thrive." She spread her arms wide. "We have a fortified position in the city, and we do not intend to give it up. The Mundanes fear our power, and their fear ensures our safety. Why should we protect you as well? What do you offer to us in exchange?"

I threw a glare in Sergius's direction, silent accusations burning behind my eyes. In front of the New Alliance, Sergius had made it sound like the Fae had already agreed to an alliance, but we clearly had some negotiating left to do.

"Their fear ensures they'll never leave you alone," he replied.

Mother Nithia raised her chin and narrowed her eyes, but her magic stayed blessedly calm.

"The Mundanes can do nothing to harm us. We took their city with minimal effort and have held it for three days. They have sent their soldiers and their weapons, and we have repelled them with ease."

"They have stronger weapons that will wipe you from the face of this Earth," I said. "They haven't used them yet because they want the city back in one piece."

Sergius spread his palms wide. "The New Alliance offers the Fae a legally acquired tract of land in the remote and natural region of Alaska for you to build a new Haven. The land is completely undeveloped, without any Mundane presence or claim for thousands of acres. Vastly bigger than the land you have taken here, and not covered in concrete."

Utter shock floored me. The Alliance had not talked about that, and I had no idea where or how he had acquired land or how he'd paid for it. The Aeternal Councilors weren't without means, but I had no idea they had that much money. I had to work very hard to hide my reaction.

Mother Nithia's brow furrowed. "If your Mundane government is so powerful, what is to prevent them from using their advanced weaponry to retaliate if we leave this city?"

"Your people can slip away, and we'll tell them you left this realm for good," Sergius explained. "You'll have the land legally, and we've arranged for it to be anonymously owned. The Lost Sect also has the knowledge to create a cloaking spell to mask any magical signature, which they have agreed to share. The Mundane government won't know where you are in order to retaliate."

His promises kept stacking up, and I struggled not to react. The Inner Circle had not actually agreed to share that spell, but if it got us the city back, they absolutely would. Sergius obviously knew that.

Nithia rocked back on her heels. "You want us to hide from the Mundanes? You think we are so weak we cannot defend ourselves?"

Sergius sighed. "Your people are isolationists. Don't pretend you want this pile of concrete you've conquered and the ongoing fight to keep it. Alaska is perfect—you'll have isolated access to nature and the legal right to occupy it. You can walk away from the mess you created when you took over the Mundane city, and you will also have a promise of support from the New Alliance. What else do you want?"

"We—"

The-floor-to ceiling pane of glass behind us shattered with the pop-pop sound of gun fire. The shifter on Nithia's left jerked backward, screeching as blood blossomed on her chest. The sound was so animalistic and wild, I knew it was fatal before the poor creature hit the ground.

At the same moment, a metal canister the size of a water bottle thunked down at my feet, and gas hissed out of it. I grabbed Sergius and dragged him away from the smoke bomb, heading for the cover of the bookshelves.

"No!" Nithia screamed as the surviving twin shrieked, transformed into a large raptor, and flew out of the broken window.

Pop-Pop-Pop! The other shifter creature screeched as it fell from the sky.

Nithia's electric power flared around her, and she disappeared. I tried to push Sergius toward the stairs, but the entire wall—multiple panels of glass—shattered, and glass rained down on us. We stumbled back in opposite directions. My back slammed against a heavy bookshelf full of books, and I dropped to the floor, covering my head as the rapid-fire popping of bullets and the whine of disruptors filled the room. More canisters flew in through the windows, rolling across the wood floor, and I choked and coughed on their thick white smoke.

As I gasped for breath on the floor, agents clothed in black tactical gear and gas masks rappelled in through the broken windows. I crawled away from them while pain radiated up my spine from the impact with the bookshelf. I needed to find Sergius. I called to him, but a burst of gunfire was the only response. I could barely see past my own face as smoke billowed into the library.

I shuffled on my hands and knees deeper into the library, away from the agents streaming through the broken windows and toward the interior stairs. "Sergius!"

"Maeve!"

Dammit. He was on the other side of the library, near the elevators, with an entire troop of agents between us. I dropped to my stomach and dug my cell phone out of my pocket. Huddled in a corner behind a pile of beanbag chairs in the children's section, I sucked in a shallow stream of fresh air from the broken windows and punched out a text to Casius.

I swore as a bright-red icon alerted me that my text hadn't gone through. DODSI must have blocked the cell signal. And taking that an obvious step further, they must have found us by tracking my phone. Sergius and I had been uselessly sneaky, leaving all the Guardians on campus despite Silas's protests, as we maneuvered carefully from the underground exit tunnel several miles away from our campus and walked to Harvard Yard. I was confident we hadn't been followed, but it was all pointless because I'd had a very convenient GPS with me the whole time.

A bullet tore into the floor right in front of me, and I dropped the phone as I scrambled backward. It slid across the floor, glowing and drawing more fire. They'd missed blowing my face off by less than an inch. I swore under my breath as I tried to slow my racing heart. I needed to get to the rear of the library, away from the windows, and around to the back staircase. I rose into a crouch then paused. I didn't know how exact the tracking was on my phone, but it wouldn't hurt to give some misdirection.

I let my magic flow around me and attached a simple skimming spell to the phone. Another round of bullets tore through the building. I scrambled out of the way as I sent a bit of magic through the spell, sending the phone to my old apartment right outside of Boston. It was a place I was familiar with, and it would be totally out of the way. It was feasible that I could have run there from the library. If I was lucky, some of the DODSI agents would chase it down once my GPS showed me on the move again.

As I crouched in the dark, trying to calm my ragged breathing, I realized I couldn't use my magic. Someone on the DODSI team, perhaps Lennart, must be able to see my flare, because every time I tried, they shot at me. I needed to find Sergius and get us both out of there, but every second ticking by seemed like an hour as I strained to hear any movement in the dark.

Eventually, the staccato pops of gunfire died down, and everything went silent. I didn't know if my trick with the cell phone had worked or if the agents were closing in on the building. Either way, I had to find Sergius. I crawled toward the other side of the library where I had last heard him. As I scooted toward the librarians' desk, I paused. The entire floor had gone eerily quiet, and the smokey haze had mostly cleared, thanks to the fresh air streaming through the broken windows. Despite my trick with the cell phone, I doubted all the agents had just left, but everything was dark, and I couldn't see anyone moving inside or out.

I didn't dare call for Sergius again. Instead, I edged out from the bookshelves, watching in all directions and listening for any sound. I spotted two people standing in front of the elevators.

I recognized Sergius Valeron, dressed in his power suit, immediately. A large DODSI agent in full tactical gear and a gas mask held Sergius in front of him with the business end of a handgun pressed to the side of his neck. From the way Sergius sagged against the larger man, I guessed he'd been hit by a disruptor blast and was unconscious.

"Maeve O'Neill!" Lennart called.

I groaned as I scrambled back into the stacks and pressed my back against the bookshelf. Of course Lennart was there, holding a gun to Sergius's head.

"Let him go, Lennart!" I called. "I don't want to have to hurt you."

"Come out, Miss O'Neill. We need to talk."

"Sure, no problem. I'd be happy to come out so you can shoot me."

"I sent the other agents toward your cell signal. It's just us, and I'm not going to shoot you... as much as I'd enjoy that."

I backtracked through the books until I could glance out the broken windows, toward the front lawn. The wide expanse of grass in front of the library was empty and dark. A small children's playground nestled on one side of the grounds glinted dully under the streetlights. I didn't see anyone out there, but that didn't mean Lennart was telling the truth. I slunk away from the windows and did a quick recon of the library floor, keeping low to avoid any potential snipers Lennart had conveniently forgotten about. "Why should I trust anything you say? You just attacked us!"

"I tried to warn you, dumbass! Look, we don't have much time. I need to talk to you."

Lennart had acted strangely when he left campus, but I'd forgotten because of the arrival of baby Sariah. I still had no idea what the hand signal had meant, but he had been trying to tell me something. I crouched near the children's books—away from the windows—and let my magic unfurl, seeking any signs of other life. I couldn't sense anyone except Lennart and Sergius, and no one tried to shoot me. "What do you want, Lennart? Spit it out!"

Lennart cursed. "Pascal has been talking to a real creeper named Four. Everyone at your compound is in danger, and a lot of innocent people are going to die if you don't come out and talk to me."

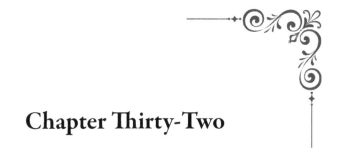

Chapter Thirty-Two

"And you believe the agent of DODSI?" Sergius's face reflected exactly how I felt—completely confused and edging close to panic.

I glanced around the library, eager to leave in case Lennart changed his mind and came back with the other agents—or Nithia, for that matter—but Sergius had barely regained consciousness and hadn't quite gotten all the way to his feet yet. He was also insisting on an explanation of what happened, despite the danger of staying at the library, where we'd been ambushed.

"DODSI had us," I said. "Lennart could have killed you or used you as bait, but he sent the other agents away and handed you back to me instead."

"Why would one of their operatives warn us?" Sergius winced as he gingerly touched the goose egg he'd gotten when Lennart had knocked him unconscious. He hadn't been hit with a disruptor, but the bump still looked painful.

"I guess he tried to warn us at the last meeting with Pascal, but I didn't understand. Four is manipulating DODSI, and Pascal is eating it up. Four convinced them the only way to get the city back is to kill anyone with magic, starting with us. DODSI is attacking the campus tonight." I rubbed Marcel's charm between my fingers. "Lennart said being freaks doesn't mean we aren't Americans, whatever that means. Turns out he does have a conscience. Plus, he has magic. I've seen it building in his aura, and I think he's realized it too. If he's got any brains in that thick skull of his, he's terrified of what that means for him."

"They won't be able to make it past the perimeter shield," Sergius said.

"I said the same thing, but I guess Four gave them a way inside. According to Lennart, it's some kind of variation on their disruptor technology. Lennart said the shielding won't be a problem. I don't know how long we have, but the alarms on campus trigger the text-alert system. If an attack were happening, we would have heard."

I remembered how the text I'd tried to send Casius hadn't gone through. "Shit! DODSI is already blocking our cell signals. It could be happening right now! We need to get back to campus!" I immediately opened myself to the magic around us and started drawing it in, but thanks to those hits from the Fae boundary defenses, I didn't have enough magic.

I was nearly blind with panic, thinking about all the families housed on our campus. If DODSI could break through our shield, we would never see an attack coming. Pascal had already threatened us... I had no doubt the government would be willing to shoot everyone with disruptors and haul them off to detention centers, never to be heard from again.

Sergius grabbed me by both shoulders. "Wait! We can't just land blindly in the middle of an attack. We'll both be captured."

"I know! I'm thinking! I don't have enough power to skim, but it's going to take too long to walk back to campus."

"Take the power from me." Sergius stood and held out his arm. "Don't gape at me. If you're right, our people are in danger and must be warned."

Surprised by his selflessness, I grabbed his forearm and drew power out of him as quickly as I could. He swayed on his feet, and I helped him sit on the ground. "Stay here until you're recovered.

Hand me your phone, and I'll give you the address of one of our safe houses. Get there as soon as you can."

"Warn them and leave. Don't be heroic." He handed me his phone, and I tapped the address into his GPS.

"Got it." I wove the magic into a skimming spell. The instant the double strand of energy formed into an archway around me, I closed my eyes, and my stomach twisted sideways. When I opened them again, I stood at the evacuation point by the auxiliary parking lot on the west side of campus. The sun had already begun to creep over the horizon, reflecting softly off half a dozen cars sitting in the lot. Someone had scrawled "Mystery Van" in bright-orange paint on the side of a broken-down Volkswagen van. That someone might have been me, but Casius would never know for sure.

The Scooby Van hid a secret entrance to the escape tunnels under the campus. With two of its wheels on wooden blocks, a cracked windshield, and peeling paint, it looked like a total junker, but Casius was a paranoid bastard, and his precautions had saved us more than once. Not only did we have multiple escape tunnels from the campus, but every family also had an assigned safe house stocked with supplies and a bug-out bag already packed.

On the far side of the parking lot, the campus's five buildings began taking shape in the morning sun, positioned like a horseshoe around the central quad area. Peering into the semi-darkness from behind the van, I surveyed the campus but couldn't see anything wrong. There were no DODSI agents anywhere in sight. Everything was silent, and the shield surrounding the campus was intact. *Was Lennart telling the truth?*

DODSI had us at the library. Lennart had no reason to let us go so he could lie about an imminent attack. And he hated me on a personal level. I figured he would have taken any opportunity to shoot me with a disruptor and haul me off, but he hadn't. He'd warned us instead, because he was an asshole but not a murderer. This was bigger than our petty rivalry.

I needed to sound the silent alarm. DODSI had a way to breach the shield, which meant everyone was in danger, and I needed to get the families out of there as quickly and quietly as possible—better safe than sorry.

I put my hand on the door panel of the van and let a sliver of my magic soak into the cold metal. The soft click of the lock sounded like a firecracker going off in the dark. I froze, waiting for some hidden DODSI agent to pop up and shoot me. After a tense moment, I slid the well-oiled door open, pulled up the metal trap door in the van's floor, then peered into the large hole in the ground.

A wave of *something* washed over me. I scrambled out of the van and looked up. It wasn't magic, but whatever had washed over the campus had completely obliterated the shield protecting us. The slight shimmer of magic that typically surrounded us was gone. There wasn't an explosion or any obviously unraveling magic threads. The spell had just disappeared, as if the entire conjuring had evaporated in an instant. I gaped up at it.

An ear-splitting alarm went off across the campus—the breach alarm, blaring like the cry of a wounded animal. My stomach dropped. I was too late.

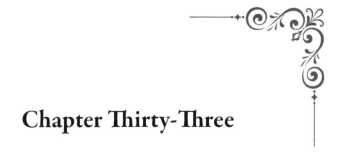

Chapter Thirty-Three

The alarm wailed as I took off in a sprint toward campus. It took several minutes to cross the parking lot, round the corner of the westernmost building, and reach the edge of the grassy central area. All five buildings on our campus were lit up in the morning dusk.

A blur of movement caught my eye as a group of black-clad agents sporting night-vision goggles sprinted across the quad like their butts were on fire, moving away from the buildings.

As I tried to figure out what the heck they were doing, a heart-stopping explosion tore through the central admin building, sending glass and chunks of concrete flying. I dropped and covered my head as debris shot out the front doors. A blazing tower of fire ripped out of the roof, straight into the sky.

My ears rang as I tried to absorb the insane amount of destruction in front of me. The administration building was engulfed in fire. The entire first floor had exploded outward through the front doors, and black smoke rolled out of the gaping hole. The deserted, previously pristine quad was covered in chunks of concrete the size of small cars, and the grand staircase that had once swept up to the all-glass front of the former hospital was a pile of rubble.

By some miracle, they'd hit our only non-residential building. Hundreds of families were housed in buildings one and two on either side, but that central structure had been used primarily for meetings.

My relief was short-lived, as people poured out of those residential buildings and onto the quad. DODSI agents decked out in tactical gear and bristling with guns emerged from the dark and surrounded them. The unsuspecting crowd on the quad didn't see the agents coming as they gaped at the burning admin building.

DODSI had used the explosion to flush them out.

"Run!" My magic rose around me to amplify my voice. "It's an ambush! Get to the tunnels!"

Those closest to me heard my warning and immediately turned and ran back into the buildings, but there were too many still pouring outside, and it created a bottleneck. I kept yelling, but the smoke and the blaring alarm confused everything, and no one knew where to go or what was happening. More people continued to flood onto the quad, like fish in a barrel for DODSI to pick off with their disruptors.

The harsh crack of assault rifles sounded as bullets ripped into the crowd without warning. Dozens were mowed down.

"No!" I yelled as my heart leapt into my throat. Terrified screams filled the quad as the DODSI agents shot the innocent. Horror froze me as my people ran in all directions, but there was nowhere for them to go. They were surrounded, out in the open.

I sprinted forward and threw my magic into a shield between DODSI and the others. "The tunnels! Evacuate to the tunnels!"

My shield was peppered with bullets as people turned back toward the buildings, dragging the wounded with them. If DODSI switched to disruptors and hit me, I would be knocked out and completely vulnerable, but they were more intent on murdering people than stopping me, and their bullets were ineffective against my shield.

"Back inside! To the tunnels!" I held the shield as the crowd finally got back inside the building, but my efforts bought us only a few minutes before the whine of disruptors powering up pierced my ears.

With only a handful of people left on the quad, I waited as long as I possibly could before I reeled my magic in, dropped my shield, and sprinted for the closest building—building three. As I ran, I yelled for everyone to take cover. A wave of magic-disrupting energy blazed toward me, and I dove behind a pile of debris, scraping my palms and arms as I rolled over broken concrete and glass.

From the relative safety of my pile of rubble, I could barely make out the dark blurs of DODSI agents as they maneuvered closer. The damn breach alarm was still blaring, along with the fire alarm, sending people out into the quad and straight into the ambush. I needed to shut it off and sound the evacuation alarm, but I'd have to reach the security control room right off the main lobby to do that. If I could, though, people would head for the tunnels instead of outside into the ambush.

As I crouched and hid from DODSI's advancing soldiers, I assessed my options. The security control room was on the right side of the admin building, but the lobby was on fire, and I couldn't run in through flames and wreckage. I would need to travel there via the adjacent building. Unfortunately, without a line-of-sight destination, I couldn't skim in and risk landing in the middle of the fire. I'd have to make a run for building three and take the interior hallway on the first floor, which let out at the back of the lobby, closest to the control room.

I eyeballed the distance from my hiding spot to the doorway, raised a shield tightly around me, and ran for it. Right then, another group of people spilled out of the building and into the quad.

I waved my arms frantically above my head. "Go back! Go back!" My yells, or maybe the sight of the DODSI agents rising behind me with their weapons, turned the people around, and we all ran back inside the building. A spray of bullets hit the shield at my back, and then I cleared the door and slid into the building.

"Get to the escape tunnels. Tell anyone you see. Go to the tunnels!" As the panicked crowd veered away from the exit, I took a sharp left and ran down the interior hallway that would put me at the back of the main lobby. I was able to run only about a dozen yards before thick black smoke filled the hallway and chunks of broken stone and debris blocked my way. I swore and backtracked to an interior stairwell. I'd have to head up one level to the balcony overlooking the central atrium and drop down from there.

I pounded up the stairs and emerged into the abandoned radiology wing on the second floor. Water blasted out of the automatic sprinklers, and I was instantly soaked. Flashing emergency lights illuminated the smoke pouring from the atrium like storm clouds. I pulled my shirt collar over my nose and mouth, trying not to cough. I wove a thin layer of magic around myself like a personal shield as I ran. It wasn't air-proof, since I needed to breathe, but it helped to filter some of the smoke and the increasing heat as I ran toward the atrium and the source of the fire. Coughing, I reached the end of the hallway and almost skidded right off the edge.

I swore as I caught myself on the twisted wreckage of the banister and levered myself back onto solid ground. The second-floor balcony overlooking the atrium had completely crumbled. The entire lobby had been smashed to bits—nothing but charred chunks of stone and wood remained of the formerly beautiful, open space. The atrium floor had become a giant crater where DODSI had detonated a very powerful bomb. Even the massive stones that had formed the portal to Aeterna were nothing more than crushed debris.

The moon peeked in from the gaping hole in the roof as flames licked up the walls and consumed the upper floors of the building, reaching for the sky. With the oxygen fueling it, the fire was going to spread fast.

Smoke obscured my view, but the door to the control room lay behind the reception area, near where the front doors had been blown out. The wrecked metal banister was hanging off the second floor like a ladder, still firmly attached to the wall on one side. I tested my weight on it with one foot then the other before climbing toward the first floor, dropping the rest of the distance at a little over halfway. I landed on uneven ground and had to crouch to regain my balance. Carefully, I crawled over piles of broken wood until I reached the reception area. I touched something soft. I recoiled in horror as I discovered what was left of the dead night guard.

I couldn't pause to digest the awfulness of the situation, but the path between the reception desk and the security room was clear. The solid metal door was locked, but the handle didn't turn when I put my hand on it. I released it and carefully put my index finger against the reader once again. Nothing.

Dammit! Casius had locked me out of the secure areas on campus, and he apparently hadn't gotten around to reinstating my access yet. I couldn't get in. My horror had to take a backseat as I backtracked to the dead guard, found his arm, and used his fingerprint to unlock the door.

A cloud of smoke spilled into the room with me, and I pushed it closed as I scanned the myriad of buttons on the security consoles. Panic threatened to choke me, but then I noticed the conveniently labeled fire-alarm switch. *Bless your hyperorganized ass, Casius.* I flipped it, and the alarm shut off. The resulting quiet was deafening.

I switched on the labeled evacuation alarm—a three-buzz bell that sounded like someone ringing an old-fashioned elevator—and exhaled in relief. Everyone would know to go to the escape tunnels and to keep running to the safe houses. We'd drilled it dozens of times since the Aeternals had joined us. They just needed time to get the hell out.

I went back into the atrium, but the smoke had gotten so thick that I couldn't see more than a few feet in front of me. And it was hot as hell. Steam came off my already wet shirt as I exited through the gaping hole at the front of the building, and I drew in a deep breath of blessedly cool, fresh air.

A disruptor blast blazed over my head. I dove to the ground, wrapping my magic around me. The shield wouldn't help if I got hit by a disruptor, but the harsh *pop-pop-pop* of automatic weapons made me weave the spell tighter as I crawled behind a broken stone column. I formed my magic into a sphere in my right palm and poked out from behind the pile of rubble long enough to sight the agents closest to me then lobbed it in their direction.

DODSI agents went flying. I ducked as gunfire peppered the stone around me, throwing chunks of marble the size of my fist into the air. I hadn't seen any Guardians, and I didn't know what Silas was doing—I focused on our bond for a moment, but all I could pick up was his steady presence. No panic or fear. I had to assume he was helping with the evacuation and was safe.

As the evacuation alarm kept ringing, I stayed on the quad, holding the ground between the agents and the buildings. I considered somehow gathering reinforcements, but Silas and the Guardians needed to help with the evacuation effort.

I could hold the line. Every second DODSI focused on me gave my people that much more time to evacuate. The whine of disruptors eventually joined the bullets, and I sank lower behind the debris. A single hit from one of those blasts would mean it was over.

I gathered magic as I waited for a break in their fire, twisting my power into a bigger and bigger orb between my palms. When the gunfire finally paused, I lobbed the ball of energy at the agents. I needed to reserve enough power to skim out if necessary, but I had enough for that and a few well-placed diversions.

The explosion and shouts confirmed I'd hit my target. I risked an extra second of exposure to scan the area and spotted a knot of agents rushing onto the quad and toward the buildings. They were covered in black tactical gear and carried bulky disruptors strapped across their backs and automatic rifles in their hands.

The sharp staccato of weapons fire and the whine of magic-killing blasts beat against my ears as I squatted behind the pile of rubble, breathing heavily. I'd been back outside for about four minutes—not long enough to help much in an evacuation. I wove magic into another orb and threw it toward the sound of gunfire, but the barrage of bullets was relentless. I crouched low as I continued blindly lobbing magic, but I was pinned down and unable to do anything about those agents headed toward the residential building.

Eventually, the whine of disruptor blasts quieted, and I risked popping my head above the rubble again. I spotted three agents with disruptors, silently working their way around both sides of my position. A wave of disruptor energy had me ducking back down. I needed to move. I considered skimming out, but I'd gained maybe ten minutes. I could do more. I needed to keep drawing their attention.

At least thirty yards separated me from the next available cover—the twisted remains of the admin building's front doors, which had been flung into the quad. Behind me, flames had finally engulfed the upper floors of the admin building and half of building one, burning out of the second-floor windows. The other buildings remained unscathed, but it would be a long dash with no cover to either of them.

Boom! Another explosion blasted into the sky, punching me in the chest. I flipped head over feet as I was tossed backward over broken ground. The entire roof of building three rained down on the quad, and flames shot out of the shattered dorm windows. Fire engulfed the building and lit up the sky.

No! I rose to my feet, choking on a scream of horror. Families lived there.

A spray of bullets slammed into my shield right over my chest, and I jerked backward. A sizzle of electricity zipped past me, grazing my left arm. I gasped and dropped to the ground, clutching my arm. My entire arm was numb, and I couldn't form a shield. I tried again, but I couldn't quite make my magic respond. My powers were fuzzy and weak, but since the blast had barely hit me, I managed to stay conscious.

"Shit! Shit! Shit!" A barrage of disruptor blasts and bullets flew over my head as I flattened myself on the ground. Thick black smoke coated the air, hiding me from the DODSI agents searching for me, but I had no idea where they were, either. I'd landed at least ten feet from my previous spot, but they would come looking. I swallowed more swears when I realized that some of them had circled the pile of rubble where I'd been hiding, guns drawn. They hadn't seen me sprawled on the ground only a short distance away, but it was only a matter of looking in my direction and the wind blowing the wrong way. I was out of time and options.

I tried to gather my magic around me and skim, but nothing happened. My head was pounding. I took a deep breath, pushed my panic down, and rolled to my feet. Gripping my numb arm with my right hand, I dashed for the entrance to the admin building, which was a good fifty yards away. There was almost no chance I could make it, but I hoped the heavy smoke would provide some cover as I leapt over broken chunks of building and raced for the flaming structure.

A spray of bullets chased me as I ran erratically, tripping over debris while I ran. I tried again to call enough magic to power a skimming spell. *Nothing.* Twenty yards stretched between me and cover. I heaved myself up the ruined stone stairs, pushing my aching legs and lungs to keep going.

A soldier in black tactical gear popped out of the smoke to my right and raised his rifle. I lurched sideways in a useless attempt to avoid the point-blank hit as he sighted the weapon at my chest.

Golden magic flashed, and Silas appeared behind the soldier, sword in hand. He smashed his left fist onto the gun's muzzle, sending the bullets slamming into the ground at my feet, then ran the man through with his sword.

I staggered backward, first shocked by his appearance then flooded with relief. Ethan appeared in another burst of magic, pulling me forward and up the stairs as his own power wrapped us in a protective shield. We took the stairs two at a time as we raced into the admin building with Silas right on our heels, throwing magic behind us.

Our backs slammed against the inside wall of the destroyed lobby. I braced my hands on my knees as I tried to catch my breath but caught a lungful of smoke instead.

"Are you injured?" Silas asked.

I checked to make sure I hadn't acquired any extra holes. "I was hit with part of a disruptor blast. I can't get a hold on my magic." I tried again, but it was barely more than a buzz of energy. I'd been damn lucky to have taken only an indirect hit, but I was out of juice. "Are you okay? Both of you?"

"No holes," Ethan confirmed.

"That's because neither of us tried taking on the enemy army all on our own," Silas groused as he wiped the bloody sword on his pant leg then sheathed it at his hip. He grasped my forearm. "You don't have time for a natural recovery. I can boost your magic."

I agreed quickly, and his magic flooded through our bond, filling me with joyous warmth.

It suddenly hit me just how close I'd come to dying and how many people were likely already dead. My adrenaline was crashing, and fear chased hot on its heels. "They want us all dead. They're trying to *kill* us." My magic rose around me, strong again thanks to Silas's boost, and I forced myself not to give in to the horror dragging its nails down my spine. "Did everyone get out?"

Silas glanced at the hole in the front of the building, but the smoke was too thick to see what was happening on the quad. "Not yet. DODSI has four towers placed around the campus, and whatever they're doing is disrupting the perimeter shielding spell. We must regroup and take them out before the shield can be reconjured. DODSI already sent in a second wave of soldiers to surround the campus. We saw them from the roof, right before you did that heroic shite on the quad."

"I was buying time for the evacuation." And ignoring Sergius's very sage advice not to do anything heroic.

Silas pulled me into his arms. "I lost at least three decades of my life by watching that. Please don't do that again."

"Can't make any promises. Got a reputation to uphold." I choked on smoke and started coughing, ruining my jaunty attempt at humor.

He shook his head. "This is my punishment for all the stupid shite I've done in the name of honor and glory."

"We can't stay here," Ethan said, glancing around the burning building.

"Is everyone out?" I coughed again. "Did building three evacuate before the bomb went off?"

"Our best drills clocked at fifteen minutes for a total evacuation. You bought us an extra ten, but..." Silas shook his head. "We don't know yet."

"We need to buy them more time!"

"Anyone who could get out already has," he said bluntly.

"Where's Casius? Did he make it out?"

Ethan shook his head. "I don't know. We need to get to one of the safe houses and figure out—"

Five agents rushed through the hole in the front of the building, spraying the atrium with bullets as they fanned out directly in front of us.

"Down!" Silas barked. Magic flared around him, and he sent a wave of it toward the soldiers. It hit two of the agents, who went flying off their feet.

The remaining three raised disruptors in our direction. Thanks to Silas's boost, I wove my magic into a shield, but Ethan put himself in front of me, and the disruptor blast hit him directly in the chest.

"Ethan!" I caught him as he crumpled.

Silas threw a second wave of magic, and the agents retreated outside as I dragged Ethan deeper into the atrium. There was no good cover and no exit. Everything was on fire. The DODSI agents blocked the only way out. We were out of safe places to hide.

There were no safe places anymore.

"We need to retreat," Silas said. "We can't hold our position any longer, and DODSI has a third wave prepared on the eastern side of campus. While those towers stand, this isn't a defensible position."

Our beautiful campus was smoldering ruins. Entire families had been killed. Everyone who was going to survive had already been evacuated. I nodded. "It's over."

I gathered my magic around me and twisted it into the domed pattern of a skimming spell. Silas scooped up Ethan and sent his own power into the conjuring. Together, we skimmed away from the ruins of our home.

Chapter Thirty-Four

Sunlight filtered through the stained-glass windows of Trinity Church, bathing Mother Nithia in its ethereal glow. Her long silver hair flowed around her shoulders. She looked like an angel, except for the edge of crazy in her green eyes as she glared at Silas and me. Even Ethan, draped over Silas's shoulder and half unconscious, didn't escape her disdain. She still wore the black bracelets and ring, but her pets were noticeably absent after our run-in with DODSI at the library. I was pretty sure that they'd both taken bullets, one was dead, and I wasn't sure whether one could survive without the other.

The Fae Queen pursed her lips as she took in our pathetic state. I was wet, covered in dirt and bloody scrapes, and hadn't slept in... well, I didn't know how long. My long auburn hair was half unbraided, and my clothes were torn. Silas was covered in dried blood and carried Ethan, who was in his pajamas, and we all reeked of smoke. We looked like the destitute refugees we were, but we had nowhere else to go.

Behind her, Nithia's people filled the cross-shaped inner sanctum of the landmark chapel in Copley Square, silent as death.

I didn't know how many had been killed in the explosions or gunned down by DODSI on the quad. I couldn't get a hold of Casius on Ethan's cell, but we were able to talk to both Tamara and Tessa and learned that almost a thousand people, including Sergius, Stephan, and Aria, had checked in at our various safe houses across the country. That left almost nine hundred unaccounted for. We discussed a rescue effort, but the chances of anyone else surviving the destruction were incredibly slim. And with DODSI likely waiting there for us, we had to focus on finding a safe place for everyone who had made it out.

"You can keep the city." I repeated the promise that had gotten me past the Fae border and in front of Nithia. "We'll help you defend it against DODSI." The Fae weren't known for their compassionate hearts, so I'd presented our case on logic alone. Helping us would help them. We had nothing left but our magic. I hated begging Nithia for help, but we had nowhere else to go. I had thousands of people to protect from a government intent on murdering them. Nowhere was safe for us anymore.

Her frown was unsympathetic. "You have nothing to offer in exchange for our help. We already have this city."

I glanced into the rafters, where the church's pipe organ loomed. More Fae had lined up along the balcony, glowing with blue elemental magic. Not only were we basically defenseless, but Nithia had already tried to kill me once, and Silas had killed her great-grandson. One word from Nithia, and they would decimate us. With some effort, I kept my own magic from rising.

"As I told you before, the Mundanes have a weapon that can disrupt magic on a large scale. They attacked us and took down the protection spell around our campus. They murdered innocent families. Children." My voice caught as I forced my emotions not to hit me yet. I had to make Nithia see why DODSI was a threat to the Fae and that they needed us despite how desperate we were. "They've declared war on anyone with magic. An alliance between our people would make us both stronger. Our only chance is to stand together against them. If you agree to this alliance, we'll help you protect the city when they inevitably use their technology against you. The only reason they haven't yet is because Four pointed them at us first."

I straightened my shoulders, refusing to show my rising anxiety. If she didn't take us in, I didn't know where we would go. Those without enough magic to skim out of Boston would have to leave the area on foot, passing the National Guard, the Coast Guard, the Boston Police, the US Army, and a handful of other military units already camped outside of the Fae's claimed territory. Even those who could skim would be on the run. Thanks to DODSIs lies, we were international terrorists.

Silas adjusted his grip on Ethan as Nithia's silence stretched on. Neither of us had accessed our magic, and it was taking a lot of my personal willpower not to.

"It would seem you need us more than we need you. What do the Fae gain from a bargain of this kind?" The question was rhetorical, and her slightly raised voice carried across the sanctuary. She'd already made up her mind. "We are safe within our territory. We fear not the Mundanes and their technology."

We were about to lose our last scrap of hope. There was nowhere to hide and no way to run quickly enough. My mind raced for the right words, for something to say or do that would make my people safe. Panic flared, wild and hot in my chest.

"Your defenses are based on Mundane technology," I replied loudly, cutting off the murmurs of agreement from the Fae. "They will find a way to disable it with time."

"Our magic is what protects us. The Fae are more than able to stand on our own."

"Not surrounded by a Mundane city," Silas said. "You took over a land where nature has been strangled. Instead of forests and waters, you have buildings and concrete. You have their cars and streets instead of animals and hunting trails. Your magic is weaker than it was under the restrictions of the Aeternal Council. This hubris will be your downfall."

A small murmur went through the Fae, and I knew he'd hit on something. I raised my voice. "We need each other, Mother Nithia. As a united people, joined by magic, we can stand against the real threat."

She sniffed delicately and lowered her voice. "A lesser person would demand an apology. I was right about the Mundanes, and you should have taken heed of my words." She arched a single eyebrow at me.

"I have no pride left. We lost too many people today, and thousands of others, including innocent children, will die if you turn us away. This is the easiest bargain you'll ever make."

The Fae had a thing about kids, and I hoped the slight tightening of her face meant I'd hit a nerve. Even more importantly, I was setting up a bargain that was clearly in her favor, and she wouldn't gain any points with her people by demanding more.

"The Mundane people will always fear us," Nithia said. "Establishing our superior power is the only way to ensure our safety. You learned that lesson the hard way, as they say."

I dug my nails into my palms as my anger resurfaced. Maybe Nithia hadn't been wrong about the Mundane government fearing us, but it had started with the Fae taking over an entire city and killing people who had done nothing to them. "You were wrong to take this city by force. Your actions pushed the Mundane government into treating all of us like terrorists." It was stupid to say, but I couldn't stop myself.

Nithia's expression went flat. "That is an unusual apology."

Silas threw me a look, warning me to back down. Nithia was baiting me. She wanted me to get angry and do something stupid so she would have a reason to turn down our bargain without appearing weak in front of her people. I took a deep breath. I could either ask the Fae to help us or try to punish them for what they'd started. In the end, the government I had trusted to protect us had betrayed us and killed innocent people while they slept. There was no choice left. My pride and anger took a backseat. "The Mundanes' bigotry and fear were already in motion before this. We need each other more than we need to point fingers."

"We're offering a bargain that is more than fair," Silas added. "You can accept us as equals and build a new alliance, or you can choose to use our current situation to subjugate your magical kin, just as you claim the Aeternal Council did to the Fae."

A tremor of unease rippled through the Fae, and Nithia's nose wrinkled, exposing the edges of her teeth. "You cannot use the wrongs of the Council to guilt me into an alliance which doesn't benefit the Fae, Silas Valeron."

Silas bowed slightly, hand over heart. His voice was barely loud enough for me to hear. "Lady Nithia, do you want revenge on the Fates for what they did—corrupting your magic and stealing your heir from you?"

A tremendous swell of magic rose around Nithia, and I had to stop myself from flinching. It felt like an electrical storm, and the hairs on my arms stood on end. The air seemed to thicken with the weight of the power she radiated. Her face transformed into a dark snarl of hatred. "You speak promises you cannot deliver."

"I know how to end them... permanently." Silas's gaze was steel as he met her disbelieving narrow-eyed glare.

"How? Tell me what you have planned."

His statement surprised me. We'd discussed binding magic to prevent them from gaining access to our realm, but we hadn't talked about a way to kill them. I wondered why he hadn't said something about it before.

He shook his head. "I cannot reveal what I know without spoiling the opportunity to end them. We need each other to defeat the Fates, and my plan requires that you accept us into the city as equals."

Nithia angrily sucked air through her teeth.

"My hands are tied, but I speak the truth," he said. "I am willing to bind my word with magic if necessary."

Her eyes gleamed. "If you know a way, I am willing to agree to the terms of your bargain."

And just like that, we had our bargaining chip. Nithia wanted revenge against the Fates, and she needed us to get it. So I added one more condition. "Our bargain includes opening the borders to my people and giving them housing in the city. And if we're going to be one people united by magic, then anyone with magic abilities—Fae, Human, Shifter, any Mundane who develops powers—*anyone* who has magic will need a haven from DODSI. We're going to be that place."

The Fae Queen bowed her head slightly. "You have bargained well, Lady Maeve of the Earthen Harvesters, and I accept the terms of your offer. Let us be agreed." Her tone shifted to match her intense expression. "Now, tell me what must be done to kill the Fates."

Chapter Thirty-Five

Mother Nithia's arms rose from her sides, her fingers spread wide as she balanced on top of the Fenway Park sign inside the stadium, right over the announcer's box. My stomach twisted. It was an awfully long fall, but she didn't seem bothered as she prepared to take the focal position in the largest conjuring circle I'd ever seen. Almost eleven hundred people, Fae, Human, and Shifter, stood arms-width apart at the highest level of the arena, ringing the entire baseball stadium.

Nithia had agreed quickly to our plan and allowed my people into the city. Within a few hours, she'd mobilized the Fae to help skim survivors from our safe houses and gave us the entire Back Bay neighborhood for housing. A few more people made it to the safe houses, including Gia with my niece, Marcille, and all of the former Aeternal Councilors, but we'd lost over eight hundred fifty people in the attack.

No one had heard from Casius or Jason, which I hoped meant that more survivors would trickle in. My throat tightened, and I struggled to breathe as I grappled with the thought that Casius might be gone. I forced myself to believe he was still headed to the safe house because I couldn't process the alternative.

With the entire city emptied, there was plenty of food in the grocery stores and other supplies to get our people settled. It was creepy to take over other people's hastily abandoned homes, but we didn't have any other choice. By nightfall, everyone who had escaped the attack on campus had a place to sleep and food in their stomachs. We were safe for the time being, and the very next morning, everyone who wasn't injured gathered at the iconic baseball stadium, standing in the chilly pre-autumn air.

Nithia had been insistent about stopping the Fates as quickly as possible, and I agreed that despite our losses, we couldn't afford to wait. I turned in a slow circle on the field, confirming everyone was ready. We had two conjuring circles set up, and all of the Harvesters had joined my circle, focused on drawing in the power that had spread outside of Boston. Nithia took the focal point on the second conjuring circle with everyone else, and their job was to hold the magic in one place until we could bind it.

The giant stone table with the sigils representing each of the layers of the binding conjuring had been placed over the pitcher's mound. Tamara, Sergius, Nero, Octavia, Alaric, Alannah, and Gia each took positions around the table. Tessa, Silas, and I planned to join them and round out the final positions, along with Nithia and one of her people representing the Fae interests, making it so the twelve of us would be able to immediately access Earth's magic once it was bound.

Silas stood with me at second base while everyone took their places. I glanced at Ethan, who had been steady and unfazed despite taking on as much risk as I had—more, if my high-powered magic mojo stunt ended up burning out his magic permanently.

"I'm here if you start to lose it," he said to me.

"Are you ready?" Silas asked.

I nodded. "I hope this works."

"It will."

I could feel his confidence radiating through our bond, and I let it bolster me. Silas handed me his cell phone, and I tapped the speaker button. "Ready, Lennart?"

"In position," he replied crisply. "Awaiting your signal."

Lennart and a small team of DODSI defectors had shown up at the Fae border, holding signs with my name on them. They'd been smart enough to keep their distance from the tree line, and eventually, one of the Fae decided to tell me about it. Lennart and some of the others had developed magic, and under the terms of our agreement, Nithia had no choice but to let them into the city. It had taken some convincing for Nithia to let in Lennart's agents, who hadn't developed magic but didn't want any part in what DODSI was doing, and all their terrified families, too, but we'd managed to relocate everyone safely inside the city limits.

It was strange to be on the same side with Lennart. He was still an asshole, but apparently, there were lines he didn't want to cross, such as murdering innocent families in their sleep. And he wouldn't have been any more welcome under DODSI's antimagic rules than any of us.

He'd taken three of DODSI's armored Jeeps and a small arsenal of weapons with him when he left, and I decided to put his team to work positioning the two new keystones the Fae had helped us create. Lennart loaded them into the backs of their trucks, and they were already standing by to place them around the city. Once they were in position, the new stones would align with the three under DODSI's control, and the boundary spell would reactivate. After that, I would work with the Harvesters to pull the magic back within the boundary, and then we could rebind it into a single source.

"Start your countdown, and remember, if you don't get our signal in twenty minutes—"

"I know the plan, O'Neill. I'll get the families out and run as far as possible before the world goes to hell," Lennart said. "But it's not going to be necessary. You're not going to let the whole world down, no matter what it takes."

He hung up before I could respond.

Silas took his phone back then placed something around my neck. I looked down to find the Heart of Valeron diamond set on a long gold chain. "It's going to work."

I grasped the stone with both hands. "I know. Because I'm not losing you again."

Confidence radiated through our bond. "Forever and always." He released me and stepped into the amplification circle he'd chalked onto the infield behind second base. His magic flared a beautiful golden yellow, and he began to work. It took him five minutes to power up the Ascension spell, and I loved every second of it. I'd seen him on battlefields, wielding his sword, but watching Silas work magic was, well, magic. He worked his way around the circle, graceful and powerful in every movement as he poured his magic into the lines of the conjuring.

Ethan's magic anchored me as I stepped into the Ascension spell with Silas, and an intense wash of amplified magic filled me. With those connections in place, I reached out to the Harvester circle, and the familiar extension of my own powers fell into place. With the circle and the amplification spell, I was aware of every life within the city—our people, Nithia's wild magic from the circle above us, and even the birds and stray dogs around the stadium.

Every ounce of that energy glowed in my mind as I let my magic grow. I was connected with every person in my circle and to every living thing within our combined magical reach. It was full of variety, like the many colors of a rainbow melding into a perfect, harmonious band of energy. When I felt like my entire being had stretched as far and wide as I could tolerate, I raised my arms high above my head and signaled the Harvester circle to pull with me.

We drew a massive amount of magic through our circle. My breath hitched as it washed over me. I allowed all that power to pass through us and then to Nithia's circle, which wove the raw energy into a huge sphere that floated above the stadium. At the same time,

Tamara and the others began building the first layers of the binding spell, preparing to work quickly once we finished drawing all of it into the stadium. We had carefully planned each step of our plan because the Fates could show up at any point and were likely to be alerted by the massive movement of magic we were orchestrating.

As if we were one being, my circle flexed ourselves outward again and called in more magic. We kept pulling and releasing until my breathing matched the effort. It wasn't nearly as desperate and taxing as it had been when I held all of the keystone's magic inside of me for a brief time, but it wasn't a picnic, either. Breathe and pull, exhale and release. The power passed through me repeatedly, like cresting waves of an ocean, and additional layers of magic formed above us, held by the circle Nithia directed. So much energy and life.

On the next draw, the power was so filling and sweet and the release so bitter that I didn't want to let it go. If I held onto the magic, it would fill me up and make me happy forever. The world flexed around me, going white at the edges of my vision.

"You're losing it!" Ethan called. "You need to pull back!"

My eyes flew open, and my entire body quivered with the weight of the magic as I lost my focus. I gritted my teeth as I surveyed the giant ball of energy building above the field. Sweat dripped down my back, soaking my shirt. Our plan was working, but I wavered under the enormity of what we were doing.

"She can handle it," Silas snapped. "Stop distracting her."

Through our bond, his steady presence held me up. He took my hands, and I exhaled shakily and released the magic.

"Keep going!" I told them. The aching need to hold onto the power was not new. Magic was addictive. I'd already faced that particular temptation, and I was stronger for it. Some things, like the connections with people I loved, mattered more to me than ultimate power. I squeezed Silas's hands and absorbed his unwavering confidence in me. I could do this. I just had to gather all of Earth's magic into one place and not drown under its weight. *No big.*

With a deep breath, I recentered myself then dragged the magic into the park and released it. Pull and inhale, exhale and release. Each draw of power decreased as we neared the end, and the magic that had slowly spread over the East Coast was contained in the middle of Fenway.

Silas checked his cell phone. "Lennart is in position."

"Tell him to place the stones."

Silas tapped out a text to Lennart then waved a hand over his head, signaling everyone that we were about to cross the point of no return.

I held my breath, waiting for Four to show up. With the boundary spell intact once more, there was no way the Fates wouldn't know we were trying to rebind magic. They would try to stop us, and we would do our best to take care of them once and for all. Silas and I stared at each other, not even daring to breathe. "Why haven't they taken the bait?"

He shook his head. "Let's not squander the gift of their inattention. Signal the next phase."

I released the last of the power to Nithia's circle as Silas and I left the amplification spell. Nithia skimmed down onto the field and placed her palm on the stone table. Silas and I joined her, taking the final two positions in the circle.

"First binding layer." Tamara had already constructed the initial layer of magic, and she tied it off quickly. "Done. Second layer—Alannah?" Tamara led us around the table clockwise, with each person finishing the layer they'd started to weave.

The binding spell was a series of twelve increasingly complex conjurings, requiring both the knowledge of how to complete each one and significant focus. We needed to move quickly, and thanks to our prep work, the less complicated layers formed quickly and slid into place around the giant sphere of magic the Fae held above the stadium. "Tenth binding. Ready, Lady Nithia?"

Nithia placed her palm on the table and began weaving the threads of the most complex layer so far. After several moments, she tied it off with a loud exhale. "It is done. Where are they?"

"They should be here, trying to stop us," Silas replied quietly. "We need them physically in this realm, or our plan won't work."

"Go ahead, Silas," Tamara prompted.

Silas completed the eleventh binding layer while our collective tension rose. It was good that the Fates hadn't shown up to stop us before we could finish the binding... unless they didn't show up at all. I had a nagging feeling that they knew what we were doing, and their absence felt ominous.

"Done," Silas said.

"Maeve? Should we start the last binding layer?" Tamara asked.

We didn't have any contingency plans for the Fates *not* showing up. I didn't know what to do. "I can at least get started."

"I agree. Start the conjuring, but don't complete it," Silas said. "Magic must be unbound for them to access this realm fully."

I was exhausted as I placed my palm onto the sigil in front of me. I'd known that harvesting Earth's magic and completing the most complex of the binding layers would be a lot, but I wanted to make sure I took the final conjuring. Because of the amount of magic required, Silas, Nithia, or I had to take it on. I didn't trust Nithia, and Silas agreed that he would be the best one to put up a distraction for the Fates when they showed. That left me to finish the binding.

It took a lot of finesse to weave the new threads of magic in and out of the others. I'd memorized the necessary pattern, but building on and through the other layers was detailed work, and I had to concentrate to make sure I didn't mess it up and cause the entire thing to unravel.

I paused without tying it off. Without the Fates, I couldn't finish the binding around our new source, but before we had to start brainstorming a way to force our guests of honor to come to the party, two glowing figures appeared on the field. Four and Two burned with power so entirely consuming that my brain couldn't quite comprehend the enormity of the magic emanating from them. My heart stuttered in their presence. I hadn't seen Two since I'd killed the oldest member of their trio, and the Fate's ageless, genderless face was creepier than ever. Four couldn't quite manage to pass as human, but Two didn't even try.

Before I had a chance to finish the binding, Four raised his palm in my direction, and ice-cold power gripped me like a clamp around my chest. I blinked, and then Silas and I were kneeling in front of the Fates in the middle of the field. I gasped as their magic squeezed me harder, barely able to breathe. All I could do was hang on to the still-unfinished final binding layer with everything I had.

"Why do you continue to fight against your fate, mortals?"

"Go to hell," Silas snapped, displaying a timely grasp of modern slang.

"What of you, Maeve O'Neill? Will you accept eternal life and infinite power to save all the souls the two of you have placed in mortal peril?" Four waved a hand, indicating the stadium full of people.

The threat was clear. One of us had to join the Fates, or he would kill everyone. "You can't do that."

"Can't I?" Four replied. "You've vastly underestimated what I can do in the past."

"You manipulate and lie," Silas replied, "but you can't take away someone's free will. You can't force us against our will, and you can't end a life directly."

"Enough. What of the other Valeron?" Two demanded in their sharp childlike voice. The Fates both glanced in Sergius's direction by home base, where he was already powering up his house's amplification spell.

"Leave him out of this," Silas said.

"We put so much effort into these two. Let us reap the full rewards." Four replied then winked at us. "We'll take you both. You will stop resisting if we grant you both the gift of our power, and in return, we will spare these mortals."

The Fates' cold tendrils of magic wound through my body, needling into my brain and wrapping around my heart. I couldn't think. My brain was full of icy fog. I should have panicked, but I couldn't feel anything. I didn't want to become one of them, but I wondered whether willingly joining them would make us able to fight their influence long enough to stop them.

Silas grasped my hand, grounding me. Through our bond, the warmth of his love brought me back from the Fates' cold temptation. When I'd first found my magic, I was willing to throw myself in front of any threat, no matter the cost, but I had learned the hard way that those instincts weren't always correct. Four had manipulated me—and so many others—over and over by using our fears and flaws against us. We were stronger together, and we had a plan. My head cleared, and I remembered what I had to do.

I looked up. The massive orb of magic above us had all twelve layers in place and only needed to be tied off. Four cocked his head as I smiled at him. "Perhaps you underestimate *us*."

Several things happened at once. I tied off the final binding layer on the conjuring containing Earth's magic, and the energy we had gathered above the stadium pulsed pure white.

The sigil on my forearm flared to life, giving me and the other eleven who had bound Earth's magic an enormous well of power to draw from. All of our auras flared with pure-white magic. Nearly within the same heartbeat, Silas hit the Fates with a blast of energy that knocked Two and Four backward and into the containment spell we'd chalked onto the grass of the outfield.

The Aeternal Councilors activated their Houses' amplification spells, which we'd also chalked onto the field, and a dome of magic slammed down over the Fates. Like the shields we'd used to protect the portal between Earth and Aeterna, the spell allowed our magic to go through, but nothing could get out. Four and Two couldn't escape.

Two screamed in rage, their shrill cry completely inhuman and piercing. An insane explosion of power surged from the Fates. The ground shook, and the shield started to waver.

"Open a portal to Aeterna!" Silas grabbed my hand. He hadn't been able to tell us exactly how we would kill them without risking the Fates interfering, but I suddenly realized his plan. We began weaving our magics in parallel, folding five threads at a time into our conjuring.

The other ten with access to Earth's Source continued to pound magic against the Fates as our portal formed on the field just behind them, leading into Aeterna, where nothing with magic could survive.

The stadium was so charged with magic that all of the hairs on my body stood on end. The shield began to quiver as the Fates continued to fight us. We were putting everything we had into stopping them, but even with all of Earth's power behind the twelve of us, we weren't overpowering them. We were all exhausted from harvesting Earth's magic then performing the binding spells, and the amplification circles powering the trap weren't meant to be a long-term power supply.

"It's not enough!" Silas yelled.

"What do we do? This is everything we have!" I cried.

"Fratch. They aren't fully in our realm! It's not holding them."

Silas and I locked gazes, realizing that we'd made a huge mistake. He had cut ties with the Fates when he'd drained the Fates' magic from him and Elias. Two and Four could no longer enter our realm fully, limiting our ability to impact them.

Nithia left her place at the table, spread her arms wide, and walked through the dome containing the Fates until she was face to face with Two and Four. She dropped to her knees and raised her face in adoration. "Accept me and complete the trio!"

"No! Nithia, don't!" Horror flooded me as I realized I'd given the Fae Queen her ultimate opportunity to become one of the Fates. I'd believed everything she'd lost would make her hate them as much as I did, but I'd been dead wrong.

Four didn't hesitate. He placed his palm on Nithia's forehead, and power sizzled between them. Nithia's aura went supernova. I threw my hand over my face as the shielding holding the Fates blew apart. Nithia's chaotic power melded with the Fates', and the entire world pulsed with magic so ancient and powerful that the moment must have embedded in the genetic memory of every living thing on Earth.

Nithia rose to her feet, glowing with cold Fate power.

"The triad is complete," Two pronounced.

"We must claim this realm quickly. Destroy the binding," Four commanded. He pointed at me, and I froze, unable to move.

"What will happen is already happening," Two said.

Nithia walked toward us, engulfed in pure energy. The air caught in my chest. Her green eyes—a mirror of Boone's—had gone completely white. Her jade iris and pupil were gone, replaced by icy magic.

"Nithia?" All I felt was sheer panic, but my voice somehow came out calm. "Their magic doesn't make up for everything they took from you. They're using you. You have to fight the temptation! Fight for your people!"

Nithia bared her teeth in a disturbing resemblance to Silas's feral smile as she reached for the diamond hanging around my neck. I couldn't move as she ripped it off of me, breaking the chain. "There's no other way for this to end, child."

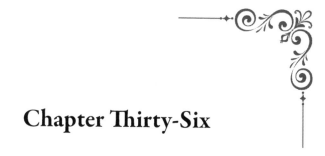

Chapter Thirty-Six

"Finish it," Nithia hissed at me.

I froze, wracking my brain for some idea of what she was talking about, but then she turned back toward Four and Two, holding up her arm that was missing a hand.

"You let me believe I could gain your powers and used me to do your bidding. Even now, you know I do not have the capacity to handle your magic, and yet you intend to use and then discard me."

Four's usual facade of emotions slipped from his face, and he looked completely alien. "We made you one of us. You cannot blame the limitations of your flesh upon us. Now, we must destroy the binding on Earth's magic to be free. Make haste!"

Nithia snarled, and magic blasted from her. Four and Two met it with a tidal wave of their own, blocking her attack.

I finally realized what Nithia had wanted me to do and began weaving the final layers of the binding around the magic contained in the stadium.

Nithia staggered backward as streaks of the Fates' power ripped through the air like forks of lightning. As I finished the twelfth layer of the binding, the magic pulsed white then cascaded through the twelve of us. The spherical ball of Earth's bound magic reached down toward her as she drew from it and the Fates' magic at the same time.

The sheer amount of magic flying around the stadium boggled my mind. The sphere of Earth's power began spinning above us like a miniature tornado. Nithia harnessed that power and the magic the

Fates had given her then threw it all at them, but they stood their ground, hitting her back with even more force.

"Push them into the portal!" I channeled magic from the newly bound source and threw it at the Fates. Silas and the other members of our new Inner Circle did the same, harnessing all of Earth's magic against them.

The Fates faltered under our assault, but they weren't done fighting. Four flung his arm out, and magic pulsed across the stadium.

"The border," Nithia gasped.

I had no idea what he'd done until at least a hundred people in tactical military gear appeared on the field in a flash of white magic, standing between us and the Fates. They were each armed with a disruptor, and in a clearly preplanned and coordinated attack, they started firing in our direction the second they landed.

"Watch out!" We scattered off the field, trying to avoid the blasts from the disruptors, but several people collapsed. Alaric and Tamara both went down, leaving us with two fewer people who could access Earth's magic.

"Guardians!" Silas roared.

"For Glory!" Tessa yelled as she charged from her hiding spot in the dugouts. Seventy Guardians followed her, weaving a battle spell big enough to level an army as they ran toward the Mundane soldiers.

The front line of Guardians shifted into their animal forms, agilely dodging the bursts of magic-killing energy from the disruptors. The bulk of our forces raced forward, toward the DODSI agents, never faltering, though many of the Guardians on two feet took direct hits and fell. The Shifters hit the front line of soldiers, and faced with teeth and claws, panic buckled the Mundane soldiers' ranks. They broke and ran as the force of Guardians reached them, and despite their outnumbering the remaining Guardians at least two to one, our forces swept through their ranks.

The fight on the field had turned in our favor, while Nithia and the rest of us continued to blast the Fates with magic, but our combined power was barely holding them, especially with two down.

"Maeve! Silas! Join me!" Nithia held out a hand. The Heart of Valeron glowed with white power in her open palm.

Hope surged inside me as I ran toward her then grabbed the magic-amplifying diamond between us. Silas grasped our hands with both of his, and the Fates' magic flowed from Nithia to us. With three of us channeling that endless well of power and our direct access to Earth's magic, we tipped the fight in our favor again and pushed the Fates toward the portal.

A primal-rage scream poured out of me as I drew more and more power until the weight of it was like lifting the world, too much yet not enough as the Fates continued to fight with everything they had. We were gaining ground, but every inch was draining our reserves.

The sheer volume of magic proved to be too much for Nithia, and she collapsed under the pressure, crumpling over the second-base plate without warning.

Our attack fell apart. The Fates' magic surged high above the field, and the binding around our new source began to disintegrate. There was nowhere to hide from the power of the Fates, and as their magic loomed above us, our community members panicked and ran.

We'd failed. We'd miscalculated our ability to stand up to the Fates, even channeling all of Earth's power. Maybe if two of our inner circle hadn't fallen or if Silas and I had channeled the Fates' powers earlier, or...

I drew in a desperate breath. I knew what I had to do.

I looked down at the Heart of Valeron, glowing in my palm with the Fates' magic, and closed my fist over it. With a deep breath, I drew all the magic inside of me, and my aura flared white. I exhaled, feeling cold from the inside out. *Love. Safety. Family.* I fixed those things in my mind and refused to lose myself to their power.

"Maeve! What are you doing?" Ethan yelled.

Silas spun toward me.

"We're getting a do-over." I twisted threads of energy into the complex, brain-bending conjuring necessary to move us through time. Before the Fates could recognize what was happening, it had already happened.

I blinked, and when I opened my eyes, we stood in front of the stone table. My palm was on the twelfth sigil of the binding spell. I had bent time around us, just as I had done when Kianna attacked us, sending us back into our own past.

"Maeve? Should we start the last binding layer?" Tamara asked.

Silas's eyes went wide in recognition and alarm.

Nithia stepped back from the table, and her nostrils flared. "What is happening?"

Two figures appeared in a blaze of white magic on the outfield. Before I could even inhale, my stomach twisted sideways, and I was kneeling on the field with Nithia and Silas. The Fates glowered down on us, glowing with their cold, pure magic.

Four's face was an angry mask. "You cannot use our powers against us. This time, you die."

"How will you complete your triad if you kill all of your candidates?" Silas stood, his golden magic glowing brightly around him as he put himself between us and the Fates.

"You are not unique, Silas Valeron. We will make another. Unlike mortals, we have infinite time. A new line can be cultivated."

Our chances of fighting the Fates and winning were zero—we'd already tried and failed. I rose and stood by Silas to face the two most powerful beings in the world, their expressions alien and angry. We couldn't do what we'd done before. I'd been making the same mistake my whole life by forgetting we were always stronger when we stood together. We'd already tried to bind magic and fight the Fates with the elite group of people we'd thought would be the most powerful, and we'd lost.

I looked up at the glowing ball of magic floating over the stadium and the upper stadium balcony ringed with a conjuring circle of over a thousand magic users, holding all of Earth's power in place. We had a chance to do this again, and I wasn't going to repeat my mistake. I had to trust our people—all of our people.

I changed our past and our future as I reached out—not for Earth's magic but for the *people*. I connected with the Harvester circle that had worked with me to draw in Earth's magic and joined them with Nithia's to create the largest circle in the history of magic. Our connection expanded to everyone and everything with any magical capacity, including Lennart and his agents out by the keystone boundary. I wouldn't have been surprised if people with only a drop of magic sensitivity felt it far outside the city.

We only needed one more layer for the spell to be complete, but instead of finishing it, I tore through the previous eleven layers. I heard gasps from those who could see what I was doing.

"Have you finally come to the inevitable conclusion that you will not win this fight?" Four taunted.

"She is undoing what was done before," Two said.

"What does that mean? What is she doing?" Four snapped at his counterpart.

"It means I am your undoing," I told them.

Four cocked his head, and I winked at him.

The expression of confused outrage on his face was insanely gratifying as I tore through the last of the binding threads around Earth's magic.

"Let the power go!" I yelled to the circle, amplifying my voice with magic.

The circle released their hold. The ball of magic floating above the stadium gushed outward like a flood of water suddenly released from a dam.

"Stop, foolish child! You'll set them free!" Nithia screamed.

The magic poured outward until it hit the new boundary spell around Boston. At the same moment, I ripped as much magic as I could from the Fates. I grabbed hold of it and transferred their power through to the conjuring circle, anchoring them in our realm. Over a thousand people absorbed their magic, and the flares of those who were capable of drawing more than others started turning white at the edges as the power continued to flow through me to them. This time, I wouldn't fight the Fates alone with only Earth's magic. I would take whatever they threw at us and use it so that all of us would fight them together.

None of this had been our plan, but it came together within the space of a few heartbeats. As the focus of the joined circles, I drew from the enormous magical capacity of our entire community, channeling both the Fates' power and all of Earth's energy, and then all of us blasted the Fates together.

Four and Two had held off from attacking us, likely trying to figure out what I was doing—unbinding magic was what they wanted, after all—but with the first wave of our combined power, they lashed out, meeting our attack with their own.

Instead of fighting against them, I opened myself to their power. I threw out my arms and absorbed what they used against us. Their magic was life and death and every moment in between as I took it all in and gave it back to my people.

"Silas! Open the portal!" I yelled.

Magic rose around him, white with the Fates' power, and he began to weave the conjuring to open a gateway to Aeterna. Nithia joined in, and the shape of it started to form quickly.

The magic between all of us and the Fates was a cloud of swirling, angry energy that had grown taller than the stadium, with the Fates at the center of the storm. I held them in place on the field as the final threads of the portal settled into place and a gateway to Aeterna appeared on the field behind Four and Two.

Silas and Nithia tied off the portal then joined the attack against the Fates. The former Aeternal Councilors powered up their amplification circles and added their magic to our attack. The combined power of the conjuring circles pushed Four and Two backward, inching them toward the portal. They continued to fight, but with our combined magic and the ties we created through channeling their magic, we were gaining the upper hand.

Around the upper edges of the arena, members of the conjuring circle were collapsing.

"The circle is failing!" Silas yelled.

I grabbed the threads of the portal and flexed. The surface surged forward like a liquid wave, ready to swallow Four and Two and send them to Aeterna and their deaths.

Four threw out a hand, and his magic flashed, freezing the portal just a few feet short of where he and Two stood.

I struggled to pull the portal forward while everyone else kept the Fates pinned and unable to escape. We poured all our magic against them, but they fought hard, throwing everything they had to keep the portal from swallowing them.

Somehow, despite the amount of magic they were already expending, Two started to weave a conjuring that looked like a skimming spell.

"They're getting away!" I yelled.

Suddenly, a black Jeep with modified armor burst out of the maintenance tunnel and onto the field. I stared in dumb shock as the driver veered wildly onto the infield. *This wasn't part of the plan.*

The Jeep didn't slow as it barreled past second base and headed directly for the Fates. Lennart leaned out of the passenger-side window and fired a disruptor. Four and Two both staggered backwards. Lennart dropped the whining disruptor onto the field, reached back inside the vehicle, then drew out another one. He fired again as the Jeep rammed into the Fates at full speed. Both of them flew off their feet. It was exactly the distraction we needed. I snapped the portal forward, and it swallowed the Fates in midair, sending them to Aeterna, where magic couldn't survive.

Lennart, decked out head to toe in body armor, stepped out of the vehicle as cheering broke out across the stadium.

"Is that it? Didn't seem so hard." He smirked at me.

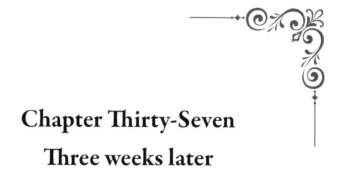

Chapter Thirty-Seven
Three weeks later

Threw conjuring circle surrounded the central keystone and released the boundary keeping all of Earth's magic trapped in the Boston area. Sweat dripped down my back as the magic purred in my chest like a content cat, freed and slowly stretching its reach across the world. My flare was no longer white, but magic belonged to everyone now. The secret was out, and we'd all agreed that not rebinding magic was the right thing to do. Mistakes were made, but together, we would heal and move forward.

"It's done," Silas said. He looked exactly how I felt—exhausted and a little beat up—but we both smiled in relief.

It had been a long couple of weeks since our victory over the Fates. Nithia's run-in with channeling their magic had left her comatose for three days. When she awoke, her magic was pure blue with no instability and no black streaks of lightning. She seemed subdued, and she didn't fight against the Fae who'd decided to stay with us in the city. She quietly slipped away one night with those who wanted to leave to their tract of legally acquired land in Alaska.

I hoped I didn't hear from her for a long, long time. We had a lot of damage to repair after what she'd done to my city.

Relief flooded me as we released magic, but it didn't wash away my sorrow. Over a thousand people, including Jason and Casius,

hadn't escaped from the buildings DODSI had bombed. I was griev-
ing that loss and struggled daily to accept that I would never see Casius again. Thousands had died, but losing my mentor weighed on
me, especially when I remembered how I'd allowed our relationship
to deteriorate since I unbound magic. At least we'd been able to start
to patch things up between us, but that was cold comfort.

Silas gathered my hand into his and kissed my knuckles. Through
our restored Aegis bond, an overwhelming flood of his love and
pride lifted me. "You need to celebrate the wins amongst the losses.
Our people are safe. We're together, and the Fates are no more. Your
plan is brilliant, and the world will be better off soon enough."

I nodded but couldn't form words. I wouldn't feel ready to celebrate until we finished the last step of our plan.

I caught Ethan's eye across the now-dormant marble keystone.
His face was grim, and I worried that he would never recover his
carefree demeanor.

"Is the media team ready?" I asked him.

"Ready. Everything is cued up." Ethan glanced at his phone. "The
press conference just started."

"Perfect." I hoped everything would eventually be okay for him
and Alannah. Ethan hadn't really had a chance to reconcile with Casius after he'd found out he was his father. Alannah was so beside herself with grief that she couldn't even help with the keystones. I was
determined not to break down, but losing Casius made for pain we
would all bear for a long time.

We hadn't recovered his body, but my mentor was a paranoid
bastard, and he'd come through for us from the other side when we
found recordings of all the phone calls and meetings with DOD-
SI. Thanks to his careful baiting, we had Director Pascal threatening
to annihilate us with the president's blessing, and we had security
footage of the destruction and death they'd caused that awful night
on our campus.

I gathered my magic around me. I would never again have the amount of power I'd channeled when I accessed the Fates' magic, but thanks to that exposure, I could draw more than anyone else in our sect—anyone except Silas. We'd spent several days in a row in his House's Ascension conjuring, and between us, we'd stored up enough magic for what would come next.

I raised a palm, and the people around us fell silent. "This is the Moment that will determine the foundation of what we stand for. It's time to build our future. Everyone knows what to do."

Silas released my hand and barked, "Legions one, two, and three, deploy! Remember, this is a zero-casualty strike. Bag and deliver only."

Tessa led the group that skimmed to the old campus, where agents still guarded the rubble. The other groups went to the two keystone sites under DODSI's control and their secret headquarters building. DODSI was about to fall to its knees.

"Infiltration team, with me!" Silas nodded at Stephan, who had moved around the table to stand by his brother. Three Guardians stepped forward and saluted Silas with their fists over their hearts.

I weaved my magic into a skimming spell, and then Silas and I pushed enough power into it to transport all six of us. Silas went through with Stephan, I followed, and the Guardians brought up the rear. My stomach twisted sideways as I blinked and opened my eyes inside the White House press room.

Stephan had already spread a heavy wave of calming magic throughout the space, and although the press pool, the Secret Service, and the president of the United States were all clearly alarmed by our unexpected appearance, no one had started shooting.

I stepped up to the podium next to the president and let my magic settle around me. If anyone got trigger happy, I wasn't taking any chances. President Lowe jerked back as I approached, revealing he knew who I was. In fact, the special press conference we'd interrupted had been called to address the situation in Boston. The three Guardians moved in front of the exits, sealing us inside with magic, and I stared into the cameras livestreaming my face across the world.

"My name is Maeve O'Neill. I am a leader of the magical community located in Boston, Massachusetts, and a legal citizen of the United States. Three weeks ago, a secret branch of the Department of Defense, Special Interests, attacked us and murdered seven hundred thirty-two American citizens. Many of those were children." More had died, but we decided to focus on those who had been in the country legally and to avoid the issue of the Aeternal refugees, who had no documentation.

My voice broke, and I had to take a deep breath. Jason would have given a more eloquent speech, but we had lost him. I was voted the next best choice since my face was already known all over the world, thanks to DODSI. No one in the room made a sound as they stared at me.

"Twenty-Three days ago, a group of Fae, led by Nithia de'Fiero, attacked and took over the city of Boston. We were not responsible for that attack and in fact tried to work with the government to resolve the situation. President Lowe authorized an unprovoked lethal-force strike team to bomb our campus. We did not receive a warning, a demand to turn ourselves in, or any chance for a peaceful resolution to whatever wrongs they believed we might have committed. This president and his secret agency attacked and murdered families as they slept in the middle of the night. They slaughtered innocent, unarmed American citizens."

President Lowe tried to shift away from the podium as the crowd murmured in surprise. Silas stepped up behind him, forcing him to stay put.

"Right now, every major news media organization in America is receiving video recordings of meetings between our leaders and Director James Pascal, the head of this secret government group—DODSI. These meetings show that the threats against us, including illegal imprisonment and threats against our lives, were sanctioned by the president of the United States. They will also receive footage of the horrendous attack on innocent families."

I stared into the cameras as my anger rose. "We are very capable of enacting revenge. I am standing inside the White House without invitation, within arm's reach of your president. The whole world saw what the Fae were capable of doing against the full might of the military. We are capable of much, much more, and we will not tolerate further acts of aggression against our people. We will act swiftly and with equal force against any attacks."

I paused, letting that sink in as the cameras fed my words across the world in real time. "We wish to build a future of peace. Therefore, we have chosen not to retaliate for the crimes committed against us. We are seeking legal and criminal charges through your own justice systems against those responsible. The media have also received a list of every active member of DODSI, and to facilitate justice, we are currently delivering each of them, safely and without harm, to local police authorities."

Thanks to Lennart and some computer hacking, we'd gotten the list of agents who had attacked our campus that night.

"We're not seeking retribution, but we can't deny the very real threat of continuing hate crimes against us and all those with magic abilities. I am here today to announce the succession of *New Boston* from the United States of America. We declare ourselves a sovereign nation as of today. We are no longer subjects of the U.S. government."

People gasped, and a few of them pulled out their phones and started making calls. Stephan pushed another wave of calm through the room.

"To the people of Boston who were misplaced and harmed due to the actions of Nithia de'Fiero, we offer our sincerest regrets. What happened in Boston was a tragedy. We have dealt with those responsible, and we welcome you to return to your homes and live with us in peace. Or you can gather your possessions and leave in peace. It's up to you. We're also offering repayment for any individuals who owned property in the city. I wish this hadn't happened, but it has, and this is the best we can do to try and make up for your suffering while ensuring a safe future for our people."

I'd insisted on that part of our exit plan, and although the former Aeternal Counselors had balked at the price tag, they had more than enough money to make reparations.

I pulled a single note card from my pocket. I had to get this part just right.

"We are not closing our borders and hiding from the world. Magic is spreading across the world, and we welcome all who will develop magic abilities to New Boston. We also welcome anyone who wants to live with us in peace, even if you do not have abilities. We want the world to benefit from our magic. In New Boston, we have opened a healing center that is free to all, without cost or obligation. Our Healers can cure any illness—cancer, physical injury, or mental ailments."

I looked up into the cameras. "'Give us your tired, your poor, your huddled masses yearning to breathe free.' Come in peace, and you will never know sickness, hunger, or homelessness again. You will be treated as equals, with access to whatever you need—for free. Lastly, we welcome the world's leaders to trade with us, and should you welcome it, we offer our support with no cost or obligation in times of famine, drought, or natural disasters. We offer all of this freely in the name of peace, and all we ask is peace in return."

The crowd stared up at me in complete shock and silence. President Lowe, firmly under Stephan's influence, gaped at me. "Mr. President, you sanctioned an illegal annihilation of my people. While you are in office, you and everyone who supports you are not welcome in New Boston. When the American people choose to vote in a new leader who will deal with us in good faith, we will open our borders and our healing center to this country. I encourage the people of this great nation to call for an impeachment of this president for his unlawful and immoral actions. I hope you go to jail for a long time."

I looked away from him, dismissing him in both action and words as I addressed the press pool directly for the first time. "In the future, we look forward to offering healing, assistance, and equal trade with the United States of America."

On cue, Tessa skimmed into the room with Director Pascal, who had already been placed under a compulsion spell. His eyes were wide as he looked around the room. The cameras continued to broadcast live.

"This is Director Pascal of the Department of Defense, Special Interests Agency," I said. "He has been compelled to tell the truth and nothing but the truth. As promised, he's being delivered without harm, and he will answer any questions you may have. Director Pascal, let's start with you telling the press who ordered you to murder innocent families in the middle of the night."

Pascal's eyes were wide with fear as President Lowe shook his head, but then he opened his mouth, and the truth was set free.

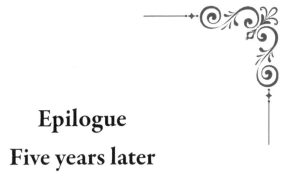

Epilogue
Five years later

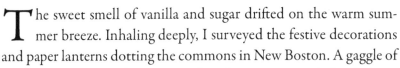

The sweet smell of vanilla and sugar drifted on the warm summer breeze. Inhaling deeply, I surveyed the festive decorations and paper lanterns dotting the commons in New Boston. A gaggle of children ran across the grass, trailing long streamers behind them, laughing and chasing each other. Booths of sweet cookies and savory meats lined the sidewalks, offering refreshments to anyone who wanted them. As with all things in New Boston, they were free. With magic, we all had everything we needed, and no one went without.

With my waxed-paper lantern in hand and the sun starting to set, I headed through the thickly forested area the Fae had grown into an elevated city and toward the open meadow in the center. Tonight, we would release the lanterns with our hopes and dreams for the year ahead. Remembrance Day was about the future, but it had a melancholy edge for those of us who had lost so many loved ones. Remembering them on that day each year was important to our healing as a community.

My list was long: my parents and my brother. My aunt Deanna and everyone who died fighting the Brotherhood. Atticus, who'd sacrificed himself to save us all and stop Titus. I also remembered Cecilia, who had fought to change the Council and then died getting her people out of Aeterna. Seth and Rhonda, whom we'd lost fight-

ing the Fae. We'd lost Jason and all the families DODSI murdered...
There were too many names. Five years later, the pain of Casius's
death still flared inside my chest, but I no longer allowed it to crush
me. I was learning to live with it.

A child ran up to me with a huge smile plastered on her face. She
held up both of her arms and looked at me with my brother's hazel
eyes. "Auntie Mae!"

I picked up my niece and swung her around in a circle, both of us
laughing. I planted a kiss in her dark, curly hair as I set her back on
her feet. "Where are your parents, Marcille?"

"Grown-up talking is sooo boring," Marci whined.

"Hey, you little munchkin, I told you to stay close," Ethan chided
as he walked up to us.

"But Daaad, you said we should help people when they're sad.
It's not my fault I did what you told me to do!" She planted her fists
on her little hips and defiantly stuck out her lower lip. "See! Auntie
Mae is smiling now!"

Ethan chuckled. "Okay, okay. I'm glad you were watching out
for your auntie. How about you go get one of those dancing ribbons
from Auntie Aria? Oh, and there's Sariah! She already has a ribbon."

Marci's face lit up, and she practically threw herself out of my
arms before she ran off to join her best friend and the other kids.
They all quickly scrambled into one of the trees and up into the Fae's
branch walkways. I waved at Aria, who was busy handing out long
ribbons on sticks to the children, and she waved back with a smile.
Her belly was swollen again with a third child on the way, which had
Stephan walking around with his own glow. Raising a family suit-
ed them, and Alaric had turned into the most adorable and doting
grandfather ever.

"Remembrance Day makes me sad too," Ethan said.

"I just wish my family could see everything we've built, you
know? I wish Marcel could see how happy his daughter is." I gri-

maced as I realized how Ethan might take that. "I'm sorry, I didn't mean... You're a great dad, and Marcille and Gia are lucky to have you in their lives."

He bumped his shoulder into mine, instantly forgiving me for my careless words. "Your brother didn't deserve to miss out on raising his daughter. How was D.C.?"

I sighed. "The new president agreed she wouldn't extend a pardon to President Lowe or Director Pascal."

"Good. Two lifetimes in prison isn't enough for all the lives they took." Ethan and I stood in companionable silence for a few moments, watching the kids twirl and run around as the last of the sun's light spread across the sky in broad swaths of orange and red. "How did Christine do?"

Christine Davina, the last newbie we'd dragged in screaming, was a lawyer and completely in her element at the White House. "Amazing. I don't know what we'd do without her. She got the House and Senate to agree on funding voluntary screenings for people who have the capacity for magic. If they pass the test, they can apply for citizenship in New Boston. That should help with the immigration delays at the U.S. borders."

"That's great news."

"Speaking of news, have you seen your mom today?"

Ethan threw me a dirty look. "You know very well I have. Everyone has. The two of them put on a total spectacle."

I managed to hold back my laughter. "Valerons do nothing by half. Proposing to your mom was a big deal for Sergius. He's never been in a committed relationship."

"But did they have to make out afterward? I'll never get *that* scrubbed out of my brain."

I couldn't hold back the full belly laugh that erupted from me, and when Ethan joined me, the last of my melancholy faded to the background.

As our laughter edged away, Ethan put his hand on my forearm and smiled softly at me. "You're going to be okay. You fought too hard not to be."

"I know. I'm just feeling more emotional than usual." I bit my lip before I said more.

"And where is your broody husband? Shouldn't he be here to dry your tears?"

"I'm not crying." I smacked his shoulder not quite gently. "Silas is finishing up with the Guardians before the lantern ceremony. He's enjoying running Lennart around, trying to earn his promotion."

The two of them had become... not friends exactly, but they both had a deep-seated desire to protect those who couldn't protect themselves, and in that shared goal, they'd built up a new cohort of Guardians, incorporating some of the Mundanes' training and weaponry alongside the Guardians'. New Boston had swelled to more than half a million people since we'd declared our independence, and we had an entire magical community to protect. Lennart was looking to be the next leader of the new cohort of graduates, but Silas was going to make him work for it.

As I suspected, Lennart hadn't let me live down his big moment of saving all our butts. He'd actually commissioned dozens of T-shirts emblazoned with obnoxious slogans like Hero of Fenway, and he wore a different one every day.

"And Tessa?" Ethan asked with a smirk. "What does she think about Lennart's big promotion?"

"I can't wait to see her face when she realizes Lennart got promoted while she was honeymooning." Officially, Tamara and Tessa were helping to set up a healing center in Geneva, Switzerland, after the city's leaders had unanimously voted to become a magic-harbor city. Along with Octavia and Nero, Silas had sent them over with strict orders to take time off after their wedding.

Thanks to Tamara's team of researchers, including what remained of the Magisters, we had brought back all the knowledge contained in the Aeternal Council's vault, and our collective magical knowledge had advanced by decades. The shielding around New Boston would never again fall to Mundane technology. We had a home where anyone with magic—and anyone who decided to live peacefully with us—would grow up not knowing fear, hunger, or inequality.

A hush grew over the crowd as the last of the sun's light slipped behind the city skyline. Ethan patted my arm. "I'm going to find Gia and Marci."

I waved him off as the crowd began to hum, thousands of voices joining in. I swayed to the song as my voice and my own power rose. I had much to mourn, but I also had hope. Our new community was thriving after years of peace and safety. With our magic, we'd helped countless people across the world. New Boston was a place of peace, and as our voices joined together, I knew what we had built would survive for our children and their children.

A familiar male voice joined in as Silas wrapped his arm around my shoulder and kissed my temple. "Sorry I'm late."

I leaned into his side, inhaling the clean, spiced smell of him as the song grew. His eyes crinkled as he smiled down at me. Like all magic users, neither of us had physically aged much in the last five years, but his easy smile and those new laugh lines made my heart soar. He deserved some peace and happiness in his life. We both did.

Our voices and our magic joined with our people's. As the song rose to its final crescendo, the blending of magic and harmony overwhelmed me with happiness. Remembrance Day was about the past, but it was also about the future. Everyone we'd lost had helped us build this future.

I held the wax-paper lantern out to him.

"What will you wish for this year?" he asked as a spark of his magic lit the candle inside. He held it in his open palm, ready to launch.

Thousands of glowing lanterns ascended into the heavens all around us, filling the air with pulses of warm light and wishes for the upcoming year. The night sky was literally filled with the hopes and dreams of everyone in the city.

"I wish..." I smiled at him as my hands cradled my belly. "I wish for our child to only know joy on Remembrance Day."

Silas's eyes widened, and he gaped at my stomach. "Are you...?"

I rubbed the tiny bump that only I could feel and nodded. "Yup."

A delighted grin spread across his face. He tossed the lantern into the air, pulled me into his arms, and swung us around in a circle. We laughed with sheer joy until tears ran down our faces.

Silas returned me to my feet gently. His overwhelming joy, pride, and a little bit of bewilderment radiated through our bond. "I love you so much, my Maeve."

"And I love you, Silas. Forever and always."

"Forever and always."

We kissed, and in that moment, surrounded by the light of our community and the love in our hearts, the future was bright and filled with hope.

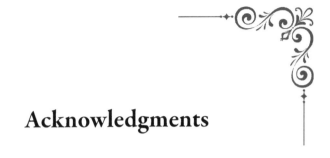

Acknowledgments

Writing this series has been an incredible journey. My husband deserves an award for seeing me through this with patience and support, and my kids for cheering me on and always asking for updates. Thanks to my "guysies" who have celebrated every step of the way with me, and especially Leslie Nielsen, president of my unofficial fan club, for reading many poorly written draft versions of *Fate Forged* and *Fate Broken*. Special thanks to my friends, and *Fate Claimed* beta readers, Christine Prather and Davina Ziegele, who caught many loose ends and asked hard questions I didn't yet have answers to.

Thank you to the many readers who have loved the series, patiently waiting for each new book. I hope you enjoyed this conclusion to the Bound Magic Series. The gift of your time and your imagination means the world to me.

Lastly, thank you to Red Adept Publishing for taking a risk on a debut author who submitted a truly terrible first chapter. Many thanks to my content editor, Alyssa Hall, who has guided me fearlessly through character arcs and out of plot holes across the entire series. She is the true hero of this trilogy. Lastly, thank you to the entire editing team at RAP, but especially Neila Forssberg, Sarah Carleton, and Kate Birdsall, who each wielded a red pen against poor grammar and taught me to be a better writer in the process.

If you enjoyed this series, please consider leaving a review on your favorite site so other readers can find my books. Exclusive content and author updates can be found at www.bpdonigan.com and by following me at www.facebook.com/BPDonigan[1].

---

1. http://www.facebook.com/BPDonigan

About the Author

B.P. Donigan was born and raised in Alaska, where real-life adventures inspired her writing, minus the magic. She left for college and spent ten wonderful years with her husband and two children in Boston, falling in love with the city. A career opportunity led to sunny California, and leaving behind her closest friends launched an escapist writing hobby that eventually became The Bound Magic Series.

She currently resides in the mountains of Salt Lake City with her two kids, two dogs, and one amazing husband. Like any good superhero, she spends her days behind a desk, building her cover story, and her nights saving the world (on paper, at least).

For author news and exclusive content and updates, visit www.bpdonigan.com or follow B.P Donigan on Facebook.

Read more at https://bpdonigan.com/.

About the Publisher

Dear Reader,

We hope you enjoyed this book. Please consider leaving a review on your favorite book site.

Visit https://RedAdeptPublishing.com to see our entire catalogue.

Check out our app for short stories, articles, and interviews. You'll also be notified of future releases and special sales.

Made in the USA
Monee, IL
25 January 2024

52315656R00201